WHAT ARE READERS SAYING ABOUT
Don't You Know It's 40 Below?

I feel compelled to write you and tell you how very much I enjoyed reading *Don't You Know It's 40 Below?* . . . I hope there will be a sequel. . . Oh please write another book for me and your other fans. **Norma Hawkins, author of *Chokecherry*, Vancouver , British Columbia**.

It was so good! I really slowed down at the end because I didn't want it to be over. **Karin Haapa Puleo, Windsor, California.**

Talking to Jack made me want to go back in time, when things were simpler. Times were tough, but they made you appreciate what you had. The book is outstanding. **Rich Deleo,** Altoona **Talk Host** at **WFB Radio, Altoona , Pennsylvania.**

A fresh breeze from the North— cool and funny. **Rich Barber**, **Radio Talk Host, KOA, Denver.**

I can't tell you how much I enjoyed the book. It was so full of memories that were so similar to mine growing up in little Cleveland, North Dakota. **Elizabeth Sinclair Miller, Aurora, Colorado.**

Your book is wonderful, delightful, and a joy to read. **June Gowryluk Feldman, Great Neck, New York.**

Jack Kates has provided a whimsical ride to a time long gone but long remembered in his *Don't You Know It's 40 Below?* It's an engaging look at life during a time when our individual worlds seemed smaller and the outside world larger, quite distant and somehow a bit more mythical.

Even if it is 50 below, *Don't You Know It's 40 Below* will warm you as you are captured by the magic of youth and the condition we refer to as growing up. It's a read with hundreds of chuckles (slightly less north of the border because of the high exchange rate) and some laugh out - louds thrown in for good measure. It's almost enough to pack the family station wagon to venture for the summer to Sheho, Canada, to see a place that produced not only Kates but a statue of a giant chicken as well. **Dream Weaver, KPAM Radio, Portland, Oregon.**

Your book is wonderful. . . . I cannot thank you enough for writing the history of life in Sheho and that part of the world. It was so well written. What detail and humor. I love it. **Elane Finley, Brockville, Ontario.**

I have only a handful of pages to read and I am saving them as my reward . . . I can't express how much I enjoyed reading your book. **Pam Johnston, Kelowna, British Columbia.**

I've just finished reading your book for the second time. . . . Never [before] have I read a book twice. **Lurena Gudmundson, Lanagan, Saskatchewan.**

Think of this as the Canadian version of John Grisham's *A Painted House.* But instead of suffering through the forces of nature to bring in a cotton crop on a farm in rural Arkansas in the 1950s, readers are treated to an unusual and memorable look at how a Jewish family dealt with life in a small town on the Canadian prairies during the Depression. You won't forget either once you have journeyed through their pages. **Godfrey Harris, Executive Director, International Publishers Alliance, Los Angeles.**

It has often been said that everyone has at least one book in him— every life holds a story worth telling. In the case of Jack Kates, that story is not only worth telling, it's worth reading. . . . *Don't you Know It's 40 Below?* chronicles the first 18 years of his life as the son of a Jewish immigrant in Canada. It is not only his story, it's history itself. At times humorous, at others reflective, it is a look at an honest and honorable storekeeper who instills in his family a sense of worth and a feeling of pride and ambition, a lesson that Kates learned well.

Having lived in Canada through the Great Depression and War II, Kates recalls the trials and tribulations that affected his family, along with multitudinous other immigrants who flocked to the new frontier.

Kates has been called the "Jewish-Canadian Garrison Keillor" and has even been compared to the likes of Mark Twain, but quite simply, Kates is a story teller—weaving his words into pictures that take the reader back to a period of western expansion, constant changes and traditional values.

At once the reader will find the book easy on the eyes, written with a poetic flow and rhythm, the colloquial dialogue unwavering in its simplicity. Its largest appeal may be the fact that, in a way, Kates's story is everyone's story. Who hasn't had a friend like the insatiable Hymie Cooperman, who, like his heroes the Marx Brothers, would place a match in an unsuspecting person's shoe sole, then light it to give them a "hot-foot"? Who didn't have at least one "out of the box" teacher like Fred Kindrachuk? It's a familiar life of skating and camping and hanging out with friends, watching parents fret over the late arrival of relatives and listening to them overanalyze small details like buying a radio. . . Wonderful memories all." **Michael T. Mosley,** *Daily Republic* **, Fairfield,CA.**

Don't You Know It's 40 Below? is a masterfully penned autobiography by word-weaver Jack Kates. It is an endearing tale of his experiences in an immigrant family in Saskatchewan, Canada. With clarity and freshness, it delightfully shares the joys, lessons, and struggles of his early life from the early 1930s through the middle part of the 20th century. . .Mr. Kates's vignettes captivatingly reveal his time-sweetened recollections—mixed with innocent childhood thoughts—documenting his maturation in a simpler time and place. It is a heartwarming story. **Roy Lewis, Educator ABC Unified School District, Cerritos, California.**

Don't You Know It's 40 Below? by Jack Kates, a literary and historical treatment of small town Canadian life over half a century ago, is deeply infused with pathos, humor, satire, and factual information. This book enables the reader to focus on a dot on the map, and then narrow in to its geography, history, and its 1930s and 1940s culture—all from the perspective of 1999. Specifically, we are given insights into the life experience of a young boy growing up in the only Jewish family in the community. Jack Kates is a storyteller who blankets everyday events with a sense of irony. Readability is especially enhanced by his frequent flights of imagination to wild exaggeration, somewhat reminiscent of Mark Twain's style. Yet most of the story is told through the eyes of an innocent youngster who excitedly shares with the reader his numerous adventures and impressions, including his passions for the rhythms of nature.

Kates' portrayal of historical events, including the Great Depression and World War II, takes the reader back in time to the actuality of how those occurrences were perceived by some of the people who were immediately involved. Indeed, the chapter dealing with the war's impact on his village was the best account I have ever read on that topic because it was so personal—narrated through the boy's eyes.. . . Jack Kates has treated his subject with great historical care and genuine love.

Don't You Know It's 40 Below? never falls into the trap of sentimentality, but it deals with the psychic development of the boy, the young man, and finally the mature man who narrates the story. Thus, an emotional element is present throughout, and it builds to an effective climax as the book nears its end.

Jack Kates has treated his subject with great historical care and genuine love.— **Lorraine Tolliver Levin, Professor of Literature, Los Angeles Community College District, California..**

For Rosanne.

I enjoyed meeting you.

Best wishes

Enjoy

DON'T YOU KNOW IT'S 40 BELOW?

Second Edition

Jack Kates

Jack Kates

Nov. 7. 2024

Seal Press

Since 1976

Cypress, California

DON'T YOU KNOW
IT'S 40 BELOW?

Second Edition

Jack Kates

Published by Seal Press
6505 Jaluit Street
Cypress, California 90630

Copyright 2002 by Jack Kates.
ISBN 0-930364-08-2.
Manufactured in the United States of America.
Library of Congress Control Number 2001118715.
First Printing 2000.
Second Printing, Second Edition 2001

CONTENTS

Chapters:

Map

DEDICATIONS.

This book is dedicated to the beloved memory of my mother and father, Rose and Louis Katz. It is also dedicated to the memory of my mentor Samuel Leckie, and my closest buddy while growing up, Walter Lys. Finally, it is dedicated to the memory of *all* Allied Servicemen who made the ultimate sacrifice during World War II, and in particular to those from my home town, Sheho, Saskatchewan, and its surrounding area, whose names are listed below.

LEST WE FORGET:

Joseph Charles Bisschop

William Butula

William Fedorchuk

Jack Ferguson ✓ *same class as author .*

Nick Kulyk

Norman Abraham Leckie ⟋ *cub master*

Albert Logan

William Maxsemuik

Hector Munro

William Oleksiuk

Joseph Sackeny

Harry Sawchuk

Allan Scramstad   *sisters' Boy friend*

SPECIAL ACKNOWLEDGMENTS

Before I acknowledge anyone, I must publicly express my utmost gratitude to my cardiac physician, Dr. Mike Vasilomanolakis, and to my cardiac surgeon, Dr. Guy La Mire, formerly of the University of Saskatchewan, for saving my life, thereby allowing me to enjoy the most precious gift of all. *L'Chaim!* To life!

First and foremost, I am deeply grateful to Professor Allan Sklove for listening to my many anecdotes over the decades and eventually persuading me to write this book, for encouraging me along the way, and for providing valuable criticism and suggestions on the manuscript. Second, I would like to express my deep gratitude to Professor John Wintterle for critiquing and proofreading each draft of the manuscript and for his encouragement; to Professor Lorraine Levin for critiquing the numerous drafts of the manuscript and for her encouragement as well; and to my sister Merle and her husband Arwin Gould, and Roy Lewis for additional proofreading. Next, my gratitude to Janet Benson, Byron Rose, Donna Bynum, and Debbie Bjerk for patiently listening to me read each new chapter I wrote over a period of seven years and for their suggestions. In addition, I thank Charlie Shnider for his extensive help by supplying me with important statistics for a particular chapter. In addition I thank Jerry Holm, Dr. C. Stuart Huston, my cousin Rachel Neumann, Merle Gould, and my wife, Marilyn, for proofreading the second edition. Finally, my deep gratitude to Marilyn, not only for her important feedback on the book but especially for listening to my many tales about Canada—and their numerous reruns—for the past thirty-three years without even divorcing me, let alone causing me serious and permanent bodily injury or worse. My profound thanks to all of you.

ADDITIONAL ACKNOWLEDGMENTS

In my attempt to be as historically accurate as possible, I have consulted with a great many people and organizations for information about various aspects of this book. Although the list is a long one, I would like to acknowledge as many of the contributors as I can, some of whom have passed on. I now express my gratitude to the following people: Alice Curry, Dr. Bernard Eisenstein, Merle Gould, Clara Holmes, George Homeniuk, Dr. Walter Hudyma, Julius Izen, Fred Kindrachuk, Larry Lackman, Sylvia Landa, Kerb Leupp, Louise Marak, Mickey Markert, Dr. Mervin Laskin, Shimon Laskin, Rachel Neumann, Seymour Neumann, Jenny Ortinski, Vera Scheibner, Betty Schotz, Emil Sebulski and the Sheho Reunion Committee, Dr. Maurice Shnider, Ruth Stern, Murray Straker, Howard Tansley, Ludwig Walkowski, and Clifford Wunder.

My gratitude also goes to the following businesses and organizations for information used in this book: Columbia Broadcasting System New York and National Broadcasting Company New York, Edmonton Public Library, The Foam Lake Historical Society, David Goldin, Producer of *Themes Like Old Times: 90 of the Most Original Radio Themes*, Recordings from the Arches of Radio Yesteryear; Radio stations CJGX Yorkton, CKCK Regina, and KFYR Bismarck; Royal Canadian Mounted Police Headquarters Regina, *Yorkton This Week and Enterprise*, University of Saskatchewan—Department of Records and English Department.

IMPORTANT NOTE ON LANGUAGE AND PRONUNCIATION

During my years as an educator, I concluded that most readers skip the "Preface" of a book; and since the Preface of this book is important, I have titled it "Important Note on Language and Pronunciation."

Diction

If a memoir is to serve any historical purpose by accurately describing the people and the times in which they lived, the language in both the dialogue and the narration must be authentic. I have therefore tried to be as accurate as possible, particularly in the dialogue, so that readers will have an understanding of what it was like growing up as the son of Eastern European Jewish immigrant parents who owned a general store in a small village on the Canadian Prairies during the Great Depression and World War II. Lest language zealots take offense, I must emphasize that to the best of my recollection, the words used are the exact ones spoken by the people depicted in this book during that era.

For example, the Chinese owners of cafes were called "Chinamen" by almost everyone because they were different than the rest of us, not only because of their color, physical features, and language, but because they rarely left their cafes and usually did not participate in community affairs. Hence, most of us never bothered to learn their actual names. Although the Chinese were at the bottom of the acceptable immigration list into Canada, there was no animosity toward them in our village. The word *Chinamen*, oddly enough, was not considered to be a derogatory term. It was used because most of us didn't bother to learn their real names.

Some readers may also take issue with me because of my continued use of the word *Jewish* instead of *Yiddish* when referring to the language spoken and read by my parents. The truth is that when they spoke *English*, they always referred to their native language as *Jewish*—not Yiddish. And when my sisters and cousins and almost everyone I knew referred to that language, we also used the word *Jewish*. We considered the word *Yiddish* —meaning Jewish—to be a foreign word like *Francais* (meaning French), or *Deutsch* (German). One says, "I speak French," not "I speak Francais." To this day, we still use the word *Jewish* when referring to the language our parents spoke and read.

Readers may notice the absence of vulgar language. We were brought up differently than the kids today. Vulgarities were not tolerated, and we rarely used them. Also lacking in the dialogue— at the end of a sentence —is the use of "eh" pronounced "a" as in hay. Although many Canadians uttered it, I don't recall my friends having used it very often. Eh? Besides, I don't think it would enhance the story. Eh?

Spelling and Pronunciation

The spelling of English words in this book is in accordance with THE RANDOM HOUSE DICTIONARY OF THE ENGLISH LANGUAGE: SECOND EDITION UNABRIDGED. The English spelling of Hebrew words is also based upon this dictionary whenever possible; likewise with Jewish words. However, because there are often different pronunciations for the same Jewish word depending upon what region of Europe the immigrant came from, that word may be spelled two different ways. For example, since my mother was born and reared in Poland, and my father near the Polish border, they both used the word *sheel* to mean synagogue, whereas many other Jews used the word *shule*. Throughout this book, *I have spelled Jewish words the way my parents pronounced them*. Translations of foreign words and editorial comments by the author will be given in brackets. Additional information and documentation will be listed in the addendum.

Although my father's anglicized first name was spelled "Louis," it was always pronounced *Louie*. My sister Etta's name was pronounced *Eeta*. Finally, in Canada my surname "Katz" was *always* pronounced *Kates* as in dates—*never* "cats." Cats are soft furred animals, and although I have an abundance of hair on my arms, chest and legs, that hair is not fur and I am not a cat. Even though I like soft furred animals, when Americans insisted on mispronouncing my name, I changed the spelling to Kates when I changed my citizenship. Please do not pronounce my original surname "Katz" as "cats." I think it's a horrible name and should be outlawed or at best referred to as the "K" word, and then only in whispers—when nobody else is around.

INTRODUCTION
Settlement of the Canadian Prairies

For thousands of years, the only humans to set foot on this vast stretch of land, from the large lakes in the east to the foothills of the Rockies, were nomadic hunters, later to be known as Indians. In the south, they hunted the buffalo grazing on the tall grass covering the flat land stretching from horizon to horizon, with barely a tree in sight. Farther north, and also west toward the Rockies, small hills rose over the prairie, and the grasslands gave way to denser growth including thick groves of berry bushes and taller birch and poplar trees. Alongside the banks of countless creeks, sloughs, and small lakes grew more bushes, bulrushes and willows. Here, in the summer, ducks and geese mated and raised their young. This was also the home of the prairie chicken, partridge, rabbit, fox, coyote, muskrat, and beaver. Farther north, in the land of the spruce and pine, lay hundreds of larger lakes, creeks, and rivers, home not only to all of this wildlife, but also to the bears, wolf, deer, moose, and elk. The nomadic hunters lived off this virgin land. Then came the Europeans.

First came the explorers, followed by the fur traders, followed by the trading posts of the Hudson's Bay Company. Next came a few brave pioneers—long before the railroads—followed by more hardy settlers, who chopped down trees, built their cabins, waited out the winter, then cleared the virgin land, by hand or with oxen, and planted crops. But these earliest pioneers were mere voices in the wilderness. Decades passed and the wilderness remained virtually unchanged. In 1867 the Dominion of Canada was born through the confederation of provinces, and the

Canadian government— eager to populate the West —advertised in East-ern Canada, parts of the United States, and throughout Europe that "Free" land for settlers was available. Under the "Dominion Lands Policy," 160 acres for only ten dollars was offered to any homesteader who could build a house and cultivate a specified area within three years.[1] Slowly but steadily, people began to arrive. They came first from Eastern Canada, next from the British Isles, and from the Northern United States—the Dakotas and Minnesota. Then, around the beginning of the twentieth century, the floodgates opened and the multitudes poured in. They came from many lands: from Iceland, Scandinavia, the Baltic states, Austria, Romania, Germany, Poland, Russia, and the Ukraine. By the boatloads they came—on steerage— like cattle, the cheapest way. Poverty stricken, they came with their life savings to buy the homesteads. But some also came for another reason. For among these pioneers were Jews who came to escape from the anti-Semitic persecution of the old country— espe-cially the Russian government sponsored pogroms of Tsar Nicholas II, which persecuted and all too often made sport of massacring Jews.

Most of the Jewish immigrants settled in the big cities of Montreal, Toronto, Winnipeg, Vancouver; and in smaller cities like Saskatoon, Regina, Edmonton, and Calgary. But for many of them who were unable to earn a livelihood in the city, there was one possible solution : Move to the "country" and open up a general store. With a few hundred dollars and with the help of wholesalers who extended them credit, they were in business.

Along with the general store came the beginnings of a community: grain elevators, the railroad, a railway station, a post office, a school, a livery stable, a lumber yard, a shoe and harness repair shop, a barber shop and billiard hall, a blacksmith shop, a flour mill, a cafe, a hotel, and eventually another general store. The grain elevator, school, and even the post office sometimes preceded the general store; but almost no other business did. And nobody was more crucial to the development of the community than was the storekeeper.

The general storekeeper not only served the community; he was its center. Without him, the community could not have existed. Not only did he stock practically everything the community needed to survive, but more importantly, he extended long-term credit to his customers—without any interest whatsoever. And there was no such thing as "regular payments." If the farmer's crop came in, and if the price of grain was adequate, and if the farmer felt like it, he would pay off his annual debt to the storekeeper. There were a great many "ifs" in the equation. And if the farmer couldn't (or wouldn't) pay off his debt in full, he might pay something on the bill to show his good faith and ask for another year's credit. Where else could he get credit? Not from mail order houses. The bank extended credit to the manufacturer. The manufacturer extended credit to the wholesaler. The wholesaler in turn extended credit to the storekeeper. And the storekeeper "carried" the farmers—not merely for months, but sometimes for years. Without the general storekeeper, the Prairies —and perhaps the West—would not have been developed.

Although a community may have had more than one general store, at least one was usually owned and operated by a Jewish immigrant. Often he lived upstairs or in the back of the store itself. He eked out a livelihood. But he was "independent." By the early 1930s, there was at least one Jewish general storekeeper in practically every hamlet, village, and town on the Canadian Prairies— a three hundred mile -wide and one thousand mile- long corridor running east to west—from Lake Winnipeg to the Rocky Mountains. Today, the Jewish general storekeepers are gone. All gone! *Only their stories linger in the memories of their surviving offspring.* This is the story of one of those children who grew up in one of those families, in one of those villages, in one of those provinces on the Great Canadian Prairies. It is a story recalled in tranquillity —in cheerfulness, in gratitude, and at times in sadness—in the sunset of my life.

In the latter part of the nineteenth century, Yankel Volf Katz, a rabbinical scholar in the tiny hamlet of Mervitz, in the Ukraine, and his wife Ronya Leah, produced twelve children, one of whom, named Schmeel,was born in 1886 or 1887. While the infant lay deathly ill, special prayers were held for him, pleading with God to let him live. In exchange, he was given another name "Leib," meaning "to live." He survived, and in 1912, along with his younger sister Bessie, he followed in the footsteps of his older brothers David and Moishe, and emigrated to Canada, where Anglo immigration officers, who frequently had difficulty with non-English names, gave him the name of "Louis," pronounced "Louie."

In 1922, at the age of thirty-five, Louis Katz married Raizell Izen, a twenty- year old, newly -arrived immigrant from Lutsk, a large city in Poland. It is from the union of these two that this story springs.

CHAPTER ONE
Our Town

How many times have you looked down from 35,000 feet in an airliner flying at 600 miles an hour (ten miles a minute), only to see a cluster of dots or pinpoints of light as you fly over a town in a matter of seconds? Have you ever wondered about that tiny dot or pinpoint? What is it? An outdoor light on a farm? Or is it a small village? How many people live on that farm or in that village? What kind of a place is it? What would it be like to live there? Have you ever wondered about the human drama? What kind of personal stories could somebody tell about life in that settlement?

That's what this book is about. It's a series of recollections about the first eighteen years of my life in a tiny village whose pinpoint of light would have been invisible to the naked eye even from a single engine biplane flying at only sixty miles an hour and a mere ten thousand feet above the ground. You would have had to descend several thousand feet before you could actually see a pinpoint of light. Then, as you got closer to the ground, that pinpoint would have become a dot, increasing in size until you could make out four large dots; and then as you flew just above the four grain elevators, you could actually see four lanterns whizzing by in less than thirty seconds. These were not only the brightest outdoor lights in town, but the only ones. Nobody at that time ever dreamed that someday our village would actually have electricity. So that's what you might have seen in the 1930s and 1940s if you had flown at night over my home town of Sheho, Saskatchewan, a farming village of about seventy families totaling approximately 350 people on the Great Canadian Prairies.

But what can you see in only thirty seconds? There's a lifetime of stories in that town. So let's slow down. Let's take a walk along the gravel highway toward Sheho. As we enter the village from the west, we notice a sign reading "Sheho." Not "Sheho welcomes you." Not "Sheho population 350." Just "Sheho."

However, if a national magazine had sent its top team of journalists to Sheho to write a feature story about this village, the printed article might have read something like this: "Sheho is a typical four grain- elevator village, which means that its population is larger than most villages with only three grain elevators. That's important to know because grain elevators are a status symbol on the Canadian Prairies. Whenever someone from Sheho visits another village with fewer than four grain elevators, the visitor proudly boasts, 'We're bigger than you are. We have four elevators. You have only three.' But if the visitor is in a village or town with more than four elevators, he never mentions the word elevator and hopes that nobody else does, either.

"But there is more to talk about than elevators in this thriving village through which the Canadian Pacific Railway (C.P.R.) runs twice a day, once in the morning—westbound toward Saskatoon, Saskatchewan— and once in the evening eastbound toward Winnipeg, Manitoba. Just north of the railway and paralleling it is the world famous Saskatchewan Highway 14, a modern graveled road (with numerous potholes and washboards) over which as many as thirty cars and two buses sometimes travel in less than a day without breaking down. In case they do, there is a garage in this ultra modern village that someday, according to wild rumors, may even have electricity, running water, and indoor plumbing. However, nobody in his right mind believes these fantastic rumors. At night the village is well lighted by four Coleman gasoline-burning lanterns, each suspended from a telephone pole spaced one block apart. That is the main function of the telephone poles because the only telephone in this village is located at the Central Telephone Office in Grumetza's Store.

"In addition to grain elevators—remember, there are four of them— Sheho boasts of a tennis court, a railway station, and an open air skating rink, all along the south side of this superbly graveled highway. On the other side of this highway, a stone's throw north of where the cement sidewalk begins, is the hand-pumped well that serves the entire village. Sheho's best kept secret and its claim to fame (within the village) is its cold, fresh, pure drinking water, which is also used for washing clothes and taking sponge baths when all the water collected from rain or melted snow has been used up. Twice each day, every family in town sends its biggest or strongest member to the well for water. Carrying two galvanized steel pails to the well, he pumps the handle up and down until both pails are full, then trudges back home with a half-day's supply of water.

"A stone's throw south of the well, at the western edge of town, is where the three-block long cement-paved sidewalk begins. It runs east from Darling's house on the corner, past Katz General Store and Katz's house, past the Massey Harris Implement Shop, past Hoop's butcher shop, the Red and White Store, the Post Office, Leckie's Store, the Elite Cafe, the Queens Hotel, the Town Hall, Lys's General Store, the pool hall and barber shop, the Provincial liquor store, and the Rex Cafe. The cement sidewalk finally ends at a tiny building, the harness and shoe repair shop. From here, a cinder sidewalk continues east for a block, past the Ukrainian hall almost to the four-room brick school which accommodates 150 students from grades one through twelve.

"Although the entire sidewalk is actually the main street, it was originally named 'Railroad Avenue.' However, nobody ever calls it that. Nobody calls it anything except the 'sidewalk' or the 'street.'

"Sheho also has five—not four but five— dirt-covered, well-worn paths running north and south. Along these 'side streets' one finds a flour mill, two livery stables, a lumber yard, a garage, two churches, and about sixty cottages, and perhaps ten two-story buildings, all of which house Sheho's total population of about 350, which might include cats and dogs.

"Besides cats and dogs, which of course run loose, Sheho is proud of its four domesticated cows which are allowed to wander off to the surrounding fields during the daytime but come home every evening to be milked— unless they are in heat, during which time they usually run off to visit Frank Wunder's prize winning bull. Sheho is also proud of its numerous chickens and roosters, especially the roosters, each one of which competes with other roosters as loudly as he can to announce the dawn, but reigns unopposed over his private flock. Consequently, behind many of the homes, there are a number of chicken coops, as well as barns and manure piles, which are not only home to millions of flies in the summer, but also give off a special unmistakable odor that will never be confused with the fragrance of French perfumes.

"Be sure to slow down if you drive through Sheho," the article concludes, " or else you'll miss it; and unless you've seen Sheho, you haven't lived."

Unfortunately, the magazine article failed to mention the vegetable gardens. In the summer every family without exception had a large vegetable garden. Fortunately, however, the article omitted something else— the most important item of all. Away in the backyard of every home, as far away as possible, almost out of sight and painted inconspicuously, there was a very tiny building, barely large enough for one occupant at a time. Inside this building was a bench in the center of which the carpenter had cut a large hole. At one end of the bench in a cardboard container, one could find various reading materials, including last year's Eaton's Catalogue, Simpson's Catalogue, and numerous outdated newspapers in different languages, depending upon which family owned this miniature house. The most prevalent languages were English and Ukrainian; the least prevalent were Jewish and Chinese. All these wonderful reading materials were now being recycled for a more important use. From time to time, in addition to newspapers, one could find several soft tissue wrappings from Sunkist oranges and lemons, precious wrappings that had been carefully saved for the most important use of all. Although this tiny house was used several times a day without fail—by every member in the family— it was never occupied for more than a few minutes at a time—certainly no longer than was necessary. As one approached this out-of-the-way house, the reason was obvious: It stunk. Chloride of lime helped to disguise the stink, but replaced it with another odor that irritated the nostrils. In time, however, one either got used to the stench or breathed through the mouth. That was it! Take your choice.

On Halloween night, some of the older kids in town took delight in tipping over these tiny outhouses. That was big-time fun. For this reason, my father attached steel bars from our outhouse to the barn. It was what one called security—ultimate security—unmatched by any insurance company anywhere in the world. Besides, what kind of insurance company would sell you insurance coverage on an outdoor toilet? Can you think of an appropriate adjective?

By now you probably have a slight mental picture of Sheho and are wondering what it was like to live in this small primitive village. That's what I hope to tell you in this memoir— a look back at the microcosm of my world when I was growing up in Western Canada. But this book is more than that. For anyone interested in sociology, it presents a contrast in our technology and lifestyles during the closing years of the twentieth century with that of my own simple life on the Canadian Prairies more than half a century earlier, during the Great Depression and World War II. For those of you who are old enough to remember, this book will undoubtedly bring back your own memories of that era, some of them perhaps similar to mine. For the younger generation, this book offers an insight into what rural life was actually like long, long before anyone ever heard the word "computer" or "jet airplane."

This memoir, then, is about a different period in our history. Canadian or American—it doesn't really matter which history we are talking about. In small town rural America or Canada, the times were the same. My story begins during what we called "hard times," an era to which historians have subsequently named the "Great Depression." Our family didn't have much money then. In fact, I almost never did. But we all made our own fun. And unlike many of the kids today who join dangerous gangs that cause serious trouble, or other kids whose parents control their lives after school hours, driving them here and there, for little league baseball or soccer practice or some other supervised activity, we were free to do what we wanted to do after we did our chores, so long as we didn't get into trouble. The only stipulation was to be back home in time for supper. Then we were free again, not only during the school year but also during the long days of summer. Our parents didn't have to worry because nobody ever bothered us, and in turn, we rarely caused any problems. It was a time of innocence. We were glad to be young and carefree, growing up in this little rural village, with so many exciting things to do.

CHAPTER TWO
My First Car Ride

How can I describe the enormous contrast in technology and life style from my childhood days on the Canadian Prairies almost seven decades ago to these closing years of the twentieth century? Sheho, Saskatchewan, at that time was a farming village of about seventy families. We lived under what today would be called primitive conditions—without electricity, indoor plumbing, or any of the conveniences that even the poorest in our country now take for granted. The pace of our simple life was slow, very slow; so slow in fact that nobody every died from a heart attack brought about by over-excitement. The posted speed limit on the gravel highway through town was only fifteen miles an hour and for a good reason. Most of the traffic consisted of horses, which would not only get exhausted at such a prolonged speed, but might become frustrated or even acquire an inferiority complex if they saw anything moving faster than that.

Can you imagine now the awe and thrill I felt on July 20, 1969, as I witnessed the most dramatic event of this or any other century—man's first landing on the moon? On July 16, the Apollo XI astronauts had blasted off into space at 25,000 miles an hour, escaped from Earth's gravitational pull, and rocketed toward the moon, circling it three days later, and landing safely the following day, all the while broadcasting back to Earth, so that six hundred million people throughout the world not only heard their voices but saw their images on television. What a way to travel! And as I sat mesmerized in front of a television screen, watching Neil Armstrong set foot on the moon, 240,000 miles away—

and listening to his voice— "One small step for Man; one giant leap for Mankind!"—I could not help but reflect on how I felt as a child taking my first ride in a car, thirty-six years earlier.

It all began more than a week before we made that momentous journey of three hundred miles round-trip. Papa wanted to visit his sister and brother-in-law, my Aunt Bessie and Uncle Abe (who like Papa also owned a general store) and their family in Inglis, Manitoba. Inglis, slightly smaller than Sheho, was 150 miles away. That was a long, long way to travel. It might as well have been on the next continent. Visits were extremely rare then. We didn't have a car, nor did they; and travel was not easy, especially since they did not live on the main East-West railroad line. The year was 1933. We were in the depths of the Great Depression. It had been only twenty-five years since Henry Ford had invented his Model T, and exactly twenty since he had introduced the first automobile moving assembly line in Highland Park, Michigan. Only five people in our entire village drove a car, and almost none of the farmers around Sheho owned one. They traveled to our village either in a horse drawn buggy, or a wagon pulled by a team of horses, or they rode horseback or a bicycle. Some walked. In the winter they used a sleigh. Nobody had ever heard of the term "traffic jam." And at the age of five, I had never even sat in a car!

Before making this journey, Papa had to make numerous plans. First of all, he discussed the idea with Mama and with his closest friend, Mr. Leckie, the only other Jewish merchant in Sheho. The vote was unanimous. Second, he wrote a letter to Aunt Bessie and Uncle Abe. In a week he received their reply. Of course, they would all be delighted to see us, especially since they had never seen my baby sister, Sylvia, who was then two years old. So far so good. Third, he arranged with our next-door neighbor, Rufus Darling, to have him drive our entire family and Mr. Leckie to Inglis and back on a Sunday in mid June, when there would surely be enough daylight for the return trip. Three hundred miles is a long way. Who knew how long the drive might take in Mr. Darling's 1922 Dodge? Who knew how many flat tires the Dodge might get? Who knew how long we might get stuck in the mud if it rained? Who knew whether the headlights would work? It would be a long trip. It could be risky. Papa wasn't about to take any chances. Sixteen hours of daylight should be enough.

Mr. and Mrs. Darling were retired. Their house was right behind our woodpile. When the woodpile was used up, there was just open space between us—one big yard. We never even thought of a fence. Good neighbors don't need fences. A fence just gets in the way. Merle and Etta, my older sisters, and I were always going over to their house. We never knocked. We just walked in any time we felt like it. You never knock when you go into your own home. Maybe their home wasn't exactly our home, but it sure felt like it because Mrs. Darling was always there and I could always sit on her lap. She was my make believe grandma. My real grandma lived in the old country, where the children of Europe were starving any time I left any food on my plate. That's what Mama would tell me. "Eat! The children in Europe are starving!" So that's why I liked Mrs. Darling. All I ate over there was angel food cake, and if I left any on my plate, she didn't scold me. Besides, she had an organ and would play "Rock of Ages." She also had a little radio and sometimes we would listen to cowboy songs. I liked Mrs. Darling even if she wasn't my real Grandma. She told me she had two sons, Frank and Floyd, who lived far away and never came home to see her. She also had grandchildren. But they lived far away, too. So my sisters and I were just like her own grandchildren. But we never called her "Grandma." That's because our real grandma lived in the old country.

Mr. Darling, I learned many years later, had moved to Sheho from Fergus Falls, Minnesota, in 1902. He had made his fortune as a builder. He had built the only hotel in Sheho, owned at one time by Sam and Harry Bronfman, Canada's most famous bootleggers and founders of the Seagram Company. He had also built the general store that Papa now owned.

Mr. Darling's 1922 Dodge touring sedan had been a fine automobile in its day, away back when Papa married Mama in Winnipeg and brought her to Sheho. By 1933, however, it was an antique. The wheels had wooden spokes, and instead of real windows on the sides, there were open spaces shaped like windows but with no glass. Instead, leather flaps could be rolled up if one wanted to see outside, or rolled down to cover the spaces and partially protect the passengers from rain or dust or flying gravel. The Dodge rested on wooden blocks in his garage. That's how seldom he drove it. In fact, with the exception of my first "journey," I don't recall ever seeing that automobile off the blocks. That's what Mr. Darling called it. An "automobile."

After arranging for the ride, Papa had to hire somebody to take care of our cow, Bossy. All milk cows must be milked twice a day; Sunday is no exception. Fortunately, Mike Haluke, who had a dairy, knew how to milk cows. Thus, Papa knew that Bossy would be taken care of. Mike Haluke could keep the milk. Or he could give it back to Bossy to drink. She gave milk and she drank milk. She was quite a cow.

Finally, Papa had to double check with Uncle Abe and Aunt Bessie. Therefore, he had to make "the" telephone call. It wasn't easy. The only telephones in our entire village were owned and operated by the Saskatchewan Provincial Telephone Company, which had a "central" telephone office in practically every town and village in the province. (A settlement of over five hundred was classified as a "town"; under five hundred, a "village"; under one hundred, a "hamlet.")

Sheho's central phone office was located in Grumetza's General Store, a few blocks away from us. The girl who operated the switch-board was also known as "Central." That's what she was called by other telephone operators. She sat on a high stool facing a switchboard which contained all kinds of switches that connected her main phone to other switchboards throughout the province and ultimately throughout all of Canada and the United States. However, the process of placing a long distance telephone call was by no means simple. Rather, it was a very complicated step-by-step process that could take anywhere from min-utes to hours.

On Friday, two days before our momentous journey, Papa took me to the central office and told the operator he wanted to speak to Abe Shnider in Inglis, Manitoba. As she began plugging in switches, Papa took out his watch. He knew it would probably take at least ten minutes if he was lucky. He knew that after our central connected with Yorkton, sixty miles away, the call would have to be relayed to Roblin, Manitoba, another sixty miles away, then to Russell, Manitoba, twenty miles away, and finally, Russell would plug directly into the party line in Inglis.

Uncle Abe, years ahead of his time, had his own telephone in his store. The phone, however, was one of many on a party line that connected all these phones so that they all rang at the same time. Fortunately, each party had its own identifying ring—for example—two long rings and a short one. Thus, the person for whom the phone call was intended knew when to pick up the phone. So could anyone else. Obviously, it was impossible to keep a secret on a party line. In fact, the best way to make a public announcement was to phone somebody and say, "What I'm about to tell you is confidential. Don't breathe a word to anyone." That way everybody on the party line heard the news instantly.

After about fifteen minutes, Papa was ushered into the little glass booth. This booth contained a gigantic telephone. The oak base was at least as high as the yardstick we used to measure the yard goods in our store. It was wider than the wooden rulers we sold for a nickel. It looked like a huge empty Sunkist orange crate attached to the wall. From the box protruded a speaker arm, about the length of a ruler. Papa lowered it so he could speak into the little black cone at the end. Then he slipped the receiver out of its y-shaped cradle and held it up to his ear. That huge telephone was too scary for me.

Papa shouted into the cone: "HELLO, ABE HELLO, ABE!" If he had shouted any louder, he wouldn't have needed a telephone. He spoke in Jewish. He always spoke Jewish at home. So did Mama. My sisters and I understood Jewish but answered in English. It was easier. Besides, Canada was an English country and everybody *should* speak English. Sometimes he mixed Jewish and English. Sometimes he mixed English and Jewish. That's how he spoke. In Jenglish. Mixed up.

"HELLO ABE! *Laaibka. Veer gte kimen tzo der mit Leckie in Darling's car Zintig. Veer vil deer zeyen nooch elef azeyger, efsha tsvelf. Zoog Bahsey* Hello. Good-bye." ["Hello, Abe. Louis. We are going to come to your place with Leckie in Darling's car Sunday. We will see you after eleven o'clock, maybe twelve. Say hello to Bessie. Good bye."]

And so, with all arrangements made, it was time to get ready for this historic journey. On Saturday night after closing his store, Papa polished his only pair of "Sunday" shoes with black Nugget shoe polish and a brush. Mr. Leckie came over and did the same, then went home. Papa then made preparations for his bath, the first "real" bath he had taken in years. He took daily sponge baths, of course, as we all did; but this was to be a real bath, like the one Mama used to give me in our little tin bathtub every Saturday night.

Papa first unlocked the engine house, located several steps from our outside kitchen. It was like a museum, the Sheho Royal Museum of Canada. At one time it had housed an engine for generating electricity. But now the engine lay idle and was simply part of the clutter and junk Mama and Papa had accumulated but were afraid to throw away. They always thought it might come in handy some day. "You never know." That's what they said. Inside, stood a large bathtub filled with shmatas [rags], old clothes, old shoes, and more clutter. The bathtub looked brand new, not necessarily because it had been protected by clutter, but because it had rarely been used. It wasn't easy to take a bath when the stove for heating water was in one building but the bathtub in another— filled with junk and clutter. So the next thing Papa did was to empty the clutter and junk from the bathtub. And that wasn't easy.

Next, he carried several pails of hot water from our wood-burning kitchen stove to the bathtub in the Sheho Royal Museum of Canada. Then he undressed and took his bath. As he soaked in the tub, he murmured, *"Es is a machaiya!"* [It is delightful!]

The rest of us sponged because Papa had used most of the hot water.

Mama then laid out Papa's only Sunday shirt, along with his only tie and suit, a two-button, single-breasted, purplish burgundy, twin striped worsted that he had bought long before I was born. After we had all bathed, we went to bed early. I was excited.

At three o'clock in the morning, we all got out of bed. I distinctly remember it was three o'clock because I have risen that early only two other times in my entire life, once by mistake, and once to go mountain climbing. And I shall never get up that early again. But at the age of five, I was in no position to exert what little free will I possessed. Besides, this was going to be the most exciting thing I had ever done in my life. Taking a trip in a car.

We carried blankets and jackets to the car, which was now off the blocks. Then each of us climbed onto the running board and began to pile in. First, Mama and Papa and Mr. Leckie got into the back seat, followed by my older sisters, Merle and Etta. Then I climbed onto their laps. Finally, Mrs. Darling climbed into the front seat, carrying my baby sister.

Mr. Darling then began the enormous job of cranking the engine to get it started. Although some of the newer models featured self starters, his 1922 Dodge had no such advanced technology. He bent down in front of the car, inserted the crank into the hole at the base of the radiator and began to crank. The engine spat and hissed and died. He cranked it again. The engine spat, sputtered, hissed, and groaned. He cranked again and again. The engine was tired. It wanted to sleep—maybe forever. But Mr. Darling was persistent. He swore under his breath. He would show the engine who was master. And so, with each crank, the engine showed more signs of life. Finally, after sputtering, hissing, shaking, and quaking, the engine roared into life—ready and raring to go. And off we drove.

Like a chauffeur for King George V and the Royal Family, Mr. Darling sat ramrod straight, peering neither to the right nor to the left. He turned the corner onto the main highway, Saskatchewan 14, and headed east through the village for two blocks until he came to the upright marker in the middle of the road, in front of the hotel, where the highway turned north. He made the right-angle turn north, and then another right-angle turn where the highway turned east again. Saskatchewan highways were engineered with only one kind of turn—a full ninety degrees. Gradual turns were never used by the Highway Department in those days. Perhaps the Highway Department had never heard of such engineering marvels. Or perhaps they had not yet been invented.

Saskatchewan 14 was hardly the smoothest highway in the world. Not only was it graveled, as were practically all Canadian highways at that time, but it had numerous "washboards"—extremely rough surfaces resembling the old fashioned washboards on which Mama washed clothes. The car bounced up and down and even sideways on these washboards, shaking us and even making us dizzy at first, until we got used to the jarring ride. We had just survived one of these washboards and were now about two miles out of town when Mrs. Darling turned around and shouted, "WE'RE DOING THIRTY-FIVE MILES AN HOUR!"

I had no idea how fast thirty-five miles an hour was, but I knew it must be faster than any car in the world because I couldn't count past twenty and it took me a long time to get even that far, and I was sure thirty-five was way more than twenty.

A car behind us tooted its horn to pass. Mr. Darling moved away over to the shoulder of the road. The car passed, kicking up gravel that flew in all directions, some of it striking the windshield. A cloud of dust followed the speeding car, practically choking us. "LOOK AT HIM GO," shouted Mr. Darling. "HE MUST BE DOING ALMOST FIFTY." I could hardly believe it. He was going even faster than we were.

We had traveled exactly sixty miles in just under two hours when we stopped for breakfast in Yorkton, a city of five thousand population. Yorkton was the only city in eastern Saskatchewan and, therefore, the hub of a huge farming area in that part of the province. Not only did Yorkton have electricity and indoor plumbing in most of its homes, but it boasted black-topped asphalt roads on its two main streets, Broadway and Betts Avenues.

There were two cafes on Broadway, the Rio and the Boston. Papa chose the Boston. His oldest sister lived in Boston. That's a big city in the United States.

I was excited as we entered the Boston Cafe. What a thrill! I had never seen or even imagined such a modern and luxurious cafe. Real leather -cushioned booths and large overhead fans and girls called waitresses who waited on you. I had never seen a waitress before. Both cafes back home were each owned by two Chinamen. They waited on the customers themselves besides preparing the meals. The Chinamen did not have any wives because I had never seen a Chinawoman.[2] Anyway our family never ate in either the Elite Cafe, next to Mr. Leckie's store, or the Rex Cafe, past Lys's store. Why should we? Mama was a much better cook then the Chinamen; and besides, we ate only kosher food. But eating breakfast here in Yorkton was a different matter. We were far from home and it was a matter of convenience. Besides, we would not order anything that was not kosher. The adults ordered toast, marmalade and tea; and we children ordered cocoa and toast. We always had cocoa and toast for breakfast at home. Fry's cocoa with hot water—no milk. It was not until many years later, after leaving home, that I learned about bacon and eggs.

After breakfast Papa picked up the check, carefully took out two folded dollars from his change purse, and gave the money to the Chinaman at the cash register. Papa received some change which he put back in his purse. [These were hard times and tipping was unheard of.]

We continued our journey east toward Manitoba. I will never forget crossing the border. Mrs. Darling pointed to the large sign, "Welcome to Manitoba." Then, to make sure we could again hear her voice above the road noise, she shouted, " WE'VE CROSSED THE BORDER! WE'RE NOW IN MANITOBA." I thought it was a different country. How miraculous! On one side of that sign is Saskatchewan, my home. On the other, Manitoba—a strange land. A different world! What about the boundary—the thin dividing line between Saskatchewan and Manitoba? Which province claimed that razor thin strip of land? And I wondered exactly where Saskatchewan ended and Manitoba began. It confused me. Perhaps I should have asked Mrs. Darling. But everyone told me that I asked too many questions. Questions like: "How high is the sky? How far away are the stars? Why doesn't God have a wife and family? What's under a woman's skirt?" Perhaps some day I would know.

Soon the terrain changed from prairie to high rolling hills and we began to climb. Although the curves were still sharp, they were not right-angle curves like those in Saskatchewan and western Manitoba. They were more gradual, as the road twisted and turned and climbed until we were high above the farms below. Then we began to descend, slowly, and Mrs. Darling shouted, "WE'RE ENTERING THE ASSINIBOINE VALLEY!" I had never heard the word "valley," but I could see that these hills were much, much higher than any back home. I could climb any of the hills around Sheho with ease. In winter, Merle, Etta, and I would take turns on our sled, sliding down the big hill near the creek by Cecil Scott's home. But these hills were huge—I mean enormous. I wouldn't dare slide down them, even if they were all covered with snow.

Mrs. Darling called them "mountains." The only time I had heard the word "mountains" was when Mrs. Darling sang "When the moon comes over the mountain." Now I knew what a mountain was. I wondered how many more things I would learn from Mrs. Darling before this trip was over. Then she shouted, "THERE'S THE ASSINIBOINE RIVER!" I was amazed. A real river! Our creek was six feet wide in the spring. In the summer it dried up altogether. But this river—it must have been at least twice or even three times as wide as our creek. And the water was still flowing.

As the car wound around these mountains, Mr. Darling frequently sounded the horn. "Uh-oo-oo-ah." It sounded like Papa trying to throw up, only much louder. Mrs. Darling explained that these were "blind" curves and Mr. Darling was warning any other driver on the other side of this mountain that we were heading in his direction and the other driver had better keep to the extreme right-hand side of the road, as we were doing, to avoid a head-on crash. Sure enough, we did meet another car around one of the curves, and its driver also tooted his horn. As we approached each other, each car moved so far over to its right that I thought we might tumble down the mountain. [Guard rails were then reserved only for the steepest and most dangerous stretches of the road. Otherwise, driver beware.] But Mr. Darling was an excellent driver. How lucky for us to have him as our driver on this dangerous road.

When we passed through Roblin, we knew we were only about twenty miles away from Inglis—less than an hour away. A light drizzle had fallen, cutting down the dust on the main highway. Although we had not encountered much traffic on this Sunday morning, we were occasionally engulfed in dust from cars passing in either direction. If we stayed a mile back from any other car driving in the same direction we were going, we avoided the dust. But we could not avoid it when we met on-coming traffic. And if we rolled down the flaps to cover the open spaces, which we called windows, we couldn't see outside unless we peered straight ahead. We therefore kept the flaps up and ate the dust. This drizzle, then, offered us relief. At least that's what we thought until we turned off the main gravel highway, twelve miles from Inglis and took a smaller road leading toward our final destination.

This road was narrower than the main highway and so thinly graveled that it might as well have been a plain old dirt road like the one going south from our school to Hoffman's farm.

The drizzle had turned into a light rain, and the rain—especially where it had come down hard—had turned stretches of the road into mud. The mud was even worse in the ditches. At least there were ruts in the road through which one could navigate if one were lucky. But not so in the ditches. And although nobody intentionally would think of driving his car into the ditch—certainly not Mr. Darling—his car started to slide. It went one way and then another, left and right, then left and too far over to the right, and we ended up in the narrow, muddy ditch. Mr. Darling tried rocking the car back and forth, but it didn't help. The wheels spun and threw mud in all directions. The heavy Dodge was stuck. There was only one solution. Find a farmer whose horses would pull the car back onto the road.

The job of finding a farmer was left up to Papa. Because each section of land [one mile by one mile totaling 640 acres] was inhabited by at least two or three or sometimes even four families, Papa did not have very far to trudge in the ankle-deep mud. Maybe as far as from the town well to Lys's store, about three blocks. But the mud was not marked off into blocks. It was just one long stretch of mud. I felt sorry for him. He had just polished his shoes the night before.

Fortunately, Papa soon reached a farm house with a red barn behind it. He was in luck. He knew what was in the barn beside manure, and he knew the farmer was home. Where else would he go, especially when it was raining? When the farmer learned that Papa was on his way to visit his Shnider relatives in Inglis but was stuck in the mud, he readily agreed to help. He knew Uncle Abe because he traded at Shnider's store. It would be a pleasure to help, especially since Papa would pay him a whole dollar. That princely sum would buy two blocks of salt (one for each horse), a package of cigarette tobacco, and a package of zigzag or Chantecleer papers to roll the cigarettes. It was "found" money. The farmer hitched up his two best horses—mixed breeds. They were not pure bred Clydesdales, manicured ever so neatly, with their tails tied in curly knots. They would never pull an empty beer wagon for the Anheuser

Busch Brewing Company. Never! Not in a million years! They were Manitoba farm horses, bred and raised for working on the farm. They were real work horses. They pulled the plough. They pulled the harrow. They pulled the cutter. They pulled the binder. They pulled the threshing machine. They pulled the wagon to town, a wagon full of Manitoba number-one hard wheat, not empty beer kegs. They took one look at the car and its occupants stuck in the Manitoba mud and snorted—a horse laugh—as if to say, "Horseless carriage. Serves you right." Then they glanced at the foreign license plates and snorted again, even harder.

The farmer hitched his horses to the 1922 Dodge, in which nine people sat and prayed. He clicked his tongue. "Giddyup." One tug—two at the most—and the car was back on the road. The mixed breed Manitoba farm horses seemed to take delight in showing off their prowess, especially in front of foreigners who didn't even have sense enough to keep their horseless carriage out of the ditch.

Carefully navigating his 1922 Dodge over the narrow muddy road, Mr. Darling finally reached Inglis less than an hour later. We all piled out of the car to the joyous greetings of our hosts, who embraced and kissed us as if we were long lost relatives who had just come over on the boat from Europe. Even though everyone oohed and awed over my baby sister, I also received my share of attention. The last time they had seen me had been four years earlier, when I, too, had been a baby.

Although Merle and Etta had told me about the Shniders every time they came back from their summer holidays (vacations), this was the first time I had met them. Uncle Abe was tall and had a bigger belly than Papa. Aunt Bessie was short, like Mama, but much plumper. My cousin Myra was also on the plump side, with a beautiful smile and a beautiful round face. Her younger brother, Maurice, also had a round face, but unlike his sister, he rarely smiled. His straight jet-black hair was combed sideways, giving him a rather mature appearance. Charlie, the youngest, was also the shortest in the family. He had curly brown hair and was grinning, always grinning. I was quite in awe of them.

Like the homes of many other general merchants in that era, the Shnider's home was attached to the rear of their store. As we walked through their yard to enter the house, I noticed their flower garden. Everyone I knew had a vegetable garden. The Shniders had one too. But a flower garden like this—I had never seen anything like it. I was dazzled by the colors. I learned later that my aunt was known throughout the area for her beautiful flower garden.

My most vivid and lasting impression of that visit was the breakfast. It featured several plates of cantaloupes cut in half. What a lavish breakfast! The only times I had ever eaten cantaloupe before were on rare occasions when Papa would return from Mr. Leckie's store in the evening with a whole cantaloupe. He would then cut it into sections so that our entire family could enjoy a piece of this delectable fruit. But here—an entire half-cantaloupe for each person! And as if that weren't enough, there was also shredded wheat with milk, rye bread, and coffee. We hardly ever ate shredded wheat at home because we didn't stock it in our store. Instead we had corn flakes. The only time we had rye bread was when Mama would return from a buying trip in Winnipeg. She would usually bring back rye bread and kosher salami. What a treat! And the only time we ever had coffee was on a special occasion when we entertained guests. But this was a very special occasion, and it obviously called for a very special breakfast—our third breakfast of the day.

After breakfast, Uncle Abe gave us a tour of his store. Although his yard-goods section was smaller than ours, he had a much larger grocery section than we had, featuring such items as bread, cheese, bologna, fresh fruit (besides apples, oranges, and lemons—which we carried), shredded wheat, and soda pop. He also had a huge hardware department. Most impressive, though, was his telephone. It was just like the one Papa had used in Sheho's central office. I wondered how he was able to get his own telephone. And as if that weren't enough, he finally showed us his electric generator in the basement. They had electricity. Imagine! And even a large cabinet radio. I was astounded. This family, obviously, must be very rich. But more to the point, the Shniders were away ahead of the times. At least twenty years ahead. That's as far as I could count.

What I enjoyed most about that visit was their dog. They had a short-haired black and white mongrel called "Tippie." He stayed inside the house. He was part of the household, except he didn't eat at the table. But he stayed under the table to get the scraps Maurice and Charlie fed him. He could even do tricks. Maurice would say, "Shake a paw." And sure enough, Tippie would extend his paw to be shaken. I never had a dog. Mama and Papa wouldn't hear of it. And even if I ever got a dog— by some miraculous Divine intervention—that dog sure as heck would not be allowed in our house. As Mama would say in Jewish, *"Ich vil nicht hooben kein hint in mine shteeb."* Translated, the edict was, "I will not have a dog in my house." And that was that. But at least here I could play with their dog. I could pet him. I could shake his paw. I could let him lick my face. He was a smart, loveable dog. I wished I had a dog.

CHAPTER THREE
The Creek That Flowed Through Wunder's Field

Shortly after moving to California in July of 1955, my oldest sister, Merle, and her husband invited me to join them and their three young children for a wiener roast. After they bought Kosher wieners, relish, buns, soda pop, lighter fluid and expensive firewood in a supermarket, we all piled into their car on a Saturday night, then drove twenty miles down the Pacific Coast Highway to Huntington Beach State Beach Park, where they paid admission to enter, then parked the car in front of a cement fire ring. Believe me, we were not alone. For miles and miles up and down the wide sandy beach, thousands of other cars were parked next to fire rings like ours, and thousands of families were starting their individual fires or already roasting wieners or marshmallows over the roaring fires on the sand, inside one-foot high cement rings spaced only yards apart. This was what Californians called "getting back to nature." I immediately felt homesick for my life on the sparsely settled Canadian Prairies. And I could not help but think back to the excitement my closest buddy and I experienced roasting potatoes on long summer evenings during my early school years.

Our excitement began at what I shall call the Western bridge, the first one you came to as you walked along the gravel highway and crossed the railway tracks to enter Sheho from the west. At the age of ten, Walter Lys and I used to crawl down the banks of the creek and stand beneath that bridge. We would just wait there and listen for a car to cross. We had to wait for quite a while since there weren't many cars entering or leaving Sheho. But when we did hear one in the distance, our hearts pounded, for we knew it would be only a matter of a minute or two before that car would drive over the wooden bridge. Then for two seconds as it drove right over our heads, the entire bridge would shake and roar. We thought it might collapse or explode. It was absolutely terrifying. But as soon as the car had crossed, we knew we were safe. What a relief! Now we had to wait for another car, and who knows how long that might take? If we were lucky, maybe only half an hour.

It was also near that bridge, just along the banks of the creek that flowed through Wunder's field where we held our famous "charcoal potato roasts." We were both Wolf Cubs (similar to Cub Scouts in the United States) and, therefore, knew how to build a camp fire without using paper and with only one match. After the dry twigs had begun to burn, we placed our potatoes alongside the tiny fire, then carefully piled larger twigs and branches in the shape of a wigwam over the potatoes and the fire. Soon the fire began to crackle then roar, and our potatoes gradually underwent a magic transformation, changing color from brown to brownish black, and eventually to charcoal. But it was not until the embers had died that we would dare take the potatoes out. We simply rolled them out of the white-hot embers. They were now as black as coal. When the potatoes had cooled off a bit, we would cut them in half, sprinkle some salt and pepper over them, and eat them—charcoal, peelings, and all—savoring each delicious mouthful, as though it were a banquet fit for a king. Perhaps you may think we were eating dirt and charcoal. Be that as it may, to us it was a delicacy. And I can truthfully say that I have never enjoyed any "gourmet" potatoes in my entire life as much as I did those home grown potatoes from our own garden, charcoal roasted to perfection by Sheho's master chefs Walter Lys and Jackie Kates. I shall give Walter top billing because it was eventually his idea how to simplify the process by using paper to easily start a roaring fire, then throw the potatoes into the fire and wait until they were thoroughly incinerated before eating what remained of them. Prepared that way, they tasted even better.

The creek that flowed through Wunder's field brings back some of the fondest memories of my early boyhood. So does Frank Wunder's field. For the creek, which ran under the Western bridge, snaked its way north then east through Frank Wunder's field, to become our swimming hole. That is where I first learned how to swim, even if I could only dog paddle. It was on Wunder's field, just above the creek, that I learned how to fire a 22 caliber rifle, how to drown gophers, and how to use plaster in building a log cabin.

Although Frank Wunder and his family lived almost one-quarter of a mile west of us—virtually out of town—I began going over to their home every day after school when I was about seven or eight. Clifford was three years older than I, and his brother Cecil about five years older than Clifford. For some reason they were building a log cabin. I think they were pretending to be pioneers, like their grandfather Peter. Since I wanted to make myself useful, I helped Clifford mix mud and straw to make the plaster which we used to pad the spaces between the logs. There were no windows in that log cabin, nor any door, even though there was a doorway. But there was a floor. It was earth. And the roof was thatched with straw. It was an authentic log cabin. And I can truthfully say that in my own little way, I helped to build it.

Because Frank Wunder owned the field through which the creek flowed, we occasionally—but only occasionally—referred to that property as "Wunder's Field" or "Wunder's Pasture." However, we did not really consider it private property, even though he raised pure-bred Hereford cattle on that land. There were no signs reading "Private Property— no hunting, no fishing, no trespassing." Even the barbed wire fence he had constructed to keep his cattle inside his property made little difference to anyone who wanted to enter his field for whatever reason. We simply lifted the upper strand of wire, pushed down on the middle and lower strands, then crawled through the fence. It never entered our minds that we were trespassing. We had never heard of that word. The only time we ever thought about it was when we spied his bull in the pasture. That huge, red bull spelled danger. It was much more effective than any sign might be in reminding us that this was really private property. And since nobody was remotely interested in becoming a matador, picador, toreador, or any other kind of bullfighter, we retraced our steps back through the barbed wire fence, back to safety. If there is one thing for which I would now like to thank the Almighty, it is simply for His cooperation in keeping Frank Wunder's bull interested in more sensual things than chasing us away from the creek which widened into our one-and-only swimming hole.

By late April the snow had usually melted and the creek had begun to flow. This was not the awesome Peace River emptying into the Arctic Ocean. It certainly was not the mighty Mississippi. And by no possible stretch of the imagination was it the St. Lawrence. It was a creek. If a college football team drank enough beer during an evening, they could produce such a creek. It might not be the same color. It might not flow as swiftly or as long as our creek did. But it would be almost as wide. And almost as deep. That was our creek.

In order to water his livestock, Frank Wunder had dredged the creek into an oval shaped hole about thirty feet long, fifteen feet wide in places, and about five feet deep in the middle. That is where I learned how to swim. But we did not go into the water until it was comfortable enough to swim, in June.

"June's the time to swim," said Walter Harris, one of my second grade classmates. So immediately after school, away we would go. We had no use for bathing suits because we didn't have any. We simply undressed, threw our clothes in a pile along the bank, and waded into the water bare naked. No girls allowed. Half a century later, I learned that a number of girls used to hide in the bushes on the hills high above the creek to peek at us. That was Sheho's greatest excitement of their young lives.

The bottom of the swimming hole was 100% pure, black, Saskatchewan mud, the softest, stickiest, and deepest mud you can imagine. The only term I can use to describe it is "quickmud" instead of "quicksand" because you sank at least a foot as soon as you entered the swimming hole. That's why I had to learn how to swim. The first time I entered that mud hole was when I was about five. I had accompanied my father and the other Jewish merchant in town, Mr. Leckie, to the swimming hole on a Sunday. We all waded into the mud hole. I had waded only a few feet before I began to sink. I cried out, "Help! I'm drowning." They pulled me out. Otherwise, I would have disappeared and you would not be reading this book. However, since I never was a quitter, I soon

learned how to dog paddle and how to swim on my back. By the following year, I could swim across that mud hole in either direction with ease.

Because of its muddy bottom, our swimming hole turned a grayish-
black color as soon as a few of us entered. (50% black would describe
it.) By early July, the creek began to dry up, and our swimming hole
began to shrink. Only a few of us continued to use it on a daily basis. By
now the color had turned to a blackish-gray—about 70% black. Worse
yet, leeches, which we called "bloodsuckers," attached themselves to
our bodies, and we had to pull them off. It was messy. By mid July, only
a few of us diehards continued to swim in the muddy hole. We told ourselves it was still fun, in spite of the nasty bloodsuckers. But by the end
of the month, we finally gave up the ghost and left the mud hole to its
rightful owner and the bloodsuckers. We would all be back the following June.

Frank Wunder, in addition to dredging the creek for his livestock,
had also built a wooden trough which could be filled with water for the
cattle. This trough resembled a crude row boat. It was long enough to
seat at least two people and stable enough to be used as a raft by two
boys pretending to be explorers.

Oh, how Walter Lys and I loved to ride up and down the creek in that
raft! We used large tree branches for poles to push and guide the raft
along, one of us acting as navigator, and the other supplying the power.
In early April, just as soon as the snow had barely begun to melt, we
would chug our way through the remaining slushy snow banks in
Wunder's Field, until we got to the swimming hole, still covered along
its banks with snow. There we would "borrow" the raft for our explora-
tions of the untamed wilderness. At times I would be Samuel Champlain
and he would be John Cabot, one in the service of France, and the other
in the service of His Majesty, the King of England. Or the roles might be
reversed. Or we would be some other explorers, bravely entering the
unknown, traveling by canoe as far as the raging river would allow before encountering death-defying rapids or impassable water falls. Perhaps the Iroquois or some other tribe might be lurking in the forest along
the banks of this mighty river, waiting to take our scalps. Danger lurked
everywhere. But we were not the ones to turn back. Not yet. Not until we

came to a turn in the creek where a fallen log barred our way, forcing our return to the swimming hole.

Although the creek was navigable for only about three hundred yards, and only in one direction (downstream), we never tired of exploring the banks along the way. They were often covered with bushes and shrubs and willow trees. Once as we floated near a particular bush, we noticed a duck flying out of the thickets. Stopping our raft, we separated the bushes and discovered her flock of ducklings. We picked one up with the greatest of care and gingerly held it in our hands. I have never felt anything so fluffy and soft. The peeping from its tiny beak told us how helpless it was. That was all we could bear. Quickly and ever so gently we put it back in the nest. It was an experience I will never forget.

In addition to being a home for ducks, crows, robins, rabbits, and other wildlife, Wunder's field was also the domain for thousands of gophers. Certainly, they outnumbered the human population in that field and other farms throughout the province by at least 100:1. Besides eating the farmers' crops, their holes—entrances to and exits from their burrows—were a life-threatening hazard to livestock and horses. If a horse or cow caught its foot in a gopher hole, the result would almost certainly be a broken leg, and the animal had to be shot to put it out of its misery.

Recognizing the menace of these teeming, dangerous rodents, the Saskatchewan government offered a bounty of a few pennies for each gopher tail it collected. For more than one reason, therefore, farmers were anxious to kill all the gophers they could, either with gopher poison, steel jawed traps, the 22 caliber rifle (simply called the "22"), or by drowning them. And since Wunder's field contained ample water in the creek and more than enough gopher holes, it provided Clifford Wunder, his younger brother, Murray, and a few other kids including me with another pastime—drowning gophers.

After school, beginning in late April and lasting through May, when I was in the third and fourth grades, a few of us kids would go to Wunder's field, just above the swimming hole. One of Wunder's dogs would usually join the hunt. The adult gophers at this time of year, having recently emerged from their winter hibernation, were extremely thin. But they were still wary of the many dangers that lurked above their burrows—long and elaborate tunnels with numerous entrances and exits. These gophers were "smart." They were survivors. They would cautiously emerge from beneath the ground, with only their heads showing. Then, slowly, they would crawl out of the hole and stand erect on their hind feet, surveying their domain. If it seemed safe, they would run for a few feet, stop, stand erect again, then continue running to a clump of grass or to another hole. Some of their litter usually followed them, slowly learning the lessons of survival. But as soon as the adult gophers noticed us near their hole, they would sound a shrill, ear piercing shriek, a warning to other gophers nearby, and almost immediately disappear into one of their many holes. If their litter had followed them above ground, some of these young would also retreat. The remaining stragglers, however, might or might not live to see another day. It all depended on the hunter—or the dog. We called these gophers "stupid." We did not go after them. Even to us, hunting had its limits. It would be like shooting rabbits or deer today with an assault rifle.

If the dog was part of our hunting party, we would wait until it chased its fair prey down the gopher hole. The dog would then begin to dig and dig and dig —relentlessly—the dirt flying between its hind legs in a torrent, like wheat coming out of a threshing machine. What a sight! That dog certainly knew how to dig. But dig as it might, there was no way it could catch the gopher. The tunnels were too deep and too numerous. There was only one way to get the gopher out. Flush it out with water.

As the other kids, armed with clubs, guarded some of the surrounding holes through which the gopher might escape, I climbed down the hill to the creek, where I filled a pail full of water, and then climbed back up. While Clifford or Murray held their dog, another member of our group or I poured the water down the hole. We waited. The dog could hardly be restrained. Usually the water disappeared quickly, indicating that the tunnel was not yet even remotely flooded. The gopher would therefore remain below. We needed more water, perhaps several pails more, before we could flush the gopher out. And so down the hill and up the hill I went again and again, each time the water disappearing more slowly than before. Now it was only a matter of time before the gopher must come up. One more pail full. At last the water began to back up. We waited excitedly. We knew the hole was full. The water swirled as the gopher, its fur soaking wet, began to emerge. First the top of its head came into view, then its large, brown slanted eyes staring straight ahead. Instantly, the dog grabbed it by the head and began to shake it—violently—up and down and sideways, again and again. Water sprayed in a fine mist from the drenched coat of the gopher, its paws and body only a blur through the violent shaking. Soon the dog threw its prey on the ground. The gopher lay still, its neck broken. Its tail would fetch a stick or two of licorice candy or some bubble gum at Grumetza's store. I felt guilty. I didn't need that kind of candy or gum. We had our own.

Another method of hunting these rodents was with a slingshot. Johnny Drobot, who had lost his mother and who lived with his grandmother in a small cabin, was one year ahead of me in school. He always came to class with his own hand-made slingshot sticking out of his rear pocket. He could put a stone in the leather pouch of this crude weapon, hold it between his thumb and index finger in either hand, stretch the rubber sling which was attached to its Y-shaped handle, close one eye and squint with the other, with his tongue hanging out of the side of his mouth as he took aim at anything—a can, a sparrow, or a gopher—release the sling, and WHAM—bulls eye. He rarely missed.

One day, perhaps because he was tired of lending me his own slingshot, he made me one. Using his jackknife, he cut a Y-shaped branch from a poplar tree, filed it down to one foot in length, cut some rubber from the inner tube of a tire, attached this rubber to the upper posts of the Y and to the leather pouch he had cut from the tongue of an old shoe, then handed the slingshot to me. He had even whittled the bark away from the Y-shaped handle, so that it glistened in the sun. The rubber, I vividly remember, was a beautiful red. That slingshot was a beauty—a true work of art. Unfortunately, one day tragedy struck. It disappeared. It is one of the very few articles I sincerely regret having lost. In fact, it was the only "weapon" I ever owned or ever shall own.

Unlike Johnny Drobot, I did not kill any gophers with that slingshot. My aim was not good enough. Nor was my aim good enough even with the "22." But I had fun firing the rifle. I liked the sound of the shot as I pulled the trigger. It gave me quite a thrill. Besides, it was only on a rare occasion that I had the opportunity to go shooting.

Once in a while, when Frank Wunder took his sons out to shoot gophers, they would include me in the hunting party. After I had asked them if I could take a shot, they loaded the 22, cocked it, then handed it to me. I held it as steadily as I could, took aim at a gopher, and fired. I remember seeing the dirt fly right next to the gopher, but I doubt if I ever hit anything except the gopher hole. That was hardly the case with Frank Wunder. I remember glancing at him as he took aim. Then quickly I peered at his target. Instantly, as soon as I heard the ear-splitting "crack," I saw the gopher fly backwards, blood oozing from its head or body, drenching its coat in a bright crimson, its feet twitching for only a few seconds before it lay still. Only then did I realize that although hunting may have been fun for us, it wasn't exactly a picnic for the gophers. But for Frank Wunder, it meant one less gopher hole and possibly one less crippled cow.

As I grew older, unlike Ernest Hemingway, my hunting career ended altogether. I found it more fun rolling tires all over town with Howard Tansley and cycling to Maas's Lake with Walter Lys than I did shooting gophers. Besides, I never had a rifle. My father was vehemently opposed to hunting. "Let Ayseff hunt," he would say, referring to the biblical brother of Jacob,—Esau—the patriarch of the Arabs— and to gentiles in general. "Jews don't hunt."

Wunder's field also provided great fun occasionally for almost everyone in our school. In early fall, the school would hold a wiener roast in that field. Anyone who wanted to attend would contribute fifteen cents to buy wieners and buns. We would meet in the field an hour after supper, and several of the older kids would start bonfires. Then everyone would break off a branch from a willow or poplar tree, borrow a jack knife from someone, and whittle one end of the branch to a sharp prong which could pierce the wiener so that it would be ready for roasting. One could then hold this branch over the fire and, hopefully, only the wiener would get roasted. After the fires began roaring, we held these crude utensils —each containing a wiener at one end—over the fire. If the branch wasn't sturdy enough, it would bend or even break and the wiener would fall into the fire and become incinerated. Or if one held the wiener directly into the fire for too long, the whole branch would catch fire. Or if one didn't rotate the wiener, it would be black on one side and raw on the other. There were a great many ors and ifs in this equation. But it was fun. I was smart enough to get Johnny Drobot to cut a big branch for me and sharpen the end. Then I waited until the fire had died down to white hot embers before roasting my allocation of wieners.

We hardly ever ate wieners at home because we kept Kosher. Twice a year, when Mama returned from a buying tip in Winnipeg, she would bring back such delicacies as Jewish rye bread and kosher wieners.

Then she would cook the life out of those thick all beef wieners, and by the time she put one on my plate, any semblance of the original flavor was left in the pot of water she threw away. Nevertheless, after I covered them with mustard, they were a treat—even without buns.

But in no way could they be compared to the non-Kosher wieners that I roasted over the bonfire we shared at night in Wunder's Field under the full harvest moon. And when I placed mine inside a bun, I did not smother it with mustard or relish. I don't remember how many hot dogs I ate that night, but I know I didn't go away hungry. And I know I've never again tasted such delicious hot dogs. In fact, even though I've since had the privilege of dining at some of the finest restaurants in Canada and the United States, I have never tasted anything so good as those roasted hot dogs I savored that night under a harvest moon. The only delicacy that might compare would be the blackened, almost incinerated potatoes that Walter Lys and I roasted in our own tiny camp fire, near the Western bridge, alongside the creek that flowed through Wunder's field.

CHAPTER FOUR
Early Country Doctors

Every time my wife and I visit someone in a hospital, she always insists on peeking into the maternity ward to view the newly born infants. (I think she's trying to tell me something, although it's a little too late.) During those times, I can't help but contrast the state-of-the art technology in medicine today with that practiced by rural family doctors when I was growing up. With rare exceptions today in the western industrialized world, practically all infants are born in hospitals. Such was hardly the case when I was a child. In rural areas, very few hospitals existed and almost all infants were born at home.

Although my oldest sister, Merle, and I were both born in a hospital in Winnipeg, Manitoba, my other two sisters, Etta and Sylvia, as well as my cousins in the Shnider family, were all born at home in Sheho. How well I remember the day my younger sister, Sylvia, was born! In fact, that is the earliest date I can vividly remember, November 23, 1931. And it is no exaggeration to say that I can remember it as clearly as though it had happened this morning.

I had been sleeping overnight on our chesterfield (sofa), in the living room. The living room—which we called a "sitting room"—adjoined our dining room without any partition between the two. A large black cast-iron potbellied stove stood at the edge of the dining room and provided the only heat for most of the house. (The bedrooms ran perpendicular to the dining and living rooms.) Since I was only 3 1/2 at the time, and was considered to be still a baby by my parents, I normally slept with either Mama or Papa. (They used separate bedrooms.) This time, however, they apparently had put me to sleep on the chesterfield.

Very early in the morning, I was awakened by a baby's cry. But since I was too sleepy to investigate, I went back to sleep. Some time later, our nurse, Inez Nesset, who had come to stay with our family, woke me up and said, "The doctor just brought you a baby sister." Without giving the matter a second thought, I retorted, "I'd rather have a dog."

My rationale was simple. I could have all kinds of fun with a dog. I could pet it. It could pull me in my wagon. It could pull me on my sled. It could even give me a "horseback" ride if it were big enough. It would be a marvelous pet, especially since I didn't have one. But what the heck could I do with a baby sister? What a stupid gift!

As I got up, I glanced outside and noticed that it was still dark; I could barely see the snow on the ground. I then peered into the dining room. What an eerie sight. On our round dining room table stood a coal oil (kerosene) lamp, feebly illuminating the room. Beside the lamp stood a small scale, just like the one in the hardware section of our store. Papa used his scale to weigh nails, bolts, nuts, staples, as well as horse hair, seneca root, and other produce that he purchased from the farmers. What was that scale doing here? And on top of the scale I could see a white bundle with black hair sticking out. Dr. Somers lifted me up to see the little creature. Sure enough, it was a tiny baby. It was even smaller than most of the dolls I had seen. It had such a tiny face, a red face. And the smallest mouth I had ever seen. And jet black hair. But its eyes were closed. It looked weird.

Suddenly the little creature began to cry. It cried and it cried and it cried. Then it began to shriek. It was frightening. How could so much noise come from such a tiny mouth? Magic!

That was my introduction to my baby sister. She could sure cry and she could sure shriek. And within a few months she could sure yell. And within a couple of years she could sure talk. My goodness! How she could talk! And to this day, well over half a century later, she has never stopped talking. I mean NEVER!

Dr. Wallace Eugene Somers was a legend in his day, one who epitomized the best in the traveling country doctor. Tales abounded about his heroic deeds in delivering babies and saving lives. Born in Waterford, Ontario, in 1880, he graduated from medical college and traveled west to Sheho, a bustling settlement in 1905, where he began his practice. He was the only doctor for at least sixty miles in either direction. Two years later, he moved to Foam Lake, eighteen miles away. Because the closest hospital was in Yorkton, seventy-eight miles distant, and because most patients were unable to come to his modest office, upstairs in his house, he traveled to the settlers' homes by horseback, in all kinds of weather, with his black medical bag tucked under his arm. In the spring, when the melted snows had caused the creeks to overflow, he forded them, using both hands to pacify his horse. In later years, he used a team of horses, and eventually a car—when weather permitted. In the early days, he would often be away from his office for days on end, tending to critical cases. About the time Sylvia was born, he could travel to his patients' homes in the winter by a crude, home -built snowmobile driven by Dinty Moore, an innovative local mechanic.

Except for my vivid recollection of his visit to our home to deliver Sylvia, and a rather vague recollection of a visit to his office on another occasion when Mama wanted him to examine me for some reason or another, I cannot remember much about this legendary doctor. Oddly enough, however, I can still picture him in my mind—a slim elderly looking man, with graying hair and a very kind face. And I can still see him as he held his stethoscope up to his ears, listening to my heart beat, and then thumping my chest, again listening for any clue to help him make an accurate diagnosis.

When I was only two or three years old, according to my two older sisters, I almost drowned. A heavy rain had flooded part of our back yard, creating a pool about two feet deep. I had been playing with a large bouncing ball, which had rolled into the pool. In an effort to retrieve my ball, I waded into the pool and apparently fell down. Both sisters screamed and Merle ran to the store, about one hundred feet away, and cried for help. Papa immediately rushed to the pool and rescued me. He was so mad, he cut the ball into little pieces. I was immediately taken to Dr. Somers to be examined, and for some time afterward I was quite frail.

Both Mama and Papa worried about me. Eventually, Mama took me to see a renowned pediatrician in Winnipeg, Dr. Gordon Chown. Although I have no recollection of that visit, Dr. Chown apparently told

Mama I was anemic. Whether it was he or Mama who prescribed the treatment, I shall never know. But in any event, both Mama and Papa decided there was only one thing that could restore my health—daily doses of "fresh" chicken soup.

In those days we had never heard of Campbell's Chicken Soup. And even if we had, it certainly was not fresh. Fresh means fresh. It means freshly killed. There was one problem, however. Both Mama and Papa were orthodox and kept kosher. And in order to have kosher chicken soup, we would have to ship the live chickens by railroad express to the *shochet* in Yorkton, a religiously ordained person who was qualified to slaughter animals in accordance with the kosher food laws —biblical instructions in the Old Testament. After the *shochet* had slit the throats of the chickens and bled them, he would ship them back to us. We would then pluck the feathers, after which we would hold the plucked chickens over the fire to burn off the "pin feathers," the small, hair-like quills that remained. Finally, Mama would remove the internal organs and prepare the chickens for cooking. Unless the bird or animal had been killed by a *shochet*, it was not kosher, and we would not eat it.

Because it was impractical to ship only one chicken to Yorkton every day and have it shipped back to us, a procedure taking up at least three days; and because the chicken would not be "fresh" enough to qualify for fresh chicken soup, Mama and Papa decided that they would waive the kosher food laws exclusively for me—more precisely, for my delicate health. Instead, they would serve me fresh chicken soup that had been freshly prepared by cooking a freshly killed chicken the goyishe [gentile] method. And so, Mr. Darling once more came to the rescue.

In his yard stood a large old stump, about three feet high and at least two feet in diameter, the remainder of what had once been a tall, stately pine tree. He used this stump mainly for splitting wood. When a block of wood was too large to burn in his stove, he put the block on the stump and split it into smaller pieces with a hatchet or ax, depending on the size of the block. He also used the stump for another purpose—decapitating chickens.

I remember Papa bringing him one of the many chickens we had in our chicken coop. In his left hand, Mr. Darling held the chicken by its two legs, with its head dangling down on the stump. With his right hand he picked up his hatchet. He held the blade of the hatchet up to the chicken's neck, measuring it. Then he lifted the hatchet high in the air, and in an instant down it came with a whack. The chicken's head flew off and blood spouted from its neck. Mr. Darling flung the chicken on the ground. It fluttered its wings and ran in all directions—in erratic semi-circles that got smaller and smaller, until at last it flopped on the ground, still fluttering its wings ever so slowly until they ceased moving altogether.

Plucking the feathers from the chicken was a messy job. I remember grabbing a fistful of feathers and trying to pull them off. It wasn't easy. I managed to pluck only a few before Mama took over the job. She had a stronger grip than I. After plucking the bird, she held it over the fire in our wood-burning stove to singe the pin-feathers that still remained and were virtually impossible to remove by hand. A pungent odor of burning flesh and feathers immediately assaulted my nostrils. It smelled worse than burning hair. I shall never forget it. Phooey!

Mama then lay the singed chicken on our wooden kitchen table, which was covered with "oil cloth," a rubber-like coated canvas material. After sharpening a butcher knife, she made one long insertion on the chicken's underside, inserted her thumbs in the slit, and spread the chicken apart, exposing its inner organs, which she then began to pull out all at once. In later years, she would identify them for me: "This is the gizzard, this is the intestine, these are the lungs, this is the liver, and this is the heart." Those anatomy lessons ignited my initial interest in the study of medicine, but that's another story. Finally, the chicken was ready for the pot.

Because Mama's house was strictly kosher, she kept separate dishes and silverware for "meat" and "milk." To be more specific, any food containing meat—whether beef or chicken—required separate cooking utensils, dishes, glasses, and silverware. Almost all other foods were classified as "milk," and were prepared and served in "milk" utensils. Fish, however, classified as pareve, remained neutral, like Switzerland, and was never dragged into the kosher conflict. Hence, it could be prepared and served either way. During Passover, these dishes were put away, and a separate set of cookware and dishes was used for the eight days of Passover. The Passover dishes were then removed and the regular dishes were put back in use. Now because "my" chicken was not killed by the *shochet*, it was not kosher and, therefore, must not be cooked in or eaten from kosher utensils. Mama therefore procured a separate pot, a separate set of dishes, and separate silverware for my *traif* [non kosher] chicken. God forbid if any of the dishes were mixed or if the wrong food was served on the wrong plate! That would be a sin of major proportions.

Mama's chicken soup apparently restored my health, and there was no further need for me to see a doctor for quite some time after that. I can readily understand why chicken soup is often called "Jewish penicillin."

When I was about four years old, a newly graduated Jewish doctor from the University of Manitoba in Winnipeg came to Sheho to begin his practice. My recollections of Dr. Charles Shaum are quite vague, but I do remember that his office and drug store were located one block down the street from us. I remember that he occasionally came to our place for Sunday dinner. What I remember most, however, was that he fell in love with a lady who was not Jewish, a *shiksa*. Not only was Mrs. Charlie Prowse a *shiksa* but worse—much worse—she was a widow with a young daughter who was almost a teenager. Obviously, Mrs. Prowse was not a virgin. My parents were quite upset, to say the least. And if my parents—who hardly knew the young doctor—were upset, can you imagine how his mother took the news? She came to Sheho to try to persuade her son how dreadful it would be if he married this *shiksa*. I remember that Mrs. Shaum stayed with us and was extremely grateful for the hospitality and moral support given to her by Mama and Papa. She must have pleaded with her son, and I am sure Mama and Papa did also. In a matter of months, Dr. Shaum moved away from Sheho and opened a practice in another Saskatchewan village, farther west. His true love and her daughter quickly followed. He soon married Mrs. Prowse and apparently was quite happy in his new environment. Mama and Papa, however, talked about that "terrible tragedy" for years afterward. I learned early that the worst sin a Jew could commit—with the possible exception of murder—was to intermarry. But the worst—the very worst—was for a *doctor* to do so. God forbid! That was not only a sin; it was a tragedy.

About a year later, Dr. Alice Woodhead, who had graduated from the University of Edinburgh, returned to the home of her parents in Tuffnell, a small hamlet of under one hundred population, located just nine miles west of Sheho. She began practicing medicine, dividing her time between Tuffnell and Sheho, spending Wednesday in Sheho. I am eternally grateful that she happened to be in town on the day I suffered my most serious accident.

In the warehouse, a separate room in the back of our store, stood a huge coffee grinder used for grinding coffee beans. Although we also stocked canned coffee, most of our customers preferred our own brand of freshly ground coffee from bulk coffee beans. Besides, it was cheaper. I had just turned five at the time and was quite curious about a number of things, including the huge coffee grinder. I remember thinking, "I wonder what's in that metal cone at the top of the machine?" I climbed up on a chair, inserted my left index finger into the cone, and with my right hand began to turn the huge wheel. Instantly I cried out from the excruciating pain and withdrew my bleeding finger. I ran into the store, crying hysterically. My finger was hemorrhaging.

"Today's Wednesday," someone shouted. "Dr. Woodhead's in town today." And the next thing I remember was this young lady clamping my finger and inserting stitches and then snipping off the thread with an odd kind of scissors. She then bandaged my finger and gave me something to ease the excruciating pain. A week later I came back to have my stitches removed. I distinctly remember howling from the horrible, unbearable pain—the worst I have ever experienced in my life. After the procedure was over she consoled me. "You'll be all right now." And indeed I was. But I still bear the scar of that operation on my left index finger. She was a saint. If she is still alive and happens to read this book, I want her to know that I am eternally grateful to her for saving my finger.

After two years of trying to eke out a living in the Sheho area, Dr. Woodhead left for greener pastures in England. She became a prominent gynecologist and later married, before returning to Vancouver, where she and her husband opened a joint practice. It would have been a miracle for any doctor to survive in our immediate area during those Depression years. Dr. Somers, however, continued to practice medicine in Foam Lake even though there was no hospital in the town. If one needed surgery, one had to travel to Yorkton, sixty miles away from Sheho, and seventy-eight miles away from Foam Lake.

Yorkton, a city of five thousand population, not only had a large, well equipped hospital, but two doctors who were more than ready, willing, and eager to perform general surgery on any patient —often it was said—whether he needed it or not. The two most common types of operations performed by Dr. Harry Portnuff and Dr. Potoski were tonsillectomies and appendectomies—in that order. Tonsillectomies by far headed the list. And at that time, practically nobody was immune to this malady. As soon as one got a sore throat and consulted either of these doctors, the diagnosis was instant and positive. "It's the tonsils. We have to take them out right away."

Thus, at the age of five, I remember lying on the operating table, looking up at Dr. Portnuff, a fairly tall handsome man, dressed in white. Beside him stood some nurses, also dressed in white. Overhead, shone a large, odd-shaped electrical light, unlike anything I had ever seen before. "Everything's going to be fine," said Dr. Portnuff. In his hand he held a rubber -like cup to which was attached a hose. "Now I want you to look up at this light," he said, as he placed the cup over my nose, "and breathe in deeply." The next thing I remember was Mama standing beside me, feeding me some ice cream. Was my throat ever sore! And that was my only surgical operation in a hospital until sixty -four years later.

The last doctor to open a practice in Sheho was Dr. Mitchell Rubin, who had just completed his internship after graduating from the University of Manitoba. With help from our village and the rural municipality of Insinger, he opened his office in late July of 1936. We were still suffering from hard times, with many people receiving Dominion Government relief vouchers. Hence, Sheho was in no better position to support a doctor than it had been when Dr. Woodhead had saved my finger just three years before. He did not have a car and, therefore, was chauffeured on his rural house calls by someone else with a car or with a horse - drawn buggy. Early the following year, at the invitation of Dr. Somers, who had gone away for surgery, Dr. Rubin moved to Foam Lake, where his practice flourished, allowing him the luxury of a car. Now, without imposing on anyone, he could accommodate his patients with house calls at any hour of the day or night, so long as he was awake. I have never seen anyone in my life more concerned and devoted to his patients than Dr. Rubin. I often wondered how much sleep he got—or if he slept at all. Like his predecessors, he did not ask his patients what kind of insurance they had or if they had enough money for the two dollar office visit or ten dollar house call. He treated them first. If he got paid, that was gravy. He was the closest person I had ever known to a "Christ-figure."

At that time and up until the end of World War II, the University of Manitoba, like most major universities—at least in Canada—was extremely anti-Semitic. It had a very strict quota for Jews entering medical school. The quota was based upon their percentage of the population in the province. If the percentage of Jews in Manitoba was only 5%, for example, the percentage of Jews allowed into medical school was only 5%—regardless of their excellent marks (grades). And since there was a very high percentage of Jewish premed students applying for medical college, most of whom were quite brilliant, only the creme de la creme would be accepted. Therefore, only the very best of the best of Jewish students ever became doctors. Although Dr. Rubin and his successor, Dr. Irving Miller, seven years later, were both only about twenty-four years old when they began practicing medicine, they were absolutely brilliant. They did not get their degrees by protesting for equal opportunity, equal quotas, or against color discrimination. They got their degrees the old fashioned way—they "earned" them.

During his short stay in Sheho, Dr. Rubin appeared to be aloof. He rarely visited our home despite special invitations and our open door policy. When he moved to Foam Lake, however, he would occasionally visit us on special occasions such as Passover. Perhaps because of his God- like power—his ability to cure one's illness and in some cases to prevent death— I was in awe of him. I remember his big brown eyes; they looked right at you, not away from you, not through you, but right at you. They reassured you that he would take care of you, and everything would be all right.

It was from him and his nurse that all the students in our school received their inoculations against small pox, diphtheria, typhoid fever, and scarlet fever. It was also his diagnosis and recommendation that saved my mother's life.

After emigrating to Canada in 1920, Mama corresponded regularly with her sister and brother in Poland. One winter day in 1938, I had come home at noon for dinner and she was terribly upset. She had just received a letter informing her that her sister had died. Mama buried her grief in housework—cleaning up our home for Passover. Shortly after I got home from school, she was hurriedly lifting a kettle of boiling water from the stove, when she slipped on the wet linoleum floor. The kettle spilled the boiling water over her breast, chest, arms and much of her body, scalding her. She shrieked in agony, and one of my sisters ran immediately to our central office to telephone Dr. Rubin. In the meantime, Mrs. Holmes, who had done some nursing in England during World War I, came over and administered what she thought to be first aid, covering the scalded skin with baby powder. Because the roads were all blocked with snow, Dr. Rubin came to our home in a snowmobile. By the time he arrived it was evening. The powder Mama had received as first aid treatment was absolutely the wrong kind of treatment. Amidst her howls of agony, he began scraping off all of the powdery dressing which stuck to Mama's scalded skin. Then, when her skin was bare, he administered the proper medication, a special jelly-like substance squeezed from a tube and known by the trade name of "tangel." It was late at night before he left. He had saved Mama's life.

As the days passed, Mama complained of a pain in her side. The pain got progressively worse, so we again called Dr. Rubin. Once more he traveled by snowmobile, this time arriving about nine or ten at night. I remember that he spent a great deal of time with her, probing her side and asking numerous questions. Finally, he said, "Mrs. Katz has a rupture. We'll have to take her to Yorkton and operate on her immediately."

Papa and the snowmobile driver hurriedly made preparations for the dangerous trip in the unheated snowmobile, over unmarked roads in the dead of night, in sub freezing weather. Heavy blankets and quilts were most important. Overcoats, warm headwear, scarves, mitts, and warm footwear were taken for granted. It was to be a long trip. I remember asking the doctor if he was hungry and if there was anything I could get him. "Just a glass of milk if you have any," was his reply. As I gave him the milk, I asked him why milk was so special. "It's almost the perfect food," he replied. "It has most of the minerals and vitamins we need." I never forgot his answer. But I still didn't care for milk. I hardly ever drank any.

They carried Mama into the snowmobile. The driver spun the propeller at the back of the crude, canvas- covered vehicle whose four skis would steer it over the unmarked, frozen, snow-covered fields in pitch blackness, the only light coming from the single headlamp of the snowmobile. They headed southeast toward Yorkton, sixty miles away, provided that they could get that far without going round in circles.

I prayed to my personal God, asking Him to protect them from the bitterly cold weather and to guide them safely to the hospital. I pleaded desperately with Him to spare Mama's life. She was only thirty-six. I was only ten.

The next morning Papa phoned our central telephone operator to tell her they had arrived in Yorkton about six o'clock. They had gotten lost several times in the snow bluffs, having gone off the main highway and over farmers' fields. But they had headed southeast anyway, and had arrived in Yorkton six hours after leaving Sheho. Dr. Portnuff and Dr. Rubin had operated on Mama, and the operation was successful. My prayers had been answered.

Papa had left my two older sisters, Merle, age fourteen, and Etta, twelve, in charge of our store. As young as they were, they assumed the responsibility, including taking care of Sylvia and me. Since he would be in Yorkton with Mama for a while, he telephoned his sister in Inglis, Auntie Bessie, and asked her to come and stay with us during Mama's recuperation in the hospital.

Very early the next morning, Aunt Bessie was driven twenty some miles to Binscarth, Manitoba, where she caught the Canadian Pacific Railway train west to Sheho, arriving at 10:00 a.m. It was comforting and reassuring to have her in our home. Besides, she spoke English. Both of my parents rarely spoke English in our home. They spoke to us in Jewish and we answered in English. The whole Shnider family, however, was different. They all spoke English. What I remember most about her visit was the morning she came into my bedroom and saw the black-and-blue bruises on my shins. "Oh my God!" she exclaimed. "How did you get those?"

"Shh," I whispered. "Please don't tell Papa. If he finds out, he won't let me play hockey any more."

Allow me to digress and tell you about my short-lived hockey career. Three years earlier, when I was seven, I had asked Papa if he could buy me a pair of skates. There was nothing else to do during the long winter nights except to go skating on our outdoor ice skating rink. As soon as the weather got cold enough, Mike Haluke would be hired to haul tankfuls of water by horse and sled from Maas's Lake, 1 1/2 miles away, to our rink. The large plug from the underside of the tank would then be pulled out, and a portion of the rink would be flooded. Then back to the lake the horses would go, again and again, until the entire rink would be a solid sheet of ice. The cost for this initial flooding was $75.00. In later years the cost of flooding went up to $100.00.

But that was only the initial cost for the skating season. There was the cost for the nightly caretaker, who lighted the lanterns and scraped the snow off the ice every night, and flooded the rink by a hand-pushed tank full of hot water twice a week.(Hot water melted the snow, thus providing a smoother surface than cold water.) Then there was the cost of gasoline for the two lanterns outside the rink and the two lanterns inside, and finally the cost for cordwood to heat the wooden shack all winter long. That's where we put on our skates and came in to get warm after skating around the rink a few times. The shack was partitioned, one side for the boys and the other for the girls. If one had to urinate, the skater simply stepped outside in the snow, alongside the shack. We boys took special pride in being able to write our first names—and sometimes even our second—in the snow.

To offset these expenses, the management of the skating rink charged the enormous sum of twenty-five cents for a single night's ticket, seventy-five cents for an entire season ticket for one person, or $1.50 for a family season ticket, allowing the entire family to skate (and play hockey) for the three to four month long season. Practically everybody in our village—except the old folks—skated. And all the boys in Sheho, including little Jackie Katz, at one time or other played hockey. [Katz was always pronounced "Kates" as in dates.]

A brand new pair of boys' hockey skates cost anywhere from $2.95 to $3.95 in the Eaton's catalogue. And so, at the age of seven, I asked Papa for a pair of skates. His reply, in translation, was, "My grandfather never had hockey skates, my father never had hockey skates, I never had hockey skates, and you don't need hockey skates." Somehow or other, Aunt Bessie learned about my predicament. The next thing I knew, I was the proud owner of my cousin Charlie's old skates that he had outgrown. They were "blades." Only the goalie wore blades. Everyone else had "tubes." Tubes—blades—who cared. Now I had skates. They even had a strap for an ankle support, and I needed an ankle support because my ankles were narrow and weak. No matter how many pairs of socks I put on, my ankles would collapse. But at least I had skates. Now all I needed was seventy-five cents, and I could skate. Never let it be said that my father was not a generous man. Or perhaps it was my mother who convinced him. At any rate, that winter I began to skate, and believe me, I was the happiest kid on the Canadian Prairies.

With skates goes a hockey stick. Mr. Leckie sold hockey sticks. He sold all kinds of good things: fire crackers during Victoria Day and Dominion Day, comic books, the Sunday funny papers, marbles, water pistols, Halloween masks, cap guns and caps that went "crack," balloons, and everything that a young boy needs. And I needed a hockey stick. He stocked three kinds of hockey sticks: affordable, less affordable, and prohibitively expensive. The seventy-five cent hockey sticks were the same kind that our senior team used. They were about as good as one could get. The fifty- cent hockey sticks were also very good, but only slightly shorter than the most expensive stick. Then there was the twenty-five cent stick—my size and price range. I wouldn't even dream of asking Papa for a more expensive stick lest he have a heart attack. Oh, how I longed for that little hockey stick! It was only slightly shorter than I, and believe me, nobody was shorter than I except my young sister, Sylvia, who was only four.

One day I finally worked up enough nerve to ask Papa for a twenty-five cent hockey stick. I will give you only one guess what his reply was—I mean the *exact* words in translation. You guessed it: "My grandfather never had a hockey stick, my father never had a hockey stick, I never had a hockey stick, and you don't need a hockey stick." In the end, however, Mama prevailed, and I got my twenty-five cent hockey stick, the *only* piece of hockey equipment I ever owned.

Please believe me when I tell you I was no Wayne Gretzky. I couldn't stick handle or skate fast enough to play center or wing. So don't ask me how many goals I scored. Don't even ask me if I ever scored a goal. Are you kidding? And don't ask me what position I played because I was always out of position. My classmate George Homeniuk, one of the best players on the team said, "You'll play defense. You stay behind that blue line in front of that goal and don't let them other guys score. When the puck goes into the corner, you go and get it out, then pass it to me or someone else on our side." That's what he said. And those were the only instructions and the only coaching I ever had during my hockey career.

Since my job was to go into the corners after the puck, I went into the corners—real upright corners with two sides—not round ones like those in modern hockey arenas. When the puck went into the corner, it stayed there until either an opposing player or I got it out. We used to play chicken—to see who would go into the corner first. Whoever went in first got slammed into the boards—hard. That was called a body check. And I got checked into the boards plenty of times. Whoever went into the corner first also got speared sometimes with the butt end of the opponent's stick. That was illegal and warranted a two-minute penalty. But we played without a referee. Did I ever get speared? To this day, whenever I see an N.H.L. player rush into the corner followed by his opponent, I cringe. I can still feel that stick going into my gut. And I can still feel the shock of a jarring body check. It hurts.

I learned about defense the old fashioned way. One day I skated with the puck across our goal mouth. George Homeniuk shouted and swore at me. "Don't you ever do that again! If you lost the puck they could score." I learned quickly. I am still appalled at the stupidity of many N.H.L. defensemen who make that mistake costing their team a goal. Yet they get paid in spite of their stupidity. George, incidentally, went on to play professional hockey, including a stint with the Detroit Red Wings number one farm team—on the same line, in fact, with the legendary Gordie Howe.

I played without shin pads. Do you think I was crazy enough to ask Papa for shin pads? I didn't even use the Eaton's catalogue for pads, as some of the kids did. I just got out there when they gave me ice time(which wasn't very often), and got in the way of the puck and everybody else and got the hell beat out of me. But most of all, I got bruised on my shins from stopping shots near the goal. Blue bruises and black ones. And they hurt. But I never showed my bruises to anyone or spoke about them. Not until Aunt Bessie saw them that winter day. "Shh," I whispered." "Please don't tell Papa. If you do, he won't let me play any more."

In three years I had outgrown my twenty-five cent hockey stick, and that was the end of my hockey career. What a loss!

[Sixty years later at the huge Sheho School Reunion, I joked with George about how my father had reacted when I had asked him for a twenty-five cent hockey stick. "My grandfather never had a hockey stick, my father never had a hockey stick, I never had a hockey stick, and you don't need a hockey stick." George paused, thoughtfully, then said, "Your father was right."]

Aunt Bessie stayed with us until Mama returned from the hospital. We had no radio. Aunt Bessie found the evenings boring. One day she said, "It's so lonely here. I'm used to a radio." I don't know what influence she had with her brother, but a few months later, in the spring of 1937, we got a radio. It was a beautiful walnut cabinet, full console, four-tube Philco battery powered radio. It changed our lives. But that's another story.

After about a week in the hospital, Mama returned. She slowly recovered not only from the operation but also from her horrible scalding. I became very, very close to her. We all did. And I was more than ever in awe of Dr. Rubin.

He was one of my earliest role models. I decided then that I wanted to become a doctor—like him. I wanted to cure people and to save their lives. I also wanted the prestige that I felt a doctor possessed. Nobody, but nobody in my estimation could possibly have the prestige that a medical doctor had. All the money in the world could not buy that prestige. I worshipped Dr. Rubin. To me, he was God.

Later that year, he was instrumental in raising funds for a ten-bed hospital in Foam Lake. That was also the year that a very pretty nurse, Dorothy Bowman, came to Foam Lake to assist him. I liked her. She was a doll.

In 1940, one year after the outbreak of World War II, Dr. Somers, who had suffered a heart attack in 1937, returned to Foam Lake to resume his practice. Dr. Rubin then joined the Canadian Army Medical Corps. In September of the following year, 1941, he married Dorothy Bowman and proceeded overseas shortly afterward. My parents were very disappointed that he had married a *shiksa*. Another tragedy! I thought so too. Although I thought Dorothy was not only very pretty but also a wonderful person, she was a *shiksa*, and Dr. Rubin had surrendered his heritage. I had not yet learned to think for myself.

CHAPTER FIVE
Starting School

My wife, Marilyn, just retired as a kindergarten-primary teacher. She was an absolutely first-rate teacher in every respect. Her preparation included many units beyond the Master's degree, continuing education seminars and workshops, a lifetime credential, and forty-one years of teaching experience in the same school district, mostly at the kindergarten level. She worked hard every day. She used to leave home about 6:00 a.m. and usually did not get back until twelve hours later. She was loved by all her students and their parents. She thought of them as "her" parents—the parents of "her" children. And indeed they were her children: *in loco parentis*. Whenever I visited her kindergarten class, I marveled at the loving bond between the children and her. What a contrast from my first teacher! Unbelievable!

On August 26th, 1933, when I was exactly five years and five months old, I started school. The reason I know it was August 26th is that Sheho Public School *always* started its classes on August 26th unless and only unless the 26th fell on a Saturday or Sunday. I began in grade one. None of the small towns had kindergarten. We all began in the first grade. I realize now that I was much too young. But at that time who knew any differently? To merely say that my first year of school was a traumatic experience would be a gross understatement.

Up until that time the boundaries of my world were quite limited, even by Sheho standards. Although I had a four-wheel kiddy car, which I could pedal and steer anywhere along the three -block-long cement sidewalk, I rarely ventured beyond that limit except when I walked a couple of blocks down a side street to make mudpies with Margaret Peters and her sisters. Otherwise, I didn't explore much more of the village. Papa had laid down the law, and I wouldn't think of disobeying him. Moreover, I had almost no responsibilities. I did not even know how to dress myself. Polly Snihur, our hired girl(live-in maid), did practically everything for me. Whether it was her idea or Mama's, I don't know. In any event, I was certainly innocent, fussed over, and protected. I was about to get a rude awakening.

Because my two older sisters often talked about school enthusiastically, I was about as excited as a child on Christmas eve when I went to bed the night before school began. The thought of beginning a new adventure was so overwhelming that I had difficulty falling asleep. I was tired when Polly woke me at eight. But I was so excited I could hardly eat my breakfast of cocoa and toast. I proudly picked up my pencil box, containing a new pencil and some crayons. My "scribbler," a thin notebook, came next. I kissed Mama good-bye, put on my Jackie Coogan Donegal tweed cap, then strutted proudly alongside my sisters all the way to school, four blocks to the very edge of town. I had never walked that far before. We entered by the south facing double-doors, walked up the steps, turned left, and entered the room of Miss Mamie Griffiths, the teacher for first and second graders. My sisters introduced me to her. She smiled like Cinderella's step mother. Her teeth were as white as snow. Then my sisters disappeared, leaving me alone with the sorceress and her twenty-nine captives.

Miss Griffiths sat me down at my desk, third from the front, extreme right-hand row. A bell clanged—not an electric bell— but a hand-held bell that clanged like a real bell, the only hand-held bell in Sheho Public School District number 953. There were three other bells in Sheho, all large bells: one in the Ukrainian church, one that served as a fire bell in the town hall, and the third, also a fire bell in the basement of our school. But this hand-held bell sounded like no other one, simply because it was the only one of its kind in the village. So distinct was its ring that it was borrowed by the officiating referee during hockey games, to call face-offs, offsides, penalties, and the end of periods. Believe me, when the referee clanged that bell, you knew the period had ended! Nobody ever thought of using a whistle. That technology was much too advanced for Sheho.

That bell was housed in the joint office of the principal or vice principal for the twelve years I attended Sheho school. It controlled my life and the life of every student who attended our school. Usually the principal would ring it promptly at nine, then twice to begin and end our recess, at noon, at 1:30 to begin the afternoon session, then twice to begin and end the afternoon recess, and finally at 4:00 P.M. Sometimes he would honor one of his students by handing him the bell. Believe me, that was quite an honor. I am proud to say that I rang that bell many times. Perhaps someday on my tombstone, engraved in fancy letters, the following epitaph may appear: *"He was always eager and proud to ring the bell."*

Immediately after the bell rang, Miss Griffiths shouted: "Good morning boys and girls. I want you all to sit in your desks and keep quiet. I am now going to 'take the register.' When I call your name, say 'present.' Do you all understand? I will begin with the first graders."

A few kids squirmed in their seats and whispered. "KEEP QUIET!" shouted the commandant. Then she began:

"Mervin Bokla."

"Present."

"Alice Curry."

"Present."

"Louis Gnip."

"Present."

And so it went, with only five or six interruptions during which she let the class know without any doubt whatsoever that we were supposed to be quiet while she called our names for "the register." Finally, after twenty-nine "presents," she turned the page in her register and began calling the names of her second graders. These twelve "presents" went much more rapidly, like a well drilled army platoon. She had been their commander the year before. Then she explained that her "register" was the most important thing in the whole school, and whenever the downstairs fire bell rang, it meant there was either a fire drill or a real fire, and we were all supposed to leave the room quickly, taking the register with us, and walk down the steps—not jump—and go outside. In the event that she forgot to take her register, her monitors would be in charge. I never achieved that honor.

When the bell rang at recess, we all went outside to play. There were four softball diamonds on the school's playground, two for the boys and two for the girls. Because the players were usually grouped by size and ability, and because I was the smallest boy in school with the least ability to hit and catch a ball, I did not find myself on many softball teams during my first two years of school. As I got older, however, I was good enough to play with the younger kids and occasionally even hit a home run when I managed to hit the ball. But my main memory of playing softball is stopping a grounder or catching the ball. It hurt because we played without gloves. The only gloves allowed under the rules then were for the catcher and first baseman. I usually played in the outfield—out of sight and out of mind. We also played "tag" and other running games. I remember playing a running game during recess with a much bigger kid from my class, George Homeniuk. I had just learned a nursery rhyme at home about Georgie Porridgie, and I thought it kind of odd that one of my classmates had a similar sounding name. So without any malice whatsoever in my innocent heart, I said to him, "Georgie Porridgie pudding in pie, kissed the girls and made them cry."

Wham! Instantly George punched me in the stomach so hard, he knocked the wind out of me and I fell on the ground, writhing in pain. When I eventually regained my wind and had stopped crying, I returned to class and reported my injury to Miss Griffiths, but to no avail. She reserved her disciplinary action for such major crimes as squirming in one's desk, whispering, and talking. By far, the worst felony was "talking." Retribution was instant—the "strap." Or perhaps it was rehabilitation. I don't believe Miss Griffiths knew the difference. They were one and the same. They both had the same results.

The strap was cut from split leather cowhide; smooth, shiny black on one side. The underside, however, was made of rough, unfinished, skin-colored grain, indented with groves to cause abrasion and inflict maximum pain when utilized. And that was the side utilized. It was about eighteen inches long and three inches wide— tapered at one end so that it could be gripped easily, firmly and comfortably by the teacher. It was only about one-quarter of an inch thick, thus allowing a certain amount of sway when the teacher snapped it on the student's hand. The sight of that awful instrument of torture would put the fear of God into the heart of even the most cynical of atheists. It was probably invented to torture heretics during the Spanish Inquisition. Can you imagine how it terrified me?— an overly-protected, innocent five-year-old child who did not even know the rules of the game! Nobody knew the rules because there were no rules.

There was no warning unless her constant shouting and yelling were meant to be interpreted as a warning. But Miss Griffiths was always shouting. That was her method of classroom control. Shouting, yelling, humiliation, and the strap. Consequently, nobody knew when it was his (or her) turn to get the strap. And rarely a week went by without Miss Griffiths calling up one of her inmates to the front of the class for the ultimate humiliation—getting the strap.

"Jackie Katz, come on up and get the strap!"

My heart pounded and my legs turned to rubber as I struggled to comply with her command. I had been sentenced to a terrible death. I did not want to go. What had I done to deserve this cruel fate? I had absolutely no idea. But nobody ever argued with Miss Griffiths. And nobody even dreamed of protesting. I'm sure it would have meant the guillotine.

"Hurry up! Hold up your hand!"

Reluctantly, I began to extend my right hand. Her left hand grabbed my fingers and twisted my hand, palm upward. She gripped my fingers tightly. "NOW HOLD OUT YOUR HAND!" She released her grip. My hand trembled. I was terrified. I tried to hold it steady.

In her right hand, she gripped the strap, then tapped it lightly on my fingers, measuring my hand. Then she lifted her hand high in the air.

SCHWISS! I felt a gust of wind on my face as the strap hurtled downward. WHACK! The explosion instantly deafened me, and the red-hot searing blow crumpled my palm like a dry twig thrown into a bonfire. I howled in anguish as scalding tears ran down my cheeks. My body trembled with pain.

"KEEP YOUR HAND UP!" she commanded. Then she gave it to me—once more with feeling.

"NOW HOLD OUT YOUR OTHER HAND!"

I sobbed uncontrollably as I returned to my desk.

Intimidation, fear, and punishment were only three of her weapons used for classroom control. There was one more. She took extraordinary delight in embarrassing students for no purpose at all except for her own gratification. One of my classmates, who recently passed away and wished to remain anonymous, was almost exactly the same age as I. I shall call her Betty Whiteford. She sat right behind me. One day she had the misfortune of losing control of her bladder. As soon as Miss Griffiths saw the puddle, she announced to the class, "Betty Whiteford wet the floor. Go stand in the corner, Betty Whiteford." Although I was only 5 1/2 years old, I cringed with embarrassment for Betty and disgust with Miss Griffiths. "How can anybody be so mean?" I thought. "How can anyone be so cruel?"

After a little while, Miss Griffiths announced to the class: "Betty Whiteford has stood in the corner long enough. Let Jackie Katz stand in the corner. He's a Jew!" So, like a dunce, for the whole classroom to see, I stood in the corner to be punished by Miss Griffiths because I had not selected Christian parents. Perhaps she wanted me to apologize.

Many years later, while reminiscing with my sisters about our life in Sheho, I mentioned this incident. They were appalled. "Why didn't you report this to our parents?" they asked.

"I didn't know any better," I responded. " She was the teacher, and I always tried to obey my teachers. Besides, I was not a tattle tale."

In July of 1992, my wife and I motored through Western Canada, looking up my some of my surviving classmates. We found several of them, including Betty Whiteford. It was a joyous but all-too-brief reunion. She had become a school teacher, she told us, because she had been so incensed at Miss Griffiths for constantly receiving the strap that she vowed she would get her revenge by punishing the children of that witch if they ever enrolled in her classroom. "She gave me the strap so often because of my spelling mistakes," Betty explained, "that the palms of my hands became red and I couldn't write. And I never did learn how to spell properly."

I must mention that her recollection of standing in the corner differs from mine. She claims that she never wet the floor, and the reason for her being sent to the corner was for getting out of her desk and walking over to a classmate to extend an invitation to her birthday party. I don't dispute that incident because I, too, was invited to her party. However, certain traumatic events are engraved in our memories forever and ever and ever. And I shall never forget looking behind me and seeing that little puddle as Miss Griffith announced to the class: "Betty Whiteford wet the floor. Go stand in the corner Betty Whiteford." Then later, "Let Jackie Katz stand in the corner. He's a Jew." How could I possibly forget such incredible and utterly malicious insensitivity?

We recalled how she used to humiliate kids who didn't meet her learning expectations by threatening to flunk them.

One of the second graders, Alex Homenuik, George's older brother, had the nickname of "Lazy," because he moved very slowly. He was an excellent goal keeper on our Pee Wee hockey team, but in school he seemed to move at a snail's pace, as though he were ill. On more than one occasion Miss Griffiths would announce to the class: "ALEX HOMENUIK, YOU'LL BE IN THIS ROOM UNTIL YOU'RE AN OLD MAN WITH GRAY HAIR." Alex became slower and weaker, and two years later he died. He had been born with a defective heart, resulting in his blood not receiving enough oxygen. I attended his funeral, as did most of the school. The service was conducted in Ukrainian, and although I didn't understand the language, it didn't make any difference. My classmate was gone.

I will say one thing about Miss Griffiths: She certainly left a lasting impression. One day instead of hanging my cap up in the cloakroom adjoining our classroom, I kept it on and sat down in my desk. "TAKE YOUR CAP OFF!" commanded my teacher. "WHERE DO YOU THINK YOU ARE? YOU NEVER WEAR YOUR CAP WHEN YOU'RE IN-SIDE A ROOM!" To this day, I have a difficult time wearing anything on my head, even in a synagogue. On another occasion, when she asked me a question that I could hardly hear, I said, "Huh?" "HUH!" she shouted.

"YOU NEVER SAY 'HUH.' YOU SHOULD ALWAYS SAY PAR-
DON." Please believe me, since that day I have never responded to anyone with a "Huh." I always say "pardon" or "I beg your pardon." She
taught me manners.

Miss Griffith encouraged story telling, a period in which she would
call upon her pupils to come up and tell a story. Cold. Without any preparation or warning. Some of the kids were so embarrassed, they couldn't
face the class; they kept their heads turned away while they mumbled
something or other that made little sense, even to the walls. Others told
odd stories that I suppose were meant to be entertaining. I remember
Annie Homenuik telling a story about a married couple who had been
given three wishes. The husband first wished for some sausage. When
he got his wish, his wife was so angry she wished the sausage would
stick to his nose. When her wish came true, the couple tried and tried to
pull the sausage off his nose, but to no avail. Their only recourse was to
use their third and final wish to ask that the sausage be removed. And it
was. I suppose the moral was that one should be careful when wishing
because wishes may sometimes come true.

If I had known the stories then that I know now, I might have told the
following one:

There was once a little old lady who lived all alone in a little room
with her little dog Jimmy. One day, on her birthday, she received a bottle
of champagne, opened it, and out popped a fairy. "I will grant you any
three wishes," said the fairy. "'Oh, how wonderful!" said the little old
lady. "First off, I wish that I could live in a big castle." There was a big
blast of smoke and suddenly the little old lady found herself all alone in
a huge castle. "Oh, how wonderful!" she said in amazement. " For my
second wish, I wish that I were young and beautiful." Another puff of
smoke followed, and as she looked in a mirror she saw her reflection.
She was now young—about eighteen—and ever so beautiful. "Oh how
wonderful!" she said. "Now you have one final wish," said the fairy, and
she disappeared. "For my final wish, I wish that my little dog Jimmy
were a young, handsome prince." As soon as the smoke disappeared, a
young, very handsome prince stood beside her. "Oh, Jimmy, Jimmy, is
that really you?"

"Yes, it is," replied the prince. "And aren't you sorry now that you had me fixed?"

Unfortunately, I did not know many stories or jokes then. I don't think our family had much of a sense of humor. As for Miss Griffiths, she had none. I never saw her laugh. Not even once.

Sometimes a student would raise his hand and announce to her—and to the class—some important news. I remember Billy Naherny excitedly informing her and the whole class about a startling piece of information. "Jews don't eat pork." Everyone stared at me with contempt as though I had just let off gas. And I can't even remember how many times I heard "The Jews killed Christ." That was a real education. Share -and -tell! When I told them Christ was a Jew, they didn't believe me. The only Jews they knew were our family and Mr. Leckie, both general store-keepers. How could a general storekeeper be the Son of God? That didn't make sense. All they knew was what they had heard from their parents and classmates, and that was all that mattered.

At exactly five minutes before twelve, Miss Griffiths would say, "Boys and girls, I want you all to put your heads down on your desk." We would all obey at first; then after a minute or so had elapsed, some of us would sneak a glance and watch Miss Griffiths powdering her nose and applying lipstick. If she happened to return our glance, we would instantly look away, sometimes accidentally banging our heads on our desks, in our hurry to pretend that we had never looked at her.

The three most exciting events of the school year were the Hallow-een party, Valentine's Day party, and Christmas concert—my very first. On Halloween some of the kids dressed up in various costumes or merely wore masks. Mr. Leckie sold Halloween masks which cost about ten cents each. Since we couldn't afford such luxuries, I brought a large paper bag from our store, cut out holes for the eyes and mouth, and put it over my head. That was my costume. For Valentine's day, we were sup-posed to buy or make a card and give it to a classmate. I remember some of the kids receiving pretty store-bought cards. I couldn't draw if my life depended on it. But I made some kind of simple card, nonetheless, and gave it to somebody, hoping to get one back in return. And sure enough, somebody remembered me with a red crayon-drawn Valentine on half a sheet of lined paper.

The Christmas concert was the highlight of the school year. Beginning in November, her two classes, along with those of Miss Yemen, who taught the third, fourth, and fifth grades, would walk two blocks down the street to the town hall, where we would rehearse for the big event. Although the other grades would also participate, my most vivid recollections are those from my earliest school years. I remember learning all the Christmas carols with ease and singing them in a chorus to the accompaniment of an upright piano, and I distinctly remember my initial irritation at having to learn these words:

"Away in a Manger, no crib for a bed,

The little Lord Jesus lay down His Sweet Head . . ."

Although Christians considered Baby Jesus a Lord, he held no such status in our home. Not even remotely. We Jews were different from the gentiles. We did not believe in Jesus. Also, we did not eat pork at any time, nor did we eat ice cream and chocolate bars at Passover. Worst of all, we did not marry shiksas. At the age of five years and eight months, I had never been introduced to pork, I had not yet learned how to steal chocolate bars from our store during the eight days of Passover, and I had no inclination to get married. I did not even know any Jewish girls except my sisters. The closest I had ever come to getting married was when I had played with Margaret and Donna Peters, but they had moved away just before I started school, so I was now safe from that temptation. But Jesus was another matter. We never mentioned his name at home. We never even referred to him as the "J " word. It was taboo. Yet here I was singing about the little Lord Jesus. The next thing I knew, Miss Griffiths would probably feed me pork and force me to marry a shiksa.

At first, I felt as though I were being forcefully converted. However, after rehearsing the song at least a few hundred times—in first grade alone—the "J" word didn't bother me any more. And I enjoyed the music. Besides, if it wasn't for Baby Jesus, we would be back in Miss Griffiths's class instead of singing and marching in drills and reciting Christmas stories and acting in Christmas plays and doing all kinds of new and exciting things that five and six and seven-year-olds enjoy. We could even talk to our classmates without fear of getting the strap. To be sure, Christmas was the most exciting time of the year, even for me, even if I hadn't selected Christian parents. Thank God for Baby Jesus!

After rehearsing for almost two months, the big event finally arrived. The Christmas concert. The Town Hall was packed to capacity.

The audience sat on wooden fold-up chairs; the students on wooden benches up front, near the stage. At the other end of the building, near the entrance, the big cast-iron potbelly stove radiated a red glow from white hot burning coals inside.

Outside the building, the temperature had fallen to forty degrees below zero. But inside, it was hot, especially near the stove. And it was stuffy. And smoky. But nobody cared. Every home in winter was hot and stuffy at one end and cold as an icebox at the other. If one could afford two potbelly stoves, it could then be hot throughout the entire house. I mean really hot. That's how much heat those stoves radiated. Yet nobody dared open the storm windows more than a tiny crack lest all the heat escape. If one opened the door for more than two seconds while entering or leaving, somebody immediately shouted, "Close the door! Were you born in a barn?" Maybe it was all right for Baby Jesus to be born in a barn on Christmas Day in Bethlehem; but Bethlehem is not Sheho, and Sheho certainly isn't Bethlehem. Not by six thousand miles and not by forty degrees below zero. If Joseph and Mary had traveled to Sheho that night instead of Bethlehem and stayed in a barn without a potbelly cast-iron stove radiating enough heat to keep both Mary and Baby Jesus warm, there would have been no Christmas and no Christmas Concert—not in Sheho and not anywhere.

How can I describe our Christmas concerts? With the exception of our Sports Day on July 12, the concert was the biggest event of the year. Sheho did not have movies when I was young and only an occasional play. Very few families even had radios. The concert, therefore, was big time entertainment, especially since most of the parents had come to see their children perform. Some had even come by horse-and-sled from as far away as six miles, a three hour round trip in the bitterly cold weather. They were hungry for a change of routine in their dreary, monotonous daily lives—any change—even if it lasted only a couple of hours. It was also the biggest social event of the year. Almost everyone would be there. It would certainly be more exciting than talking to the horses and cows. .

We first and second graders had practiced and rehearsed for two months; and now, backstage, the show was about to begin. In the wings, the pianist began playing "O! Canada" and everyone stood up and joined in singing our National Anthem. We heard the rustle of the audience sitting down, followed by a long hush. Then someone backstage began pulling on a rope which was wound around a pulley and then attached to the curtain, which in turn was wound around a large pole, like a huge piece of toilet paper on its rolls. The curtain slowly rose, exposing the wooden stage upon which some of us first-graders, accompanied by the pianist, began to sing:

"It came upon the midnight clear

That glorious song of old,

With angels bending near the earth,

To touch their hearts of gold."

As we finished the carol, the curtain slowly began to fall and the audience clapped and clapped. We took a bow, and the curtain held steady for a minute or two before rolling down to the stage, the end of our performance. Hurriedly, we were ushered backstage so that a new act could begin. Someone recited a poem about Christmas, and somebody else told a story about the meaning of Christmas, and each time the curtain fell, the audience clapped and clapped.

But the biggest applause came after our "drill." We marched in columns across the stage: first in one direction, then in another; and then we criss-crossed, first in one direction and then in another; and then up one end and down the other, and then down one end and up the other, and then sideways and then horizontally and then vertically and every which way the compass could read, from any direction in any hemisphere on Earth. Thanks to Miss Griffiths, we outdid ourselves. I always knew she had missed her calling. She should have been a drill sergeant.

After we first and second graders were through with our performances, we joined our classmates on the wooden benches, just beneath the stage. Although we had to strain our necks to see the rest of the concert, we wanted to be as close as possible to the stage so that we wouldn't miss anything. When you're in first and even second grade, sitting up front is a matter of life or death. You dare not take a chance on missing anything—especially Santa Claus. We knew he would make a special appearance here, right after the concert had ended. I was as excited as anyone else, because Miss Griffiths had told us all about Santa Claus. She also told us that storks brought babies, and although I had never seen a stork or heard of such a bird before entering her class, I believed her. I had no reason to doubt her word. Perhaps the stork also brought Santa Claus. At the age of five years and eight months, I was not overly sophisticated and did not question my teacher about Santa Claus or the origin of life until Johnny Drobot told me about Santa Claus and babies six months later, while swimming naked in our swimming hole in the creek that flowed through Wunder's field. Until that time I really believed in the stork and Santa Claus, and both of my parents and older sisters supported my conviction.

As the last act ended, the principal took the stage and shouted, "Santa Claus is coming!" Everyone jumped up and looked toward the door near the potbelly stove. The door swung open—just for a moment—and in he rushed, all dressed up in scarlet with white cuffs, and a huge belly and a full white beard and black overshoes (like the ones we sold in our store). What a magnificent sight! On his back he carried a white sack that swung up and down as he trotted along the aisle and climbed the steps to the stage. Were we ever excited! All of us kids started shoving our way to the stage to be as close to him as possible. We couldn't take any chances. We might miss our presents.

He lay his sack down, opened it, and then began to take out the presents, one by one, while calling up the lucky winner. " Jenny Lys, will Jenny Lys come up and get her present?"

While he waited for Jenny to claim her present, the rest of us grew impatient. "Howard Tansley, will Howard Tansley come up? " It was taking too long. We shoved our way up to the stage itself, blocking the way for anyone who wanted to come up and claim his present. Unless one stood up front, right at the stage, it took forever to shove oneself through the pack. Fortunately, the principal and teachers came to the rescue. They cleared an aisle, then began taking out presents from Santa's bag and calling out names. "Alice Curry. Audrey Bokla. Eddie Grumetza."

It was going a little faster now, but my name still hadn't been called. Some of the kids had been called up twice, some even three times. I waited, then slowly began to walk back to the bench. I sat down and jealously wondered how some of the kids could get two or three or even more presents, while I had been left out altogether. Then I remembered that word had gotten around that they would be exchanging gifts among themselves and Santa would be delivering them. Obviously, these kids had a lot of friends. I wished I had a lot of friends. Howard Tansley was my friend, even though he was in second grade. And Walter Lys was my friend, but he hadn't started school yet. I waited. Perhaps Santa had forgotten me. So had everyone else. Maybe next year?

Suddenly I heard "Jackie Katz." I fought my way through the thinning pack, right up to the stage. "Jackie Katz," Miss Griffiths, announced, and she handed me a fancy envelope with my own name on it, in her own fancy handwriting. I thanked her and walked back to the bench. Inside the envelope was a store-bought Christmas card, signed by Miss Griffiths, the only Christmas card I received that year and the first store-bought card I had ever received. I hadn't been forgotten after all. Christmas really was a wonderful time of year, even if I didn't believe in Baby Jesus.

A few nights later on Christmas eve, I hung up my long woolen stocking alongside the two long cotton stockings of my older sisters and the small one worn by my baby sister. We attached them with clothespins to a wooden panel in our living room. As I went to bed, I knew with absolutely certainty that Santa would visit our home late that night. As soon as I woke up the next morning, I hurried to the living room and grabbed my stocking. It was full. So were all the other stockings. During the night Santa had filled all of them with mixed nuts— the same kind that we sold in our store: Brazil nuts(which we called "nigger toes"), almonds, walnuts, filberts, and peanuts. In addition, each stocking contained one Cadbury milk chocolate bar, also sold in our store, and two Japanese oranges (tangerines) that we stocked only once a year—in December. What a treat! That was the most exciting Christmas I ever enjoyed in my entire life —even without a Christmas tree.

CHAPTER SIX
My Train Ride To An Amazing City

If you happen to live almost anywhere in Canada and need to travel to another town or city, you have one of two choices: take the bus or drive. In a large city, of course, there is usually an airport nearby and you can fly. But forget about traveling by train. Except for the main Canadian National Railway line from Vancouver through Calgary and on to Winnipeg, train travel is now almost impossible. Practically all of the thousands of miles of railway tracks connecting all of Canada are now used only by freight trains, if used at all. The same situation exists throughout most of the United States. What a contrast from the days when I was growing up in Sheho! Traveling by train then was not only the main method of getting from one place to another, but in the winter when the roads were blocked with snow, it was the only way to go.

How can I describe my first overnight trip on a train? It was in the early fall of 1933 when Papa had to go to Winnipeg, Manitoba, to see the wholesalers and while there, he spent Rosh Hashanah, the Jewish New Year. For some reason, he decided to take me. Until I started school at the age of five, I had stayed home with Mama and my young sister, Sylvia, during the High Holy Days, while Papa, my older sisters, and Mr. Leckie all went to Yorkton for the two days of Rosh Hashanah and the holiest of days, Yom Kippur. Papa closed his store during these Jewish holidays, but Mr. Leckie's store remained open, with his son Norman looking after it. Then, in 1933, about a month after I had started school, when I was exactly 5 1/2 years old, Papa took me with him to Winnipeg for Rosh Hashanah.

Because this was the first time I had traveled alone with Papa, I have vivid recollections of that trip. I remember the green plush seats on our coach and the overhead rack where he put his suit case and the water fountain with little paper cups on top that I could pull out to get a drink of water. I loved pulling them out. They were so tiny. I remember getting up from our seat many times and swaying from side to side with the rocking motion of the train each time I got up to walk over to the far end of the coach where the water fountain and those little tiny cups were located. That was great fun. Finally Papa ordered me to sit down. That was boring. But the train was always stopping, and each time it stopped I could see another station, almost identical to ours, except the name on the station was different. I asked Papa what the sign said and he told me it was the name of the town. So each time the train stopped I asked him what town we were in and he named each one: Insinger, Theodore, Springside, and Yorkton. We were in Yorkton a long time, but the train just stayed there and stayed there, forever, and ever. I was getting tired. And sleepy.

Instead of having to sit up all night in the coach, Papa had bought a sleeping car ticket. So we shared an upper berth in the sleeping car. I remember crawling into that berth and hearing the swish of steam immediately followed by a tug on our coach which sent me sliding backward as the locomotive started up from zero to a few feet per second, yanking its coaches—one at a time— until they all fell into line like dominoes. I remember listening to the clickity, clickity, clickity of the wheels as they passed over the joints between the tracks as the train gradually picked up speed until the only sound I heard was one rapid, continuous clickclickclickclick. Then, a few minutes later, just when I was getting used to the rhythm, I heard the shrill blast of the steam whistle, which sounded like an ear-piercing "TOOT," followed by another two TOOTS, and the train gradually began to slow down until the clickity, clickity, clickity sound returned, and each interval between sounds became longer, until the train gradually came to a jerky stop, jerking me forward, my head now off the pillow.

"Why are we stopping?"

"We're in another town."

"Which one?"

"I don't know. *Gay schloffen.*" [Go to sleep]

" How long will we be here?"

"Five or ten minutes."

"How far away is Winnipeg?"

"A long way."

"When will we get there?"

"Tomorrow morning."

"What time is it now?"

"It's late. *Gay schloffen.* "

Gradually the swaying of the coach and the clickclickclick lulled me to sleep. When I awoke, it was daylight. "How far away is Winnipeg?"

"Not far. Maybe like twice from Sheho to Yorkton."

"When will we get there?"

"Not long. Maybe like twice from Sheho to Yorkton."

"What time is it?"

Papa took out his silver pocket watch and put on his glasses, then stared at the numbers. " *Ziben ah zeyger.*" [Seven o'clock.] Sometimes he spoke to me in Jewish; sometimes in English. But I rarely spoke Jewish. That was an old fashioned language from the Old Country, and only people from the Old Country spoke Jewish. They should learn to speak English. They were now in Canada. Everyone in Canada should speak English. Then he wound up his watch and put it back in his pants. He let up the window blind and we watched the farms with their barns and their cows and the stacks of wheat go by, one after another. Gradually, we started to get dressed. It wasn't easy. We were tightly cramped in this small sleeper and there wasn't much room. But we curled and bent in one direction and then in another and eventually got dressed. We both went into the tiny little toilet with a silver colored metal basin and silver colored metal water faucets and a small toilet seat which had a cover that could go up and down. And each time I flushed the toilet, I could see the railroad ties underneath and feel the cool air coming up through the toilet hole. That was sure a funny toilet. It was so cramped, I could hardly do anything. But at least it didn't stink. Finally, we went back to the coach.

I had noticed that the porter had a black face, just like the other porters my classmates and I had observed during recess, when the west bound train stopped in Sheho at exactly ten in the morning. The station, just on the other side of the road, was less than a block away from our school. Occasionally, the porters stepped off the dining car and walked up and down the platform for a few minutes before returning. At other times we saw them as they stood outside, on the platform of the train's observation car. None of us had ever seen a black face before except when a local actor had blackened his face with burned cork for a particular play in the Town Hall. Tarres Koropatniski insisted that the porters actually were white like us but had to blacken their faces with cork for their job, just as our actors did. He spoke with such authority that who was I to question him? But now, when I stared at our porter, his face seemed to be an even black all over, and even his neck and his hands were black. I was beginning to doubt Tarres. He had never been as close to a porter as I was right now. In fact, he had never even been on a train. But just to confirm my discovery, I asked Papa.

"Does that man rub his face and hands with burned cork, or is his skin really black?"

Papa laughed. " No. *Er is tahka schvartz. Er is a schvartza.*" [He is really black. He is a black person] Then he added, "*Schvartzas* are called Negroes."

"Where do they live?"

"In Winnipeg."

There, I had learned the truth. Porters were really black all over. They were called Negroes and they lived in Winnipeg. Wait 'til I tell Tarres.

I waited for Winnipeg. I didn't know what to expect. Although Mama had taken me there a couple of years before to see "a specialist," Dr. Gordon Chown, I had no recollection either of that trip or of Winnipeg. All I knew about Winnipeg —besides what I had just learned—was that it was a big city and Mama's relatives —the Leachmans—lived there, at 713 Selkirk Avenue. She was always writing to them, and my older sisters would address the envelope. I had heard Mama dictate the address so often, I had memorized it. 713 Selkirk Avenue, Winnipeg, Manitoba. I had been to Manitoba earlier in the year, before school had started, when the Darlings had driven our whole family to visit Papa's relatives, the Shniders, in Inglis, Manitoba. Now I would be visiting Mama's relatives, the Leachmans.

Auntie Leachman was really Mama's aunt, but we also considered her our own aunt, just as we did Papa's sister, whom we called Aunt Bessie. But unlike Aunt Bessie, Auntie Leachman couldn't speak English at all except for a few words. Uncle Leachman was Auntie Leachman's husband; so we called him Uncle Leachman. I didn't think they had first names. Uncle Leachman could speak English better than Auntie Leachman, but not better than Uncle Abe.

Uncle and Auntie Leachman used to come to visit us in Sheho. I liked them because they made a fuss over me and brought us fancy candies, each one individually wrapped in fancy white paper with a colored picture of cherries and oranges. The wrapper was twisted so tightly at one end that I had to keep on untwisting and untwisting it until I could pull out that delicious sweet and sour hard candy which I sucked until I could taste the jelly inside, and then I just chewed the whole thing and kept on sucking until it was gone. It was a real treat. It was better than any candies or suckers we had in our store. Much better. It had to be better. After all, it was from Winnipeg.

They also brought *koochen*, which Auntie Leachman had baked and which I called Jewish cookies. They were big and shaped kind of funny and had sugar all over. They tasted sweet, but not too sweet. And they brought little round corn starch cookies, which weren't nearly as sweet, and tasted a little bit like corn starch, but were still delicious. Sometimes they were covered with poppy seeds. And sometimes they brought strudel filled with apples or cherries and with a crust so delicate, it began to flake when you picked it up, even before you could put it in your mouth. It was wonderful. And they brought *pletzlach*, round buns covered with fried onions or poppy seeds. It was always a real treat whenever the Leachmans visited us.

They would hug me and kiss me and pat me on my head and call me "Yankella." My Jewish name was Yankel. I was named after Papa's father, Yankel, meaning Jacob. He had died in Russia before I was born. I really didn't care for the name Yankella which meant "little" or "small" Yankel or the "child" Yankel. I already knew I was small and that name only reminded me of it. Besides, I really wasn't a child. My baby sister Sylvia was a child. She was smaller than I was. But they never called her "Sylvia." They called her "*Faygella*," which means a little bird.

The name Yankel, though, wasn't too bad. Once in a while Papa would call me Yankel. But Yankella! The only people who called me Yankella were Uncle and Auntie Leachman. So even though I didn't like that name, I didn't say anything. You know how older people are, especially from the Old Country. I didn't want to hurt their feelings. Besides, I knew they called me that because they loved me.

Uncle Leachman would get up early in the morning and put on his yarmulke and Lay *Tfillin*. [phylacteries] That's a Jewish custom that only the most orthodox Jews still practice, twice each day. Once in the early morning and once late in the afternoon. He would wind those funny looking long, slim leather straps around his arm, round and round, until they were all used up, and his arm looked like a huge piece of bologna sausage with heavy twine wrapped around it that Hoop the butcher hung in his butcher shop. Only Uncle Leachman's arm was a different color and so were the funny looking leather straps that he wound around his arm. Then he would fasten a funny looking tiny square black box to his forehead. The box was about half the size of a can of Copenhagen snuff, only it was square. Then he would put on his large *talis* [prayer shawl],white with long black stripes and with fringes on the ends. Then he would open up his *siddur* [prayer book], stand in front of our piano, and begin to pray in a strange, funny sounding language called Hebrew. It sounded like someone was coughing. He would mumble and mumble away, sometimes swaying back and forth, for a long, long time. He was praying to God. I already knew all about God. He was supposed to be everywhere, except that nobody could see him, like he was hiding. But Uncle Leachman knew *exactly* where He was. And so did I. He was hiding inside the piano.

Uncle Leachman taught me the Hebrew alphabet, even before I started school. He repeated it and I repeated it, until my mind soaked up all those funny sounding names like a sponge. *Aleph, bez, gimmel*, and so on. He was extremely kind and always praised me when he taught. He was a good teacher.

Uncle Leachman liked eggs. For breakfast, he always had a soft boiled egg, I mean really soft. It was gooey. Ugh! Sometimes it got on his mustache. I couldn't stand that. I hated eggs. Except hard boiled eggs. And they had to be really hard.

When Uncle and Auntie Leachman got ready to go back to Winnipeg, we would pack a crate full of eggs and give it to them. That's a lot of eggs. The crate had two sides, and each side was called half a crate, and each half- crate held five flats or layers of eggs, all packed one on top of the other. Each layer had six funny rows of folded cardboard going up and down and also sideways, so that it looked like six rows of tiny square rooms all open at the top. Each egg was protected from breaking because it was in its own tiny, little cardboard room. When we filled one layer, which held three dozen eggs, we would put a flat cardboard on top of that layer, then add a folded cardboard on top of it, and then start all over again. I could put in only one egg at a time, and I had to be careful not to break any. My older sisters could put in two eggs at a time. But Papa had bigger hands and he could put in six at a time, three with each hand. When we filled the crate, Papa would put a wooden top over the crate and pound it shut with nails. Then Mike Harris, the drayman, would pick up the crate and take it to the C.P.R. station, where Mr. Curry, the station agent, would put it in the baggage car and ship it to Winnipeg.

Uncle and Auntie Leachman's youngest daughter, Susie, was Mama's cousin. But she was also my cousin, just like my cousins in Inglis. She was a beautiful girl with a full round face and freckles on her nose and jet black hair and the softest, sweetest voice I had ever heard. She was just a few years older than Merle, and she also visited us. I distinctly remember her last visit. It was in the winter, around Christmas time, the year before I started school. I was 4 1/2 at the time. Like her father, she, too, was extremely patient and kind and made a fuss over me, especially when I learned the A,B, Cs from her without any difficulty at all. She also taught me how to count to twenty. I thought she was an excellent teacher, except when she tried to teach me a Chanukah song and the meaning of Chanukah. I had never heard of that holiday. Mama and Papa observed Rosh Hashanah and Yom Kippur and *Pesach* [Passover] and even Purim—the holiday on which they were married. But Chanukah! They had never even mentioned it. Never! I thought that Christmas was the only holiday in December even though we didn't celebrate it. But I knew that Santa Claus always visited us then, and I didn't think it was fair that Susie didn't even mention Santa Claus and tried to confuse me when she said Chanukah was a holiday. So I never bothered to learn the Chanukah songs or anything about Chanukah even though Susie thought it was a Jewish holiday.

But now Papa and I would be visiting the whole family as soon was we got into Winnipeg. I had absolutely no idea what Winnipeg was like, except that it was much bigger than Yorkton, and Yorkton was much bigger than Sheho—a whole lot bigger. So I stared out the window at the telegraph poles that flew past us so fast I could hardly count them. And I stared at the farms beyond the telegraph poles. I stared at brown stooks of wheat and the men in the field pitching the stooks higher and higher onto the wagons. I stared at the horses pulling the wagons to the threshing machines. I stared at the barns, mostly red like ours but much larger. And I stared at the cows all gathered together, black ones all over, and black ones with white patches—and some were red with no patches and some were red with white patches. And some were light brown all over and some were cream colored. There were all kinds of cows. I had never seen so many cows. And there were large, long, strange looking buildings unlike any I had ever seen. And high metal tanks, as high as our house. And gradually these farms went by slower and slower, and instead of farms I saw all kinds of houses, like the houses in Sheho, only some had two stories and some were much larger—even larger than Wunder's house or the hotel. There were all kinds of buildings now, big ones and small ones, hundreds of them, in all directions. And there were cement sidewalks, not just the one like in Sheho, but on both sides of the road, with people walking on them, and roads with more sidewalks on every block. There must have been a hundred sidewalks at least. And at least a hundred roads. And there were all kinds of cars on all these roads. And colored lights that changed from red to green and sometimes orange. I had never seen colored lights before. And soon we crossed a bunch of railroads and bridges and more railroads and the train tooted its whistle and slowed down, and it went slower and slower and I knew we were about to stop. I didn't have to ask Papa where we were. There was only one place that could be this big. Winnipeg.

Everybody got up at once. It was crowded. Papa took his suitcase down from the overhead rack, just like everyone else. He took me by the hand and we slowly made our way to the door which the conductor had just opened. The conductor pulled a chain and lowered the portable steps from the coach to the station's platform and then laid a small black stool at the bottom of the steps. He then held out his hand and began helping passengers off the train. He didn't help everyone, though. Papa didn't need his help. But I did. He was a nice conductor. He smiled at me and said "good-bye." I liked him.

I had never seen so many people get off a train before. Every time the train stopped at Sheho— the morning train from Winnipeg or the night train from Saskatoon or the Peanut from Nipawin or Yorkton — a few people would get off. Sometimes one or two or three or maybe even four; and once in a great while as many as eight. I had never seen more than eight people get off at once. But here—in Winnipeg—I couldn't even count that many. There were hundreds getting off just one train. Honest!

Then we entered the huge C.P. R. station. I had never heard so much noise or commotion before. All I could see were people. People greeting people, hugging and kissing each other. Hundreds of them. Maybe even thousands of them. They were coming and going in all directions. I felt dazed. Then Papa and I walked down a flight of steps and there were even more people there. Again, they were coming and going in all directions. More confusion. But why had we walked down the steps? In the Sheho station and even the Yorkton station, there were no steps. We walked from the station's platform right *into* the station. Here in Winnipeg, first you walked into the station, then you walked down the steps into another part of the station. It was huge. Maybe it was built on more than one level. What level were we on now? Where was the ground? I was baffled. I forget whether we then walked up a flight of steps or not. But I remember we walked quite a long way before we finally walked through a huge door, and suddenly there was daylight. Not phony light (which everyone called electric light)—the kind we had on the train and in the huge Winnipeg station—but real daylight. We were outside at last. And we were really on the ground. Now I knew we were actually in Winnipeg.

All kinds of cars, some of which Papa called "taxicabs," were lined up along the curb. Papa, however, his suitcase in his left hand and my own hand in his right, led me along the sidewalk to a corner where we started to cross the road. We crossed only partway, then stopped and waited at some yellow painted posts that were connected by thick rope-like strands of wire. In the middle of this wide paved road (much wider than the road next to our store) were two sets of railroad tracks. They were not quite as wide as our railroad tracks and not quite as high and they didn't have ties with cinder between the ties, but they were real steel tracks that looked like railroad tracks. Papa called them "streetcar" tracks. And there were dozens of cars zipping by on each side of this wide road that Papa called "Main Street." I thought it odd that Papa called this very wide road a "street." Back home it would have been called a highway. A street was the same as the cement sidewalk that ran three blocks from Darling's corner to the shoe repair shop. Back home people walked on the street but cars and teams of horses used the high-way. Now suddenly, in Winnipeg a highway is a street. How come? I asked Papa why? He said *"Hack mir nisht kine chanek."* That means "Don't chop me a tea kettle." But what it really means is "Don't keep on talking like a tea kettle." Then he said, "You ask too many questions." Everybody says I ask too many questions.

A funny looking railroad car without an engine and with a long pole attached to overhead wires was coming toward us, right on the tracks. It clanged and clanged until it stopped. It sure made a lot of noise. I asked Papa what it was and he told me it was a streetcar. I asked him if this was the one that would take us to the Leachmans, but he said "no." I asked him why not. "We have to wait for the Selkirk car. It goes along Selkirk

Avenue, right past the Leachmans." That made sense to me. So we waited. Finally it came.

I don't remember how many people got off the streetcar or how many like us got on, but there were quite a few. Some of the men were dressed in suits, and some of the women in fancy dresses. What I remember most is that everyone seemed to be in a hurry. It sure wasn't like Sheho. After we climbed the steps of the streetcar, Papa gave some coins to the conductor then guided me to an empty seat. I sat on the inside so I could look out the widow. It was exciting. There was so much to see.

The conductor closed the door and clanged a bell two or three times and the street car started to move, not with a real big jerk like our train, but with a smaller jerk until it quickly picked up speed. But not for long. The conductor kept clanging that bell and clanging that bell, and soon the streetcar slowed down and came to a jerky stop. We hadn't gone far at all. Maybe one block. Not more than two. Some passengers got off and others got on. Then the conductor clanged the bell and we were on our way again. I soon got used to the clanging and the starting and stopping and it didn't bother me any more. There was too much to see.

On both sides of this real wide road that Papa called Main Street, I could see all kinds of different buildings, one right after the other. They were packed together with no space in between. Not like Sheho. A lot of them were two stories high, like our store, but many were much higher. And there were so many people walking along the sidewalk, entering and leaving these buildings. I had never seen so many buildings or so many people. I had never imagined there could be that many. It was more than I could count.

Some of the buildings had lights all around them and the lights were going off and on, round and round, in a circle.

"What kind of building is that?"

"It's for moving pictures. They show movies there."

"What kind of buildings are those?"

"They're business. Stores and cafes and factories and all kinds of business."

I was amazed. Main Street must be the biggest street in the whole world.

I was just getting used to Main Street when the streetcar turned left. "Where are we now?"

"Selkirk Avenue."

"How far from the Leachmans?"

"Not far, seven blocks."

I thought of counting the blocks, but there was too much to see—not only business buildings but also houses. Mostly two story houses even bigger than Wunder's home. And there was almost no space between the buildings.

I noticed, however, that Selkirk Avenue wasn't quite as busy as Main Street, and more and more of the buildings were homes. I could easily tell the difference between business buildings and homes. Businesses were built of brick or large stones or cement and had flat roofs. But homes were built of wood and had slanted roofs and verandahs.

Suddenly Papa reached up and pulled a cord and said, "We get off at the next stop." As the streetcar came to a stop, he picked up his suitcase, took me by my hand, led me toward the open door, and helped me off. We walked across the road that he called Selkirk Avenue, and suddenly we were on the sidewalk, which was also called Selkirk Avenue. A few more steps and there we were. Uncle and Auntie Leachman's home at 713 Selkirk Avenue.

It was a large two-story house, not quite as big as Wunder's house, but much bigger than ours. And the steps were also higher than ours. Papa rang the bell and soon Auntie Leachman came to the door and called me Yankella and patted me on my head and hugged me and kissed me on my mouth, as though I was the most precious child in the world. I still hated the word "Yankella," but what could I say?

My recollections of my first visit to the Leachmans are rather dim except for meeting the rest of their family and my first visit to a synagogue. I vaguely recall meeting their son Harry, who owned a bingo-type of business at Winnipeg Beach, which he called "Tango" and which he ran during the three months of summer. I also remember meeting their three other daughters —all older than Susie. Ethel seemed quite a bit older than Susie and was rather high strung. She was still single. Mabel, a little older than Ethel, was an extremely beautiful lady, whose voice was every bit as sweet as Susie's. Mabel was married to Bill Cutler, a tall, slim, very handsome man with a mustache. He looked like a movie actor and talked so loud I could hear him in the next room.. They lived around the corner, on Pritchard Avenue.

Finally there was Mama's oldest cousin, Bessie, who had moved to Long Beach, California, with her husband, Sam Lackman, shortly after he had become a lawyer in Winnipeg. Bessie looked a lot like her sisters, only a little plumper and a bit older. She also spoke so much faster than they did that I had a hard time understanding everything she said. Mama was always telling me about how wonderful Bessie and Sam were and how mature their son Larry was, even though he was not quite two years older than I, and what a wonderful appetite he had and how he ate everything without being coaxed and never left any food on his plate because he knew the children in Europe were starving. And since the Lackmans didn't keep kosher, he even drank milk after eating meat. Jewish people weren't supposed to do that, but they lived in California where everything was different, so that was their business. Yes, Larry was a chubby, healthy boy, not skinny like me. And now, after hearing such wonderful things about my cousin Bessie and her son Larry, who was also my cousin, I finally met them. She had traveled with him on the bus, all the way from California. And even though I didn't know exactly where California was, I knew it was in the States, somewhere down south, far, far away.

Her son Larry, her only child, who was really my "third" cousin, was much, much heavier than I. He was certainly chubby, as Mama had said. In fact, I thought he was fat. And he did have an appetite. No question about that. What impressed me most about him, though, was his attitude. He always seemed so knowledgeable and confident. He knew exactly where the sheil [synagogue] was on Selkirk Avenue. We would all be going there tomorrow. He knew which streetcar to take to go all the way downtown—to the big department stores, Eaton's and the Bay. And he knew which streetcar would take him back. He was smart. He even spoke with more authority than Tarres Koropatniski. I asked Larry how he knew so much about Winnipeg, and he told me he came here quite often with his mother for summer vacations. We called them summer "holidays." But Americans called them "vacations." Americans also had a funny accent. They said "cowent" instead of count and "soweth" instead of south. But at least they spoke English.

I don't remember whether or not we went to *sheil* that night, but I distinctly remember going there the next morning. It was a small building and it was crowded inside. I mean really crowded. The women all had hats or fancy scarves over their heads, and they all sat along the sides of the room, separated from the men by a ledge. The men were all dressed in suits, like Papa, and they all wore caps, like Papa, or hats, like Uncle Leachman. They all had *talises* [prayer shawls] draped over their shoulders, and sat by themselves, or with their sons, on long, wooden benches. And they all *dahvened* [prayed] in Hebrew. At times they all *dahvened* aloud, all together. I couldn't understand them. To me, it sounded like a bunch of people shouting different words that nobody could understand. At other times they prayed silently. Or they mumbled like a swarm of bees. Sometimes they all stood up and swayed, just like Uncle Leachman in front of our piano. But most of the time they just sat there and prayed all day long. It was really boring.

It was so boring that I was glad when Larry took me outside and we walked away from the *sheil*, back to the Leachman's home. I don't remember what game he was trying to play, but to the best of my recollection, he was trying to show me how far he could throw a stone, and it hit somebody's window. Or he might have gotten into some other trouble. Anyway, I do remember that he did get into some kind of trouble because the neighbors complained and Auntie Leachman really scolded him. And I distinctly remember what he said: "Honest, Baba, it wasn't my fault." He sounded so convincing that she apparently believed him. I could never get away with telling such a lie. Right then I knew he had a very special talent. I thought that someday he would become a lawyer, like his father, and convince a judge that night was day and day was night, and up was down and down was up, and outside was inside and inside and was outside. [Believe it or not, my prediction came true. Today he is a well known, successful real estate trial attorney, and he wins most of his cases.]

In addition to meeting the Leachman family, I also met Mama's only brother in Canada, Uncle Dave. He was younger than she was, and I knew he adored her. He lived with the Leachmans. He was shorter than Papa and rather thin, like me, and he could speak English better than Papa or Mama or Uncle Leachman, even though he still had a thick Jewish accent. And when he called me "Yankella," it sounded like he was speaking through his nose. He spoke very slowly so that I could understand everything, even though every now and then he would pronounce certain words through his nose. He was the third uncle I knew and the only one who was not yet married.

My final and most vivid recollection of that trip is marveling at the hundreds of bright lights the last night of my visit, when Papa and I took a taxicab back to the C.P.R. station. I had never imagined there could be so many lights. In Sheho we had four gas-burning Coleman lanterns that our village constable, Mr. Howe, hung up each night—one at the beginning of each block. Four lanterns. That was all. But here in Winnipeg, every block had dozens of lights—each one as bright as a Coleman lantern, and there were hundreds and hundreds of lights just along Selkirk Avenue and Main Street alone. And there were side streets also with dozens of lights. Every business building had a lighted neon sign, and some glowed a deep red or purple or bright green in big letters that I could see blocks away. But of all the lights I saw, the ones that I will never forget were the rows of plain electric lights that went off and on and off and on and seemed to be going around and around and around the entire front of the building. I thought it was magic. I knew that building was a movie theater, and I marveled at how many movie theaters there were just on Main Street. And as our taxicab passed the last of those magic lights, I felt a twinge of sadness in having to leave Winnipeg, where everyone had treated me like a favorite relative, as if I were the best little boy in the whole world.

It is now more than sixty-two years since I first saw those revolving lights, and my memory blurs as I try to recall the details of my second visit to Winnipeg. It was in January of 1934, when I was in second grade and still under the harsh day-to-day threats and corporal punishment of Miss Griffiths, that I accompanied Mama to Winnipeg for the wedding of Uncle Dave and his bride, who was about to become my new aunt—Auntie Sarah. The reason I even bother to mention Miss Griffiths is that during this trip I stuttered—for the first and only time in my life. In retrospect, I must have stuttered for a good reason: Miss Griffiths.

I remember that Aunt Sarah wore a long white gown and there were a lot of people at the wedding. But what I remember most about that wedding was my offer—out of the sheer goodness of my innocent heart—to help with the crowded sleeping situation that night at the Leachmans. I don't recall how many rooms were in the Leachman home, but I knew that in order to accommodate everyone who was staying at their home, people doubled and even tripled up. I slept with Mama, and I believe someone else also slept in the same room. At home Mama and Papa rarely slept in the same room, and I often slept with Papa. [I never knew why they slept apart until many years later, when I learned about the rhythm method of birth control.] In any event, there was some discussion about where all of us would sleep. And so I thought my suggestion to Susie might solve the problem. "Uncle Dave can sleep with me."

Susie laughed, then without any explanation she merely said, "Oh, no. Uncle Dave is going to sleep with his wife Aunt Sarah."

I thought that was strange and felt like asking her why. But Papa had told me that I asked too many questions, so I kept my mouth shut. And so at the age of almost seven, I learned that husbands were supposed to sleep with their wives. But I still thought that storks bring babies because that's what Miss Griffiths had told us. It was not until later that year, while swimming in the creek that flowed through Wunder's field, that Johnny Drobot explained to me exactly how babies are made and where they come from. And he used a bad word I had never heard before.

During Uncle Dave and Aunt Sarah's wedding reception, I remember trying to say something that I thought was important but it wouldn't come out. All I could do was stutter. And I remember Bill Cutler scolding me: "Don't stutter. Think about what you're trying to say, then speak slowly." His reprimand didn't help but only made me more conscious about my stammering. When I tried to concentrate on what I was trying to say, I stuttered all the more. I don't remember how long I stuttered, but eventually that problem disappeared, probably about the same time as I got used to getting the strap from Miss Griffiths.

Another memory I have of that trip is meeting Mama's *zeyda* [grandfather], my great-grandfather, for the first and only time. He had a long beard and wore a black suit and hugged me and kissed me and blessed me and gave me some coins. That's all I remember about him. I couldn't quite understand my relationship to him except that he was related to both Auntie Leachman and to Mama, and they both called him *zeyda*. I really had no concept of a grandfather, because it had never been explained to me. Papa always referred to him as the *Schatchin*, the matchmaker who had introduced him—Papa—to the beautiful young brunette who not long afterward became Mrs. Katz. Apparently Zeyda Izen had done quite well because it was he who had paid for the steamship tickets for both Mama and Uncle Dave. Yet at the age of almost seven, I knew very little about him except that he was a very, very old man—almost 100. And he was somehow related to Mama.

During that visit, my cousin Susie took me downtown to window shop at the expensive stores along Portage Avenue. I marveled at the window displays and how the women and men and even boys and girls in the window looked so real. Susie told me they were fake. They were large dolls and were called "mannequins." Although I was supposed to believe her, I watched them for a few minutes to see if they were breathing or if they moved their fingers just a tiny bit. But they didn't move at all.

Then we went to both Eaton's and the Bay (Hudson's Bay Company). She told me they were the biggest department stores in all of Winnipeg. I tried to count how many rows of windows went up from the main floor of the Eaton's building, but there were so many I had to squint before I got to the top, and then the traffic light changed and we had to hurry across the street. Eaton's looked almost as high as our grain elevators, and so did the Bay. Susie told me they were even taller. But I didn't think so. Nothing could possibly be taller than grain elevators. I remembered my previous visit when Larry Lackman had told me there were buildings in New York called "skyscrapers" that were so tall a person had to bend his head away back to look up at the top, and sometimes the tops of the skyscrapers were even above the clouds. I didn't believe him, but I didn't say anything. He told me that it never snowed in California—not even in the winter. I couldn't imagine how that was possible, especially in the middle of winter when it got to be forty and fifty below zero. I wouldn't argue with him any more than I would argue with Tarres Koropatniski. I didn't know who was the worse liar. Probably Larry. He thought that just because I was from Sheho and he was an American, he could tell me anything and I would believe it. But I wasn't stupid. I was beginning to realize that Americans were full of it. But I never told anyone. Why should I?

Susie took me by my hand and led me inside a glass door, and we went around with that glass door until we got inside the building and then let go of that door. It kept on going round and round, with people pushing it to get inside or to go outside. She called it a "revolving" door. It was the strangest door I had ever seen. I don't remember whether that door was in Eaton's or the Bay or whether both stores had that kind of door. I don't remember which store was which because they both looked alike inside. They were both huge and crowded. I never saw so many people in all my life—even at the Winnipeg C.P.R. station. And they both had stairways that moved, some going up and others down. You had to be careful on these moving stairways. Susie called them "escalators."

But that wasn't the strangest thing I saw. Both Eaton's and the Bay had a row of small rooms, each about half the size of our bedroom, with a light above each room that would turn red or green. As soon as the light turned green, the doorway to the room slid open and some people got out and others entered this room. They were all in a big hurry. They pushed and shoved until the room was full. As soon as it was full, the man in uniform, who always stood at the front of the room, pulled a handle and the door closed. Then he cranked the handle again and the whole room started going up or down toward the next floor. I had a funny feeling in my stomach as soon as the room started to go down.

When it went up, my feet felt like they were pushing through the floor. It was the funniest feeling I ever had.

Almost immediately after the room started to move, he shouted "second floor" or "third floor" and cranked the handle and the room came to a jerky stop. Then he cranked the handle again, and the door slid open and he shouted "Watch your step." About half the people in the room—men and women alike —pushed and shoved to get out of the room, onto this new floor. Then a whole bunch of different people pushed and shoved to get into this same room before the man yanked the handle and closed the door. Susie called this room an "elevator." I had always thought an elevator was a very high wooden building, like the one across from our store, where farmers took their wheat. I was beginning to learn that there were many words in our language that had different meanings.

Back home we all used to look at the thick Eaton's catalogue. It had pictures of everything—clothing, shoes, radios, skates, hockey sticks, all kinds of hardware, and just about everything a person could possibly need or want. I wondered if this Eaton's would stock the same items, and I was surprised that it did. I found it simply amazing that one department store—a single building—could contain such a variety of items. Eaton's not only carried everything they showed in their catalogue but even carried groceries. All kinds of fruits and vegetables and groceries that I had never seen before. And you could pick out your own groceries. All by yourself. And you could pick out whatever you wanted to wear—or almost anything—all by yourself. I could hardly believe it.

I wondered how much money Eaton's lost through stealing. Back home Papa and Mama personally waited on each customer. Almost nothing was displayed in the open for people to steal. On Saturdays my job was to watch for anyone who might steal. But here—people could pick up anything they wanted. And if they didn't want to pay for it, who would know? It was so easy. But on second thought, Eaton's probably had policemen, like me, who were watching everyone. They were probably dressed in everyday clothes, and nobody knew who they were. Otherwise dishonest people could empty the store and Eaton's could go broke. But I still couldn't get over it. So much of everything and all out in the open. Amazing! Everything in Winnipeg was amazing. If I told my classmates what Winnipeg was like, they wouldn't believe me. It was like a fairy tale.

When I returned to school a few days later and Miss Griffiths asked me where I had been, I said "Winnipeg." Then she asked, "Did you see the traffic policeman on the corner?"

"What's a traffic policeman?"

"He's a special policeman who stands on the corner and holds up his hand to stop traffic so people can cross the street. You must have seen him."

"No, I saw many policemen, but they were just walking up and down the street. They didn't direct traffic. We crossed when the traffic lights turned green."

"But you must have seen the traffic policeman."

"No. There was no traffic policeman."

She was disappointed I had not seen " the traffic policeman" that she apparently had heard about or read about in one of the readers. Then she turned to Jenny and Walter Lys and said, "When you were in Winnipeg, you saw the traffic policeman, didn't you?"

Both nodded their heads. I was disgusted because I knew they had lied. I guess they were probably afraid of getting the strap if they didn't agree with her. Or maybe they didn't want to embarrass her. Then Miss Griffiths turned to me and said, "See, I told you so. It's too bad you didn't see the traffic policeman."

Right then I knew she had never been to Winnipeg or any other large city and had no idea at all how huge Winnipeg was or what the traffic was like or how many policemen there were just on Portage Avenue alone. I knew she didn't know anything at all about that city. I suspected that the farthest east she had ever been was to the edge of her home town, Saltcoats, Saskatchewan. But I didn't want to argue with her. I didn't want to get the strap. So why argue? Besides, people will believe what they want to believe, even if it's not the truth.

CHAPTER SEVEN
Reading And Writing And Forty Below

Although I taught the three "R's" in high school many years ago, and my wife taught them at the kindergarten-primary level for over four decades, I am still amazed at the mystery of learning. Some children pick up the secret of reading quite easily while others never pick it up at all. Writing, however, is a different matter. I can teach anyone who can read how to write, at least up to a certain level of proficiency; and I have done so in my career as a teacher, professor, and consultant. But mathematics is another problem altogether. Again, to some children arithmetic comes almost naturally; to others, it comes ever so slowly and sometimes not at all. Does a particular teacher make the difference? Sometimes I wonder. But to give credit where credit is due, Miss Griffiths did teach me how to read, write, add, and subtract. It occurred not overnight, but gradually, almost imperceptibly, like sunrise turning into daylight, and not entirely in the first grade. By the end of my second year in her class, I had no difficulty with the three "R's."

I remember sitting in my desk, looking up above the blackboard at some cards with large marks on them.

I stared at them day in and day out. I had no idea what they were or why they were there. Then one day Miss Griffiths put some marks on the blackboard, similar to those I had been staring at. She told us these were letters of the alphabet and we were supposed to copy them in our "general work books." This was called "printing." I tried to copy them. Some of the big letters were easy, especially C, I, O, T, U, and V. But the rest ranged from difficult to impossible. I didn't know why we were copying these funny marks, or "Capital Letters," as she called them. But I eventually learned how to print them. It helped that I already knew how to recite some of the letters of the alphabet which my older sisters had taught me before I had started school. I could also count to twenty. So far, so good.

Then one day she began to put some much smaller marks on the blackboard. She called these "small" letters. They were absolutely impossible for me to copy. As hard as I tried, I might as well have been copying Chinese. I hate to admit this, but I never did learn how to print lower case letters until my first biology class at university, twelve years later. So much for fast learners.

One day she handed a book to everyone in class. The cover was hard and smooth, but the color was ugly. It was an ugly, muddy yellowish gray. "This is your *"reader,"* she announced. I want you to take this *reader* home and put a cover over it, then bring it back. You must take special care of this *reader*. Don't scribble in it, don't put any marks in it, don't tear it, and don't lose it. Now be sure to put a cover over it, and bring it back tomorrow." That was my introduction to THE CANADIAN READERS, BOOK 1. No wonder she wanted it covered. It was the ugliest color I had ever seen.

For the cover, most of the kids used heavy brown wrapping paper, which they got free of charge from their friendly storekeeper, including Papa. But my "reader" was special. My sisters covered it with white "oilcloth," the same kind of heavy oilcloth that covered our wooden kitchen table. Then they sewed the inside flaps together, tightly, so that the oilcloth cover would never fall off and would last forever and ever. When the oilcloth got dirty, it could easily be wiped off with a damp rag. It was a masterpiece. Alas! At the end of the school year, when I finished grade one, I had to take the cover off before handing the book back to Miss Griffiths for her new first graders who would inherit these readers. Ironically, I remember that the new first graders received an entirely new set of readers with a pretty bright blue and orange cover. The CANADIAN READERS BOOK I that I had used had been retired. May they rest in peace!

Every day, right after school, I took my reader home and, as Miss Griffith had requested, practiced my reading. I usually practiced in front of my sisters, who corrected any of my mistakes. Then I practiced and practiced until I memorized the selection. The next day when I was asked to stand up and read, I had no trouble at all. I cannot say the same for many of the other kids, who read word for word, or mumbled and stumbled and needed a great deal of prodding from Miss Griffiths. I felt sorry for them. I also memorized the poems she had asked us to memorize, both in first grade and in second. To this very day, I still remember most of them. I especially liked poetry. I liked the rhythm of the words and the sound of the rhyme. And I never tired of listening to everyone in class trying to recite the same poem.

Since we first graders all listened to the second graders when they read their selections or recited their poems, most of us found the second grade much easier than the first. We learned "The Little Red Hen" and "The Fox and the Grapes" and "The Bag of Feathers" and "Little May" and so many fables and wonderful stories that all had a moral. Every story had a moral which I never forgot. To this day, whenever somebody asks me to do something and I want to procrastinate, I never say "in a minute." I may say, "I'll get around to it later," or "I'll do it just as soon as I can." But I never say "in a minute." Never! I remember what happened to Little May.

Whenever her mother asked Little May to do something, Little May would always reply, "In a minute." One day her mother asked her to close the door of the bird cage. "In a minute," replied Little May. But the cat did not wait. Instantly, it leaped up and grabbed the bird inside the unlocked cage. By the time Little May looked up it was too late. Her bird was gone. And that was the last time Little May said "in a minute." Her tragedy left a lasting impression on me.

It was in the first grade that I learned how to add and subtract. I remember turning around and watching Alice Curry counting on her fingers to get the correct answer to some problem. We all counted on our fingers, especially for "take-away" problems, but I remember that I could do some of them in my head—without the help of fingers—whereas she would stick out her tongue and count on her fingers. That's all I remember about my arithmetic class in Miss Griffiths's room.

Finally, there was the subject that has forever remained a mystery to me—spelling. Although I never had too much difficulty in my primary grades memorizing the daily spelling list in our "Speller," the rules of logic seemed to give way to exceptions to the rule as I grew older. Whoever invented spelling for the English language must have been drunk at the time. Why should the spelling for one word have different meanings? and why should the same sound be spelled differently? Unfortunately, I never mastered spelling, but have compensated by using spelling-dictionaries and proofreaders.

With the exception of my first several months in Miss Griffiths's class, I don't remember having any particular difficulty learning the three R's; and by the end of my second year—not first—I was able to read and write as well as almost anyone in my class. Students who did not meet her expectations were "flunked." Several of my classmates failed. There was no such thing as "social promotion." If one didn't achieve certain standards, one failed—even in grade one. It was as simple as that. "You'll be in here until you're an old man with gray hair," Miss Griffiths would shout. And she meant it for boys and girls alike.

Although I was ranked third in class at the end of grade one, I don't think that I could actually read. I believe I had relied on my memory and recognition within a context, and could not actually read something I hadn't seen before. I remember Mrs. Darling handing me the Saskatoon *Star Phoenix* shortly after school had ended. She pointed out the heading underneath which appeared the names of our first graders who had passed. "See, your name is there," she said. I looked at the list of names but could not recognize my own name until she pointed it out. That is why I suspect I could not really read, even though I had been ranked near the top in of my class of twenty-nine. Annie Homeniuk had been ranked first. I don't remember who was second, but the following year and every year thereafter right through grade twelve, I always ranked second. Even when Annie Homeniuk left school after completing grade ten and I thought that at last I would be first in class, Destiny conspired against me. Walter Hudyma, a transfer student from a one-room farm school entered my class. Not only was he smarter than I, but he studied all the time. It was no contest. I was still second best.

At the age of seven, I entered Miss Yemen's room, right across the hall, for grades three, four, and five. It was like going from a battlefield to an emergency hospital. Even though there was a certain amount of noise and commotion, Miss Yemen was Florence Nightingale in contrast to our previous drill sergeant. She spoke slowly and quietly and occasionally raised her voice. But only on rare occasions did she resort to yelling and even the strap. I got the strap from her once or perhaps twice, probably because I whispered too much.

As soon as we entered her room to begin the afternoon session at 1:30 P.M., she would read us a selection from one of her books about animals and birds. Since we all listened intently, it eliminated any whispering. The author had personified nature and wild animals and birds by giving them names such as Mother West Wind, Reddy Fox, and so on. Her characters were portrayed in such a heart- wrenching, sympathetic manner that some of us cried when Father Goose lost his mate when she was shot by hunters during the fall migration. To this day, I wouldn't even dream of hunting. Miss Yemen would occasionally ask for volunteers to read part of the chapter. I remember the excitement of standing up in front of the room and proudly reading to the entire class a page that I had never seen before. This was a real book—not our reader. And I hadn't even practiced. Suddenly I stumbled over some of the words and my face felt hot. I was so embarrassed, I wished I could disappear. But with a little help from Miss Yemen, I continued to the end of the page.

It was exciting to be in her room because we were learning new subjects: health, history, and geography. In order to be healthy and grow up big and strong, we should get ten hours of sleep a night (eight was more than enough for me), and eat three good meals a day, including four glasses of milk (which I never drank unless it was with Kellogg's corn flakes, Quaker puffed wheat, or Nabisco shredded wheat—topped with plenty of brown sugar). We should eat at least a daily serving of meat (which I ate only when it was smothered with ketchup), and eggs (which I also hated unless they were boiled hard as a rock). We should also eat fish and cheese because they contained protein. I hated fried fish but I liked the tiny King Oscar sardines that we sold in the store, as well as canned red salmon from British Columbia. I also hated the cottage cheese we made at home because it tasted awful. However, I loved cheddar cheese, and whenever Papa brought some home from Mr. Leckie's store, as a treat for all of us, I devoured it.

Fresh fruits and vegetables were also good for us, we learned in our health class. I never cared for oranges or apples or lemons, the only kinds of fruit we sold in our store; but I loved bananas, grapes, and cherries, which Papa also brought home from Mr. Leckie's store when they were in season. That was a treat. As for fresh vegetables, I loved eating all kinds of them, fresh from our garden in June and July and August, especially green peas while still in their pods. In winter, we had no fresh vegetables. Nobody did. My favorite foods, however, were not on the health chart. There was probably a conspiracy against peanut butter, ice cream, Cracker Jack, chocolate bars, rye bread, and kosher salami. As for fast foods, nobody on the Prairies, I'm sure, had ever heard of them.

I also learned that we should brush our teeth at least twice a day and see a dentist once a year, wash our hands with warm water and soap before eating, to kill the germs which cause disease, and never drink from somebody's else's cup because we don't want to catch their germs. I couldn't stand it when Polly, our hired girl, would drink water from the dipper in our water pail at home. The dipper was meant to pour water from the pail into a cup. "You shouldn't drink from the dipper," I told her. Then I explained why. But she was not impressed. Everybody on the farm always drank from the dipper, yet grew up big and strong. What kind of nonsense was little Jackie Katz talking?

The most intellectually exciting day in Miss Yemen's class was the day—in grade three—when she said, "Now take out your history note books and copy the notes I'm going to write on the blackboard." We had never copied "notes" before. This was a brand new subject, and it was really exciting. She had previously told us a story about why and how Christopher Columbus discovered America.

I loved stories. I could listen to them all day long. But suddenly the story ended. "I want you all to take out a new scribbler. That's going to be your history notebook. Now open your history notebook and on the first page copy the notes I'm going to write on the blackboard."

HISTORY

1. Christopher Columbus.

2. An Italian sailor.

3. Born in Genoa, Italy.

4. Wanted to find a western way to India by sea.

5. Received help from the queen of Spain.

6. Sailed west.

7. Discovered America in 1492.

Then we put our scribblers away. When we wrote our final exams in June, I knew all the answers to Christopher Columbus. History was exciting.

In our geography class, she rolled down the large map above the blackboard and pointed out the countries belonging to the mighty British Empire. For the third consecutive year, we learned that the sun never set on the "Mighty British Empire," which included Canada, Australia, New Zealand, South Africa, India, and of course the British Isles. These countries were depicted in red. They were all over the place and took up most of the map that covered the blackboard. I was proud to be a Canadian since we were part of the Mighty British Empire. Although England was the strongest and most important country in the world—it was really small. Canada with only ten million people, was the largest country in the British Empire, even larger than the United States, our neighbor to our south, which was green. The United States wasn't important anyway. That's why we never learned about it, even though my Lackman cousins lived in California, and Uncle Moishe and Auntie Bayla lived in Boston. The largest country was Russia, where Papa came from. It was huge. China was the second largest and had four hundred million people, but to me it didn't look any larger than Canada. I thought Canada was larger. Maybe whoever drew that had made a mistake, but I didn't want to tell Miss Yemen. Besides, she knew more about China than I did. Greenland was also big, but it was mostly ice. If we lived there, we wouldn't have to hire Mike Haluke to haul water to flood our skating rink, and we could skate all year round. I didn't pay much attention to the countries in South America. They were even less important than the United States. So who cared?

All of the five continents and five oceans were pointed out to us. [Antarctica was not yet considered as a continent.] The Pacific Ocean was really big. Huge! I wondered what it looked like besides water. The only body of water I had ever seen was Salt Lake, three miles north, and it wasn't any bigger than Sheho. The Pacific must be enormous. Maybe someday, if I was really lucky, I'd get to see it. What I liked most about geography, however, was looking at the National Geographic Magazines. Some of the African natives didn't wear many clothes and the women sure had big breasts.

There was no such thing as separate textbooks for the students. In fact, there was no such thing as textbooks. The only books we used— loaners—were the speller, the reader, and an arithmetic book. Other- wise, there simply were no books. The teacher told us a story, then put some notes on the board and had us copy them. Sometimes she didn't even tell us a story. Not until the ninth grade did we have textbooks for each subject, and then we had to buy them ourselves. As politicians would say, " There was no free lunch."

At noon, as soon as the bell rang, we all went home for lunch, which we called "dinner." That was our main meal of the day. Since we had an hour-and a half, we ate leisurely and well. Dinner included soup, roast beef or ground beef or chicken, potatoes, navy beans or canned peas or corn, bread, Jell-O or pudding, and tea. Because we ate only kosher food, we did not have butter or milk with meat. I was a skimpy eater. I picked and picked. When I left food on my plate, Mama would scold me with the command: " Eat! The children in Europe are starving." I didn't feel sorry for the children in Europe. If it weren't for them, I wouldn't have to eat all my food.

When we returned to school, normally about 1:15 P.M., there was usually a softball or volleyball game in progress in the fall and late spring. Although I was usually excluded from softball because I was smaller than the others in my grade, I occasionally played on Johnny Drobot's team, especially if I returned to school within thirty minutes. He had his own ball and bat, which he carried almost everywhere he went, in addition to his slingshot. He would rush home to his grandmother's little shack, get something to eat, and be back in ten minutes flat. Then, as captain of his team and commissioner of his own league, he would choose up sides with another captain he appointed from the fifteen or more farm kids who had brought their lunches to school. Everybody, eager to be included in the game, would huddle up close to Johnny or the other captain. Carefully, each would survey the group and choose the best player available. Believe me, I was not one of the best players available, but I often had a place on his team. When a player would run for home plate after his team-mate had hit the ball, and if he had barely slid home safely before the catcher caught the ball, somebody would yell, "Safe as a dollar in a Jew's pocket." That remark always irritated me, but I attributed it to ignorance. Besides, I rarely got to slide home. In fact, I rarely got to first base.

I often envied the farm kids who brought their own lunches in a pail, which at one time had contained Roger's Golden Corn Syrup or Empress Jam or Swift's Lard. Some of these kids carried a black metal lunch kit containing a thermos bottle, the same kind of kit that the section workers on the C.P.R. took with them to work. I often wondered what it would be like to eat lunch at school. One very cold winter morning, when Mama had come into the room to make sure I dressed warmly enough, Papa followed her and said, "Rosa, pack lunches for the children. It's fifty below."

How cold is fifty degrees below zero Fahrenheit? It's extremely cold. It's even colder than that. Please believe me when I tell you there are no words in the English language or any other language to give you the feeling of how cold fifty below is. It doesn't get that cold every day or every month or every year or even every several years. But once in a great while, the temperature falls to an unimaginably frigid fifty degrees below zero.

In Sheho, Saskatchewan, twenty below is considered cold. But it's normal for Sheho—like eighty-five above in California. Thirty below is very cold. It's getting there. You need to keep your ears and nose covered or they'll freeze in minutes. The cold air creeps right up under your coat or jacket, right up to your crotch. Forty below is extremely cold. It's almost there. But not quite. Only a seven year old crazy fool goes skating on an outdoor rink when it's forty below. That's because he's seven years old, he's crazy and doesn't know that it's forty below. But fifty below! That's something else. Nobody goes skating when it's fifty below. Nobody even goes outside unless it's absolutely necessary—and I mean ABSOLUTELY NECESSARY.

Fifty below is it! It translates into eighty-two degrees below the temperature of ice. It's the straw that can break the camel's back. It's miserable and it's dangerous. The air is so frigid that your nostrils freeze when you inhale, and your lungs feel as if they're catching fire. So you take short breaths. When you exhale, your breath turns to ice immediately. Your eyes water and your eyelashes—frozen with ice—stick together and you can't see. So you cover your mouth and nose and most of your eyes with a scarf and leave only a narrow slit through which to squint, allowing you to glimpse where you want to go. If there's any wind, you walk backwards, turning around occasionally to see where you're going. You tie another scarf around your forehead, even though you're already wearing a fur-lined helmet, so that you are now all covered from head to toe except for the narrow slit above your eyes. In seconds, the scarf is covered with ice. You chip at the ice with your hands, which are protected by two layers of woolen liner mittens inside the leather outers. But your fingers still get cold. Your feet are inside heavy woolen stockings which are inside felt boots, which are inside canvas and rubber overshoes. But your feet still get cold—and your toes are freezing. I mean freezing. The cold permeates everything and stings, no matter how many layers of clothes you have on. It's unbearable for more than a few minutes at a time. If any part of your body is exposed for more than a few minutes, it freezes immediately. That's how cold fifty below is. But life goes on. There are no "snow days" or "cold days" on the Sheho School calendar. Saskatchewan is not Indiana, and Sheho is not Evansville. And that's why Papa said, "Rosa, pack lunches for the children. It's fifty below." [During the winter of 1977, when I was in Evansville, Indiana, to conduct a district-wide workshop on the teaching of writing skills, it snowed on the day scheduled for the workshop and all classes were canceled for the entire district.]

After Mama and Papa had bundled my two older sisters and me so that we looked like upright preserved mummies, and after they had handed us our lunches, separately packed in empty cans of Roger's Golden Corn Syrup, Crisco, and Empress Pure Strawberry Jam, we darted outside and hurried down the block, past the Massey Harris Implement Warehouse to the first building in the next block, our first stop, Hoop's Butcher Shop. We darted inside for a moment, then outside again, past the Red and White Store, past the Post Office, and into Mr. Leckie's store. Like Hoop the butcher, he was also up, stoking the fire in the potbellied stove. He greeted us and grinned. Then we darted outside again, past the Elite Cafe, and up the steps of the Queen's Hotel, into the lobby. Peter Peters, the elderly owner greeted us. Then we were off again, past George Lys's Store at the first corner of the next block, past the barber shop and pool hall next door, operated by Mildred Hesper's father, and into the Rex Cafe. We stomped our feet and warmed up, then hurried outside again, past the town hall, past the two-story red brick building, which had once been a bank and was now the provincial government liquor store operated by Audrey Bokla's father. We hurried by. Only a short way to go now. We passed the little shoe and harness repair shop, past the Ukrainian hall, past a few homes, including the one owned by Mr. Lusak, the section foreman, past Howard Tansley's home, at the end of the block. At last. There it was. Right across the road. The yellow brick school. Merle and Etta entered through the first entrance—the one facing west. I was supposed to enter through the other—the one facing south. But enough was enough. I joined them. We walked up the steps, and entered our own rooms.

Only a few of my classmates were absent. Somebody was always absent. But I was surprised to see that practically all of the farm kids were here. They had come by horse and "cutter," a narrow sleigh that had been converted from a buggy whose wheels had been replaced by two narrow steel runners (one inch wide blades) that cut through the snow like skates. The horses remained outside. Their owners covered them with heavy horse blankets. These blankets had been converted from some horses' hides after the animals had either died from old age or had been dispatched after reaching the age when they were no longer useful on the farm. After the horse had been skinned, its hide had been scrapped, cleaned, salted, and dried, then cut into the shape of a huge blanket which could cover an animal's back or a king size bed. There was no substitute for a horse blanket when it was fifty below.

After the bell rang at noon, most of the kids who lived closer to school than I did went home. But I remained in my room. This was a new experience for me—eating with the farm kids. I suddenly felt important, as though I belonged here. I opened my Empress Pure Strawberry Jam lunch can. Mama had made two sandwiches; one was peanut butter and the other jam, my favorites. They tasted good. I wished I could bring lunch to school more often.

However, I hardly ever got that chance. The temperature rarely fell to fifty below; and even if it did as I grew older, my father felt that I was no longer a child and, therefore, did not need to be overly protected. In retrospect, I sometimes wonder who needs more protection from the cold—the youngster or the adult?

I remember coming home from skating one cold moonlit night. I was walking home slowly with one of my classmates, Tarres Koropatniski, who lived about half-a-mile out of town. His father ran the Federal Grain Company elevator, directly across the road from our store. Tarres, who was quite a bit bigger than I, was the goal keeper on our Pee Wee hockey team. We were both kicking the ball-like, flash-frozen horse droppings which lay all over the hard, icy, snow-packed road. These droppings were about the size of a small orange. We were trying to see who could kick each piece the farthest. If I kicked it too hard, it would shatter into a number of smaller pieces. Then I'd have to get another piece to see how far I could kick it before it broke up. And if I didn't kick it hard enough, it didn't go very far, and I'd lose the game. Because he was our goalie and was accustomed to kicking out pucks that were shot at him, he had an unfair advantage over me. But because my kick wasn't as hard or as accurate as his, my horse turd didn't shatter as often as his, and I remained in the game.

Normally, I could walk home from the skating rink, a quarter of a mile away, in about five minutes. If I was really tired after skating for two hours, it might take me a little longer. But this night was different.

Although it was very cold, we had an exciting game going, with the horse droppings flying all over the place. It took time to find just the "right size" of horse dropping after the previous one had disintegrated. That's important. Besides, the full moon was so bright, it lent a magic feeling to the night. In between kicks, we would sometimes pause and look up in wonder at the bright huge moon. We could see what looked like clouds or huge hills on the moon. "You can almost see the man in the moon," I said.

Tarres stared intently at the moon for a long time, then proclaimed, "The moon is made of orange cheese."

I knew he was full of horse manure, but because I didn't want to get beaten up, I didn't argue with him. "If the moon was made of orange cheese, "I thought," how come the mice haven't eaten big holes in it?" I was no dummy.

Soon after we parted, I walked up our narrow, snow-packed walk-way to the back door of our home. We always entered through the back door—never the front door. The front door opened onto the living room, or "sitting" room as we called it. And we never entered that way. I climbed the steps of our outside porch, which housed a stack of one-foot long firewood logs, some of which had already been cut into smaller pieces for the stove. This small woodpile was covered with icy snow. I pounded my feet on the steps to get the icy snow off my overshoes, then scraped them again before entering the "summer kitchen"—our indoor porch—which contained our ice box, cream separator, and extra pots and pans. I took off my overshoes, opened the kitchen door, and entered, carefully laying my overshoes and skates down on a nearby rug.

A blast of hot air greeted me as I began to take off my fur-trimmed helmet. No sooner had I taken it off, then Papa and Mama came in from the dining room and stared at me as if I were an intruder. "Look at him," said Papa, as he turned toward Mama. " Look at the way he's dressed." Then he angrily confronted me. "What's the matter with you? Don't you know it's forty below?"

In all honesty, I don't remember whether I was wearing my heavy, all wool mackinaw or a lighter jacket. But underneath whatever I wore was a cotton sweatshirt over a flannel shirt and underneath it all was my cotton fleece-lined Penman's combination underwear. But Papa was staring down at my blue denim overalls. I remember that distinctly. (They cost $15.00 a dozen from the Henderson Manufacturing Company in Winnipeg, and we sold them at $1.50 each, for a gross profit of twenty-five cents a pair.) All the farm kids wore overalls, and so did I much of the time. Although they were certainly not as warm as the all wool bedford cord breeches that I wore to school in winter, they were more resistant to snow—that is, snow did not cling to them as it did to my wool breeches. And it was much easier to brush off any snow that remained. Furthermore, when I fell down on the ice, the dampness did not penetrate my overalls as readily as it did my breeches, which absorbed everything. That's why I often wore overalls when I went skating.

Unfortunately, however, I was not cut out to be a defense attorney, and so I had no case. The evidence was clear. I had gone skating when it was forty below and—worse yet—I had not dressed warmly enough. I had worn $1.25 wholesale blue denim overalls instead of expensive all wool bedford cord breeches. I was guilty. Even if I had had six million dollars at the time in U.S. funds, and even if I had been able to hire the entire O.J. Simpson defense team, with Johnny Cochran trying to persuade the jury that Sheho was not Sheho but really Palm Springs, and it was not winter but really the middle of summer, and the temperature was not forty below, but really 120 above, and the police had tampered with the thermometer, and my father was a black racist, Papa would never have acquitted me. No way. He knew what he knew. I was guilty. Beyond any shadow of a doubt.

I bowed my head to admit my guilt and received my punishment—a proclamation by Papa in Jewish. *"Foon deer vil zyen a richh as foon myna tzserisinna schich."* The literal translation is something like this: " You will amount to as much as my torn shoes." However, since torn shoes are still of some use, a more accurate translation would be this: "You will amount to as much as the torn soles of my shoes."

More than six decades have passed since that uncontested trial in which I was found guilty. I have often wondered how my father knew it was forty below. To me, it is the mystery of the century; yet neither the Canadian nor the United States government has investigated it. We didn't have a radio then nor a thermometer. My father, therefore, probably got his information from Mr. Darling, our next door neighbor, who was retired and not only had a thermometer but also a radio, and knew everything there was to know—especially about the weather—and had plenty of time to tell anyone who had time to listen.

On second thought, my father may have gotten that critical information (or misinformation?) from a regular customer—since there wasn't much else to talk about besides the weather. I can visualize the scenario now. Mr. Bodie [pronounced Bowdee], who lived a mile west of town, and who came into our store almost every day either to buy snuff or chewing tobacco and to enlighten my dad about the great philosophical questions of civilization, probably came into the store late that afternoon before closing time, just as my father was stoking the coals in the cast-iron stove and said, "Good day, Louis. Sure is cold today." [Louis is pronounced Louie.]

"Sure is. What can I get you before I close?"

"I ran outta snuff. Gimmie a can of Copenhagen."

"Here you are. That'll be ten cents."

"Thanks, Louis. Sure is cold today. "Must be at least thirty-five below right now."

"You think so?"

"At least that. I'd say by nightfall it'll get down to forty."

"You really think so?"

"You betcha. Forty below. Take my word for it."

Ladies and gentlemen of the Jury, I rest my case.

CHAPTER EIGHT
Sundays, Mr. Leckie, And The Magic Box

My wife and I live in Cypress, California, a city of forty thousand in Orange County, which is part of the huge Southern California megalopolis whose population numbers about twelve million. One might think that since we are surrounded by so many people with so many activities going on all the time in this giant sea of humanity, our social life would be overwhelming. However, this is not the case. Sometimes one becomes so busy one doesn't have time to smell the roses. And sometimes it's hard to make close friends in such a populous area.

By contrast, I was brought up in tiny Sheho, surrounded by farming families whose total population within a twelve mile radius was probably about three thousand. With the exception of Mr. Leckie, the closest-living Jewish families were twelve, eighteen, fifty, and sixty miles away. Since we were so isolated from other Jewish families and did not have a car, one might think that our Jewish social life would be almost non-existent. The irony is that although we were largely isolated, we got together with other families much more often than I visit my own sisters today, even though we live only a few miles from one another. And our social life in Sheho was much fuller than mine is at the present.

Sunday was a special day. It was a holiday. All businesses through-out practically all of Canada were closed, except for some gas stations, cafes, hotels, and a few drug stores in larger cities. We had "blue laws" then. Sunday was virtually a religious holiday, and it was meant to be a day of rest.

For Mama, however, it was not a day of rest. Instead, it was her day to prepare and serve her "special" one o'clock dinner, not only for her family, but also for Mr. Leckie, Papa and Mama's oldest friend in Sheho—who was virtually part of our family—and for any other Jewish families who visited us. And believe me, we were the host to many a Jewish family for Sunday dinner, families from as close as twelve miles and as far as 150 miles away.

On one of the 1939 visits by the Orloffs, who owned a large general store in Foam Lake, eighteen miles away, they brought along the Teskey family from Wynyard, thirty-two miles farther west. Jack Teskey, a short gregarious, likable man spoke English not much better than Papa, and his wife had a worse accent than either Papa or Mama. Their daughter, Helen, was about the same age as my younger sister, Sylvia. The Teskeys and we Katzes took an immediate liking to each other, and for years afterward, regardless of the weather—unless and only unless the roads were blocked in winter—the Teskeys were regular Sunday visitors to our home.

You see, both Mama and Papa were so starved for Jewish company that they considered all Jews on the Prairies to be part of our extended family. Sunday, therefore, was a special day—a day for socializing.

My earliest memories of the Sunday holiday are of Dr. Shaum coming to our home for dinner—a huge dinner that I barely picked at. I was only four at the time. Mama was concerned that I hardly ate. The doctor tried to assure her that I would not starve and would eat when I got hungry enough. I remember asking him a bunch of questions, but I don't remember what his answers were. Then I remember his mother coming to stay with us while she tried to convince her son that he should forget about the *shiksa* [gentile woman] he had fallen in love with, and I remember how delighted Mama felt at having another Jewish woman to talk to. Shortly afterward, much to the disappointment of my parents and his mother, Dr. Shaum moved away and married his sweetheart.

My next memory of the Sunday holiday was of Mr. Leckie coming to visit us regularly about ten, almost every Sunday morning without exception. Because it was the highlight of the week for him, he usually dressed up for the occasion in a dress shirt, dress pants, and dress shoes.

He loved babies, and I remember that when Sylvia was one or two, he would hold her hands and put her astride his foot, then swing her up and down. She loved it. But as she got older, the swinging game ended.

Next, I recall his knocking on the kitchen door once—maybe twice—and immediately entering and greeting everyone warmly. Then he would sit down on a white-painted wooden kitchen chair, take some Ogden tobacco out of its green package, pull out a leaf of Zigzag paper from its black folder (or Chantecleer paper from its red folder), roll the tobacco back and forth into the cigarette paper ever so neatly until it was a perfect cylinder without any bumps whatsoever. Next, he would lick the edge to seal it and tap any loose tobacco back into the cigarette. Finally, he would scratch a match on his thumbnail, and after the initial flare died down, he would hold the flame up to the cigarette while puffing two or three times, to make sure the cigarette was lighted. After receiving an ash tray, he would begin a conversation in Jewish with Papa and Mama, often switching to English to include my sisters and me. These conversations lasted until dinner was served—shortly after one.

What a dinner! I have very few regrets in life, but one of the biggest is that I was such a fussy eater. I never really appreciated how tasty Mama's cooking was. What I wouldn't give today if I could indulge myself—just once more—in her famous Sunday dinner!

It began with her delicious beef borscht, always served hot in the fall and winter. She made it from cabbage, big chunks of beef, lemon juice and sometimes beets. In the summer, she served cold beet borscht with sour cream, followed by a *milicha* [milk] meal—dairy products only. But during the rest of the year, the dinner was *flaayshick* [meat-based]. Since she "kept kosher," she never served any milk products with meat.

Although we all dined leisurely, the adults ate with zest. I can still hear the slurps as they emptied their bowls of borscht. If anyone tried to compliment Mama on her cooking, she would immediately recite the entire recipe to everyone—in English. "It's not hard to make. First, you take a chuck roast and then some cabbage, and then you cut up three beets. . .," and so on. While she was dictating her recipe, she would lift the large serving bowl of borscht, which had remained on the round walnut table, and say to whoever had paid her the compliment, "Here, have some more." Before the person had time to refuse, Mama would have dished out more borscht—or whatever she had just served.

After removing the borscht, she would bring in a huge platter of pot roast smothered with gravy, roasted potatoes, and carrots. Again, she would serve everyone first, then herself. You didn't argue with Mama. She went around the table, personally serving everyone, and she wouldn't take no for an answer. "Here, have a little more. It's good for you." After the pot roast came the *keegel*. [Some Jews pronounce it *kugel*. As my buddy Dr. Milt Spector in Edmonton says, "Some call it *kugel* and others call it *keegel*. But ve foon da Glenora Club, ve call it poodying."] Again, she would go around the table and dish out to everyone a piece of this baked noodle-or- potato pudding with a hard, crusty topping. Sometimes she made a raisin keegel, my favorite. When my two older sisters were big enough, they would help Mama bring out the platters, but Mama always served the entrees and side dishes herself. One of my favorites was *kasha* and *varnatschkass*—buckwheat and pasta and onions fried usually in schmatlz [goose fat]. It's still one of my favorites—but without *schmaltz*. (My oldest sister, Merle, makes it for me on special occasions. That's only one of the reasons why she is so dear to me.)

My all time favorite dish then was my "bean cake." Mama always included cooked white navy beans with the dinner or occasionally big white lima beans, my very favorite. I would then add some *schmaltz* and mash the beans with it until the mixture became a soft paste. Next, using my fork and knife, I would shape the paste into a brick-shaped cake. Finally, I would add salt and pepper and smother tomato ketchup over the top of the cake. It was absolutely delicious. Sylvia soon followed my lead. To this day, my sisters and I still laugh when we recall what I did with those beans.

Mama also served her own homemade challah bread, baked from locally milled Foam Lake flour (which we sold for $2.40 per hundred pound sack) and plenty of fresh eggs from our chicken coop. The thick, egg-rich crust was covered with more than enough poppy seeds from our garden. I loved to tear a hole out of the center of a slice, eat the torn part, and then peer at Sylvia through the big hole remaining. She soon copied me. I guess the game was to see who could manage to get the biggest hole in the bread before the crust broke. Mama never scolded us; she was too busy serving everyone else. And Papa was too busy eating.

Finally came the dessert—Mama's own home-canned fruit. She always canned her own: apricots, crabapples, peaches, pears, and plums. In July and August, wholesale grocery companies would have boxcars full of fruit shipped direct from the Okanagan and Kootenay valleys in British Columbia to the stations along the Canadian National and Canadian Pacific Railways. Any town large enough to purchase an entire boxcar full of fruit would usually be targeted by a wholesaler, who would then pre-sell the fruit at carload price discounts to the different merchants. Each merchant, including Papa, would then pick up dozens or sometimes hundreds of cases of fruit direct from the boxcar. He would then sell the fruit at virtually wholesale prices to his customers, not by the pound, but by the case, each wooden case— weighing anywhere from twenty-five to forty pounds—full of Okanagan or Kootenay peaches or pears, or whatever fruit had been picked only days before. Every housewife canned her own fruit.

I remember Mama, her face drenched in sweat, as she stood over our hot wood-burning stove in July, pouring sugar into the mixture of peaches and water, as it boiled in a large copper tub. Outside, the temperature was well over eighty; and inside, only two degrees cooler than the temperature of the sun. The aroma of sweet syrup permeated the kitchen, the summer kitchen, and even the verandah outside. Swarms of flies outside the screen door buzzed and buzzed; they were going crazy. Every time the screen door opened—even for a second or two—some flew in. But their lives were short lived. Sticky, gooey, adhesive, spiral- shaped "fly catchers," extending their full length of three feet hung from the ceiling, and every time a fly flew into this trap, it buzzed and buzzed, trying to free itself, but to no avail. Although each fly catcher would soon be almost full of flies, it continued to trap more until it was covered black. Then it was carefully taken down and wrapped in paper before being discarded into the slop pail and finally thrown into the enclosed slop well at the far end of our yard adjoining the back alley. Immediately afterward, another fly catcher was slowly and carefully pulled out of its bullet-shaped casing and attached to the ceiling with a tack, ready to keep the kitchen clean of the insufferable pests.

Mama usually canned enough fruit to last for an entire year. After she filled each jar of fruit to overflowing, she fitted a quarter -inch wide red rubber ring over the mouth of the jar, then placed a thin glass lid on the top of the rubber ring, thus covering the jar and making it temporarily air tight. Next, over the lid itself, she clamped a one-inch wide ridged metallic ring, just slightly larger in circumference than the glass lid, and turned and turned until the jar was permanently sealed air-tight. Finally, the jar, along with dozens of others, was ready to be stored in our cellar, where the temperature was usually about fifty-five degrees the year around.

Mama's canned fruit was far tastier than any commercially canned fruit I have ever eaten. Maybe it was the fruit itself; maybe it was the Sheho water; maybe it was her recipe. But it was delicious. And it was served with loving care by the master cook herself.

Mama served only cold water or hot tea and lemon with her dinner; never milk. Toward evening, if Mr. Leckie was still around, she again served tea with lemon, as well as cake. She might also serve a light supper then if we were still hungry. But one big meal on Sunday was usually adequate.

After dinner, Papa and Mr. Leckie often went next door to the Darlings, where they played whist, a card game, with Mr. and Mrs. Darling. Sometimes the Darlings would come over to our place after dinner to play. Papa usually teamed up with either Mr. or Mrs. Darling, but not with Mr. Leckie, who in turn teamed up with the other Darling. The reason was that Papa and Mr. Leckie often carried on a running commentary on the game in Jewish, and speaking a foreign language to one's partner could be interpreted as cheating. I distinctly remember that at the end of one particular hand, Papa excitedly threw down a card toward Mr. Leckie and shouted, " *ICH VIL DIER BEGROOBEN.*" The literal translation of this Jewish expression, probably borrowed from the Russian, is "I will bury you." However, that is *not* the correct connotation. A more accurate translation would be " My card will trump yours," or "I will triumph over you." Twenty some years later, at the United Nations headquarters in New York, during the height of the cold war, Soviet Premier Nikita Krushchev pounded his shoe and uttered the same proclamation in Russian, a proclamation which really meant, "We will triumph over you" or "Our system will outlast yours." Instead, interpreters unfortunately and mistakenly misinterpreted his words to mean "We will bury you." This literal but incorrect translation resulted in lack of communication; and the cold war continued.

It was late in the afternoon by the time the card game ended. Only then would Mr. Leckie go to the outhouse. I often wondered how he could control his bladder for such a long period of time. I am even more amazed now that I have reached the age where I must go regularly and often. By early evening, he would go home, and that would be the end of our Sunday.

At that time the only person in this group who had a radio was Mrs. Darling. I always considered her to be my grandma —the only one I ever knew—even though we were not related. I remember sitting in her living room in December 1936, listening with her to the small radio on the shelf, during the abdication speech of His Majesty King Edward VIII. He had given up his throne for the woman he loved. I thought it was a very touching speech. Mrs. Darling, however, was absolutely furious at Mrs. Wally Simpson, as were many Canadians. Shortly afterward, just before Christmas, I remember visiting the Glass family in Insinger, twelve miles east of us. Irving, the youngest in the family, who was some years older than I, said, "Have you heard the latest Christmas Carol?" Then, to the tune of the "Hark the Herald Angels Sing," he sang, "Hark the Herald Angels Sing/ Wally Simpson stole our King."

About four months after I had listened with Mrs. Darling to the abdication speech, she fell seriously ill. I remember Papa saying, "Her chances are less than fifty-fifty. Although I had little knowledge of statistics, I understood that my beloved Mrs. Darling was too ill to see me and might soon die. Nobody I had known had ever died. I had seen gophers and rabbits die; I had seen a dead cat and dead mice, but never a dead person. I wondered what a dead person looked like. I asked Papa what a dead person looked like, and more specifically what Mrs. Darling would look like when she was dead. Papa told me that I was a *Kohayn*, a descendant of Aaron, the brother of Moses, the highest ranking tribe among the Jews, and that a *Kohayn* was not permitted to view the dead. "What about *Kohayns* who are doctors?" I asked.[3] "That's different," he said. It was obvious their profession required it. At that moment I wished I were a doctor so I could see Mrs. Darling after she died. But since I was not a doctor, I wished God would at least spare her life until I became a doctor so that under Jewish law, I would be permitted to view her in her coffin.

God, however, did not answer my wish. One day Papa brought the sad news. "She passed away." We all cried and cried. For the first time in my life I knew I had lost a loved one. I could never sit on her lap again. I could never talk to her again. And under Jewish law, I could never see her again—not even in her coffin. It was not easy to be a Jew. There were too many restrictions. If only I could see her again—just once more—for the last time!

The funeral was held in the town hall. Almost everyone in town, as well as dozens of farmers and their families who had enjoyed her warm friendship and hospitality, came to pay their respects. Mr. Darling sat stone faced. He did not cry. I found that very strange. The Darlings' son Frank, along with his wife and their son and daughter, Beryl and Fern, were also there. They had come from Lac Vert, Saskatchewan, to be with Mrs. Darling during her last days. She had mentioned them to me so often, but I had never seen them before. Then suddenly, when Mrs. Darling's chances were fifty-fifty, they appeared— in person—as if by magic. Frank was a tall, husky, handsome man with a ruddy complexion; his wife was quite pretty; and their children—almost adults now— were also tall and very good looking. Although they had anticipated her death, they did seem to be as upset about it as I was. At least that's the way it appeared to me.

Now here they all were, packed into the town hall for her funeral. Somebody gave a sermon, but I don't remember who it was or what he said. Then somebody played her favorite hymn, "Silent Night/Holy Night." I looked around. Mr. Darling still sat stone faced. His son Frank was also stone faced, and so was his wife and their son and daughter. I found that really odd. Why was I the only one crying? Why didn't adults cry? Maybe they're not supposed to cry? Some day I, too, would be an adult. Then maybe I wouldn't cry. But I still couldn't understand how they could control their emotions and not cry.

The coffin was open, thank God! We all began to file past it, to pay our last respects. I don't believe Papa was with me, but at that moment I couldn't have cared less—even if I was a *Kohayn*. I wanted to see Mrs. Darling again for the last time. Equally important (or maybe even more important), I wanted to see what a dead person looked like. I stared at her in amazement. She didn't look dead—not like a gopher we had drowned in Wunder's Field or a rabbit Frank Wunder had shot, or a mouse I had caught in a trap. She looked as if she were asleep, only a little more pale than when I had last seen her. Perhaps she was asleep. Forever.

We drove to the cemetery just out of town, high on a hill overlooking the creek that flowed through Wunder's field. Somebody had dug a huge rectangular shaped hole, big enough to bury that black, lovely coffin inside of which Mrs. Darling lay asleep. Several men carried her coffin toward the hole. Then somebody said something and they attached some straps around the coffin and lowered it inside the huge hole, around which lay piles of dirt that had just been dug up. Then they pulled the straps up and began shoveling the dirt on top of the coffin. They shoveled hurriedly without stopping, and soon the coffin was covered with dirt. And soon the hole was full.

And that was the last I saw of Mrs. Darling.

I believe it was in the late fall of 1936 when Mr. Leckie bought a radio. It was a momentous event because it changed our Sundays forever. His battery powered Rogers 6-tube mantle radio virtually ended our isolation in Sheho and —for me—made Sunday evening the most exciting evening of the week. I felt as if I was now really part of a much enlarged Canada and even part of that great and powerful country to the south, the United States. It pulled in not only neighboring Canadian stations like CJGX Yorkton, CKCK Regina, CFQC Saskatoon, but also American stations like KFYR Bismarck, North Dakota; KOA Denver; KSL Salt Lake City; and WHO, the 50,000 watt clear- channel station, Des Moines, Iowa. On cold winter nights it could even pick up the WBBM

Air Theater, Wrigley Building, Chicago; and KNX, Columbia Square, Hollywood.

Mr. Leckie no longer went home alone on Sunday evenings. Instead, we would all eat a light supper about five o'clock, and then Merle, Etta, and I would accompany him to his store. He would pump up his Coleman gas-burning mantle lamp, hold a lighted match up to the nozzle, and slowly turn the knob controlling the flow of gas. A continuous hiss from air pressure was followed instantly by a narrow blue flame that quickly turned to red and ignited the carbon crusted mica filaments, turning them into a blinding white luminescence. As he hung the hissing, blinding-white glowing lamp to a hook in the metal ceiling, the whole store became bathed in a brilliant white light. Night had become day.

How can I describe my sensations as Mr. Leckie turned on the radio about a minute before six o'clock? Then, seconds later, we heard three loud resonating gongs spaced one second apart that sounded like someone trying to play the scale of C, but hitting the wrong notes. They were followed almost immediately by a deep baritone voice. "THIS IS THE NATIONAL BROADCASTING COMPANY. KOA, DENVER." And then, about two seconds later, a singing group shouted "J. E. L. L. O," followed by another voice excitedly and hurriedly shouting, " THE JELLO PROGRAM, STARRING JACK BENNY. WITH MARY LIVINGSTON, KENNY BAKER, PHIL HARRIS AND HIS ORCHES-TRA, AND YOURS TRULY, DON WILSON." It was magic!

Here, sitting on a crate of Macintosh Red Delicious apples right next to his fruit stand, just under his brown mantle radio secured in a corner high on top of a ledge, I could hear the music and words of a live program being broadcast thousands of miles away. And I could hear it at the same instant his audience did. I was really not in Mr. Leckie's store. I was in Hollywood. I was listening to Jack Benny in person. I was actually part of his audience. To an eight year old, it was more than amazing. It was unbelievable.

Jack Benny was unique. Unique means like nothing else —anywhere— at any time. It cannot be compared. There was nobody else like Jack Benny, and there never will be. He was the lovable cheapskate of his radio show who hid his money and would do almost anything to save a few pennies. He would pause, thereby creating perfect timing for his jokes.

Robber: "This is a holdup. Your money or your life!" Long pause. Robber: "What are waiting for?"

Jack Benny: "I'm thinking, I'm thinking."

He would never be the first to pick up a restaurant bill and would never pay for anything without arguing over the price. Because he was such a cheapskate, he was always the butt of criticism and good natured fun; and it was all the more humorous because his wife, Mary Livingston, was the antagonist. In turn, everybody except Mary seemed to be the butt of humor. Jack always teased Phil Harris about Phil's drinking, accusing him of being a drunk. Jack poked fun at Don Wilson because he was overweight. And years later, when Kenny Baker was replaced by Dennis Day, it was Dennis who was always being teased because he was so naive.

A cast of unbelievable characters became part of the show almost every week, and as the audience and listeners became familiar with these people, they knew what to expect. The same situation and even the same joke may have been used over and over again, yet the audience and listeners laughed as if they had never heard it before. The name " Mr. Shlepperman" always drew a laugh. (The world shlepper in Jewish means a cheapskate.) And who can ever forget the ticket agent sarcastically telling Jack Benny that the tickets had all been sold or the train had already left? Perhaps the biggest laugh of all came when the conductor, appearing regularly, would announce, "Train now leaving for An-A-Heim, A-Zu-Sa, and Cu-Ca-Mon-Ga." Thirty minutes passed all too soon, as The Jack Benny program became an integral part of our lives every Sunday evening.

After the Jack Benny program, came Walter Winchell spitting out his words in urgent rapid fire succession, like a 30 caliber machine gun firing its bullets. "Good evening Mr. and Mrs. North America and all the ships at sea! Let's go to Press! Flash!" And for thirty minutes he would hold his listeners spellbound with his inside "exclusive" gossip about movies stars, politicians, gangsters, and anyone who was supposedly rich, famous, or infamous. I didn't know whom he was talking about most of the time nor did Mr. Leckie. But Walter Winchell sure sounded as if his entire program was not only important, but urgent!

At seven o'clock came The "Chase and Sanborn Hour. With Edgar Bergen, Charlie McCarthy, and Robert Armbruster and his Orchestra." Mr. Leckie told us that Bergen was a ventriloquist who projected his voice through the mouth of Charlie McCarthy—the dwarf-like wooden dummy that sat on his lap. I found it hard to imagine the scene until Mr. Leckie showed me a picture of Bergen and Charlie some weeks later. We all enjoyed the program, but after sitting on a wooden box of apples for another hour, I was ready to go home.

Although his living quarters were upstairs, Mr. Leckie spent practically all of his time in his store. He purchased home- cooked meals from Mrs. Holmes, who brought them to him and placed them right on his counter every day except Sunday. If he had time, he would eat them while they were still hot. But if there were customers in the store, it might be a long time before he ate a warm meal, let alone a hot one. He rarely left the store except to go the outhouse. Even before he got his radio, during the long fall and winter nights, he would stay in his locked store after the 7:00 P.M. closing weekday hour and read until late at night. Besides reading the newspapers and some magazines he sold in his store, he purchased and read serious books, including Freud's *Introductory Lectures to Psychoanalysis*, Spangler's *Decline of the West*, Sir James Jeans' *The Universe Around Us*, and *Gray's Anatomy*. Sheho did not have a library and so he accumulated his own.

Papa would often visit him after hours. They always called each other Katz and Leckie, never Louis and Sam. They would converse in Jewish about life in the old country and about how difficult it was to make a living during these hard times. From Mr. Leckie, Papa would learn the latest Canadian and world news which had been reported in the Winnipeg *Free Press*, the Saskatoon *Star Phoenix,* and the Regina *Leader Post*. Before leaving, Papa would usually buy some fruit such as bananas, cherries, watermelon, or whatever was in season, because the only kinds of fruit we carried were apples, oranges, and lemons. Then just before going home, Papa would take the soft tissue wrappers off the Sunkist oranges and lemons in Mr. Leckie's fruit display and put them in his pockets to take home to our outdoor toilet for a more important use.

After the snows had melted and the long winter nights gave way to long hours of daylight, Mr. Leckie would often come to our home after he had closed his store and join Mama and Papa in a conversation about anything and everything. During balmy July evenings, we would all sit outside on our white kitchen chairs, while slapping the mosquitoes that regularly landed on our faces. Then Mr. Leckie and Papa would begin talking about Rosh Hashanah and Yom Kippur. "Who should we get to drive us to Yorkton?" Mr. Leckie would ask.

"Bill Filney. He drives straight," Papa would say. "He's as good as gold."

"Yes. But maybe he's too busy in the elevator," Mr. Leckie would say.

"Maybe Norris we should ask then?"

"Frank Norris is a good driver."

Papa would nod. "As good as gold. But Filney likes to go. He likes to see Abe Shnider."

"Where will we eat?" Mr. Leckie would ask.

"At Dachas."

"Maybe she can't take us?"

"Why not?"

"I don't know why not. Maybe it's too crowded with the Laskins."

"So it's crowded. With the Laskins we'll eat at Dachas."

"Maybe with Coopermans if Mrs. Dachas can't take us," Mr. Leckie would say.

Papa would nod. " With Cooperman maybe we could eat."

They talked and planned and talked and planned for over two months. Going away on the annual two-day trip was the most exciting event of the year, and the talking and planning were more fun than the actual event. Often, Mr. Leckie would bring some fruit for all of us. At other times he or Papa would give me thirty-five cents to buy seven ice cream cones from the Elite Cafe (next to Leckie's store). Sometimes he and Papa and I would take a walk from our home to the school and back, or in the other direction, to the Western bridge. Although he was one of our business competitors, he was virtually a member of our family. And the bond between us could not have been closer, even if we were related by blood.

Because Mr. Sam Leckie never told me much about himself, I know very little about his background. What I do know is that Sholom Lehovich was born into a very large and very poor Jewish family in the Russian seaport of Odessa, probably in 1888. Like most boys his age, he attended *chayder* [Jewish school]. I recall that he mentioned something about the *gymnasium* [Russian public school], but I'm not sure if he actually attended it. From his youngest daughter, Ruth, who is now widowed and living in Winnipeg, I recently learned that her father had walked across the Ukraine, supporting himself by painting fences, barns, and homes, and doing any kind of work that paid anything at all, in order to get to a seaport, from where he could board a ship and escape from the anti-Semitic tyranny of Tsar Nicholas II and the horrible poverty that permeated the country. He borrowed money from someone, bought a steerage ticket, and eventually sailed away, possibly to England—nobody seems to know—and eventually to Canada, where the immigration officials — unable to spell his name— changed it to "Sam Leckie." He came to Winnipeg, where he was taken in by the Jewish community. He opened a small grocery store, got married, and struggled as he tried to support his wife and his growing family of five children: Nessa, Irene, Norman, Leon, and Ruth.

Around 1920, in the hope of improving his lot in life, he moved to Tuffnell, Saskatchewan, a hamlet of about one hundred people, only nine miles west of Sheho. He either purchased or opened a grocery store, but was still unable to earn much of a livelihood. About a year later, he moved to Sheho, where he rented a building and opened a larger grocery and confectionery store. His wife and my mother, who had just moved to Sheho, were quite close. In 1923 his wife died, leaving him alone with his five children, ages: two, four, five, six, and ten. He took his children with him to Winnipeg when he went there to bury his wife. After the funeral, he was persuaded to temporarily leave his two youngest children, Leon and Ruth, at the Jewish Orphanage, while he returned to Sheho to decide what to do. His sister-in-law took his daughters Nessa and

Irene to live with her; and another relative took his oldest son Norman. However, Norman did not like the arrangement and in time returned to live with his father. The temporary arrangement with the Jewish orphanage turned into years which turned into more than a decade, until both Leon and Ruth had completed high school. The Jewish merchants in the greater Yorkton area contributed generously to the Jewish Orphanage, and in turn the Leckie children were not treated like storybook orphans. Nobody was. According to Ruth, "It was like a big happy family; everybody was treated well. But I often got the impression that Leon and I were treated as if we were teachers' pets."

Because Mr. Leckie was alone and could not leave his store unattended for any length of time, he never traveled to Winnipeg to visit his two younger children, nor did they visit him until after they had completed school and were on their own. Nessa and Irene, however, visited him occasionally, and Norman lived with him all the while I was growing up. But Norman was independent. He came and went on his own. He played hockey, baseball, and tennis; he went shooting and participated in everything there was to do. But he hardly ever came to our home, and I rarely saw him with his father after the store had closed, when my older sisters and I would go there to listen to the radio.

Besides going to Mr. Leckie's on Sundays, we often went on Mondays and regularly on Wednesday evenings to listen to Bob Hope and his rapid fire jokes, and to Fred Allen, with whom Jack Benny had a mutually contrived feud. Much of Fred Allen's program featured a stereotype cast of characters who all lived in an imaginary neighborhood called "Allen's Alley." Fred Allen would knock on a door and out would come Mrs. Nussbaum, who would expound on the latest gossip in a Jewish accent thicker than Mama's. Another door, and out came Senator Claghorn from the deep, deep south. "I say, I say there. I'm so far south, if I stepped back, I'd fall into the Gulf."

As my two sisters and I went home from Mr. Leckie's store after listening to the radio on Wednesday night, I wished that we also had a radio. I mean one that worked.

We did in fact have an old mantle radio that at one time had worked, long, long ago. It had been placed on top of our china cabinet in the dining room, where it had died and gathered dust. I distinctly remember that it contained three knobs and possibly a few other gadgets that were supposed to control its operation. One day when I was four, somebody played around with the dials, and I remember a voice coming from that radio shouting at me: "I want YOU to listen." And I distinctly remember joking, "Who, me?" Almost instantly I was shocked to hear the announcer shout, "Yes YOU." For years afterward, I wondered how he knew that I had replied. That incident was one of my earliest memories, and it was the last time I remember listening to that radio. Finally, it was retired to our engine house, where it lay next to our old retired generator, part of the clutter and junk in the Sheho Royal Museum of Canada.

We also had a big black gramophone which stood on four ugly, curved black legs, the funniest legs I had ever seen. In addition, we had some big black dusty records whose labels pictured a little dog listening to "his master's voice." I wished I had a little dog like that. It could listen to my voice. It would be a heck of a lot more fun than cranking the handle on this big black gramophone, then watching the record on the green felt covered turntable go round and round, as I placed the steel arm with a needle at the end onto the big black record. Then I could hear a scratchy, tinny noise that sounded like some people inside a vinegar barrel who were shouting to get out.

The man inside the barrel had a super low basso voice that sounded like someone trying to sing while simultaneously gargling with a mouth full of gravel: " I'm Barnacle Bill the Sailor." I remember how he bragged about his drinking: " 'I drink my whiskey when I can/ whiskey from an old tin can/ for whiskey is the life of man,' cried Barnacle Bill the Sailor."

In between his verses, the girl inside the barrel cried out in a timid, pleading voice: " 'Won't you come down and let me in? Won't you come down and let me in? Won't you come down and let me in?' Cried the fair young maiden." She was just asking for trouble.

That was some song. That was some record. I don't remember if we had many other records, but if we did, they were probably worse than "Barnacle Bill the Sailor." No wonder we rarely listened to the scratchy, tinny sound that came out of the old, ugly, big, black gramophone with the funniest looking legs I ever saw. That gramophone was certainly no radio.

I sure wished we would get a radio. But I wouldn't dream of asking Papa. I remember what he had said a few years earlier, when I had asked him for a twenty-five cent hockey stick. Asking Papa for a radio was out of the question. These were hard times, and a radio cost a lot of money. But who knows? Miracles sometimes happen! Thousands of years before, God had parted the waters of the Red Sea, allowing Moses and his people to flee from Egypt. And there hadn't been too many miracles since. Perhaps it was time.

CHAPTER NINE
How We Got Our Radio

My wife and I have five radios in our home—one for every room in our house except for the bathroom and my office. In addition, we have a radio in each of our three vehicles, as well as a number of radios stored in our garage, leftovers from my days as an electronics distributor. Some of our radios are called "tuners" and are part of complex custom stereo sound systems which we assembled. Others are portable Am/FM cassette players often referred to as " boom boxes." I don't believe that as a family we are unique in the number of radios we own. Almost every family I know has several radios. In fact radios are so common today that it would be extremely rare to find even one household in any industrialized country in the world that does not have at least one radio. What a contrast from the early 1930s when there were no more than ten radios in all of Sheho!

Back then, there were only AM radio stations, and radios were just beginning to gain popular acceptance on the Canadian Prairies. Uncle Abe in Inglis, whom I considered to be away ahead of his time, had a radio as early as 1933, and Mrs. Darling got one about a year later. Papa also had bought one of the earliest versions (with three dials) probably before I was born; but by the time I went to school, that museum piece had been assigned to permanent retirement amidst the junk in our engine house—the Sheho Royal Museum of Canada.

In 1936, Mr. Leckie got a radio and it changed our lives forever. Although I felt that my isolation in Sheho had temporarily ended whenever I went over to his store on Sunday, Monday, and Wednesday evenings to listen to our favorite programs, I still felt that our family was isolated from the rest of the world. We did not have a radio, and there were no indications that our situation would change in the foreseeable future. Radios were expensive. As far as Papa was concerned, in these hard times they were prohibitively expensive. And so, like a stoic, I accepted our predicament.

However, I still prayed for a miracle. Perhaps the Almighty in His infinite wisdom and compassion would understand our plight. Even though I realized there were worse catastrophes in the world, such as "the children in Europe who were starving," according to Mama, whenever I left any food on my plate, I thought it wouldn't be asking too much of God if He could see His way clear to persuade Papa to get a radio. I wasn't asking for a car. I wasn't asking for a million dollars. I wouldn't know what to do with a million dollars, although I knew it was enough not only to buy a radio but also a seventy-five cent hockey stick —the best one in Mr. Leckie's store—and even a pair of shin pads and even hockey gloves. What more could anyone want! But I wasn't asking for a million dollars. I was being considerate. All I was asking for was a radio. Perhaps if God caused enough rain to fall so that the crops would grow, and killed the grasshoppers before they ate the crops, and prevented rust from damaging the wheat, and prevented any hailstorms that could wipe out the farmers' crops, and delayed the frost until the crops had been harvested, and kept the price of wheat high enough so that the farmers would have a lot of money when they took their wheat to the elevator, perhaps then the farmers would buy everything we had in the store so that we could make a lot of money—at least enough to buy a radio. Surely, that wasn't asking for too much.

But I was still a realist. God probably had more important things on His mind. And so, I did not hold my breath.

There is usually a reason for practically every historical event. This phenomenon is known as "cause-and-effect." We did not get our radio by random chance. No way. And to the best of my knowledge, we did not get it by Divine Intervention, although it is said, "God works in mysterious ways." When Papa finally considered getting a radio, he did not order it overnight. He gave it "serious" thought. It was expensive. The radio that he eventually bought from Bill Finley for the enormous sum of fifty dollars—on installment payments—was the biggest purchase he had ever made with the exception of our house and our furniture.

The word *persuasion* might be the best word to describe why Papa eventually bought a radio. Papa's sister and brother-in-law, Aunt Bessie and Uncle Abe in Inglis, had owned a radio for several years. At the time Aunt Bessie came to stay with us, when Mama was rushed by snowmobile to the Yorkton Hospital for emergency surgery, Auntie complained about how lonely it was without a radio. I suppose she was the first to put the bug in Papa's ear. Then when my older sisters and I started going over to Mr. Leckie's store every Sunday, Monday, and Wednesday night, he probably gave the matter some consideration. But his ultimate decision was almost certainly the outcome of the repeatedly wise counsel and friendly persuasion from Sheho's own Justice of the Peace—Bill Finley.

Bill Finley, one of the early pioneers in Sheho, was without question Sheho's most prominent and influential citizen. Not only was he the area's Justice of the Peace, but he ran the McCabe Bros. Grain Company elevator, he owned the local flour mill, the local garage, an automobile agency, a farm implement agency, and a number of farms around Sheho. But most important of all, as far as I was concerned, he owned the agency for Philco Radios.

Everyone in town—even children—while speaking about him called him "Bill Finley"— never Mr. Finley. Papa, however, could never seem to pronounce the "n" before the "l" Thus, to Papa he was Bill *Filney*, Papa's very dear friend, the town's godfather. He was the driver Papa hired most of the time when we occasionally went to Inglis and when we regularly went to Yorkton for Rosh Hashanah and Yom Kippur. He was the accountant who calculated whatever taxes we paid. He was the sage who advised Papa on important civic or political matters. And he was the salesman who eventually persuaded Papa that it was high time to become part of the twentieth century.

Bill Finley planned a sale the way a general would plan a military campaign—very carefully. It was the long range outcome that mattered. If on his first attempt he failed to make the sale, he probably said to himself, "I may have lost the battle, but ultimately I shall win the war." And that is most likely how his campaign began when he entered Papa's store early one morning, probably in late February of 1938.

"Good morning, Louis." [pronounced Louie]

"Good morning, Bill."

"It's gonna be a nice day today. It's going up to only fifteen below."

" Only fifteen below! Sure is better than forty below."

"Sure is. Say Louis, how much is my bill?"

Papa would have opened his alphabetized ledger and after peering at the name "Filney" would have responded, "Four dollars and thirty-five cents."

"Here's five dollars."

"Thanks."

After receiving his change, Bill probably said, "Gimmie a can of Prince Albert pipe tobacco. And charge it." Then after opening the can and stuffing his pipe with Prince Albert and using at least two matches to light the pipe, Bill would have puffed and puffed and puffed and let the pipe dangle from the corner of his mouth, and in between puffs, slowly mumble, "Louis, you should get a radio."

"I got a radio from you a long time ago. Remember? Just after Jackie was born. It never worked."

Bill would have puffed and puffed and slowly replied, "That was a long time ago. Say, how old is Jackie now?"

"He'll be ten next month."

"Ten! My goodness, seems like yesterday when Rose brought him back from Winnipeg. How time flies! He's a good little boy."

"He's too skinny. He looks like TB. [tuberculosis] He doesn't eat enough."

"He'll eat when he gets older. Don't worry about him." Puff, puff, puff. "You know, Louis, that old radio is ten years old. It's as old as Frank Wunder's bull. And that's an old bull."

"Yeah, it's an old bull. But it can still do the job. Better than my radio."

"You got a point there, Louis. But one of these days Frank will have to retire that bull and get a young one. Nothing lasts forever. Not even a radio. You should think about getting a new radio. See you later, Louis."

About a month later, when an unexpected warm Chinook wind had suddenly fanned over the Prairies from the Rockies, pushing the temperature up to fifty degrees, Bill Finley probably came into the store around noon, puffing on his pipe, and said, " How d'ya like this weather, Louis? It was zero early this morning, and it's almost fifty above now. Look at the water on the sidewalk. Look at the slush on the road."

"Some weather. Sure changed fast. It's just like spring. Time to take out your rubbers."

"Yeah. That's why I came in. I need a pair of rubbers. Size eight, I believe."

Papa would have pulled out a box from under a counter displaying rubbers, overshoes, and rubber boots, and handed the box to Bill. "Here, try these on."

After tugging on the rubbers which barely stretched over his wet shoes, Bill would have said, "They're kinda tight. Gotta size larger?"

Papa would have handed him another pair that stretched more easily, covering Bill's shoes.

"That's alot better, Louis. How much?

"Dollar-an-a half."

"Charge it."

While Papa leaned on the counter, writing up the sale in his hand-sized, single carbon-copy salesbook, Bill would have lighted his pipe and in between puffs probably said, "Louis, you should get a radio."

"I got a radio. It doesn't work. It's in my engine house. Remember?"

"Yeah, but it's an old radio. It's real old. Like Anderson's old model T Ford. They didn't know how to build radios back then. Times have changed." Bill would have continued puffing on his pipe. And in between puffs he would have slowly but distinctly said, "There's no comparison to the radios built today, Louis." Puff puff. "They work. And they're simple to operate. Only two dials."

As Papa tore out the original sales slip (without requiring a signature) and handed it to Bill, he might have raised his eyebrows and said, "Only two dials?"

"Only two dials. Even a kid can turn on today's radio and pick up almost any station."

"Really?"

"It's true."

"I don't need a radio. "

Puff, puff, puff. "You should think about getting one, Louis. *Everybody* is going to have a radio before long. It's called progress."

"I owe the wholesalers too much money. I can't afford one."

"Every storekeeper owes the wholesalers money. If you didn't owe them money, you'd be rich. Think about it, Louis. You give them enough business. And you always try to pay your bills on time. It wouldn't hurt them to wait. You should get a radio."

About two months later, after all the snow had melted, Bill would have come into the store in the late afternoon and in between puffs on his pipe he would have said, "Looks like the farmers are almost finished seeding their fields, Louis. Looks like they might have a good crop this fall."

"You think so."

"Yeah, I'm quite sure. They had a lotta snow this year, enough to give the crops a good start. If it doesn't hail and if grasshoppers or frost don't harm the crops, the farmers should do real well."

"Sure hope so."

"I need a good shirt, Louis. Size sixteen.

"Work shirt or Sunday shirt."

"Work shirt. Light weight, not flannel."

"Come over here. I just got these in. Good cotton, light and strong."

"That's chambray, isn't it?"

"Chambray, shambray, how should I know? Who cares? It's good cotton and it's strong. And it's cheap."

"How much?"

"Ninety-five cents."

"How much for two?"

Papa would have looked carefully at the small three-line pin ticket he had recently fastened to bottom of the shirt. The ticket, from top to bottom, read: OD

95

16.

The cost code on the top line indicated that the shirt cost seventy-five cents. Because he had to compete with Eaton's catalog, even though he had to buy these shirts from Kays Limited, a wholesaler who extended him long term credit but who charged considerably more than the manufacturer would, Papa's markup was always small. But twenty cents profit on a shirt wasn't too bad. And even by giving a discount, if he sold two shirts at only fifteen cents profit on each, he could still make thirty cents total, which was more than he would on one. That was merchandising. "I'll give you a bargain. I'll let you have two shirts for only ninety cents each. "

"Good. Charge it."

"How about some socks, Bill? Come here. Look at these socks."

"Yeah, I could use some socks. Gimmie a couple pair."

Papa would have pulled down one pair at a time from the bundle of twelve pairs which were sown together by thread and then reinforced by a number of more threads, forming a parachute -like bundle that was then tied to a narrow metal rod suspended about an inch from the ceiling and running the length of the store. He then would have walked back to the grocery counter on top of which the sales book lay, inserted a carbon in between two pages, and probably written the following:

May 13, 1938

BILL FILNEY

2 shits 90 = $1.80

2 sox 25 = .50

* $2.30*

tax   .02

total $2.32

Papa's spelling was not the best in the world. He never did learn how to spell the word "shirt."

After writing the bill, Papa would have torn out the top sheet and handed it to Bill. Papa never—ever—asked the customer to sign the bill. And the customers never questioned Papa's figures. If the customers wanted to pay their bills, they eventually paid them. And if they didn't want to pay—for whatever reason—they didn't. There were no small claims courts available; and even if there were, Papa would never sue anyone. He trusted people. And people trusted him. His word was his bond.

Papa then would have torn a piece of thirty-inch wide brown wrapping paper from its roll at the edge of the counter, placed the shirts and socks neatly in the paper, folded the paper neatly into a package, and then tied the package with string, first lengthwise and then across its width, finally tying a knot and breaking off the string with his fingers. Then he would have handed Bill the package. "Thank you, Bill."

"Thanks, Louis." Then, just as Bill Finley got up from sitting on a block of salt near the counter, he would have taken the pipe out of his mouth and slowly and distinctly said, "You should get a radio, Louis. There's lots of good programs now. Your kids would love it. They could stay at home every night instead of going over to Sam Leckie's."

Papa might have nodded his head. Then he would have said, "A radio costs alot of money. Even wholesale at Walter Woods. But I'd rather get one from you. How much would you charge me?"

Bill would have put the pipe back in his mouth and after puffing at least three times said, "I'll tell you what, Louis. "I'll give you a better deal than Walter Woods. If you bought it from them, you'd need someone to put up an aerial. That cost money. And you'd need somebody to install it. That cost money. And you'd need the right kind of batteries. Two B batteries—dry cells—and one wet cell, the A battery. Would you know what kind of batteries to use? Would you know how to plug them in? When you get your radio from me, you don't have to worry. I take care of everything." He would have puffed on his pipe and waited for the question which he knew would follow.

"So how much is it going to cost me?"

"The radio will cost you only fifty dollars."

"FIFTY DOLLARS! That's alot of money."

"It's not that much when you consider what you're getting. The radio will last you a long time. Maybe a lifetime. Besides, it's a beautiful piece of furniture. The cabinet is walnut. It's gorgeous. Rose will be proud."

Papa paused, probably for a minute, then said, "What about the batteries? How much will that cost?"

"I'll give you a deal on the batteries."

"But fifty dollars! That's alot of money." He would have scratched his chin and then added, " I don't know. I owe the wholesalers too much money."

"They can wait. They're not worried about you. They know you're honest. They know you'll eventually pay them."

Papa nodded his head and said, "I don't know. I'll have to wait to see how the crops are doing. Maybe this fall."

A few weeks later, toward the middle of June, when the fields were heavily carpeted in green with newly sprouted wheat, Bill Finley came into the store on a Monday morning. He knew that Saturday was the biggest sales day of the week and that our store often took in as much as one hundred dollars or even $150 on a busy Saturday. He knew Papa was extremely conscientious and that the money would then be held over until Monday morning, when Papa would take most of it to the post office, to buy money orders he sent to the wholesalers, as partial payments on his bills.

"Good morning, Louis."

"Good morning, Bill"

"I need a good pair of work gloves."

Papa would have pulled out three pairs from behind the counter in the grocery section and handed them to Bill. "This is split leather. Sixty five cents. This is cowhide. Eighty five cents. This is the best. Horsehide. Ninety five cents. Try them on."

"I'll take the cowhide. They're softer. And gimmie a can of Prince Albert. Charge it." After filling his pipe, lighting it, and puffing away,

Bill would have said in a slow and very distinct voice, "Looks like the farmers are going to have real good crops this fall, Louis. Real Good." Puff, puff. " The best in years."

"You think so?"

"Sure do. Best in years. I was just looking at Hoffman's field.

He'll probably get twenty-five bushels to the acre."

"Twenty five! You think so?"

"At least. Maybe even thirty."

"Thirty!"

"Could be. Wouldn't surprise me at all." Then taking his pipe out of his mouth, Bill would have said, "So when do you want to get a radio?"

"Maybe this fall."

"Why wait 'till fall? Why not now?"

"I can't afford it now. I owe too much money."

"I'll tell you what, Louis. Your wholesalers know they're going to get paid. They know you'd never cheat them. Your credit is as good as gold. Gimmie thirty dollars now and ten dollars a month for two months, and I'll install a new Philco cabinet radio for you this week."

"That's alot of money, Bill. How about twenty dollars now and ten dollars a month. "

"Twenty dollars now and ten dollars a month. You got a deal."

"What about the batteries?"

"I'll give them to you wholesale, same price as Walter Woods."

"I'll pay you cash for them."

As Bill extended his hand, he said, "Louis, you got a good deal. I'll have George Holmes put up an aerial today. And you'll have your radio before the end of the week."

Whether or not this scenario actually happened, nobody will ever know. However, what I do know for certain is that one day in June— and I believe it was on a Monday—just as I came home from school at noon for dinner, I distinctly remember Bill Finley standing on our small wooden walkway which ran along the length of our house from the cement sidewalk to our back yard, between our house and our front garden. He was staring first at the roof on our house and then at the roof on our engine house. I asked him what he was doing.

"I'm looking to see where George Holmes can put up the aerial."

I liked Bill Finley for many reasons, one of which was that he respected people and never talked down to anyone. He paused for a moment and then, as if to include me in his decision, he added, "I think I'll have George run it from the front of your house above the garden to there," pointing to our engine house. "That should be long enough."

Normally, one might think that after I had hoped and prayed for a radio all these many years, I would have been surprised and excitedly asked the obvious question: "Are we getting a radio?" But I wasn't stupid. Who else would Bill be putting up an aerial for in our own yard? And so, in a matter-of-fact voice which I hoped would mask my excitement and illustrate my maturity, I merely said, "I think that's a good idea." But try as I might, I could not hold back the overwhelming thrill I felt at this moment. And so I blurted out, "When are we getting it?"

Bill grinned, then slowly said, "We should have it installed in a couple of days."

CHAPTER TEN
THE GOLDEN AGE OF RADIO

With all the radios my wife and I have available at our fingertips and with over thirty radio stations in our immediate area, whose broadcasts come in very clearly, without any static or fade out, one might think that we spend a great deal of time listening to the radio. The fact, however, is we rarely even bother to turn it on except when we are driving, and then only to listen to traffic reports, news, classical or the popular music of the big band era. We don't care for most of the programs being broadcast today. Neither of us can stand rock and roll music or most of the insipid radio call-in talk shows that feature confrontation instead of conversation. At home we occasionally listen to an important guest being interviewed on one of the better talk shows. In my opinion, despite over sixty years of technological progress, the radio programs today can in no way compare to the enjoyment and sheer excitement they produced for us during the golden age of radio, from the late 1930s through 1940s.

It has been said that "the radio unified America." How true! Not only did it unify America —and that includes Canada—but it brought comedy, drama, music, live interviews and discussions, news, sports and all kinds of entertainment to both of our countries. In short, it brought in culture. Radio was the theater of the mind. It was the window which enabled us to view the outside world through the magic of our imagination. I can think of no other medium that has had such an enormous impact on the lives of my generation as the radio has had. It was overpowering. The only word I can think of to describe the importance and wonder of radio during its golden age is magic. Through the magic of radio, the world was now at our fingertips.

How can I describe our new radio? It was a four-tube Philco battery operated radio inside the most beautiful walnut cabinet that one can imagine. The top of the cabinet curved downward to resemble a water fall. I thought our Philco was the most beautiful piece of furniture we had in our home. We were all proud of it.

The Philco's tone was wonderful. It sounded so realistic that if one listened from another room to Lorne Green reading the CBC news at 9:00 P.M. Central Standard Time, one would swear that he was in our sitting room, not in Toronto. And when Arthur Rubenstein or any pianist was featured with the N.B.C. Symphony Orchestra from New York, one would swear that the soloist was actually performing in front of us. In all honesty, until the advent of hi fidelity, I had never heard a better sound.

Unfortunately, however, our four-tube Philco, was not the most powerful radio on the Prairies. Unlike Mr. Leckie's six-tube Rogers radio, which could easily pick up many American stations most of the year, and at least a couple even during the long summer hours when reception was at its worst, our Philco was underpowered. During daylight, it could barely pick up any American stations with the exception of these powerful 50,000 watt affiliates of CBS and NBC respectively: KSL Salt Lake City, and KOA Denver, both about 1,200 miles away. We could also pick up the much weaker 5,000 watt signal from KFYR Bismarck, North Dakota, 550 on our radio dial. However, all these signals were often so weak that they faded in and out and in and out until, disgustedly, we turned to a Saskatchewan station instead.

Bismarck was about four hundred air miles away, a very long way for a weak A.M. radio signal to travel in the daylight hours of summer. It has something to do with physics. Although the signal bounces off the stratosphere and can easily travel that distance during the cold, long dark hours of winter, it simply won't reach that far during summer's long daylight hours. That's why our Philco could barely pick up KFYR Bismarck during most of the year, but could pick up all kinds of American stations at night, especially when the temperature dropped to below zero. On those cold nights we could pick up stations that were located even as far as two thousand miles away, including Chicago, Los Angeles, and Mexico.

Reception, especially at night, was accompanied by a great deal of interference from static and other neighboring stations. The powerful 50,000 watt stations usually interfered with and often drowned out our weaker neighboring stations, including Bismarck, operating on the same frequency as those on an adjoining frequency as well. That's why KFYR Bismarck became but a memory a year after we got our Philco.

During the daylight hours, we would usually turn our dial to 550 whenever we wanted to listen to a particular program being broadcast by the National Broadcasting Company. Because the signal was so weak, we would turn the volume up as loud as possible. Even then, we could barely hear the program. When the program was over and we turned the radio off, we simply left the dial there —tuned to 550—with the volume turned up as high as possible. It saved time because we would be listening to the same station usually within a matter of hours. Then one day as I turned on the radio, the loudest shouting I had ever heard in my life frightened me so badly that I immediately jumped backward and almost fell over. It was in French. I was stunned.

"EE SEE RAD-IYO CAN-AH-DAH. THIS IS THE CANADIAN BROADCASTING CORPORATION!"

What happened? What the hell! Swearing, I hurriedly tried to turn down the volume. "C.B.K. WATROUS, SASKATCHEWAN. BROAD-CASTING ON 540 KILOCYCLES WITH 50,000 WATTS OF POWER."

I was in shock. Fifty thousand watts! That was fifty times as powerful as CKCK Regina, which came in so loudly that we had to turn down the volume. Fifty Times stronger! Good God!

The radio was supposed to be tuned to 550, not 540. Where was KFYR Bismarck? I checked to make sure. The dial was still tuned to 550, but there was no KFYR. The announcer at CBK sounded as if he was still shouting. Reluctantly, yet curiously, I turned the station dial slightly to the left. His voice was much louder than before. I turned down the volume as low as I could. It was still loud enough to be heard in the next room. The Canadian Broadcasting Corporation had entered Saskatchewan with a surprise bombardment of 50,000 watts that had obliterated KFYR Bismarck, North Dakota. Throughout practically all of Saskatchewan, KFYR was now only a memory.

However, 'tis an ill wind that blows no good. Now instead of being able to pick up only three (Saskatchewan) stations at any time, any season, we had four.[4] And CBK Watrous was by far the clearest and loudest of all. It was deafening. I wondered if my friend Milt Spector who lived in Watrous even had to turn on his radio to hear the station.

The Canadian Broadcasting Corporation had silenced any competitor anywhere near the 540 radio dial. Canada, with a population only one tenth that of the United States, was now a mighty world power.

I wondered why the CBC had picked the small town of Watrous for its regional station, thereby bringing added fame to this little resort town. It was already famous for another reason. Just outside of Watrous was the most famous resort area in Saskatchewan, Lake Manitou. Its water, like that of the Dead Sea, was so salty that anyone could float in the lake. It was impossible to sink. And when one got out of the water, one's entire body was covered with salt. Sick people throughout Canada and even some from the United States came to Watrous in the summer to bathe in the health-giving waters. For the Jews in Saskatchewan, especially those with aches and pains and all kinds of imaginary illnesses, "Votrous" was the place to go in the summer. Lucky husbands (who had enough money) would send their wives and children there for at least a couple of weeks, while they (the lucky husbands) stayed home to look after the store and to get some peace and quiet. Nobody complained. That was Watrous.

But why had the CBC decided to place its regional transmitter there? I glanced at a map. Watrous was almost the center of the populated part of Saskatchewan and the Prairies for that matter. Like the 50,000 watt clear channel station WHO Des Moines, Iowa, CBK could probably be heard not only throughout the Prairies, but certainly throughout the Dakotas, possibly throughout the intermountain states, and even as far away as the Great Plains. Now our neighbors to the south could have the privilege of listening to such original Canadian programs as *The Happy Gang* from Toronto, The *CBC News*, read by Lorne Green in Toronto, the latest reports from the Toronto Stock Exchange in Toronto, the Toronto Symphony Orchestra in Toronto, and all kinds of other wonderful programs that originated in Toronto. Now Americans, too, could learn all about Canada—from Toronto. They would think there were only two cities in Canada—Watrous and Toronto. Little did they know that Watrous was hardly a city. But Toronto, of course, was a different matter. Not only was it the largest English speaking city in Canada, but the financial center of our country and, according to the CBC, the only cultural city in Canada. Welcome to Toronto!

How well I remember listening to *The Happy Gang*! I thought it was one of the better Canadian variety programs. It came on every weekday morning, about ten or eleven, and lasted for half-an-hour. My sisters and I listened to it as often as we could during the summer holidays or at other times when there was no school. It began like a knock-knock joke: "Knock, knock!" Immediately someone would respond "Who's there?" Then the announcer would shout, " It's The Happy Gang, with Bob Farnam on the trumpet, Kay Stokes at the organ, Les Foster with the accordion, and Bert Pearl—five foot, 2 1/2 of sunshine." The group would immediately break into the theme song, accompanied by the band, led by Bob Farnam. I enjoyed Bert Pearl's singing and especially liked the jokes.

Toronto maintained its position as the center of Canadian radio culture for a number of years. But Western Canada resented the impression that a great cultural desert stretched west from Ontario to the Pacific Ocean. Eventually, in 1943, thanks to radio producer Fred McDowell, Vancouver made its bid over the CBC with his *Nabob Harmony House*, one of the first network programs—if not the very first—to originate from Vancouver. This program featured a singing group of four called "The Nabobettes," with Susan as soloist and Pat Morgan as a featured singer. The group began the program with this song:

"Nabob, N. A. B. O. B.

Nabob, spices, coffee, and tea.

And there's plenty more

to be found in your store

We're singing N. A. B. O. B."

Although we sold Nabob products in our store, we rarely used them, except for their spices. We ground our own coffee and my father preferred Red Rose or Salada tea. But if there is one thing I have learned about advertising, it's that a good singing commercial often can be re-membered forever and ever and ever.

A year after the *Nabob Harmony House* began, Fred McDowell pro-duced another favorite musical from Vancouver, the *Burns Chuckwagon*, sponsored by Burns and Company, one of Canada's largest meat pack-ers. [5]

Fred McDowell had opened the doors of the Canadian Broadcasting Corporation to other programs originating from the West. I remember listening on Friday nights to this introduction of one of Canada's top dance bands: " From the Banff Springs Hotel, mile high in the Canadian Rockies, we bring you the music of Mart Kenny and his Western Gentle-men." Banff, Alberta, far away from Sheho, was Canada's most plush mountain resort. I never dreamed that I would often spend my vacations there, let alone one day climb one of its highest and most photographed mountains, Mount Rundle.

Besides musical programs, a few producers from Vancouver added outstanding dramas to the CBC repertoire, and thus Vancouver became known as Canada's other radio cultural center.

American programs, however, were by far the most popular, not only in our family but with everyone in Sheho and probably everyone on the Prairies. And of all the programs broadcast from the United States, I am sure that during the summer months, the soap operas had the biggest listening audience. Because they were also broadcast over Canadian sta-tions, they became an integral part of our daily lives whenever we had the time to listen.

Our favorite was *Big Sister*. It came on in the morning just after *The Happy Gang*. After a brief commercial, four gongs resonated, followed by the announcer's voice: "Now soapy rich Rinso presents *Big Sister*. The clock in Glen Falls' town hall is telling us it's time for Rinso's story of *Big Sister*." For a while the husband of Big Sister was Dr. David Brewster, as I recall. He was a wonderful person, very happily married to a wonderful woman who was also in love with him, that is, until she met someone else, John somebody or other. But adulterous relationships were not condoned on soap operas, not even if the woman's husband was dying from an incurable disease. So she was in a dilemma. We all sympathized with her but really felt sorry for her husband who was dying and had no idea that his wife now was really in love with someone else. Then one day, during the Easter holidays, Dr. David Brewster passed away, and we all cried. Even my mother cried. He was such a wonderful man. He was a saint. But I don't think his widow cried. Now—at last—she and John somebody or other could get married and consummate their love. To tell you the truth, however, I can't recall what happened next. And since there's no point in speculating, let's just leave *Big Sister* with this reminder: "The new soapy rich improved 1938 Rinso gets your clothes RIN-SO-WHITE."

Although I never did laundry, I preferred Rinso to Oxydol, not only because I liked the simple green box of Rinso and hated the gaudy yellow and purple colors on the box of Oxydol, but also because I didn't particularly care for ***The Proctor and Gamble Hour***. It began at one o'clock with *Ma Perkins*, followed fifteen minutes later with a short piano selection introducing *Pepper Young's Family*, "the story of your friends the Youngs, sponsored by Camay soap, the mild beauty soap for a smooth, softer complexion. "Next came *The Story of Mary Marlin*, sponsored by Ivory Flakes. The final program was *The Guiding Light*, "presented by Proctor and Gamble, the makers of P and G soap, the white naphtha soap." Believe me, one hour is a long time to listen to four different soaps, especially when you think that the first two are so bad you simply lose interest in the remaining two. All I remember about the third soap, *The Story of Mary Marlin*, besides the opening theme, Debussy's "Claire De Lune," was that Mary was riding in a sleigh through the snow in Siberia, of all places, and either she or somebody else had amnesia. That was too much for me to swallow. We had all the snow we wanted in Sheho and it lasted until May. We didn't have to go Siberia for more. Enough was enough. So I never listened to that program again.

Pepper Young's Family was probably only slightly better. [6]   But let me tell you about the worst one of all— Oxydol's own *Ma Perkins*. A few seconds after 1:00 P.M. Central Standard Time, a few long resonant chords of an organ were followed immediately by the announcer's voice: "Now everyone ready for Oxydol's own Ma Perkins—America's mother of the airwaves—brought to you by Proctor and Gamble, makers of

Oxydol." As bad as it was and as incredible as it may seem, it ran continuously for twenty-some years, I believe. Why, I'll never know. It was the worst soap opera I ever listened to. The setting was a small town somewhere in America, where Ma Perkins, a gentle, kindly old soul, owned the lumberyard. I believe she was a widow. No wonder. She spoke so slowly and never had anything interesting to say that her husband probably died from boredom or committed suicide. Her friend Shuffle (that was his name, honest!) and her daughter Faye were the supporting characters. After the announcer completed his Oxydol commercial and a recap of what happened the previous day (which wasn't much), he would usually begin the program like this: "And now let's look in on Ma. She's in her lumberyard with Faye. Right now they're looking out the window. Ma is talking to Faye. Let's tune in and listen."

Ma: "Look Faye, there's Shuffle. He's comin this way."

Faye: "That's right, Ma. He's comin this way. "

Ma: " I wonder what's on his mind."

Faye: "You know Ma, I was wonderin the same thing."

Ma: He looks kinda serious. Like he's worried about somethin."

Faye: "He sure does. I wonder what it could be."

Ma: "Well, maybe we'll find out soon. He's comin up the sidewalk."

Faye: "Oh, here he is now. Hello, Shuffle."

Shuffle: "Hello, Faye. Hello, Ma. Nice day today, isn't it?"

Would you believe this type of insipid dialogue continued for almost ten minutes? Then, just before the closing commercial, if we were very, very lucky, we might find out what was on Shuffle's mind. But don't bet on it. More than likely, we would learn that Shuffle was just about to tell us what was on his mind. But such an earth shattering event would have to be continued—the next day.

Soap operas were not the most exciting programs for ten, eleven, and twelve-year-old boys. We liked action programs. Walter Lys told us about a new and exciting program, especially for us kids. So shortly after I came home from school, I would often listen to *Dick Tracy*, who would send us secret code messages that could be deciphered only by regular listeners who had received their decoders after they had sent away for them with a box top from Quaker Puffed Wheat or Quaker Puffed Rice. That was exciting. But more exciting were the promotions which we could receive through the mail from the sponsor, the Quaker Oats Company. If we saved three box tops and sent them to the sponsor, we would be rewarded by being promoted to Sergeant. Along with the promotion came the Sergeant's badge. It was an impressive badge that looked just like the badges we saw in the comic strip. Walter Lys, who got that badge in less than three weeks, was the first in town to get that promotion. We all were proud of him and forever after called him "Tracy." I got mine about a week later. It was one of the proudest moments of my life. Now I would work on my Lieutenant's badge, which required three more box tops. And some day I hoped to reach the rank of Captain and get the most prestigious badge of all. But that required another three box tops. It was the ultimate promotion, and it was a long way off— six box tops away. Perhaps if I persuaded my sisters to join me in eating more Quaker Puffed Wheat, I could get my Captain's badge in only a few months.

About a week after I had made Sergeant and had saved up another box top and was now only two box tops away from Lieutenant, Robert Heron came to school with a proud smirk on his face. Conspicuously pinned to his shirt were all three badges. He had canvassed the town and collected all nine box tops. That wasn't fair. I was deflated and mad. And I never listened to *Dick Tracy* again.

I did, however, listen to another cops-and-robbers program, much more exciting than *Dick Tracy*. Although *Gang Busters* was intended for adults, staying up until eleven on Wednesdays to listen to *Gang Busters* became a status symbol for my classmates; hence, most of us listened to it regularly. At exactly three seconds after eleven o'clock, we heard the sound of marching men, followed by the shrill, piercing sound of a police whistle, and then the announcer excitedly shouting: "Palmolive Brushless and Palmolive Lather Cream, the shaving creams made with olive and palm oils present." Three machine gun bursts interrupted him before he completed shouting "GANG BUSTERS." The staccato sound of a final machine gun burst was followed by the announcement "at war, marching against the underworld" followed by another police whistle.

For the next thirty minutes, my ear was glued to the radio as my mind witnessed bank robberies, get-aways, shootouts and finally the capture or killing of one of the nation's most notorious criminals and the end of his career. The lesson was clear. Crime does not pay.

It was now 11:30 and everyone in our home was in bed, sound asleep. Everyone except me. But I wouldn't dream of turning in yet. My adrenaline was still flowing, and my imagination was on high. I needed another fix. Now it was time for *Lights Out*. So I left the radio on, barely audible. If Papa woke up, he would shut the radio off and send me to bed.

Slowly the announcer commanded "LIGHTS OUT EVERYBODY!" I was so frightened now, I wouldn't turn out the lights if my life depended on it. Almost immediately came the loud resonating sound of a gong. Slowly, ever so slowly, it struck the hour of midnight. My curly hair stood on end. Then came the scary sound of the wind, followed by the eerie howl of a lost dog. Thank God we didn't live near a graveyard. Finally, in a voice that would scare even Boris Karloff, came this warning: "This is the witching hour. It is the hour when dogs howl and evil is let loose on a sleeping world. Want to hear about it? Then turn out your lights." Are you kidding? I wouldn't dare turn out our lights even if we had electricity. And I certainly wouldn't turn down our coal oil lamp. In fact, after the program ended, I was so scared that I took the lamp into my bedroom and kept it lit all night. There was no way I would sleep in the dark. I was terrified. The next morning it was all I could do to get up.

Lights Out was not the only scary program I listened to. Some programs added another element—mystery. One of these began with: "Roma Wines of Fresno, California, presents— a tale well calculated to keep you in SUSPENSE." [7]

The very best of all the mystery programs, even though it was not the most frightening one, was the series *I Love a Mystery*. An organ theme introduced the program followed by the announcement: "Fleischman's Fresh Yeast presents the latest adventures of Jack, Doc, and Reggie, specialists in crime and adventure." Written by Carlton E. Morris, an absolutely superb writer, his fifteen -minute mysteries were broadcast nightly, Monday through Friday at 9:00 our time, as a series all dealing with a particular mystery. ("And now, follow the Chinese private map of P.Y. Ling.") Each mystery, "P.Y. Ling," for example, or "The Widow with the Amputation," would be solved only after weeks of adventure and intrigue. Each carefully plotted program built toward its own climax that particular night, leaving us listeners—Sylvia and me—anxious to find out what would happen the next night. But the following night presented another twist to the mystery which ended on a cliff hanger—every night, again and again. Finally, weeks after listening spellbound to a particular installment, we were able to breathe a sigh of relief. The mystery was solved. We also felt as though we had lost a friend, for we had followed this particular adventure, it seemed, forever. But we knew that a new adventure would begin the following week.

Unfortunately, this program was broadcast only on American stations and, therefore, we were unable to hear it clearly during much of the year. It is one thing to be deprived of an experience when you know it is impossible for you to have that experience. Thus, although we were disappointed because we couldn't hear the program during the late spring and early fall, we took our disappointment philosophically. There was nothing we could do about it. It is another thing, however, to be frustrated because you are constantly being teased. When the program fades in-and-out, and in-and-out, right at the climax, just when the mystery is about to be solved, you know you're being teased. You want to strike back. And sometimes you do. Then you feel better because you've succeeded.

One evening in early fall, while throwing a tennis ball up at the aerial, I discovered that I could usually hit it two times out of three. And each time I hit it, the aerial vibrated like a plucked guitar string. It hummed. The vibration lasted for at least four minutes. My underhand pitching arm was getting good. Then one day just after pitching a four minute serenade, with the aerial humming a new tune, I went into the living room, turned on our Philco, and heard an American station that had faded out only five minutes before. It was now coming in as loudly as most of our neighboring stations. It was magic. But within five minutes both the magic and the program began to fade. Then there was nothing but static. I ran outside and hit the aerial again with another four-minute serenade. I quickly ran back into the house. The magic had returned. I had learned how to bring back to life an American radio program that had just died. I had performed a miracle.

When I showed my magic trick to Sylvia, she took her own ball—a large rubber bouncing ball—and practiced her own magic act that even rivaled my own. From that time on, whenever the airwaves teased us by causing a fadeout, especially during *I Love a Mystery*, we would take turns running outside as quickly as we could to hit the aerial, and then immediately run back inside to hear the remainder of the program before it began fading out again. We perfected our game until it took us only seconds to rejuvenate the fading signal. Eventually, we were able to listen to almost all of each nightly episode with scarcely an interruption.

I remember the names of only two of the stars of that series—Martin Yarborough and the leading female, Mercedes McCambridge. Her deep husky voice lent character and drama to any role she played, whether on radio or the movies. I never forgot the sound of that magnificent voice. More than fifty years later, I saw her in a Neil Simon play on Hollywood Boulevard. She was marvelous. Her voice hadn't changed. I went backstage to meet her and we reminisced about her earlier days on radio. She was gratified that I had remembered. We also spoke about Carlton E. Morris's other famous program *One Man's Family*, a weekly program about the family of Father Barber living on Seacliff Drive in San Francisco. I had even remembered the slogan: "This program is dedicated to the fathers and mothers of the younger generation and to their bewildering offspring." Although I was now in my sixties and she was somewhat older, I was as thrilled as a teenager meeting his favorite movie star. To me, she was still a star—the best of the golden age of radio.

Space does not permit me even to list most of the wonderful radio programs which bring back such fond memories to those of us who listened and learned and used our imagination to travel to far away places on a magic carpet when radio was king. However, I feel I would be doing a disservice to my contemporaries and perhaps to students of history who are interested in that culture if I did not mention just a few, which I shall list in the addendum.[8]

We were thrilled when we listened to sportscasters like Red Barber who were so good they made you feel that you, yourself, were actually in Yankee Stadium in the seventh game of the World Series, you your-self were on the mound, winding up, with the count three and two, the bases loaded, the score tied, the bottom of the ninth and two out. And you were facing the pinch hitter. This was it! Now or never. Or you, yourself, could be the pinch hitter—facing that relief pitcher. You've waited all your life for a chance like this. Now it was all up to you. Television—heck! It doesn't come close.

And who can forget Clem McCarthy in his staccato voice bringing us all the excitement and pageantry of the Kentucky Derby from Churchill Downs? Nor will we ever forget how he made us part of the crowd at ringside in Madison Square Garden when the world heavyweight box-ing champion Joe Louis, the Brown Bomber, demolished another oppo-nent with " a jab to the head and another jab and a punishing right to the body and a left hook to the body and he's in trouble and there's a sharp right cross to the jaw and he's down. He's down. He's down for the count. Eight, nine, ten, and it's all over. And Joe Louis has scored an-other knockout."

During the winter on Saturday night, the C.B.C. broadcast *Hockey Night in Canada* "with Foster Hewitt in the Gondola at Maple Leaf Gar-dens." Although he was an excellent hockey announcer, I was not the student of hockey that I am today and found hockey rather hard to fol-low. Therefore, I usually listened to something else. But on one particu-lar Saturday night, I listened to a game that I shall never forget.

To be sure, my most vivid impression of the golden age of radio is the night I listened to *Hockey Night in Canada*. I had just returned from Bill Finley's garage after picking up our own "A" (wet cell) battery that I had taken there earlier in the week to be recharged. The six volt battery, about one quarter the size of a regular twelve volt car battery, weighed about fifteen pounds and could be carried by its handle, like a pail of water. It had to be recharged every couple of months. After our battery had been recharged, I would first pick it up, come home to reconnect it in the back of our Philco cabinet, and then return the loaner. On this particular night, for some reason or other, I just happened to turn on the radio to the C.B.C. and found the hockey game rather exciting. It must have been exciting or I must have been lazy, because there I sat on the chesterfield, with our wet cell battery flat on my lap, listening to Foster Heuitt for at least an entire period, which usually lasted forty minutes. When one of my legs got tired from the battery, I would switch legs. And if both legs got tired, I would balance the battery on my shins, one at a time, or cradle it on my stomach and chest. The only part of my overalls that had not been exposed to the battery was the back. And a few hours later when I went to bed, instead of neatly hanging up my overalls, I must have crumpled them so that the back touched the front. I had completely forgotten about the sulfuric acid in the battery. The next morning when I awoke, I looked in vain for my overalls. Except for a few remnants of blue denim to which were attached the metal fasteners that had held up my overalls the night before, there was nothing. Not even holes. My overalls had disappeared.

CHAPTER ELEVEN
What It Means To Be A Jew

There are probably hundreds of books that have been printed on various aspects of Judaism, including "what it means to be a Jew." And every year more are published by authors professing special knowledge and a unique insight into this subject. Because most of you have neither the time nor the slightest inclination to read all of these books—or even one of them, or even part of one of them—I shall relieve you of that burden by giving you the inside scoop in this chapter on what it really means to be a Jew. My credentials are impeccable. My grandfather in Russia, after whom I was named, was a pious *Roov*, that is, a biblical scholar. According to my dad, his father spent practically all of his time studying the Torah and Talmud and making twelve children who did all the work to eke out a living so that their father could continue his life-long study of Judaism. As a result, my dad, who had worked hard since childhood, had little use for the deep philosophical questions posed in the Talmud. He knew exactly what it meant to a be a Jew and had no time for elaborate answers or explanations. My mother, born in Poland, kept kosher, read the Jewish newspapers, and told me horror stories about what could happen if one married a *shiksa*—a gentile girl. On Rosh Hashanah and Yom Kippur they closed their store, and we all made the annual sixty-mile pilgrimage to Yorkton, where we went to *sheil*—the synagogue. And I even had a bar mitzvah. They brought me up to be a good Jew. What else is there to know about Judaism? So as you can see, I am eminently qualified to tell you all there is to know about "what it means to be a Jew." Oh, perhaps I've omitted a few minor details such as the sanctity of life and the Ten Commandments. But I'm not talking about trivialities. I'm talking about the really important issues here. The most important ones. Take my word for it.

My instruction began at a very early age—three to be exact—back in 1931. The first thing I learned was that I was Jewish, my sisters were Jewish, Mama and Papa were Jewish, and Mr. Leckie was also Jewish. However, Mr. and Mrs. Darling were not Jewish, Polly Snihur our hired girl was not Jewish, and Papa's customers were not Jewish either. Being Jewish meant being different from other people. I knew I was different because I was small. I was small and Mama and Papa were short. Jewish people were small and short.

Next, at the age of four, I learned that Dr. Shaum, who frequently came to our home for Sunday dinner, was also Jewish. He was Jewish even though he wasn't small and short. When he stopped coming to our home and instead spent most his spare time with the widow Mrs. Prowse, who not only was a *shiksa* [gentile lady] but also had a young daughter, he was doing something wrong. And when he left town and married her, it was a sin. Thus, at the age of four, I learned that it was sin for a Jewish doctor to marry a *shiksa*. For years afterward, Mama and Papa spoke of it as being a " tragedy," and even a "major tragedy." A tragedy was worse than a sin, and a major tragedy was worse than a tragedy. I was getting an education in what it means to be a Jew.

Being a Jew also meant obeying the Kosher Food Laws, and that meant a lot of "don'ts" and "can'ts" and "couldn'ts." There were three kinds of meals: meat, milk, and *pareve* (neutral foods). Meat meals included poultry and neutral fish. Milk meals meant dairy products and neutral fish. Kosher meant we couldn't butter our bread if we were eating meat, and we certainly couldn't drink milk with a meat meal or even immediately afterward; we had to wait two hours. On the other hand, if we had a milk meal, we could eat meat immediately afterward. Don't ask me why. I never made the Law. The Law was "meat after milk but not milk after meat." Otherwise it was a sin. At least a minor sin; almost a major one. But not a tragedy. Fish, however was neutral like Switzerland, and stayed out of the wars.

The Kosher Food Laws also required separate dishes for meat meals and for milk meals, and also separate pots, pans, cutlery and silverware.

But not separate glassware. Maybe glassware had not yet been invented when Moses and the Children of Israel fled from their bondage and the wicked Pharaoh in Egypt. Or maybe they had never heard of it. Or maybe they didn't have time to carefully pack it in Pharaoh's newspapers before they fled. Or maybe the newspapers were late. Or maybe glassware doesn't travel well in the desert and got broken along the way. Who knows? Your guess is as good as mine. In any event, glassware doesn't count. It's neutral. Not like dishes, pots, pans, cutlery, and silverware. No siree. If you mixed the dishes or silverware or pots or pans and served meat on milk dishes or milk on meat dishes or served meat from a milk pan or milk from a meat pot, or if you used the wrong silverware—God forbid!—that was a sin. A minor sin, not a major one, but still a sin. It could be a major sin if Mama found out about it. (That's why I never told her.)

But that's not all. I'm not through yet with the dishes and silverware and pots and pans. Not by a long shot. During *Pesach* (Passover), we put away all our dishes and silverware and cutlery and pots and pans because they were *Chametz* —forbidden on pain of death to be used during *Pesach*. Then we went next door to our store and climbed the stairs in the warehouse to the vacant second floor, where we took out a special set of everything— for both meat and milk —to be used exclusively for *Pesach*. After bringing everything down and unpacking it, we washed all the eating utensils thoroughly and put them in the cupboard for the eight days of Passover. After Passover, we repacked everything and *shlept* [lugged] it back upstairs. Then we unpacked the *chametz* dishes, and began a new cycle. It was a sin to use the wrong utensils. I don't know what kind of a sin, but it was a sin. It was probably a special kind of a sin—a Passover sin.

It was also forbidden to eat certain foods called *chametz* during Passover, and chocolate bars were *chametz*. I waited as long as I could. Eight days would be an eternity. Seven days unthinkable. Six days were out of the question. Five days would be impossible. So I tried for four. But on the third day, I couldn't hold out any longer. That Cadbury's milk chocolate bar which I took from our store when Papa wasn't looking was the best tasting chocolate I ever had. I knew I had committed a sin—maybe two. I didn't know which was worse—stealing a chocolate bar or eating it. And I wasn't sure God would forgive me. So I never told anyone. Until now.

Keeping kosher meant getting our meat from a kosher butcher shop. We got ours from the Service and Quality Meat Market, owned by Uncle Abe's brother in Yorkton. Papa would send a letter to Harry Shnider, along with a money order, and within two days the order would arrive by railway express. If Ed Howe, one of the two draymen in town, was on duty, he would deliver all the other orders but take his time in delivering our meat, even though he knew it was perishable. He didn't particularly like us, probably because Papa and Mama spoke with an accent. However, if Mike Harris was on duty, he would bring the meat to us immediately. He was Ukrainian and Papa spoke Ukrainian.

According to Kosher Law, the only part of the animal one is allowed to eat is the front end. Hence, steaks cut from the rear end of the animal such as New York cut, sirloin, tenderloin, T-bone, porterhouse, and filet mignon are *traif*—forbidden by Kosher Law. The Jews may have been God's chosen people, but He sure wasn't playing favorites when it came to the Kosher Food Laws. While the gentiles dined on filet mignon, we ate chuck. Round steak was a "gourmet" treat.

After Mama got the meat, she would soak it in a salty brine to get all the blood out. Then she would pound the meat with a rolling pin, again and again—unmercifully—as if she were taking out all the frustrations the Jewish people had suffered over the past three thousand years on that poor piece of meat. I felt sorry for that poor round steak, but what could I do? It was innocent. What had it done to deserve such a pounding? Nothing. But Mama didn't care. She kept on pounding. She pounded it and pounded it until it was as flat as a pool table. Finally, when she was through with the pounding, she would fry it in *schmaltz* [goose fat] with onions and potatoes, until it was not only well done, but very, very, well done. We used a lot of ketchup. That was Kosher steak.

We never ate non kosher meat. Not even in a restaurant. That would surely be a sin. Probably a major sin. Almost a tragedy. But not quite. Eating pork, therefore, was absolutely taboo. It was a major sin, and maybe worse. Even Billy Naherny had blurted out to the whole classroom in my first grade that "Jews don't eat pork." I would never eat pork. Not on your life! Eating bacon or ham was probably as bad in the eyes of the Almighty. But somehow those words—especially "ham"— didn't sound quite as bad as pork a few years later, when I was ten and was visiting my Shnider relatives, in Inglis, Manitoba. Maybe that's because I had accompanied my cousins Maurice and Charlie to the neighboring town of Russell, eight hundred population, and we were all seated on stools inside the delicatessen owned by Louis Malinsky and his brother Jack. So there I was, alongside Maurice and Charlie, who were carrying on a conversation with Louis Malinsky behind the counter, when Louis picked up the menus and said, "What'll you have?"

"I'll have a ham sandwich and a Wynola," replied Maurice.

"I'll have a ham sandwich and a Coca Cola," said Charlie.

I was on the spot. I didn't know what to order. I had never even dreamed of eating ham. Yet here were my cousins who were about to commit a sin. Not a minor sin. This was big time. It was a major sin for sure! They had ordered a ham sandwich. I didn't know what would happen if I joined them—if I dared to challenge God Himself and taste the forbidden meat. I remembered the story of Adam and Eve in the Garden of Eden and the serpent that had led her astray by tempting her with the forbidden fruit. I looked around for a snake, but I couldn't see one. All I could see was Charlie, grinning like a Cheshire cat, and Maurice, scowling as if to say, "What's the matter with you? Afraid of tasting something new?" They were the ones who were tempting me—not the serpent. I was surely being led into temptation and I could barely resist. I wondered about the punishment. Would I go straight to hell if I disobeyed the Law by tasting a ham sandwich and thereby committing a major sin? Or would the angel of death come down through the ceiling and strike me dead before I even ate the sandwich? Or would I first be struck dead and then go to hell? It would certainly be a major sin. No doubt about it. I was frightened. But I was curious. I mean really curious. My cousins had led me into temptation and I could no longer resist. It was therefore not my fault. Not entirely. I would commit that sin and find out what would happen if I tasted the forbidden meat. Besides, I would show my cousins that I was no ordinary ten-year- old, but almost a teenager, like them. So, in as calm and mature a voice as I could manage, I said to Louis Malinsky, "I'll have a ham sandwich and a coca cola." Then I took out my handkerchief and wiped my forehead.

Louis Malinsky brought our sandwiches. Maurice and Charlie lifted the top layer of bread and poured ketchup over the ham, then put the bread back on top of the ham. They bit into their sandwiches and chewed. Nothing happened. I started to pour ketchup on my ham, all the while glancing at the ceiling. I was terrified. That's where the angel of death or God Himself would come down to strike me dead if I even dared to taste my ham sandwich. But I had already put the bread back on top of the ham. Breathlessly, I kept staring at the ceiling. But nothing happened. So far so good. But my forehead was wet. And so were my hands. I couldn't back out now. I was no coward. So, with one glance at the ceiling and the other at my ham sandwich, I bit into it and chewed. It was delicious. In between bites, I kept looking up at the ceiling. It hadn't moved. Was I ever relieved! And after finishing my sandwich, I came to the conclusion that even though I had committed a sin, God would not punish me after all. Obviously, He didn't really care what I ate. Even if it wasn't kosher. And I began to wonder what obeying the Kosher Food Laws had to do with one's religion, and more specifically with one's relationship to God.

For a boy, being a Jew means undergoing circumcision exactly eight days after he is born, at the hands of a *mohel*—one who has been specially trained and ordained to perform this religious surgical procedure in accordance with Jewish Law. There is a story about a *mohel* in Europe who had just moved into a new town, and after having rented a house he put up a lovely window display featuring a watch. A neighbor stared at the watch for a while, then said, "*Mohel*, why on earth did you put up a window display of a watch? What does a watch possibly have to do with what you do—your profession?" The *Mohel* sarcastically replied, "What would you like me to put there instead? A *putz*? [penis]

The circumcision ceremony —called a *bris*—includes giving the baby boy his Jewish or Hebrew name. Most Jews name their children after a dead relative, thus perpetuating that name and thereby honoring the deceased. The English translation, however, usually bears little resemblance to the original name except for the sound of the first letter, and sometimes not even that sound remains. My cousin Maurice was named after his uncle *Moishe*, from the biblical Moses. I was given the Jewish name of *Yankel* after my grandfather, whose Hebrew name was Yacob, which translates into English as Jacob; but my parents anglicized it to Jackie, and eventually when I got tired of being the smallest kid in my class, I insisted on being called Jack. At this stage in my life I don't care what anyone calls me, so long as it's not Jake or Cats. When I moved to the States, Americans insisted on mispronouncing my surname, Katz, which in Canada was pronounced "Kates" like dates. They pronounced it "Cats." That's why I changed the spelling of my surname to Kates. I think "Cats" is a horrible name for a human being and should be outlawed. How would you like to be called "Cats" or "Dogs" or " Rats" or "Mice?" But forgive me. I was talking about the circumcision ceremony, the *Bris*.

Obviously, I don't remember that procedure, but I know I was circumcised. Although nobody had ever told me, it was quite obvious that mine looked different from everyone else's when we went swimming bare naked in the creek that flowed through Wunder's field. I looked different because something was missing at the end. That's when I realized that being Jewish really meant being different.

The *bris* is held either at the home of the parents or at a synagogue, depending on how many people are invited. It can be a simple affair with as few as ten men present for the required *minyan* [quorum]. I'm sure mine was a very simple affair. My parents did not believe in making a mountain out of a molehill. What a contrast from some of the lavish affairs today on the occasion of the infant's *bris*! Some of these celebrations can be as expensive as a big bar mitzvah or even a big wedding, with feasting and drink afterward. If the parents have a lot of relatives, friends, and associates whom they would like to impress, they hold the ceremony in a synagogue. Otherwise, it's performed at home.

The "good" *mohels*, like highly skilled surgeons, are usually in great demand. Therefore, one must reserve the services of this very important dignitary as soon as the mother gives birth to a boy. The ceremony will take place exactly eight days after the infant's birth. But scheduling the exact time is a different matter. It's at the convenience of the mohel. He keeps his calendar open so he can schedule as many appointments as possible on that particular day. And in a large metropolitan area like Los Angeles, he must make allowances for traffic tie-ups when traveling to outlying cities or counties. When his calendar is full, then he makes the appointment, telling the parents approximately what hour to expect him. He runs on Jewish Standard Time—somewhere between one and two hours late. After securing his services, the parents make other arrangements, with the synagogue if necessary, and with whoever is catering the affair or buying the food and drink. Finally, they invite the guests—by telephone or fax or e-mail.

After the guests arrive, they wait for the mohel. And they wait. And they wait. Then the father, grandparents, uncles, and other relatives and guests speculate on why he is so late. "I wonder what happened to him."

"Who gave him the directions?"

"Maybe he didn't understand the directions."

"Why shouldn't he understand them?"

" Maybe he didn't write them down."

"Why shouldn't he write them down?"

" Maybe he forgot the directions."

"Has he ever been to south Orange County before?"

"Yes, he's been to Seal Beach."

"That's north Orange County. It's not even close."

"What time did they tell him to come?"

"One o'clock."

"Maybe he got the time wrong."

"Why should he get the wrong time?"

"Maybe he took the wrong freeway."

"Maybe he got off on the wrong exit."

"Maybe there's an accident."

"Maybe he's not coming."

"He's got to come. It's a bris."

"So where is he? Tell me, where is he?"

"How should I know? He'll come. I tell you he'll come."

"What kind of a car is he driving?"

" A black one."

"Not the color. What make?"

"I think it's a Cadillac. Or maybe a Lincoln."

"Look out the window for a black Cadillac or Lincoln. You're sure it's black? Not blue?"

"It's black. It's black. He's coming in a black car. He'll be here when he'll be here. Maybe an hour or two late, that's not so terrible, but he'll be here. See! I told you. Here he comes."

The *mohel* enters with a flourish. Then he notices the anxious stares and realizes he is almost two hours late. "Oh, you should see the traffic on the freeway. You wouldn't believe such traffic. In my life, I never saw such traffic. So where are the proud parents? I'm waiting. Oh, here you are. *Mazeltoff!*" [Congratulations] He hurriedly consults them to find out what Hebrew name they want to bestow upon their newborn son. Then everyone crowds around the parents for the big event.

The basic procedure is similar for both the lavish affair and the simple one. First come the preliminaries. The mother hands the tiny infant to the father, who then honors the grandparents—if they are present—by handing the infant to them. Quite often the mother tells her husband to give the infant to her *own* mother (one of the grandmothers), who then tries to keep the infant to herself, thereby refusing to share that honor with the other grandparents. That way all the guests will notice how important *she* is. Then the other grandparents usually whisper to their son, the father, "Tell that witch of a mother-in-law to give me that damn baby or I'll kill her and you both." This kind of friendly persuasion usually works and the infant is handed over immediately. Finally, the last grandparent holding the infant hands him to the *mohel*, who then consults the parents to make doubly sure what Hebrew name they want to give their newborn. The *mohel* then blesses the infant in Hebrew and pronounces his newly given Hebrew name.

Then the *mohel* goes to work. He opens his medical bag and removes a piece of cheesecloth and a bottle of sweet kosher wine. He saturates one end of the cheesecloth with wine and inserts it into the infant's mouth. The infant begins sucking on the wine-soaked cheesecloth. The theory is that the wine will anaesthetize the infant so that he will feel little or no pain when the *mohel* cuts off the foreskin. That's the theory. But don't you believe it. The *mohel* then sterilizes his scalpel, says another prayer, takes hold of the infant's tiny penis, and in a matter of seconds slices off the foreskin and wraps cotton batten and a tiny bandage around the bleeding penis. Finally, he says another prayer and hands the howling infant back to the proud parents.

By now, the infant with his tiny mouth and tiny lungs screams like nobody has ever screamed before. And he howls and cries out to heaven for all the world to hear: "Why did you do this to me? Why? Why?" But nobody understands him. Not even God. And all the wine in Australia, California, Chile, France, Germany, Hungry, and Israel cannot ease his pain nor stop his cries. Yet this is only the beginning of what he will have to endure to be a Jew. After all, the Jews are God's chosen people. He chose them to suffer, and He wants the infant to know He means business—right from the start. The mother puts more wine-soaked cheese cloth in his mouth. But to no avail. It merely mutes the sound, making the guests less uncomfortable.

Meanwhile, Uncle Jake keeps on filming with his video camera. He's got the entire ceremony preserved for posterity. Why not? It's not every day he gets to go to a *bris*. And some day, when his newly born nephew grows up and gets engaged, he can show the film to the fiancee. "See, this is what it once used to look like. Before. And after. In all its innocence."

So now you know it's not so easy to be a Jew.

CHAPTER TWELVE
The Jewish High Holy Days.
ROSH HASHANAH

There is much more to being a Jew than a lot of "don'ts" and "can'ts " and "couldn'ts." Being a Jew also means having a good time by celebrating certain holidays, especially the Jewish High Holy Days of Rosh Hashanah and Yom Kippur. To me, that was what I enjoyed the most about being Jewish. And as I look back over half-a century at how our family celebrated those Jewish Holidays, I cannot help but sigh with nostalgia over some of the happiest times of my life. Perhaps that's because I have given up that ritual, along with just about everything else that I once accepted as a requirement for being a Jew and have found nothing to replace it. More important, though, I feel deeply nostalgic over the fellowship and affection I once shared with so many wonderful friends.

The last time I went to the synagogue for the Jewish High Holy Day services was in the fall of 1955, shortly after I had moved to Long Beach, California. I still believed in my personal God then and felt that in order to be a good Jew, I must at least put in an appearance, if only for a few hours, at the "temple" —the California name for synagogue. It was hot. September is usually our hottest month of the year. It was stuffy. It was boring. And except for my sisters and their husbands and in-laws, I didn't know a soul. I was lonely. And I felt out of place. Like a stranger. What a contrast from the wonderful times I had while growing up in Saskatchewan and celebrating our Jewish Holidays of Rosh Hashanah and Yom Kippur! I still feel a twinge of nostalgia for those long ago days whenever someone points out to me that next week it's Rosh Hashanah or Yom Kippur.

Yes, those were good times. We didn't have much money during the Depression and were in no position to buy a car. Unless other Jewish families visited us, we felt isolated from the Jewish community and deprived of Jewish social life. My parents felt as though they were strangers in a foreign land. Perhaps that's why we all looked forward to getting together with other Jewish families to celebrate the Jewish high holidays. It gave us a feeling of security and a sense of belonging. And over the years, as we kids from all over the greater Yorkton area got to know each other, we felt as though we were one big happy family filled with affection toward one another.

Until I was five, I stayed home with Mama and my young sister Sylvia while Papa and Mr. Leckie and my older sisters went to Yorkton for three days to celebrate Rosh Hashanah and for two days during the Yom Kippur holiday. Then when I was five, I went to Winnipeg with Papa for Rosh Hashanah. The following year and every year thereafter for a number of years, I joined Papa and Mr. Leckie in their annual trips to Yorkton, usually accompanied by my older sisters as well. Mama stayed home with Sylvia until she was about eight or nine; then both of them joined us. Our entire family continued this tradition until my older sisters moved to Winnipeg.

Although we always closed our store for the Jewish High Holy Days, Mr. Leckie left his open, with his son Norman in charge. Norman had not been brought up Jewish and, therefore, never observed any of the religious traditions or holidays that we did. I don't know if he considered himself Jewish or not. On the other hand, even though Mr. Leckie never made a fuss over any of the rituals, he had strong positive feelings about his heritage and never considered himself anything other than a Jew.

The first time I accompanied Papa and Mr. Leckie was when I was six and in the second grade. All my sisters had stayed home with Mama because Papa felt it was just too expensive to take the entire family to Yorkton. Since I was a boy and would have a bar mitzvah in another seven years, it was time to begin my Jewish education by associating with other Jews, and there was no better time to meet them than during *Yon Tif.* [The Jewish Holidays.]

I was shy and felt lonely. I didn't know many people in the packed synagogue except my Shnider relatives from Inglis, Manitoba, and their Shnider relatives in Yorkton and the Laskin family, who frequently visited us from Rose Valley, some eighty miles north and west of Sheho.

The Laskins were almost like cousins. Besides owning a general store, Bill Laskin also owned some land around Sheho which he rented out to local farmers for a share in the profits. He used to visit us in the fall, after the crops had been harvested. I liked the Laskins. They always made a fuss over me. But unlike my previous Rosh Hashanah spent in Winnipeg, this time almost nobody else paid much attention to me here in Yorkton.

Papa referred to the synagogue as *sheel*, while others called it *shule*. I wondered why the same word had two different pronunciations. Years later I learned that pronunciation of certain Jewish words depended on what part of Europe the Jews came from. Those from Poland or who had lived near the Polish border pronounced certain words with an "e," while others used an "o."

Papa hired Bill Finley to drive us to Yorkton. We arrived in the late afternoon and checked into the Yorkton Hotel. This was the first time I had stayed in a hotel. Our room had a dresser on top of which were two bars of soap, two large white china basins inside of which were two large white pitchers filled with water. The toilet was down the hall. In the morning, two smaller pitchers of hot water for sponging and shaving would be placed in the hallway next to our door. The room also had an electric light with a cord stretching down far enough for me to reach it. I liked pulling on it because every time I pulled the cord, the light would go on, and when I pulled again it would go off. I must have gotten on Papa's nerves because finally he said, "*Geneeg*." [enough]

After attending the first day's services of Rosh Hashanah early in the evening, we all went back to the home of Harry and Etta Shnider for their holiday supper. Harry Shnider, Uncle Abe's brother, owned the kosher butcher shop. Nobody went away from the table hungry. I don't remember much about her meal because I was such a fussy eater and was rarely hungry. Perhaps if I hadn't filled up on Etta Shnider's gourmet, mouth-watering strudel, I might have done justice to her feast. But how could a six year old boy resist that delicacy? The crust was so thin and delicate that I had to pick it up with tender loving care or it would flake off and crumble. Each small piece, filled with either apples or cherries, was just enough for a bite. That' s why I kept going back for more and more. I think I ate most of it. Although I have nothing but praise for Auntie Leachman and Aunt Bessie's strudel, Etta Shnider's strudel was in a class by itself. It was the best of the best, and I have never tasted anything nearly so good.

Yorkton's Shnider family included two children: Pearl, the same age as my cousin Maurice; and Mervin, about a year younger than my cousin Charlie. Since the Shnider kids were all first cousins, and since I was a first cousin of the Shnider kids from Inglis, we were therefore all related, either directly or indirectly. And because the entire Shnider family from Inglis also ate supper there, Rosh Hashanah turned out to be more than a religious holiday; it was also an extended family reunion.

After the late evening feast, Pearl, an excellent classical pianist, would play the piano, often followed by our cousin Myra. Then her brother Maurice would join in with his own rendition, jazzing it up with his own words. He couldn't play any piece straight—not even "God Save the King."

One of the highlights of visiting Yorkton was taking in a "talking picture." Sheho rarely had talking pictures. Sheho did not even have regularly scheduled silent movies, and the ones we occasionally saw must have been invented by Edison. Even when an enterprising traveling movie mogul occasionally tried his luck in Sheho by showing a silent film—or on a very special occasion a talking picture—in the town hall, for the exorbitant price of twenty cents for adults and ten cents for children, half of the kids tried to sneak in to see the cowboy film for free.

The plot was always the same. Roy Rogers (or some other cowboy) in a white western Stetson hat would be riding along on his white horse, strumming his guitar, minding his own business, until the bad guys wearing black Stetsons and riding black or brown horses would appear from behind some rocks and start shooting. Roy Rogers would take out his two six shooters and shoot back, and they would chase each other until one-by-one, all the bad guys in black hats had been shot dead and had fallen off their horses. Then Roy Rogers would put his two six shooters back in their holsters and continue riding along on his white horse Trigger, all the while strumming his guitar, as if nothing had happened. It was all in a day's work. The moral was clear. Don't screw around with Roy Rogers!

I didn't know there was any other kind of movie. So when we visited Yorkton, I was in for a treat. Yorkton's two movie theaters, the Roxy and the Princess, both showed talking pictures. The Princess, on a side street, showed double feature "B" films, some of them starring Roy Rogers and his horse Trigger. But the Roxy, right on Broadway, showed "A" movies, usually within a few months of their release from Hollywood. As Papa, Mr. Leckie, and I bid our goodnights to everyone at the Shniders, I excitedly bragged to Mervin that we were going to see a movie at the Roxy Theater. It wasn't every year that I got to see a movie. I was as thrilled as if I had tickets to the World Series.

Mervin seemed shocked. Do you know what they're showing?" he said. I shook my head. "THE INVISIBLE MAN!" he gasped. "It's a real horror movie. It's so scary, you'll have to cover your eyes. You won't be able to sleep tonight."

He was right. The main character was the most frightening person I had ever seen. He wore dark sunglasses over the bandages which were wrapped around his face and his head. Only he didn't have a face or a head. When he unwrapped the bandages, there was nothing underneath. His head was invisible. All we could see were the bandages falling to the floor. And when he took off his shirt, again there was nothing underneath. Only the shirt, slowly fluttering to the ground. And the same with his pants. Underneath all his clothes there was nothing. He really was invisible. I was terrified. I covered my eyes. Through an experiment, he had accidentally become invisible, but he could not reverse the process. So he took advantage of this situation and began to commit all kinds of crimes without being caught. The police tried to capture him. But how can you capture somebody you can't even see? Finally a farmer discovered some hay moving all by itself in his barn and notified the police. They set fire to the barn, and as soon as they saw new footprints on the snow leading away from the barn, they began shooting their revolvers in the direction of the footprints. When the footprints stopped, they knew they had shot the invisible man. Then, as he lay dying, he finally became visible and looked like anyone else. Not like a mummy all wrapped up in bandages. But I was still scared. I remember I was so scared that I gripped Papa's hand and held on to it tightly, all the way back to the Yorkton Hotel. That night I cuddled up to him as closely as I could. But I still couldn't sleep. Every time I looked at Papa's white shirt hanging over the chair, I was afraid. I was sure the invisible man was in the room.

The following year we went to another movie at the Roxy. I was now getting spoiled. Two movies in two years. The movie was *A Star is Born*, starring Frederick March and Janet Gaynor. Mervin Shnider said it was one of the first movies to be filmed in color. Unbelievable! A talking picture in color! What next?

The ceiling of the Roxy Theater was painted black with faint white blinking stars that spread from end to end. It looked sort of real. But not quite.

The movie began with the red flashing lights of a telephone switchboard in a Hollywood studio and the narrator telling us how many telephone calls the studio gets every minute or so from young girls hoping to become movie stars. Janet Gaynor played one of these girls who got lucky. And Frederick March played an older actor whose star was fading. He had problems. He drank too much. So, to solve his problems, he eventually waded into the ocean as the sun was setting, and he just kept on going, deeper and deeper toward the setting sun. I guess he couldn't swim. Or maybe he didn't want to swim. Anyway, he just kept on going as the phony red sun was setting over the dark blue ocean, casting a purple hue over the gentle green waves that lapped at the light brown sand beneath his snow white legs. The colors were interesting. Like my own water colors in Miss Griffith's room when she would ask us to use our imagination and paint something that looked real.

Anyway, he kept on going into the ocean, deeper and deeper, farther and farther away, toward the setting sun—not like the ones we have during the long daylight hours in Saskatchewan. No! Hollywood cannot possibly reproduce that spectacle. It's unique. A Saskatchewan summer sunset takes forever and ever to sink, then is followed by a long pinkish twilight that slowly darkens into magenta, then purple, and gradually becomes dark blue and gets darker and darker and lasts until eleven o'clock, when it slowly becomes a midnight blue that gradually turns into black; and eventually the sky is as black as black can be, and you can see millions and millions of bright stars in every direction, and the milky way lining the sky like a long faint gray cloud high above, stretching north as far as you can see, and the Northern Lights dancing their magic dance like stardust sprinkled across the sky all the way to the northern horizon, and dozens of shooting stars like huge flares that streak across the sky, then disappear just before they land in Wunder's field. And you don't have to pay to see this unbelievable display. It's free. That's the way the summer sun sets in Sheho, Saskatchewn.

But not in Hollywood. No. Frederick March waded into the ocean toward a Hollywood sunset that suddenly ended over the ocean, followed abruptly by the title "The End." That was my introduction to Technicolor.

Another vivid memory I have of my first or second Rosh Hashanah in Yorkton was the crab apple tree that grew in Shnider's back yard and the trouble some of us kids got into because of that tree. Following Rosh Hashanah services which ended around one or two o'clock in the afternoon, Papa, Mr. Leckie, and I would join the Shniders for dinner, after which the adults would visit with one another while we kids played outside. The Laskin family would come over to visit; and since their two younger sons, Shimon and Mervin, were about the same age as my cousins Maurice and Charlie, and just a little older than Mervin Shinder, they were all quite congenial. That tree fascinated us. It was the first fruit tree we had ever seen except for chokecherry or gooseberry bushes, which really aren't trees. But this was a really big fruit tree. And it had real crab apples on it. A few near the bottom, but a whole bunch near the top. Shimon and his younger brother, Mervin, decided to show the rest of us how many crab apples they could pick by climbing the tree. The fact that they were wearing their annual new suits which their parents had just bought them especially for the Jewish Holidays didn't enter their minds. About halfway up the tree, their pants got caught in the branches, and by the time they got down, their brand new suits were torn. But they had proved their point. They could sure climb a tree. And they got more crab apples then anyone else.

A year or two later my older sisters joined us in celebrating the Jewish High Holidays in Yorkton, and a few years later, when Mama and Sylvia also joined us, it made our celebration complete. I no longer felt lonely. In fact, I now felt quite at home since I had gradually come to know all the kids and most of their parents. I felt as if I was really part of a happy, extended family. And indeed I was.

Our family and Mr. Leckie all stayed at the Yorkton Hotel, the men in one room, Mama and my sisters in the other. The Shnider family from Inglis stayed at the upscale Balmoral Hotel. My cousins boasted that they had a room with a bath, and when I looked at them skeptically, they took me there. It was true. A real bathtub—right in their room. Amazing! I learned later that Uncle Abe had been a personal friend of the owners—Harry and Sam Bronfman— as well as a long-time personal friend of the manager, and regularly sold the hotel carloads of cordwood for heating. To return the favor, Uncle Abe always patronized his good customer. I never dreamed that I would ever be able to afford to stay in a hotel that had a room with a bath. Talk about luxury!

Our family got up at our usual hour, and before nine o'clock we were all eating breakfast in the Boston Cafe. My sisters and I had cocoa and toast, while Papa, Mama, and Mr. Leckie had toast, marmalade, and tea with lemon. The bill totaled almost two dollars—almost as much as a hundred pound sack of flour. Tips were out of the question. Then, with Papa, Mama, and Mr. Leckie carrying their prayer books and *talesim* [prayer shawls] in a purple velvet bag, we all went to *sheel* [the synagogue].

I loved that purple velvet bag. It looked just like the purple velvet bag that I had seen Uncle Abe take off a brand new bottle of Seagrams Crown Royal whiskey the night before. Only the writing on the bag of Seagrams whiskey was different. I asked Mr. Leckie if the owners of Seagrams Crown Royal also made the Jewish prayer bags. He said "no" and guessed that they had probably copied their own bag from the Jewish prayer bags which had been around for a lot longer than Seagrams.

He added that the Bronfman brothers, Harry and Sam, had started their business in Yorkton by bootlegging whiskey to the United States and had become so successful that they were now multi-millionaires and owned Seagrams. Papa said "*Geneeg.*" [Enough] "We shouldn't talk about such things on *Yon Tif*, not when we are on our way to *sheel.*"

The white painted wooden sheel with its purple Star of David etched on its east-facing glass window was located between Broadway, Yorkton's main street, and Yorkton Collegiate, on the west side of Betts Avenue, just a few blocks north of the home of Harry and Etta Shnider. We entered the synagogue through its south side door—the only one—which happened to face a vegetable garden behind a two-story private home. In the fall of the year during our Jewish holidays, all that remained in the garden were some small potatoes, leftovers from the harvest, and several large sunflower stalks with huge heads of ripened sunflower seeds waiting to be picked. The owners of this private home were good neighbors. They never bothered anyone. And they were quiet—as quiet as synagogue mice. In fact as far as Hymie Cooperman (one of us kids) was concerned, they were too quiet. Something should be done about that. He would see to it.

After climbing the steps of the synagogue, we entered a large hallway whose walls contained a row of metal coat hangers, next to which a wide wooden stairway led up to the second floor. This floor was divided in two: the western half for *chayder* [Hebrew school] for those youngsters who attended in the late afternoon, and the eastern half for the women who would come to pray during the High Holy Days or on other special occasions. The women sat in four rows facing each other around a U-shaped balcony, which overlooked the main floor of the synagogue seating the men and their sons.

During the High Holy Days, the balcony was full. From here the women, all wearing hats or head scarves, could look down upon their husbands. The men also had their heads covered, by hats or caps, and were draped in large *talesim*. They sat with their sons in long wooden benches, row upon row, separated by a wide aisle leading east toward the *bimah*, behind which was the Ark of the Covenant containing the holy scrolls—the Torah. [The *bimah*, sometimes called the Jewish altar, is the platform supporting the reading table used when chanting or reading portions of the Torah and Prophets.] So, whenever they prayed, they faced east, in the direction of Jerusalem, the holy city from whence the Jews had been forced to flee three thousand years ago. And ever since, the Jews have faced the East while praying and have uttered these words: "Next Year in Jerusalem."

The men looked up with pride at their wives and daughters and at other wives, occasionally waving at both. But they could not sit together. It was forbidden. The different sexes are segregated while praying in an orthodox synagogue. God is a man. Men are superior. Therefore, they must not commingle with their inferiors. Or perhaps they must not be led into temptation. Or perhaps they cannot concentrate on the prayers with their wives besides them. Or perhaps the women seated above the men are actually superior since they can look down upon the men. I never did figure it out. And so our parents prayed in Hebrew for long hours on end, heaping praise upon praise upon the Almighty, over and over and over and over again, in the language of our biblical forefathers, a language that nobody except the rabbi understood. It was called *dahvening*. And it went on forever and ever and ever and ever. And ever. And even longer. The Jews must be God's chosen people. He chose them to try their patience by making them suffer every year during Rosh Hashanah and Yom Kippur. There they sit all day long, on hard wooden benches in a stuffy synagogue, droning on and on in a language they don't understand. Yet nobody complains. They are a patient people. And patience is a virtue. No wonder God chose them. Can you blame Him? No wonder they have survived.

Now and then some of the men left their seats and wandered into the hallway. There they discussed the problems of making a living or other problems, both local, national, and international. As the hours dragged on, more and more men came out and joined in different discussions. When two Jews get together, there are at least three different answers to a question. Multiply that by fifty, and you have a Jewish discussion. But there is always a *maven*—an authority. And so, even though there may be 150 different answers, the *maven* knows the right one. Take my word for it.

Although I sat with Papa and Mr. Leckie for part of the morning, it wasn't long before I discovered much more interesting things to do than squirming on a hard bench while watching Papa and the rest of the men chant and mumble something or other, occasionally in unison, that sounded like a swarm of angry hornets coming after me because I had knocked down their nest.

The wooden stairway leading to the second floor was wide enough for two kids to race up or down, not only to see who was the fastest but more importantly, to see who could make the most noise stomping on the steps. It was Hymie Cooperman who discovered that it takes a certain skill to stomp on wooden steps while wearing brand new shoes. But that was only half the fun. When the noise got loud enough—and that didn't take too long—Mr. Harry Ferman would come out, his face beet red with embarrassment or rage—I couldn't tell which—and shout: "SCHCH! SCHCH! SCHCH!" Then, just in case we couldn't understand what "SCHCH" meant, he explained the term in English: "QUIET! THAT'S ENOUGH! DON'T MAKE SO MUCH NOISE!" His translation was quite accurate. And effective. Until we got bored.

Now if I asked you how much more trouble can a group of kids get into in a synagogue on Rosh Hashanah or Yom Kipper, you would probably answer, "Not much!" Wrong!

Upstairs was a gold mine. That was where we kids spent most of our time after we had gotten tired of irritating not only Mr. Ferman but other powerful members of the Yorkton congregation while the rest of the members prayed or took time out for a Jewish discussion involving, of course, the *maven*. After Mr. Ferman was worn out from SCHUSCHING us kids (and from *dahvening*), he would either initiate a discussion or join one. And guess who was the *maven*? At least he was an informed one. He could recite facts and statistics and tables like nobody I had ever heard before or since. I liked to watch his "discussions." They sure beat watching Papa and the rest of the men *dahvening*.

Anyway, on the western half of the second floor—our gold mine—was a large window facing due south—right into the blinding late morning Saskatchewan sun. Now it so happened that right across from this large window was the two-story house whose occupants were much too quiet for Hymie Cooperman. He liked to shake things up. Nobody should be that quiet. While rummaging through a large box of junk on the second floor, Hymie had discovered a perfectly good mirror, about a foot square, that could be held in his hands and easily reflect the sun's rays directly into the windows of the house facing the synagogue. Now since these windows of the house faced north, and the sun does not shine from the north, Hymie reasoned that its rooms had suffered from lack of direct sunlight ever since the house had been built. This discovery was too good to be true. He would show those occupants what they had missed all these years.

Like a burglar who has just come upon the keys to the bank's safety deposit vault, Hymie grinned sardonically as he focused the mirror at the sun, then slanted the reflected sunlight into the kitchen window below. He carefully moved the beam until he found and then focused on his target—a woman. Like a rabbit at night caught in the glare of headlights, the woman was instantly trapped in this blinding floodlight. She covered her eyes then screamed. Hymie was ecstatic. He continued to focus for about a minute then turned the beam on the other windows, slowly searching the house for other victims. He was out for another kill.

Suddenly a commotion erupted below. The woman had entered the synagogue, shouting, "Somebody upstairs is shining a mirror in my window. If you don't stop shining that light in my house I'm going to call the police." Hymie hid the mirror and we all hurried away. The girls ran into the next room to join their mothers, while we boys scurried downstairs and then through the doorway on the left to the synagogue, where we innocently took our seats besides our fathers. Soon word about the commotion filtered into the main room of the synagogue, and in between continual dahvening to the Almighty, the investigation began.

"Who was shining that mirror?"

"What mirror?"

The *dahvening* continued only momentarily.

"Upstairs. The mirror upstairs. Who was shining the mirror upstairs?"

"Upstairs? What mirror? I didn't see any mirror upstairs."

More *dahvening*, then, "Somebody upstairs was shining a mirror in the window next door. Who was it?"

"Upstairs. I've been outside. Now I'm here. You can see. I didn't see anybody upstairs."

"It wasn't you?"

"Of course not."

"It was Hymie Cooperman, wasn't it?"

"Hymie Cooperman? I haven't seen Hymie Cooperman since early this morning. I haven't seen any mirror."

The investigation was useless. Nobody had been upstairs. Nobody had seen a mirror. Nobody knew anything. Yet everybody suspected Hymie Cooperman. But how could one prove it? Unless one could prove it, he was innocent. But everybody *knew* it had been Hymie Cooperman who had shone the mirror into the window next door. Everybody—especially his father. He didn't need proof. He *knew*.

Hymie Cooperman, an exceptionally "cute" boy with milk white skin and curly red hair, was the adopted and only child of Mr. and Mrs. Cooperman. He had a magnificent boy's soprano voice and had won many local singing contests. In fact, he was constantly being compared to the well known Hollywood child singing star Bobby Breen, and was known as "Yorkton's Bobby Breen." His mother babied him and doted over him, while his father tried to balance this loving attention with stern reprimands and the occasional slap on the arm each time his son got into trouble. Hymie loved playing mischievous pranks on anyone, including his parents. He had once telephoned a large order to a grocery market and had asked for it to be delivered to his parents' home. "We never ordered this," protested his parents when the order arrived. "But somebody did," explained the delivery man. "Take it back," said Mr. Cooperman, "and I'll make sure it won't happen again." It didn't. But there were other pranks. Hymie had learned his antics from his favorite movie idols—the Marx Brothers—and had modeled his behavior after what he had seen on the screen. He would stick a match between the sole and leather of somebody's shoe when that person wasn't looking, then light the match, to give the victim a "hotfoot," just as the Marx brothers had done. And he loved an audience. It therefore didn't take Mr.

Cooperman long to find out who the person was behind the mirror. "Sit down!" he commanded, as he slapped his son on the arm. "And stay here!"

But Hymie could not sit still. Within a few minutes he was back upstairs looking for more trouble. He had cut off a large ripened sunflower head, one of the few left standing from the garden next door, and was sharing the seeds with a few of us kids who had joined him. There is nothing that compares to ripened sunflower seeds that have just been stolen from a garden next to a synagogue on Rosh Hashanah. What next? God only knows.

Suddenly, from the main floor of the synagogue below, we heard a blast that sounded like the horn of Mr. Darling's 1922 Dodge was shorting out because of bad wiring or a dead battery. ("UG" Long pause. "UH " Shorter pause. "OO-00 -AH.")

There goes the rabbi blowing the *"shofar,"* said Hymie. "He's almost as good as Harry James. Listen to him."

Again we heard the blast from the *shofar*. [curved ram's horn] The short-circuit wiring had been repaired. "UH. OO-OO—AH" We all stampeded downstairs to see the rabbi hold the *shofar* up to his lips and blow with all his breath. Harry James and Tommy Dorsey and even Benny Goodman would have been proud of him. The battery of Mr. Darling's 1922 Dodge had been completely recharged, and the blast from the horn was loud and clear—better than ever—with no breaks in between. "UH -OOOO-AH."

The rabbi proudly blew the *shofar* several times that morning, signifying the beginning of a new year. His final blast, around one o'clock in the afternoon—his best of the day—marked the end of the first day's service of Rosh Hashanah.

After our parents put back their *talesim* and prayer books in the purple velvet bags, they gathered in the hall and visited with each other for quite a while, and wished everyone *"Geet Yon Tif"* [Happy Holiday] before slowly leaving the synagogue. Since Yorkton itself had approximately thirty-five Jewish families, who were all present, and another ten or more had come in for these holidays, the crowd numbered approximately two hundred. We all slowly walked down Betts Avenue. Nobody drove his car on the high holidays. Driving was considered work and, therefore, it simply wasn't done. Besides, Yorkton, population five thousand wasn't that big. Walking three or four long city blocks never hurt anybody, and no one was in a hurry. Thus, the crowd, taking up an almost entire city block on one side of the street, just ambled along. It looked like one long mass of humanity slowly moving along Betts Avenue.

Dinner in the late afternoon at the home of the Yorkton Shnider family was another feast, after which there was another get-together, this time with very close mutual friends of everyone—Bill and Sarah Laskin and their family from Rose Valley.

I had always thought Papa was fat. Short and fat. Uncle Abe, however was fatter. Taller and fatter. But Bill Laskin was really fat. He was corpulent. He really had a *boch*. [belly]. We called it a "corporation." Years later I learned that because my parents' generation in Europe lived on little more than a starvation diet, they made up for it in Canada as soon as they could afford to. Perhaps that's why they loved to feast. And being fat was an obvious sign of wealth. It was something to be proud of, like owning a big business—a corporation. Perhaps that's why we called a big belly a "corporation."

Bill Laskin had married Sarah Dachas from Yorkton and had settled in Rose Valley, a frontier village on a minor railway spur line about eighty-five miles northwest of Sheho. Every Rosh Hashanah and Yom Kippur, the Laskin family would drive back to Yorkton, where they would stay with Mrs. Laskin's family—her mother, sister, and two brothers. The trip involved driving almost fifty miles over dirt—not gravel—roads, until they linked up with Highway 14, the gravel covered road full of pot holes running west and east, through Sheho to Yorkton. But at least one could not get stuck on this gravel road. However, the fifty miles from Rose Valley to Highway 14 was practically an all day's journey, involving several unexpected side trips in-and-out of the ditch. At night it was dangerous. On one occasion, Mr. Laskin's car struck a cow, killing it. He had to report the accident to the Mounties. "There was another car coming toward us and he didn't dim his lights, " he explained. I was "blindfolded." The Mounties took him at his word.

Bill Laskin was one of the more progressive general merchants in our part of Saskatchewan. As well as stocking groceries, footwear, and yard goods, he carried a few men's and ladies' suits and coats, whose sales generated a greater profit than the entire profit on a pair of overalls, a pair of boots, five yards of cotton broadcloth, and a sack of flower—all of this combined.

But no country merchant in all of Saskatchewan and Manitoba could compare his store to Norman Croll's. He did not sell groceries or yard goods. He sold ladies' furs, men's and ladies' clothing and footwear. He stocked hundreds of men's suits in all sizes. And they weren't cheap. Although his store was one of the very few Jewish owned stores in Yorkton which remained open on the Jewish High Holy Days, the Croll family always attended services.

On the way to the synagogue one morning, Mr. Leckie, who usually ordered his clothes from Eaton's mail order catalogue, decided he needed a new shirt. He entered the store and bought one, then proudly boasted that it was an Arrow shirt. We also sold dress shirts in our store for $1.25 each. Eaton's dress shirts retailed from $1.15 up to $2.95. But the lowest priced Arrow shirt at Croll's was $3.50. Papa and I couldn't understand why he would pay so much for a shirt when he could have bought one from us at our cost—an even dollar. But then if he had bought a shirt from us, he couldn't brag about how much he had paid.

Bragging about how much one had paid for a shirt or a pair of shoes or a hat or a suit—or anything—was the thing to do. All the young men wore green suits, brown shoes, and green or tan Stetson or Biltmore fedora style hats, with a bright feather sticking out of the wide headband. Green suits with cable stripes and twenty-two inch bottoms on the pants held up by braces were the height of fashion in the mid and late 1930s.

I don't remember exactly what year it was during Rosh Hashanah services, when I was sitting with my cousin Maurice Shnider, along with Shimon Laskin and Kenny Croll, while our parents were *dahavening*. I must have been about ten or eleven then because it had only been about two or three years since Maurice had had his bar mitzvah. That would mean both Maurice and Shimon would have been about fifteen or sixteen, and Kenny a couple of years older. They were discussing the new fall styles. They all wore the same colors, green and brown. "My suit is double breasted," said Shimon." Then he proudly added, "It's made by Walter Blue. It cost $35.00." Thirty-five dollars was an enormous amount to pay for a man's suit then. The suit may have retailed for that amount at an upscale clothing store like Croll's, but the actual wholesale cost would have been about ten dollars less, and the cost direct from the factory would have been about twenty dollars. There was no way the Laskins ever paid retail for anything. Never. They weren't stupid. But who cared about little details? It's the impression that counts. He had thrown down the gauntlet and was ready to duel. He waited for a reply. He looked at Maurice Shnider as if to say, "I dare you to accept my challenge."

Maurice felt obliged to answer. In a low timid voice filled with humility, he said, "Mine cost $30.00."

One down and one more to go, thought Shimon. He waited for Kenny Croll to respond. And he waited.

Kenny Croll wore very expensive suits. He spent most of his time after school in his father's store and knew exactly how much men's clothing cost and how much it sold for. He glanced at their suits, then turned away. Unimpressed, he remained silent.

Although the years seem to blend into each other as I try to recall my first few Rosh Hashanahs, I remember wishing everyone "*Geet Yon Tif*" at the conclusion of the second day's services, then as on the previous day, joining the entire Shnider family for dinner. Our visit, though, was short. We had checked out of the Yorkton Hotel in the morning and had taken our suit cases to the Shnider home, for we would be returning to Sheho as soon as Bill Finley came to take us back. When he did arrive, he was in no hurry because both he and Uncle Abe had been cowboys together during their bachelor days. Finally, however, it was time to go. A new beginning to a new year.

YOM KIPPUR

A week later we all returned for Yom Kippur, the Jewish day of atonement—the holiest day of the year. This was the day that practicing Jews around the world would fast from sundown to sundown for twenty-four hours. That meant not eating or drinking anything at all. This self-in-

flicted punishment was a symbolic atonement for the sins they had committed during the year, while asking God to forgive them.

Just before sundown, the adult Jews at our table, including everyone
who had had a bar mitzvah, as well as grown-up females, all ate heartily
and drank plenty of water because this food and drink would be the last
they would taste for twenty-four hours. I remember holding my elders in
awe. They were heroic. Twenty four hours without any food or water at
all! How could they stand it?

After this feast—just after sundown—we all went to *sheel* for the
beginning of the Yom Kippur service which was ushered in by the
cantorial singing of *Kol Nidre*. [All Our Vows] Mr. Rosenblattt, who
owned a dry cleaning plant and tailoring shop, had a beautiful tenor
voice—the best voice in the area. He was our cantor—the one best qualified to sing this most holy of holy songs: the *Kol Nidre*. The synagogue
was packed. The men with their sons, the women with their daughters,
all stood as one when he began singing this solemn and most moving
lyrical prayer, pleading with God to cancel all the vows, oaths, and promises which we had made to Him from Last Yom Kippur to this Yom
Kippur and were not able to fulfill. Unaccompanied by any musical instrument, his voice, filled with emotion, was music itself, as it rose and
fell and resonated throughout the synagogue. We all stood spellbound.
Nobody stirred. Although very few of us understood the meaning of the
foreign words written centuries before, and now sung by Cantor
Rosenblattt, the emotion was universal. There was only one song that
could evoke such a feeling emotion in all of us. The *Kol Nidre*. [9]

Although *Kol Nidre* was sung three times, it lasted only for a short
while. Perhaps ten or fifteen minutes. Nobody looked at his watch. Then
it was over. And the spell was broken. The prayers continued, with each
person asking God's forgiveness not only for his own personal transgressions, but for the sins of all mankind. And so it went for the remainder of the service on Yom Kippur night.

Although boys were not required to fast until after they had reached
their thirteenth birthday, I decided to fast when I was only ten. I remember leaving the synagogue after services that night with my family and
Mr. Leckie around ten o'clock and thinking to myself: "It's not too bad.

I'm not hungry at all. I could use a drink of water, though. But I'm not supposed to drink anything. I'll wait until morning and see how I feel."

The next morning I still wasn't hungry. (I never ate much when I was a kid.) But I sure was thirsty. And I had a foul taste in my mouth. Maybe if I brushed my teeth, that taste would go away. But that would mean putting water in my mouth and possibly swallowing some, thus breaking the fast. So I gave up the idea of brushing my teeth even though I knew my breath would smell bad.

When I got to the synagogue, almost everybody had halitosis. It was awful. Some of the kids who were over thirteen admitted that they had brushed their teeth that morning, but were still fasting. That argument didn't seem too logical to the rest of us whose tongues were so dry we could hardly spit.

"That's not fasting. You broke your fast."

"No I didn't. I never drank any water. I just brushed my teeth. There's nothing in the Torah about not brushing my teeth on Yom Kippur."

"But you put water in your mouth. You must have swallowed some. Maybe only a few drops. That's like drinking."

"No it isn't. I never swallowed any water. Not even a drop. I spit it all out. Every single drop."

"Every single drop? How do you know?"

"I know! I know! I know how much water I put in my mouth to brush my teeth. And I know how much I spit out. All of it. Every single drop. So I never broke my fast. But I wish I could. I'm so thirsty, I can hardly stand it."

"Don't talk about being thirsty. It just makes it worse."

"Only nine more hours to go. Then I can drink all the water I want."

"Nine more hours Don't think about it. Don't talk about it. It just makes it worse."

"Are you hungry?"

"Of course I'm hungry. Aren't you hungry?"

"Not much. Just a little bit. But I'm sure thirsty. Only nine more hours."

"Nine more hours isn't bad. We've already fasted for fifteen hours. Nine more isn't too bad."

"Only eight-and-a-half hours more for me. We ate early."

There wasn't much else to argue about, so we decided to join our parents who were *dahvening*. My father periodically kept striking himself very lightly on his chest. He would mumble in Hebrew while simultaneously making a gesture of beating his chest. It seemed so strange. I asked Mr. Leckie why. He said it was meant to symbolize self-inflicted punishment for the sins he had committed during the past year. I thought fasting was punishment enough, especially not being able to have even a sip of water. Not even a drop. Only eight hours more to go.

But why was *I* punishing myself? I hadn't committed any sins. At least none that were serious enough to warrant punishing myself by fasting. No! I was fasting for another reason. To prove to myself and to everyone that although I was only a little ten-year-old scrawny kid, I could be as tough as any thirteen-year-old, or even as tough as any grownup in the entire synagogue. I would show everyone that I had at least as much perseverance and stamina as any of the adults. That's what counted. Perseverance. One could overcome all kinds of deficiencies and handicaps just by persevering. It could make up for a lot of things. So although I was now beginning to feel hunger pangs and was dying for a drink of water, I did not break my fast. "What time is it?" Papa pulled out his pocket watch, wound it once or twice, glanced at it, then returned it to his vest. "*Tvonntsig minute noch tzvelf.*" [Twenty minutes after twelve] Let's see. I counted on my fingers. Six hours and forty minutes left.

The sounds of the *dahavening* had softened almost to an inaudible mumble, punctuated occasionally by a recognizable mumble. Gone was the exuberance of the night before. The enthusiasm with which Cantor Rosenblatt had begun the Yom Kippur service permeating the entire congregation had evaporated. There was nothing left. After sitting on a hard bench all morning, straining one's voice, counting the hours until one can break his fast, how can a half-starved person whose parched throat is dying from thirst with no relief for another 6 1/2 hours be enthusiastic about anything? No way. It was time for recess. It was time to give the cantor a break. It was time to give everyone a break. No more *dahvening*, no more chest-beating for another hour and-a-half. No more nothing. But no cheating. No eating. No drinking. Nothing must enter the mouth. Cigarettes excluded. As long as you don't swallow the tobacco. It was time to congregate and visit. It was also time to go home to rest. Especially for the women. They looked pale.

Their husbands came prepared. They brought out smelling salts. "Here. Take a sniff. You'll feel better."

"No. I'm all right. Just a little dizzy. Just a little hungry. Maybe a little thirsty. My throat is so dry, I can hardly speak. I sure wish I could drink something."

"Here. Smell this. You'll feel better."

"No, it's too strong. Maybe I'll feel better this afternoon."

"You should take these smelling salts now. It keeps you awake."

"I'll be awake this afternoon when I get back. I'm going home to lie down now. I've got a headache. I'll be back in a couple hours."

"Maybe you should break your fast. Drink some water. Eat some bread. God will forgive you. You're not supposed to fast if you're sick. God doesn't want you to become sick."

"I'm not sick. I'm just dizzy and I've got a bad headache and I'm kind of hungry and I'm real thirsty. But I'm not sick."

One by one, about one-third of the women in the congregation, especially the older ones, gave up the fast. When they returned, after two o'clock, their cheeks were bright and their voices strong. But the women who continued to fast looked like ghosts. They could barely speak.

Some of the men, especially the older ones, had also dropped out. But Cantor Rosenblatt and Rabbi Eisenstein were up at the *bimah*, *dahvening* away, with renewed vigor in their voices, leading the congregation down the home stretch, with only 5 1/2 hours to go. My father who was a *kohayn*, supposedly a descendent of Moses' brother Aaron and, therefore, a member of the highest ranking Hebrew tribe, had also been up to the *bimah*. But for most of the afternoon, he paced himself, *dahvening* and occasionally gesturing toward his chest.

Ever so slowly, the hours ticked by. Every now and then Cantor Rosenblatt's voice began to break and to fade, as did the other voices.

Only three hours to go. They paced themselves to conserve their strength and their voices. Two hours. I was really hungry now. I didn't know which was worse—my hunger or my thirst. I spent most of the remaining time out in the hall or upstairs. Time seemed to stand still. One-and-a -half hours left. I returned to sit with my father and Mr. Leckie for the final hour. It took forever. Then Rabbi Eisenstein took out the *shofar*—the ram's horn—and began to blow. [10] The first note cracked. He seemed to be out of breath. He waited, took a deep breath, and blew that *shofar* so hard, it sounded like a blast from the horn of Mr. Darling's 1922 Dodge. Again and again. It shook the whole building and woke up the entire congregation. I had never seen such elation. Everyone was ecstatic. The High Holy Days were over. Yom Kippur had come to an end. Now we could all drink as much water as *we* wanted and make real pigs of ourselves at the supper feast.

I had proved that I could fast with the best of them. I proved it again the following year, and the year after that, when I was twelve. But after I was thirteen and had celebrated my bar mitzvah and was expected to fast, I gave up that custom. I reasoned that I had not committed any major sins but only few very minor ones. I had not eaten any ham, I had not even stolen or eaten any chocolate bars during Passover, I had not eaten meat on milk dishes, nor had I drunk milk with meat or even immediately afterward; I had not yet married a *shiksa*, nor had I committed any crime except stealing a cigar from the store and trying to smoke it, causing me to vomit so badly that I never touched one again. I was almost perfect. Virtually without sin. So I never fasted that year. Or the year after. Or the year after that. Well, that's not exactly true. I have always fasted in between meals—except for snacks. And God has punished me. Today, I'm thirty pounds overweight and find it impossible to lose that weight. That's punishment enough. Why should I punish myself further?

But I still miss those wonderful autumn days when all of us Jews gathered together in Yorkton, and all of us in our own way celebrated the Jewish High Holy Days of Rosh Hashona and Yom Kippur. I miss those wonderful days—when I was young and innocent and we lived in a different world.

CHAPTER THIRTEEN
Summer Holidays In Inglis, Manitoba

Southern California is a Mecca for tourists from all over the world, many of whom spend much of their time fishing, sunbathing, swimming, and body-board surfing at my favorite beach—Seal Beach. Over the years I have had the pleasure of talking with many of them, not only the adults, but their children as well. If there is one common denominator to be discovered, it's the pleasure of "going somewhere"—getting away from home. For youngsters, especially, nothing is as exciting as getting away from their parents and going someplace else. In this respect, not much has changed in the sixty plus years since I first went away from home during my summer holidays to visit my Shnider relatives in Inglis, Manitoba.

Our school year ended during the last week of June, often just a day or two before July 1st, Dominion Day. Since it didn't start again until August 26 (unless the 26th fell on a weekend), our summer holidays lasted almost two months. At first we were all delighted. Who wants to go to school? We could still swim in the creek that flowed through Wunder's field. But in a couple of weeks as the mud hole continued to dry up, we abandoned it to the bloodsuckers. Now there wasn't much to do, and life was boring. I mean *really* boring.

Until I was seven, I stayed home during the summer holidays while Etta and Merle, three and five years older than I respectively, went to visit the Shniders in Inglis, Manitoba. I envied them. Life was cruel. But my pleas to Mama and Papa fell on deaf ears. "You're too young now. But someday when you're old enough, you'll be able to go." And so, heartbroken, I would watch my older sisters carry their suitcases to the hotel where they would board the greyhound bus. They would be gone for two or three weeks, but it might as well as have been two or three months. I was lonely.

I didn't care to play with Sylvia, who was three years younger than I. You really can't play with a baby sister. She liked to play with her doll. It had rosy cheeks and snow white arms and legs, and one day when I was shaking hands with it, the whole arm came off and I got into trouble. That's why I left her alone. It's not fun to have a baby sister.

I don't remember much about summer holidays during my early years except that life was boring. I had some fun by balancing myself on an empty coal oil (kerosene) drum in our back yard and rolling backwards. I pretended I was in the circus. I petted our mother cat and fed her milk and scraps from the table. In the evening I watched Polly, our hired girl, milk our cow, Bossy. Then afterward when Bossy was led into our small outside corral next to our ice house, I counted how many times she chewed her cud before swallowing it. I spent part of the day in our store, digging out the eggs from the pails of wheat that the farmers had brought in, and then packing them in a crate to be picked up by Harry Soifer or other produce buyers from Melville. I kept an eye on some customers whom Papa told me to watch because they liked to steal when nobody was looking. I never caught them in the act. I sat on the cement step in front of the store with Papa and watched the sparrows sprinkle dust over themselves. Papa said they were doing that because they knew it would rain soon. It never rained. When he wasn't looking, I threw stones at the sparrows but never hit any. I picked weeds in our garden, but there were so many, I gave up. I set mouse traps in our flour shed every morning and by noon proudly showed Papa how many I had caught. I asked Papa for a nickel every afternoon and then went to the Elite Cafe for an ice cream cone. But I was always alone. Except for Howard Tansley.

Howard was my closest buddy, next to Walter Lys. He was one year ahead of me in school and the tallest kid in class except for Eddie Grumetza. Almost every day Howard would come over to our home, rolling a tire, and I would accompany him, taking turns rolling the tire until I had enough of that tire. Or we would play checkers. Or snakes and ladders. Howard liked to play those kinds of games. But I found them boring. Maybe that's why I usually lost. I was dying a slow, natural death from boredom, but nobody cared. The whole world was against me. It's not easy to spend summer holidays at home when you're five, and it gets worse by the time you're six.

Then one day when I was seven, just after Sheho's sports day, which was always held on July 12, Papa said, "We're sending you to Inglis with Merle and Etta." That's exactly what he said. There were no qualifications like "Be a good boy," or "Eat all the food on your plate; the children in Europe are starving." I was seven and had grown up. I was going to visit the Shniders in Inglis. How lucky can a boy get!

The trip was uneventful except for my recollection of crossing the border. I could read the sign now. "Welcome to Manitoba." I no longer considered Manitoba a strange land. But I still thought about the dividing line—the boundary—between Saskatchewan and Manitoba. Whose land was that? And *exactly* where did Saskatchewan end and Manitoba begin? I was two years older now, about to begin grade three, but I still didn't know the answer. I didn't know the answer to a lot of things. I wondered if I ever would.

After getting off the bus in Russell, we were driven to Inglis by Jack Malinsky, a very close friend of the Shniders. When we reached Inglis late in the late afternoon, the sun was still high in the west. I was glad we had finally arrived. Aunt Bessie and Uncle Abe looked the same as they had two years ago. They hugged my sisters and me and kissed us and made a big fuss over us, just like the last time. And they patted me on my head and said "Look how you've grown." Maurice and Charlie were taller than they were the last time I saw them. And Charlie was still grinning like a Cheshire cat. They kissed my sisters and hugged me. Then they patted me on my head and said "Look how you've grown." That made me feel good. Like I was no longer a little boy. I felt sort of grown up. I knew I was going to have the best time I had ever had.

I was right. It started with Aunt Bessie's supper, the best I had ever tasted. She didn't have to say, "Eat; the children in Europe are starving." I was the one who was starving. So I ate all the food on my plate. I hoped that would make the children in Europe feel better.

The next morning I was treated to a whole cantaloupe for breakfast, in addition to all the brown sugar I wanted on top of my shredded wheat and milk. And Aunt Bessie even let me drink some coffee. No more Fry's cocoa and toast for me. I was now lapping it up in the land of luxury.

After breakfast I set three mouse traps in Uncle Abe's flour warehouse, and within a couple of hours I showed him my three trophies. I was rapidly acquiring a new reputation—Jackie the giant mouse killer. If I kept it up, I could eventually become a big game hunter. No doubt about it.

At noon Aunt Bessie served the best dinner I ever tasted to all of us. Unlike our family at home, the Shniders usually all ate dinner together because Uncle Abe had hired help who were able to look after the store in his absence. Besides his regular clerk Johnny Zrudlow, who had been with him over a year, Uncle Abe had recently hired Leo Leckie, Mr. Leckie's younger son.

Leo, along with his younger sister Ruth, had been taken to the Jewish Orphanage in Winnipeg immediately after their mother's death, where they had been reared since childhood and had received not only an excellent education through the Winnipeg Public Schools but also a first-rate Hebrew education at the orphanage. Upon Leo's graduation from high school, he immediately joined the Shnider family as a live-in clerk and Hebrew tutor for both Maurice and Charlie, since Maurice's bar mitzvah was now only nine months away, and Charlie's would follow two years later. After school in the late afternoon, Leo would spend about an hour teaching them the fundamentals required for their future day of glory—being "bar mitzvahed." During the summer holidays, however, his teaching schedule was shortened to allow them more free time to visit with my sisters and me.

Unlike Sheho, which was on an east-west transcontinental railway line with a train from each direction passing through daily, Inglis, smaller than Sheho, was a frontier village at the end of a spur line from Winnipeg, and was serviced only three times a week by the train, which arrived every Tuesday, Thursday, and Saturday evening. Those were exciting nights for everyone in and around Inglis because that was when everyone in the entire area came in to meet the train and to get the mail. Consequently, those were the busiest nights of the week for Uncle Abe and the other storekeeper in Inglis, who kept their stores open until ten o'clock then. So after supper on Tuesday, Thursday, and Saturday, my sisters and I joined the crowds who swarmed into Uncle Abe's store for their shopping or to exchange gossip with their neighbors.

Among the languages spoken by Uncle Abe and his customers, I recognized only English and Ukrainian, as well as Polish, which Mom sometimes spoke in our store. Another language, however, sounded something like Jewish but not quite, since I could understood only the odd word. I asked Charlie what language that was. He explained that Jewish was slightly similar to German, and since many of the customers were German, his father had mastered it. I also detected a strange language and asked Charlie what that was. He told me it was Rumanian, his father's native language. Inglis was a real melting pot. Its settlers had come from practically all over Europe.

Although Uncle Abe and Aunt Bessie spoke different languages to their customers, they otherwise almost always spoke English—even at home. They never spoke Jewish in the presence of their hired girl or Johnny Zrudlow. In fact, they hardly ever spoke Jewish. And unlike Mama and Papa and Auntie Bayla and Uncle Moishe, they spoke English without any trace of a Jewish accent.

Auntie Bayla was Papa and Aunt Bessie's oldest sister. She and her husband, Uncle Moishe, lived far away in Boston, on the Atlantic coast of the United States. I knew all about the United States. On our map in Miss Griffiths's room, it was green. It was not nearly as big as Canada, which was a huge red country, part of the mighty British Empire on which the sun never set. I was proud to belong to the British Empire because we had a king and queen—King George the Fifth and Queen Mary—and the British Empire included all those other red colored countries spread all over that big map which she unrolled over the blackboard when she taught us geography, then rolled up again when she was through. We were important because we belonged to the British Empire. Not like that little green country—the United States— which didn't even have a king or queen. Only a president whose name was Roosevelt. The United

States was below Canada. That meant it was south. Even though it was much smaller than Canada, it had a lot more people. They were called Americans. And they all spoke English—without accents—not Ukrainian or Jewish.

Auntie Bayla and Uncle Moishe were Americans. They had traveled by train all the way from Boston to visit her relatives in Canada. They had come first to Sheho and had stayed with us for almost a month, and then had traveled farther west to Guernsey, where they stayed for a few days with my Katz cousins before coming back to Sheho, and then traveling east to Inglis, the final leg of their journey before returning to Boston.

Auntie Bayla was short and plump and looked almost exactly like Aunt Bessie, except that she looked just a little bit older and wore dark rimmed glasses like Mama's, whereas Aunt Bessie wore rimless glasses like Papa's. Uncle Moishe was short and stocky and had a mustache. He spoke English better than Auntie Bayla and Mama and just a little bit better than Papa did. But not much better. I was surprised and disappointed because I thought all Americans spoke perfect English without accents. I now realized I didn't know everything about Americans. Maybe I shouldn't believe everything I had heard.

July was the month for strawberries. Some people grew their own. But since wild strawberries were everywhere, farmers would pick them right off the vines with worms still clinging to the fruit, and then bring pailfuls of fruit into the store for trade. Nothing tasted better than wild strawberries, even though some worms looked at you with disgust and squiggled as you separated them from their strawberries.

One day Maurice and Charlie invited me to come along with them to pick wild strawberries. Uncle Moishe, not wanting to be left out of the fun, asked if he could also come along. "It's hard work," said Maurice. " It's hot and we'll be gone all day."

"You think you're talking to an old man," said Uncle Moishe.

"I can keep up with you any day. I'll show you."

He showed us all right. He kept up with us for a while, but as the day grew hotter, Uncle Moishe began to sweat. I mean really sweat. First he took off his navy blue suit coat. (He always wore a navy blue suit.) Then he took off his vest. Then he took off his tie and unbuttoned his collar. Then he rolled up his shirt sleeves. And then he began to huff. And then he began to puff.

And then he began to huff and puff. And soon he put down his pail and sat down under a tree. He just sat there and watched us fill our pails with wild strawberries. And when we got home, Uncle Moishe went to bed early. He didn't even bother to eat his strawberries.

What I especially liked about Maurice and Charlie was the way they treated me. Like an equal. They took me with them when they went out of town to shoot gophers with their ".22" and even let me shoot the rifle myself. I don't remember if I actually hit any gophers, but it was pretty hard to miss them; they were everywhere. I had never seen so many gophers—not even in Wunder's Field. I thought Inglis was the gopher capital of the world.

Besides treating me like an equal, they liked to challenge me. "How'd you like to box Davy Hawkins?" they asked. "He's about your age and is the best boxer in town. His dad used to be a boxer and gives him boxing lessons. Nobody has ever beaten him."

Although I had never seen a boxing match and didn't know a left hook from a right cross or a jab from a roundhouse right, and had no idea how big or how heavy my opponent was, I immediately accepted. "Sure, I'll box him. I'll bet I can beat him."

When I saw how tall Davy was, I had second thoughts. But it was too late now. I was not a quitter. They laced on our boxing gloves, which were like pillows and just a little smaller than my head. Then they told us not to punch below the belt and said, "Go ahead."

Before Davy had time to start jabbing, I raced in and flayed away with both fists, like a buzz saw. He backed away, but I just kept coming, throwing punch after punch with both fists. Some of them even connected. But I don't think he ever hit me more than once. And that's all it took. One round. I was now the new featherweight boxing champion of Inglis.

Maurice especially liked to challenge me. He liked to run a mile every day. "See the stockyard, over there," he said. That's a half mile from here. So from here to there and back is a mile. Have you ever run a mile?"

"No, but I think I can."

"Wanna try?"

"Sure."

At first I began to run as fast as I could. I looked back and soon realized I was away ahead of him. He was simply jogging along, hardly moving at all. But he kept moving and I was almost out of breath. I felt like quitting but I was not a quitter. I would show him. So I slowed away down. He kept coming and was soon jogging alongside me. "Pace yourself," he said, "or you'll run out of steam." I paced myself and jogged just behind him. But I kept falling farther behind. He slowed down, I'm sure, on purpose. By the time we reached the stockyard, I was almost out of breath but realized I had already completed half the race. I was not about to quit now. I was determined to finish the race. So I slowed way down and just kept on jogging. Maurice had also slowed down and was now even with me. He kept jogging alongside me. We were both hardly moving. But we *were* moving. We kept coming closer and closer to Shnider's store, our starting point. It was now only a hundred yards or so away. I started to sprint. So did he. I wanted to win the race. We were both neck and neck. Then, with my remaining strength, and almost completely out of breath, I ran as fast as I could and reached our finish line before he did. I sat down on the steps in front of the store and panted. I could hardly catch my breath. Maurice reached the steps a few seconds later. "That was quite a race," he said. "I guess you won." He was not panting. In fact, he wasn't even the least bit out of breath.

Every day was an exciting new adventure for me. The only problem was there weren't enough days. Charlie had warned me. "This is your last week here. You'll be going home next week." But I didn't pay much attention. I still had another week left and I was having such a wonderful time. I never bothered to count the days. Then all of a sudden Aunt Bessie said, " I hope you've had a good time here. You'll be going home tomorrow." Before I realized what was happening, tears came to my eyes. I tried to control my feelings, but I couldn't help it and I began to sob. She held my head close to her and said, "Don't cry. You'll be back again next year." I ran into the bedroom and closed the door. I had tried to act as a grown up, and I didn't want her to see me cry like a child.

I had the strangest feeling the day my sisters and I arrived back in Sheho. Everything looked different, especially our back yard and our garden. The grass in our yard was much taller than it had been three weeks before. And so were the weeds. And so were the vegetables in our garden. They had sprung up as if overnight and were now ready to eat. I picked the pea pods right off the vine and split the shells and shoveled the whole thing into my mouth to save time. That was the fastest way to separate the peas from the pod. Then I spit out the pods and devoured those deliciously sweet tender peas. I was supposed to pick them and put them in a pail for supper, but I guess I just lost control of myself. It's hard to pick brand new peas off the vine without tasting them first. That's the trouble with trying to pick fresh vegetables. They're just too delicious to put in a pail.

The corn was now taller than I was. And the cobs were ready to be picked. It didn't take me long to fill my pail. I helped Mama pull off the outer sheaths with tufts of hair at their tips. After we had stripped about ten ears of corn, she put them into a big aluminum pot and filled it with water from our drinking pail on the stand next to our kitchen table. Then she put another stick of wood in the stove and placed the pot of water on the stove. It took about ten minutes for the water to bubble around those ears of corn which turned and tossed like corks as they floated in that pot of steaming, hissing, water. She placed another stick of wood in the stove. Then we waited another ten minutes before she took a large fork and pulled out the ears, one at a time. We smothered each one with our home-made butter and sprinkled salt and pepper over it and devoured that sweet corn until there was nothing left but the empty cobs. I don't think anything ever tasted as good as that freshly picked corn from our garden when cooked in fresh, pure water from the town well, over a wood-burning stove in the middle of summer. Of course, homemade butter from our cow, Bossy, made a big difference, too. You just can't buy that kind of butter anywhere. Bossy was more than a contented cow. She was my pet. And I think she knew it.

Every evening after Papa had milked Bossy and had led her outside to the small corral he had built between the outhouse and the ice house, I would climb the wooden fence and call her name. Sometimes she would just stand there ignoring me, while she chewed her cud. At other times, she would come right up to the fence where I stood and look at me with her huge, brown loving eyes. I would pet her head and put my cheek right next to her neck and hug her. She didn't mind that at all. But when I climbed on top of her and pretended that I was a cowboy and she was a horse, she shook me off and once I almost fell into her pile of manure. I guess she thought I was too heavy.

Early in the morning, before Papa opened the store, I used to watch him milk Bossy, pulling one teat down with his right hand and then releasing it before pulling the other teat down with his left. His rhythm was perfect; he didn't miss a beat. At first, as each squirt of milk hit the large aluminum pail, it made a tinny sound, like the shot from a water pistol hitting a tin cup. But as the steady stream of milk began to fill the large pail, the tinny sound gave way to one of liquid pouring on liquid, and the pail was soon full. Then he would lead her out of the barn and open our long steel fence wide enough for Bossy to leave our yard. And away she would wander to the wide open field, toward Wunder's pasture, about a quarter of mile away. In the late afternoon she would usually return, waiting by the gate until someone opened it.

Occasionally, Bossy would be late and I would go to look for her and bring her back. Once in a great while, she would go away somewhere, and Papa would hire Mike Haluke or someone else to find her. Sometimes she would wander off to a farm miles away. At other times, she would be found in Wunder's pasture, with Frank Wunder's bull nearby, smiling most contentedly. Several months afterward, usually in the spring, she would give birth to a calf. Papa would come in excitedly from the barn and say, "*Da key hot gekelbed.*" [The cow has had a calf.] I would run to the barn and just as I entered, sure enough, there it was. Wobbling unsteadily on its spindly legs, right under its mother, sucking away, was the smallest, most beautiful red calf you ever saw. It was silky smooth all over, as if someone had poured melted butter over its entire body and head. I had never felt anything so silky soft and moist before. Bossy must have been proud. I could sense it the way she looked at me. But she seemed tired, too. And worried. Then, in about a week, the calf was gone. Papa explained that unless a cow had a calf, it would dry up and couldn't give milk any more. But there was not enough milk for both the calf and us. That was why he had sold the calf. I wished he had kept it. I could have had another wonderful pet. But at least I still had Bossy.

Papa kept Bossy for a number of years. I don't remember exactly how many, but it must have been about ten. She had been our cow as long as I could remember, and she was still around for at least a couple of years after I had started going to Inglis for my summer holidays. In time, Bossy grew old and dried up and could no longer give milk. One day I looked for her but she was gone. Papa had sold her to a cattle buyer for beef. I don't think he realized how much I missed her. He got another cow, a skinny red one. He fattened her and she gave good milk. But she just couldn't take the place of my Bossy. That's why I never gave her a name. And I never got close to her. As far as I was concerned, she was just a cow. There's a difference between a cow and a pet. My Bossy was both.

Shniders never had a cow, but they had a real pet—a little black and white dog they called Tippy. I loved Tippy. He could do all kinds of tricks. I could pet him and say, "Shake a paw," and he would immediately hold out his paw. I could make him roll over on his back or lick my cheek. Maurice and Charlie knew I loved him, so they never played any tricks on me. But they knew Etta didn't care for him, so one day Maurice tried to force her to bend down and smell his breath. Etta, however, had a mind of her own and resisted. She shouted as loud as she could: "Stop it, Maurice! Stop it!" Aunt Bessie was in the kitchen, not far away and heard the shouts. Almost immediately, out she came with a broom and started chasing Maurice. He outraced her, then climbed under the porch where he hid until after supper. Maurice finally apologized to Etta, but she never forgot the incident—to this very day—and she never liked dogs for a long, long time afterward.

Every summer through 1941, four months after my bar mitzvah, I spent part of my summer holidays in Inglis. My older sisters usually accompanied me for the first few years, but later on they stayed home and I traveled alone or occasionally with Sylvia. To merely say that the Shniders were hospitable would be an understatement. Although their home, attached to the rear of their store, wasn't very big, they somehow managed to accommodate all of us. This included at least three from the Katz family, as well as Mervin Shnider, Uncle Abe's nephew from Yorkton, who was two years older than I and who also spent part of the summer holidays there. Even though there were occasionally ten of us living under one roof, with two, and sometimes three, sleeping in a bed, I don't remember it being crowded. We were one big happy family, and every vacation seemed to be better than the one before.

When I was eight, Maurice had already been bar mitzvahed and had even more spare time to spend with me than the year before. He and his brother showed me how to make a toy telephone that actually worked. After collecting two empty Campbell's soup tin cans, they punctured a tiny hole at the closed end of both cans. Then they got about two hundred feet of string and threaded it through each can and finally knotted the string tightly so that it would not slip through the hole. "Here, hold this can up to your ear—real tight— and we'll walk away until the string is so tight it won't give any more," said Maurice. He was the first to speak into the can. "If you can hear me, answer me by speaking into your phone." I was amazed. I could hear him clearly. I spoke into my can. "It really works. Let me speak to Charlie." He understood and handed the telephone to his brother. We played all kinds of games with that string telephone until it was time for supper.

They introduced me to baseball. We called it "hardball" as opposed to "softball." At home I played softball—never baseball. Only the big kids in town and the grownups played hardball. I wouldn't dream of standing at the plate with that tiny hard ball hurling toward me so fast I could hardly see it. I didn't even play catch. But here, with my cousins, it didn't seem very dangerous. We started off by playing catch. Eventually I could catch that tiny hard ball even when Maurice hurled it as fast as he could. It made me feel good. Like I was a grownup. And when I stood at the plate, holding that big, thick, heavy bat on my shoulder, I really felt grownup. And what a thrill I felt when I heard that "crack" and felt the sting of my bat as it connected with the ball, sending it flying up and away toward the outfield.

Another thrill was riding in Uncle Abe's truck. Besides owning the largest general store in the area, he had now gone into the produce business as well. He had purchased a 1936 Chevrolet 1 1/2 ton truck with which his hired man Johnny Zrudlow used to pick up and haul produce from the farms to the store or to other towns for market. Produce consisted of grain, cattle, cordwood, and anything else that could be used either in his store or those in neighboring towns, or sold to larger produce dealers and hotels. Produce, therefore, was considered a cash crop. Farmers could be paid for it in cash or use it as barter in his store. Uncle Abe believed in the old axiom: "If you can't come to me, I'll go to you."

Farmers paid Uncle Abe from one to two cents a bushel for their grain to be picked up and hauled to the elevator. Although this cost them as much as 5% of their selling price, it was worth it. A truck could complete the round trip from the threshing machine to the elevator and back in an hour or so compared with half-a day's journey by a team of horses. Since the farmer usually didn't have enough storage space for all his grain, the time saved by the truck enabled him to get his grain to the elevator without holding up his threshing crew, a delay which might result in further delay by autumn rains, and even a crop loss because of hail, early frost, or sometimes an unexpected snow storm.

Occasionally I joined Maurice or Charlie when they accompanied Johnny Zrudlow on those trips or on his other trips to pick up cattle on Tuesdays and Thursdays for delivery to the stock yards, where the cattle would be loaded onto boxcars the following morning, when the train returned to Winnipeg. I often thought of Bossy when I saw those cattle being loaded first onto the truck and then into the boxcars. Although I felt sorry for them, I knew they had been deliberately raised for specific purposes; otherwise, I wouldn't be wearing leather shoes or eating meat. I felt I could do without meat, but I knew the canvas running shoes we sold in our store weren't nearly as comfortable or warm or long lasting as leather ones. Nevertheless, I still couldn't help feeling sorry for those cattle whose days were numbered. One thing I will say about Johnny's job. The cattle certainly left one heck of a stinking mess in the back of the truck, and he sure had one heck of a job cleaning it up. I sort of felt sorry for him because nobody offered to help, but I had no intention of being the first volunteer.

With cordwood, however, it was a different matter. It didn't stink. In fact, it smelled good. It didn't moo. And it didn't make a mess.

Cordwood was one of the main products Uncle Abe handled. When homesteaders or other new settlers acquired a quarter section (or more) of land, the first thing they would have to do before planting crops would be to "break the land." This meant clearing it by cutting down the dense growth of native poplar trees. Then they trimmed the branches and sawed the trees into four foot logs, which they stacked into cords—eight feet long by four feet high—ready to be picked up as cordwood for one dollar a cord. Or they could sell the uncut trimmed trees which could later be sawed into logs by someone in town who owned a gasoline-powered, machine-driven huge buzz saw that could slice through the tree—or someone's hand—in seconds. Cordwood, therefore, was abundant. More important for produce buyers, it was always in great demand because when it was cut up into smaller pieces, it became "firewood," and eventually when piled neatly in rows several feet high, it became part of a large wood pile that everyone in rural Canada accumulated. Wood was the only fuel burned for cooking (and usually heating) throughout not only the rural areas of Western Canada, but in many cities as well.

Cordwood, therefore, was as good as gold. Each new farmer could count on selling from ten to thirty cords of wood to Uncle Abe for a dollar a cord, in exchange for merchandise at his store, or for instant cash if needed. Ten dollars would buy four one-hundred-pound sacks of flour, enough to bake bread for an entire family of six for at least three months. As for Uncle Abe, he sold cordwood to outlying towns and cities within a ninety mile radius, including Yorkton. In fact, both the Yorkton and Balmoral Hotels, owned by the Bronfman Brothers, were among his regular customers. In time Uncle Abe became known as "King of the Cordwood," and later on simply "King Cordwood."

At age eight or nine, riding in King Cordwood's truck was a new adventure for me. Johnny Zrudlow slid behind the steering wheel and waited as we all climbed in from the right hand side—first Charlie, followed by Maurice and me. I sat on Maurice's lap. Then we were off, bouncing along on dirt roads and on cattle trails and on virgin land with no trails at all except for new tree stumps through which Johnny maneuvered the truck until he reached a pile of newly-cut poplar logs at the end of the clearing. We all got out and stretched. The farmer, waiting, took off his pointed straw hat and wiped his forehead with a blue bandanna, then shook hands with Johnny. They both walked around the pile of logs a couple of times. Then Johnny measured it with a carpenter's retractable tape measure. Finally he wrote something on a sheet of paper and handed it to the farmer, after which we all loaded the logs onto the truck. I didn't have gloves, but I still helped load a few logs. They were almost the same height as I was and almost the same weight. Soon we were off. Johnny drove to Russell, where we unloaded the logs near the hotel. Then we went to Louis Malinsky's delicatessen for a salami sandwich and coca cola before driving back home. I was tired, but I felt good, as though I was part of the team.

On Sunday, Johnny drove the entire family to the river. The three adults sat in the front seat, while the rest of us stood in the truck bed, balancing ourselves as the truck bounded along on the dirt road.

Although the Shell river, in the Assessippi Valley, was a tributary of a much larger river, the Assiniboine, which joined the Red River in Winnipeg, to me it was a huge river—much wider and deeper and faster than the creek that flowed through Wunder's field. The very word "river" excited me, and to realize that it still flowed in late July—I mean flowed—left me in awe. I couldn't wait to get in. It was cold at first, but I soon got used to it. What a wonderful feeling. Not like the creek. No bloodsuckers. No black, thick Saskatchewan mud. This water was clean, and refreshing. And it flowed.

Charlie said, "Be careful. It's deep, and there's a current." I could feel the current tugging at my feet, almost pulling me. I was kind of scared, but I bluffed and said, "Don't worry. I'm a good swimmer." I had told all the Shniders how well I could swim in our creek and I guess they sort of believed me. Now I had to show them that I could swim even in this river. I dived in and started dog paddling across. It was more difficult than I thought. I was moving but the current kept pulling me along the bank. I got kind of frightened and paddled harder than ever. By the time I reached the other side, I was panting. But I had shown everyone I could swim.

The years flew by and every summer I spent in Inglis was a new adventure. When I was twelve, Johnny Zrudlow's brother Bill arranged to take a group of kids my age camping by the river. Although I belonged to the newly formed Boy Scout Troop in Sheho, which offered a two-week summer camping trip for ten dollars, I never dared to ask my father if I could join those who could afford that enormously expensive trip. I knew exactly what he would say in Jewish. Translated, the exact words would be: "Ten dollars! Are you crazy? My grandfather never went camping, my father never went camping, I never went camping, and you can't go camping!" Aunt Bessie was Dad's younger sister. Surely they must think alike. So I timidly moped around for a couple of days, afraid to ask her.

But I debated the problem. Were they really alike? Then a little voice inside told me that Aunt Bessie and Uncle Abe had a somewhat different outlook on life and its luxuries than my father had. They had denied their children nothing. My cousins had a ".22" rifle, a real baseball and bat, along with a catcher's mitt and two—I mean two—real first baseman's mitts. They also had two tennis rackets and even a man's bicycle. And that's not counting the family truck! It was evident the Shniders were better off than the Katzes. I finally came to the conclusion that Aunt Bessie would not have a serious heart attack if I sort of hinted in an offhanded manner that it would be nice if I could go camping. I had nothing to lose. So for the next day or so I began working up enough nerve to ask her. Finally, with my heart pounding, in the most timid voice I had ever used, I said, "The kids in town are going on a camping trip. I don't suppose there's any possibility that I might go."

Immediately—I mean without any hesitation whatsoever—she exclaimed, "Why not? Of course you can go!" Those were her exact words. And I'll never forget them to my dying day. "Why not ? Of course you can go!" That was my Aunt Bessie. She didn't mince words. I could hardly believe it.

"Really?"

"Of course you can go. It'll be good for you."

"Thank you." I couldn't think of anything else to say. And I don't remember if I hugged her or not. But I think she knew how I felt. It was the happiest moment of my life.

I don't remember much about that camping trip except that it was all too short. I could have stayed by the river forever. We slept in tents, cooked our meals over an open fire, washed our dishes and utensils in the river before soaking them in boiling water, and spent most of the day swimming and just lounging around or taking short hikes. Late in the evening, we roasted marshmallows or wieners, then sang and sat around the roaring camp fire, watching it flicker and fade and burn itself out. Then, as the sky turned from midnight blue to black, we sat up and watched the stars and the spectacular Northern Lights. Finally it was time for bed. If we had to take a pee, we just left our tent and walked a short way to the bushes. Nobody stood on ceremony. It was so dark, we could barely make out our tent. But that's what I especially liked about that camping trip—the pitch black night. I could see millions of stars, and I could make out most of the constellations I was studying to qualify for my Astronomer's Proficiency Badge with the Boy Scouts.

When I returned to the Shniders from that camping trip, I continued to star gaze, studying the constellations that were becoming more and more familiar to me. One particular night, probably around eleven o'clock, I left the house taking the one-and-only key to their outdoor toilet. After completing my urgent business, I thought I would just star gaze for a few minutes before returning. The sky was so black and so clear I could even make out some faint constellations I had never seen before. I took my bearings from the two pointers of Ursa Major, the Great Bear (Big Dipper), and from Polaris, the North Star. Then ever so slowly, I began tracing the outline of the faint constellation Draco, right between the pointers and Polaris. It was amazing. I could make it out. Draco the Dragon. It really looked like a dragon. I was spellbound. And there were other faint constellations just as exciting. Hydra the Water Snake. What a sight! I completely lost track of time. Suddenly Myra came out of the house, took one look at me, and shouted, "What the heck are you doing?"

"I'm gazing at the stars."

"Gazing at the stars! I've had to go to the toilet for over half an hour but I've been holding it in. I couldn't go because you had the key. I wondered what happened to you. I thought you had constipation or had fallen in. And all this time you've been gazing at the stars! Gimmie that godamn key!"

Of all the adventures and thrills I experienced in Inglis, none can compare to the day Maurice and Charlie taught me how to ride a bicycle. Back home, some of our customers rode to town on bicycles, but I never got up the nerve to ask them how to ride one. And it was the same with Jenny and Walter Lys, who shared a new bicycle. I guess I was afraid of falling down and damaging their bike. But with the Shniders it was different. So one day I said to Maurice and Charlie, "Walter Lys has a girl's bike, and if I learned how to ride it, we could take turns pedaling and even go all the way to the lake. It sure would be nice if I could learn to ride your bike."

I guess all along they had been thinking about teaching Merle, Etta, and me how to ride their bike. Without hesitation Charlie said, "Here, get on. Peddle, and turn the handle bars toward the side you're falling. Maurice and I will hold you up so you don't fall." True to their word, they held me upright for the first few minutes. And within half-an-hour, I was riding all over town on their bike. What a thrill! It seemed miraculous. I could now ride a bike.

Next came Merle. It took her a little longer to learn. "I told you to turn to the side you're falling," said Maurice in a stern voice." Don't turn the other way." She tried again and soon she, too, was riding without any help.

Finally it was Etta's turn. Her balance wasn't exactly perfect.

As she began to fall, Maurice shouted, "Don't turn that way! Turn to the side you're falling! Turn the other way. To the side you're falling."

"Don't shout at her," said Charlie. "Here, I'll help you. Let's try it again. Don't be afraid. When you feel like you're falling, just turn the handle bars in that direction. The bike will straighten out and you won't fall." Charlie was a born teacher. His patience paid off. Soon Etta, like the rest of us, was wheeling Shnider's bike around Inglis as if she had been riding for years.

The last time I spent my summer holidays in Inglis was in July of 1941. I had recently had my bar mitzvah, Maurice had just completed his first year of college in Winnipeg, and Charlie was about to enter his final year of high school. We were all growing up. What stands out most in my mind was the war.

It had begun on September 1st, 1939, when Germany invaded Poland. Great Britain and France sent Germany an ultimatum demanding that the invading troops withdraw within forty-eight hours; otherwise both Great Britain and France would declare war on Germany. Hitler ignored the ultimatum and his troops advanced into Poland. On September 3rd, both Great Britain and France declared war on Germany. Canada had some warships on its Pacific Coast and they would not be allowed to cross through the Panama Canal if she were at war. Hurriedly, these ships sailed from Esquimalt, British Columbia, down the Pacific Coast, and through the Panama Canal. As soon as they reached the Atlantic—on September 10th— Canada joined the rest of the British Empire in declaring war on Germany.

After ten months of staring at the impregnable Maginot Line, Germany, in June of 1940, conquered not only France but the outlying countries of Belgium, Holland, and Norway. A year later, in the early summer of 1941, Germany startled the world by breaking its non-aggression pact with the Soviet Union and invading that huge country, steam rolling through it in a *blitzkrieg* . [lightning war] Most of the radio commentators predicted that Germany would overrun the Soviet Union in a matter of months, since nothing had stood in the way of Hitler's conquest up until now—except the English Channel and the Royal Air Force.

"I think those commentators are wrong," said Maurice. "I heard H.K. Kaltenborn the other day. He said, 'This time it's going to be different. It's not going to be that easy. It's going to be a long, long war.' He thinks Hitler has made a strategic mistake. A big one. ' Russia is too big to conquer.' That's what Kaltenborn thinks. And I agree with him."

Aunt Bessie was worried about her brothers and sisters and their families who had remained in the Ukraine. Neither she nor Dad had heard from any of them recently. With Germany's advance and with Hitler's proclamation against the Jews, their fate seemed to be sealed.

A few days later Maurice, who had turned eighteen less than three months before, announced that he was going to join the air crew of the Royal Canadian Air force as an observer. He explained that an observer had the dual role on a bomber of being not only its navigator but also the bombardier. He was responsible for getting the bomber to the target, then aiming and dropping the bombs on this target. Good math skills, especially in trigonometry, were a pre-requisite for the observer. Maurice was exceptionally good in math. He welcomed the challenge.

His parents, however, were hardly elated with his announcement. Aunt Bessie had seen her brother David conscripted into the Czar's army and sent to fight the Japanese during the Russian -Japanese War. He had returned a shaken man, having witnessed wholesale carnage and death. He was never the same. There was nothing glamorous about war. Words failed her. Tears came to her eyes. Uncle Abe said, "Why do you have to go now? What's the hurry? Can't you wait?"

"I've got to go. We can't let Hitler go on forever. We know what he's doing to the Jews." He paused. There was no answer. "Besides," he added, almost as an afterthought, "If I get shot down, I can speak German quite well with a real good German accent. And my name 'Shnider' sounds German, so I could pass as a German."

I envied Maurice and wished I were old enough to join up.

Secretly, I hoped that the war would last long enough for me to get in. It sounded exciting. I would join either the Air Force or the Navy. I liked the uniforms of both. It certainly would be more glamorous than receiving the Dick Tracy Captain's badge from the Quaker Oats Company for three box tops from either Quaker Puffed Wheat or Quaker Puffed Rice. Yes, I envied Maurice. But at the same time, I was saddened. Summer holidays would never be the same again, for I knew that this was the last time I would ever spend my summers with the Shniders.

CHAPTER FOURTEEN
My Adopted Brother And My Bike

Every young boy should have a pet, preferably a dog. But if he can't have a dog, at the very least he should have a brother. And if he can't have either, he should find a very close buddy who has a dog he's willing to share. That way his buddy can eventually become the brother he never had, and the dog can take the place of the pet he wished he had. It's really quite simple.

Just before Sylvia was born, our nurse, Inez Nesset, had come to stay with our family. When she woke me up and said, "The doctor just brought you a baby sister," I immediately shot back, "I'd rather have a dog." For even at the age of 3 1/2, I knew what I wanted. I could have all kinds of fun with a dog. It would make a wonderful pet. But what the heck could I do with a baby sister? What a stupid gift!

When I was about five, I remember petting a big, black long-haired dog that had followed its master from the farm to our store. The farmer apparently forgot about his dog and returned to his farm, leaving the dog behind. Finders keepers. I never gave the matter a second thought. I quickly named the dog "Blackie," and Blackie was now mine. We kept Blackie outside and fed him scraps from our table. I loved Blackie as much as a boy can love anything or anyone and thought I was the luckiest kid in the world. Then one day, a couple of weeks later, the farmer returned to our store. When he and his team of horses turned around to go back home, Blackie followed them. I ran after Blackie, calling out to him: "Blackie, Blackie, come here Blackie, come back!" But he ignored me. I cried and cried. There was nothing I could do. I was heartbroken. Why had my own dog left me? Then Mama reminded me that Blackie wasn't *really* my dog. But I still didn't care. Despite my love for Blackie, he had not been loyal to me, for he had chosen that farmer instead of me. I had lost. And I didn't get over that loss for a long time.

When I was five, I used to peddle my little four-wheel kiddy car down the three-block long cement sidewalk to the very end of that walk-way. But I never went past the end because it was too hard for me to peddle and steer on the cinder sidewalk that continued for another block. So I turned around. On the way back, I often stopped in front of the orange-and-black general store owned by Walter and Jenny Lys's parents. The Lys family lived behind their store. Jenny was a year older than I, and her brother six months younger. They had a big three-wheeled tricycle and a red metal wagon. They also had a little white-and-brown smooth- haired dog they called "Tootsie." So whenever I got to Lys's store, I stopped and opened their gate and went in to see them. Walter let me ride their tricycle and I let him ride my kiddy car. I didn't care to ride his wagon, though. It was hard on my knees. And Walter let me pick up Tootsie whenever I wanted to. She acted as if she were my dog as well as Walter's. That's why I always liked to visit him. [I still have a group snapshot of a bunch of kids my age. I'm the one holding Tootsie.]

They also had a big tent in their yard. So when I got tired of riding his tricycle and he got tired of riding my kiddy car, we could play in the tent. We could make as much noise as we wanted and nobody would bother us. That's another reason I liked to visit Walter Lys.

One afternoon in early autumn, about a month after Walter had started school, we were both admiring the bright gold and orange leaves which were falling off the poplar tree in his back yard. Some of the leaves on the tree were still green, some had barely begun to turn color, and the rest had already turned into their fall shades of yellow, gold, orange, rust, and red. But Walter and I thought that something was missing. The colors weren't bright enough or varied enough to suit our taste.

We decided to improve on Nature and paint our own leaves. We picked several off the tree. Some were still green and others had already begun to turn color. We also chose some leaves that had already fallen to the ground. Walter brought out his set of paints with two tiny brushes. He poured some water into a saucer, dipped his brush, then stroked the red paint with his brush and began to paint his green leaf until he thought it was red enough. But the red paint kept dripping off the leaf onto the kitchen table. The paint would not stick as it always did on paper. Then he tried to paint it purple. It still dripped. He handed me the other brush and I began to paint another leaf, one that had barely begun to turn color. I used mostly brown and blue. Some of the paint stuck. But most of it didn't. We tried black. It seemed to cover the leaf a little better, but it ran into the other colors and looked ugly. So we tried to paint the leaves that had already fallen. But they were so crisp that they crumpled in our fingers if we weren't careful. We had to use a lot of leaves and a lot of paint until we got used to painting those fragile leaves. When we got through, our ugly leaves were scattered all over the place. But the kitchen table was the most colorful one I have ever seen. It was a masterpiece of modern art. However, I didn't think Mrs. Lys would appreciate our masterpiece, so I hurried home and decided not to go back to Walter's place for quite a while. Not until the trees were bare and the snow had fallen.

Walter was my closest buddy by far. For many years, especially from the time we were about nine until he and his family moved away when he was sixteen, we were practically inseparable. We navigated the creek through Wunder's field together and discovered the wild ducklings. We swam in that creek every afternoon during early summer until it dried up. We built a small bonfire near the western bridge almost every night to roast potatoes and marshmallows. We studied together for our final exams next to a bonfire we had built on the open prairie. We rode our bicycles to the lake every afternoon and rafted across Maas's Lake. We were in the same Wolf Cub Pack and slept in a makeshift pup tent until my father bought a real one for me, after which we took turns sleeping in his tent and mine all summer long, except when it poured, forcing us inside. We played tennis against each other and paired up in doubles. We did just about everything together and never, never got into a fight. Walter and I were more than buddies. We were brothers.

It may seem ironical that his parents were in competition with mine, for each claimed to own the largest general store in Sheho. But neither his parents nor mine ever spoke an unkind word about the other or tried to take advantage of one another, much less than force the other out of business. Both stores had their own customers, and both sets of parents were merely trying to make a living. And despite the ethnic and religious differences and business competition between the two families, I never heard a single negative word from my parents or my sisters against his family, or a single negative word from anyone in his family against mine. Although my parents did not socialize with his, they all respected each other. Their children were more than friendly. And their sons were closer than most brothers.

As I mentioned earlier, Walter was the first one in town to discover the Dick Tracy radio program, the first to get the secret decoder, and the first to wear his Dick Tracy's Sergeant badge, which cost him three box tops from Quaker Puffed Wheat or Quaker Puffed Rice. For this accomplishment, all of us kids bestowed upon him the highest honor anyone could possibly receive. Forever after, we called him "Tracy."

About the time Tracy was promoted to lieutenant, for another three Quaker box tops, or it may have been captain for an additional three, he had something else to be proud of—a new bicycle. The snow had already melted in late May when Tracy came riding up to the school just before the opening bell rang and parked a brand new red lady's bicycle in front of the west-facing double doors, for all to see. The only other bike parked there belonged to Louis Maas, who lived on a farm 1 1/2 miles away. Walter lived two blocks away. Faster than our station agent, Bob Curry, could send a telegram announcing this historical event, the news spread throughout the school: "Tracy's got a new bike."

The bike wasn't really Walter's alone. He was supposed to share it with his sister, Jenny. That was why Mr. Lys had ordered a lady's bike, which had no obstructing horizontal bar to hold up a girl's skirt or dress. In time, Jenny also rode the bike. But only on rare occasions—when her brother wasn't using it.

Since I hadn't yet learned how to ride a bike and Tracy didn't want to take a chance of my falling down and possibly damaging the new bike, he did not offer it to me until late that summer, after I had returned from Inglis, where my cousins had taught me how to ride. Then, perhaps to the surprise of Mr. and Mrs. Lys and especially Jenny, it also became my bike. However, I did not take unfair advantage of Tracy's generosity. I did not keep the bike at our home, nor did I ride it to school, nor take it away from Jenny when she wanted it, mainly because she hardly ever rode it. Perhaps the reason she hardly ever rode it was that it was never available—except late at night when everyone was asleep. She never complained. That's what I liked about her.

Although that bicycle was not built for two, Tracy and I never gave it a second thought the day we decided to see how far we could go on his bicycle built for one. We headed north out of town, onto the dirt road which we knew went past Paul's Lake, also known as Salt Lake, over three miles away. One of us would sit on the seat, holding onto the other's waist, while the other stood up pedaling and steering the bike until he got tired. Then we would change positions until whoever was pedaling got tired. Thus, every two hundred yards or so, we took turns pedaling, all the while discovering new territory as we advanced farther and farther into the wilderness, like the great explorers of old. We did not lack for imagination, especially since not even one car or team of horses appeared on this dirt road to disturb our dialogue. Finally, it came into view—that great body of water which we told ourselves led to the Northwest Passage. We were the first to discover it. On second thought, maybe it led directly to the Pacific Ocean. We couldn't decide which.

The sight of a large stone mansion on the edge of the lake brought us back to reality. It had been built almost forty years before when speculation arose that the Canadian Pacific Railway would be built along this route, north of Sheho, and this area would be the center of the new village. The speculators were wrong. And Mr. Paul was left with his mansion, next to Salt Lake, which in time also bore his name.

Thousands of rocks, big and small, lay along the shoreline and even underneath the lake. Since we didn't want to bang our shins against the rocks while wading or worse, slip and fall on the rocks, we gave up the idea of swimming in it. And after deciding that the lake was neither the Northwest Passage nor the gateway to the Pacific, Tracy and I turned the bike around and began pedaling back home.

We had just begun pedaling when a big black dog came out of a side road about fifty yards ahead and began barking at us. There was nothing we could do to persuade it that we had not come from the bank to foreclose on the mortgage and seize the farm. It barked and barked and snarled at us. We thought it might attack us. We were terrified. There was only one solution. "Let's pray," I said.

I looked toward heaven and asked the Almighty to spare us. Walter crossed himself and prayed to Jesus and the Virgin Mary, whose pictures I had seen above his bed. Jesus was a handsome looking man with blue eyes and blonde hair and a neatly trimmed blonde beard. He looked Ukrainian. The Virgin Mary had a halo around her head and also looked Ukrainian. I didn't believe in either, but now was not the time for religious analysis. Who knows? Gradually, the dog stopped snarling and barking and just stared at us. Then it apparently ran out of patience or got distracted and ran back in the other direction, toward the farm house.

We had not pedaled more than a mile when we spotted a skunk coming onto the road. It was making its way ever so slowly across. We stopped dead in our tracks and waited. And waited. But the skunk was in no hurry. It stared at us for the longest time, as if daring us to approach. Again we were terrified. If it sprayed us, we would literally stink like a skunk. And so we waited. We were just about to start praying when the skunk swished its tail and crossed the road into an open field. We waited until we knew the skunk was out of range for its firing mechanism to be accurate enough to hit us. Then we resumed our homeward journey.

The following summer we again took turns on his bike, frequently traveling to Maas's Lake, only 1 1/2 miles away. Since there were almost no rocks along the shoreline where we entered and none in the lake itself, we knew we would not have to avoid such hazards to swim in perfect safety. So we pedaled to the lake and back at least twice a week in the afternoon. But it was hard and uncomfortable work for both of us. I wished I had my own bike. I began to build up enough nerve to ask my father for a bike—one bike for all four of us. Finally, I approached him on the subject. I realized that the twenty dollars it would cost for a bike wholesale from Walter Woods was a heck of a lot more money than twenty-five cents for the one-and-only hockey stick I had asked him for five years before. So I expected his answer might be: "Are you crazy? Do you think I'm made of money? My grandfather never had a bike. My father never had a bike. I never had a bike. And you don't need a bike."

But that was not the answer I got. Not at all. Without going into hysterics, he merely said, "We can't afford one this year." And that was all he said. The year before he had bought a Philco radio from Bill Finley for fifty dollars— a king's ransom. Another twenty dollars the following year was out of the question. And so I decided not to pursue the matter and gave up hope of ever having a bike.

Mama, however, knew how much I wanted a bike. I think my older sisters may also have played a role in her decision to get us one. She had her own solution. She collected all the old shoes that were now too small for us and polished them until they shone almost like new. Then she gathered all the old clothes we had outgrown and carefully washed, ironed, and folded them. Finally, she stored these second hand shoes and clothes in the small room in our warehouse in the back of our store, and one-by-one-began to sell them to some of our customers whom she knew had children about our age but could not afford new clothes. "Mrs. Demonsky, I've got a pair of Jackie's pants. They're too small for him. They're just right for your youngest son. Wait here and I'll get them for you. Look, almost like new. You can have them for only fifty cents. And here's a nice cotton dress Etta, my middle one, used to wear. Only seventy-five cents. Do you need shoes for your little girl? Here's a pair of Sylvia's. Only twenty cents."

One-by-one, in just over a year, she sold them all. Twenty cents, and fifty cents, and seventy-five cents and another fifty cents added up to two dollars. In time two dollars became four, and four became eight, and so on, until one day in early August of 1939, during our summer holidays, she said, "I've sold enough old shmatas [rags] for a bike. Walter Woods traveler will be here tomorrow. We're going to order for all of you from Walter Woods a new bike."

I couldn't believe it. Mama had performed a miracle. I could hardly wait.

The next day, the traveler from Walter Woods Wholesale Hardware Company Limited came into the store. He greeted my father, shook hands with him, and chatted a while before getting down to business. First, he laid his huge catalog on the grocery counter. Next, he took out his order book and pencil. Then he put on his glasses. Finally, he began turning the pages of the catalog, ever so slowly. He wasn't flipping them. He was barely turning them, like a boy licking his ice cone, one small lick at a time, teasing another boy whose mouth was hanging open. It was taking forever. Gradually, he began going through the items he knew we stocked, as well as others he hoped to sell. Would he ever get to the bike?

"How are fixed for plate glass, Louis?"

"Yeah, I could use some."

"Same size as last time?"

"Yeah, same size."

"How many?"

"Same as last time?"

"Is that enough?"

"Yeah, that's enough this time."

Slowly the traveler inserted a sheet of carbon paper in his order book, picked up his pencil, wrote the stock number in the order book, then the quantity, then the item, then the unit price, and finally the total price. Then he put down the order book, flipped a couple of pages in the catalog, and said, "How are you fixed for nails?"

Dad ambled over to the nail section—taking his time—and inspected the wooden kegs. Then, slowly he returned. "Gimmie some one inch and two inch."

"A keg of each?"

"Yeah. One of each."

"What about three inch?"

"No, I have plenty left. Just one inch and two inch."

"What about spikes?"

"No spikes. Just one inch and two inch."

"What about staple nails?"

"Yeah, I could use some."

"A keg."

"Yeah, same as last time."

Once more the traveler picked up his pencil and began writing. He was taking forever. He was teasing me. Like the boy licking his ice cream cone, one lick at a time. I felt like shouting, "What about my bike?" But I controlled myself. It's not easy when you're eleven years old and you've been waiting for the biggest thing in your life for almost two years.

So it went, item after item.

"What about pails? Galvanized steel and aluminum pails?"

" Steel, yes. Half a dozen. No milk pails this time."

Who cares about milk pails? This was sheer torture for me. I was dying a slow, horrendous death. I would be dead before they were through. I felt like shouting, "WHAT ABOUT MY BIKE?"

"How's your stock of house paint and enamel?"

"Yeah, we need some. I'll have to check it."

I couldn't stand it any more. I just couldn't stand it. So I blurted out, "We're going to order a bike from you."

The traveler, who had been writing in his order book, stopped dead in his tracks. He immediately put down his order book, took off his glasses, and stared at me in shock, as though he had just discovered a bar of gold while digging in his garden for potatoes. He was speechless.

"We're going to order a bike from you TODAY!"

"A bike? A real bike?"

"Yeah, a real bike. A man's bike. Here, I'll show you."

I ran behind the counter. I took out our own Walter Woods wholesale catalog and immediately turned to the page which I had studied for months. "Look! This is the one I want." There it was. A brand new man's Champion bicycle for only twenty dollars. It was $4.95 less then the cheapest one in the Eaton's catalog. It came in one color—red— and in four different sized frames. "This one. It's the smallest one, the eigh- teen- inch frame. It's my size. I can reach the pedales when the seat is down. That's exactly what I want. When will I get it?"

The traveler forgot about the house paint and enamel and the paint brushes and the horse collars and the wash boards and wash tubs and everything else. This sale was the biggest one he'd had all afternoon. He shook hands with me when he left and patted me on the head. I had made his day.

Even though I would be sharing the bike with my three sisters who would have preferred a lady's bicycle, like Jenny and Walter's bike, I never gave the slightest thought of asking for their choice. I wanted a man's bike. It was heavier than a lady's bike and would hold the road better. Besides, I would be the one who would be riding the bike most of the time. But I would generously share it with them whenever I wasn't using it. When I say I never gave it the slightest thought, I mean not even the slightest. Not until almost sixty years later, while writing this very chapter, when my sister Sylvia reminded me. "There were three of us and only one of you, but you never thought about us. You only thought about yourself. You always had your own way. When I sat on the seat, I couldn't reach the pedals, so I had to put my legs through the crossbar and pedal. If we'd had a lady's bike, I could have stood up and pedaled to ride it, like you and Walter did. But I couldn't do that. No! Not with a man's bike. But you never thought about that. You only thought about yourself."

What can I say? That's my sister Sylvia. A real diplomat. Fifty years. Sixty years. She *never* forgets.

Waiting every day for my bike to arrive was worse than waiting for Passover to end so that I could eat ice cream and chocolate bars without committing a sin. With Passover, you know it will end in eight days. And you can take a chocolate bar from the store when your father isn't looking, even though it might be considered stealing. But nobody cares about that chocolate bar because the only one who knows besides you is God and He really doesn't care. But when you're waiting for Walter Woods to ship your bike, it's different. Nobody knows when—not even God. And nobody cares except you. So you wait. And wait. And you count the days. But nothing happens. Then you start thinking and asking questions.

"Maybe the traveler forgot to write the order."

"He didn't forget." My dad didn't mince words.

"Maybe they forgot to ship my bike?"

"They didn't forget."

"So when will it come?"

"It's coming."

"When?"

"When it comes. With the rest of the order."

That was my dad. If he had been caught spying, even in war time, nobody but nobody could have extracted any information from him. "What's your name?"

"The one I was given at birth."

"What is it?"

"The same one I have now."

"So what is it?"

"The one I was born with." He sure knew how to keep a secret.

About a week later, he happened to mumble something about an invoice.

"You got an invoice."

"Yeah."

"From whom?"

"Walter Woods."

"When did it come?"

"Yesterday."

"So when are they shipping the bike?"

"When they ship the rest of the order."

"When's that?"

"Today."

"That means the bike will be here tomorrow."

"Yes. Tomorrow, with the rest of the order."

If you think it was easy for me to sleep that night, I can tell you it wasn't. Tomorrow would be the biggest day of my entire life. That was all I could think of. And when I awoke the next morning, all I could think of was, "Today is the most important day of my life. My bike will soon be here."

The west-bound passenger train from Winnipeg, which also carried shipments of merchandise for every town along the railway line, arrived every morning just after ten. It often took about an hour or two for Bob Curry, the station agent, to transfer the shipments for Sheho from the baggage car to the large flat-car wagons on the station platform and then process them for delivery. From there they would be placed either on Mike Harris's or Ed Howe's flat-bed dray, pulled by a team of horses. Both took turns as drayman. By the time the drayman delivered the merchandise to the last customer on his route, Katz General Store, it would be sometime in the afternoon. It might be early in the afternoon. It might be mid afternoon. It might be late in the afternoon. It all depended on how much merchandise the drayman had to deliver.

I knew the schedule. I knew there was absolutely nothing I could do to expedite the process. I wasn't stupid. My bike would arrive sometime this afternoon. And so, as soon as I had finished nibbling at Mama's dinner served promptly at noon, I rushed to the store and waited for Mike Harris's dray to arrive, bringing the order from Walter Woods that included my bike. I waited. And I waited. In my entire lifetime, I had never waited for anything so long during an afternoon. And during this time, the only thing I could think of was, "My bike will be here sometime this afternoon. Soon!"

Merle and Etta joined me for the final countdown. They, too, were anticipating the arrival of our bike. But somehow the word *our* had been absent from my vocabulary all along. I now decided to include them in my eager announcement to any customer who came into the store. And so I said to George Nickorak, who had pedaled six miles that afternoon from his farm to our store, "*We're* getting a new bike today. It should be here anytime." Ordinarily, he would have left the store much earlier, but I guess the anticipation in my voice prompted him to stay and to share in the excitement. His cows would still get milked, maybe an hour or two later. It wasn't everyday that somebody in Sheho got a new bike. This was a big time event.

Mercifully, the big event finally arrived. Mike Harris pulled up alongside the store and hollered "Whoa!" to his horses, just before winding the reins around the front post of the dray. He began bringing in our order. I recognized the kegs of nails and the crate of plate glass and the crate of house paint and enamel and other material Dad had ordered. But where was the bike? Finally, he brought in the last wooden crate and left.

"Where's the bike?" I asked.

"It's packed in that crate," said George Nickorak. I looked at the crate in astonishment. It was about four feet long and two feet wide and three feet high. I had expected a brand new red bike, all ready to ride. But here was a wooden crate. "Gimmie a hammer and screw driver, and I'll open it," he said.

I stood over him, anxiously watching the operation. He opened the crate and began removing packages wrapped in brown kraft paper. "Where's the bike?" I exclaimed.

"Right here. These are the parts. That's how they ship them. They have to be put together. Get me a wrench and I'll put them together for you."

God works in mysterious ways. In His infinite wisdom, He knew that nobody in the Katz family was even remotely mechanical enough to ever assemble that bike—not in a day, not in a year, not in a lifetime. And He knew that little eleven year old Jackie Katz was aging prematurely by the minute. And so, in His infinite compassion and infinite mercy, on this eventful day, He persuaded George Nickorak to pedal the six miles from his farm to Katz General store to buy a pair of size 11 cotton socks, two packages of Ogden's cigarette tobacco and zigzag papers, a box of matches, a pound of coffee especially ground from the huge coffee grinder that six years before had almost ground off Jackie Katz's finger, and say to Louis Katz, "Charge it." And then, after learning that little Jackie Katz was expecting a new bike any minute now, George Nickorak would say, "I think I'll stick around until your bike arrives." For God in His infinite wisdom knew that George Nickorak knew how to assemble the various parts of a man's bicycle to fit properly. In short, God (or Destiny—take your choice) had decreed that it would be George Nickorak who would put together the bicycle that little Jackie Katz had been praying for, a bicycle to be ridden by little Jackie Katz who couldn't wait any longer. As an afterthought, God also decreed that on very rare occasions Jackie's sisters might also ride this bicycle when it was available.

"Here, it's ready to ride." George Nickorak handed me the brand new shiny bike, the most beautiful bike I had ever seen in my life.

"Thank you." That's all I said. But I'm sure he knew how I felt, not by the way I said it, but by the grin on my face and the gleam in my eyes. I was elated. I carefully lifted the bike from the wooden floor down to the cement step and then down to the sidewalk, and finally onto the graveled road, Highway 14. I pointed the bike west toward the end of the block, took a running start, put my left foot on the pedal, threw my right foot over the seat, mounted it, and began pedaling. And away I rode. I made a U-turn at the corner, then headed east toward the hotel and Lys' store. But when I got to the end of the first block, I turned around. I remembered that it was not my bike alone. I must share it with Merle and Etta who were on the sidewalk watching me, waiting for their turn. Their first ride, like mine, was short, but I'm sure we all shared the same thrill on that very first ride.

My second ride was longer. I rode to the school, 1/4 mile away, then on the way back stopped at Lys's store and parked the bike next to the entrance. I hurried into the store and excitedly interrupted Mr. Lys who was talking to a customer in his usual low, barely audible tone, which sounded as though he was whispering.

"Excuse me," I blurted out, " Where's Walter?"

"Inside the house," he whispered.

Mrs. Lys, who was standing nearby, amplified his answer in her usual strident voice. "He's inside the house."

Without asking permission, I walked through the back of the store and entered the house, where Walter was reading a comic book. As soon as he saw me, he grinned and said, "Did it come?"

"Come on outside and see."

As soon as he saw it, he grinned and said, "Maas's Lake tomorrow. See you at one."

CHAPTER FIFTEEN
Biking, Scouting, And Tenting

The summer days of 1939 passed all too quickly, and on August 26th, our new school year began. I was now in the seventh grade with a new teacher, Mr. Fred Kindrachuk— the first male teacher I had ever had except for Steve Giverego, whom I had been lucky enough to have for grade five. I liked male teachers better than the ladies who had taught me for most of my previous grades because men were able to control the class much better without yelling. Mr. Kindrachuk sounded as if we were all going to have a lot of fun, and he seemed to take a special interest in me, calling on me for answers more than he did with the others. For the first time, it appeared that I was the teacher's pet. One evening about three days later, Walter and I were playing catch with a tennis ball, just outside the tennis court, pretending we were outfielders for the Brooklyn Dodgers and New York Yankees. He now answered to the name "Tracy." After the game we discussed the war rumblings in Europe. We always listened to Lorne Green read the C.B.C. nightly news from Toronto at nine o'clock, and I also absorbed Mr. Leckie's Sunday commentary on the weekly news. We therefore considered ourselves experts on world affairs. Nazi Germany was telling the world that it would soon have to intervene in Poland to protect its German citizens who were being persecuted. Nobody except the Germans believed this propaganda, which sounded like an excuse for another takeover by Hitler. What would happen then? The question was, would Great Britain and France stand by their pact with Poland? And if they did, would Germany still invade?

"I don't think it will come to war," I distinctly remember saying. "Surely, they haven't forgotten the awful bloodshed of the Great War? I think another World War would be too horrible to imagine. I don't think there will be a war."

I believe Tracy may have agreed with me, but to him the signs were too ominous. He was reserving his judgment. A couple of days later, on September 1, 1939, we heard that German troops had crossed the border into Poland. On September 3, both England and France declared war on Germany. Exactly one week later, Canada declared war on Germany. If we had been old enough, both Tracy and I would have joined one of the services immediately. The question was, which one?

"I'd like to join the Royal Canadian Air Force as a fighter pilot," said Tracy. "I'd love to fly a Hurricane or a Spitfire."

"I'd like to be a fighter pilot also," I replied, "but I like the uniforms of the Navy better. They're not so common."

"But if your ship got sunk and you couldn't reach a lifeboat in time, you'd drown in the cold waters of the Atlantic."

"And if your plane got shot down, you'd crash."

"Not if I was a better pilot than the German. I'd shoot him down."

"But suppose he shot you down first. You'd crash."

"Not if I bailed out with a parachute."

"What if the parachute didn't open?"

"I'd make sure it would open because I'd fold it myself, and I'd even take a spare along just in case."

That was the closest Tracy and I ever came to getting into a serious argument. And that was as close as we ever got to joining the Royal Canadian Air Force or the Royal Canadian Navy. We hoped the war would last long enough for us to join. [We missed it by a year.]

1939 was a most eventful year for another reason: the organization in Sheho of the Wolf Cubs and the Boy Scouts of Canada. It was Mr. Munro who was primarily responsible. He had just moved to Sheho after being hired as a full time minister for the Sheho branch of the United Church of Canada, whose congregation consisted almost entirely of people who claimed British ancestry. He became the Boy Scout Master of the local troop and appointed Norman Leckie not only to be his assistant but also to head the Wolf Cubs with the title of Wolf Cub Master of the pack.

Tracy and I, at ten and eleven, were just the right age for the Wolf Cubs. I was one year away from being able to join the Scouts, so in the meantime the Cubs sounded exciting. They were the next best thing to the Canadian Armed Forces. We would not have to worry about being shot down in flames or being torpedoed in the North Atlantic or what uniforms to wear. It was as close as we could get to war. We joined immediately.

Unlike his father, Norman, now in his early twenties, had usually seemed aloof. Whereas Mr. Leckie came to our home every Sunday without fail for dinner and for the first night of Passover, the only time I remember Norman joining his father was one particular year during the first night of Passover—the "first Seder." Mama had just finished benching lecht —the ceremony of lighting and blessing the candles. That was the extent of our first Seder. That was all! But apparently it seemed a little long or a little strange to Norman, who had not had any religious upbringing. He predicted that because my sisters were all being brought up in Canada, by the time they grew up and married, not one would continue that tradition. I didn't agree with him. My older sisters began quite an argument about his prediction. But since it didn't concern me, I remained silent. His father had once told me, "Silence is golden."

Norman was a regular guy. He participated in every sport and had equipment for everything. He even owned a .22 caliber rifle. He would often take a group of us kids with him when he went out of town with his ".22" to shoot gophers and crows and tin cans, at which time he would give all of us a turn. So I knew he wasn't always indifferent. He could be friendly. And when Tracy and I joined the Cubs, we took to him immediately. He was a warm and exciting Cub Master and an excellent teacher.

At our first meeting, in the town hall, he told us about Lord Baden Powell, founder of the Boy Scout Movement. He had fought for the British in the Boer War and had been so impressed with the Army's scouts, who were noted for tracking animals and the enemy, that shortly after that war ended he founded the Movement, named after those scouts. His goal was to prepare boys to become scouts; hence their motto, "Be Prepared." We boys in Norman's group were not quite old enough to become Boy Scouts, but we were preparing for the day when we would. In the meantime, instead of belonging to a Boy Scout Troop, we were now part of a Wolf Cub Pack.

Norman then explained that the symbolism of the Wolf Cub Pack was based on Rudyard Kipling's famous *Jungle Book* in which the little boy Mogli, who had been lost in the jungle, was raised by a pack of wolves whose leader was Akela. We boys were a pack of wolf cubs whose leader was Akela. Since Norman was the leader of our pack, he would henceforth be called "Akela."

The first thing we did was to group ourselves into sixes and then to pick a leader of that "six." The leader would be called the "sixer." The sixer would then pick his assistant called a "second." Walter and I and four other kids, all of whom were younger than we were, joined one group. I became the sixer and appointed Walter as my second. I called him "Walter" during our Cub Pack meetings; otherwise, he was still Tracy. Sometimes I called him "Dick Tracy" or " Dick" and eventually "Dixie."

The second thing we did was to pick a color to designate our particular six. "I like green," I said to Walter. "It's my favorite color. It's bright and cheery. Let's pick green. Okay?" He nodded his head. We didn't ask the others. We never asked them anything. We just *told* them. So we became the "green" six.

After we had all been grouped into sixes and had picked our colors, Norman told all of us to get into a circle. Then he got in the middle and taught us the Wolf Cub howl. Following him, we all got down on our hands and knees, with our hands just slightly in front of our knees, and our heads looking up, imitating the way a wolf or a dog sits. Then, making a fist except for our index and third finger which touched the floor and protruded like a V that resembled a wolf's ears, we howled: "Ah kee lah. We'll do our best."

Norman, our Akela, stood as we all howled like wolf cubs. Then Akela responded: "Dib. Dib. Dib." That was a wolf command for "Do your best." Then we all leaped to our feet, holding our fists up to our ears, with the two fingers still pointing outward, and answered him: "We'll dahb, dahb, dahb." That was wolf cub language for "We'll do our best."

Finally, we learned the Wolf Cub Promise. "I promise to do my best, to do my duty to God and the King, to keep the law of the Wolf Cub Pack, and to do a good turn to somebody every day."

I took that promise to heart. But I didn't know what my exact duty to King George VI was, nor did anyone else. I knew he was my king and like everyone else, I always stood up and sang "God Save the King" at the conclusion of any special event at school or in town. Even at the end of any movies I had ever seen, King George's picture immediately came on the screen and everyone stood at attention while the first few bars of that song were played. Sometimes the entire song was played and it took forever to get out of the theater. So the people who were in a hurry to get out simply rushed out of the theater as soon as they saw "The End" on the screen or— at the latest— when his picture came onto the screen. However, once the music began, everybody stood at attention and nobody moved. Not only would it have been in bad taste and unpatriotic, but an affront to our gracious, wonderful, loving king—long may he reign! —if we had not honored him by standing at attention when anyone played "God Save the King." And as far as I was concerned, it certainly would have broken part of the Wolf Cub Promise, because that was the only thing I could think of that would fulfill my "duty to the King."

As for the other promise—besides doing my best—I tried to do a good turn for somebody every day, However, there weren't many people in Sheho who needed help or would appreciate my good intentions. I couldn't help a blind old lady cross the street because there were no blind old ladies in Sheho or blind old men or anyone who was blind or deaf or physically or mentally handicapped in any way. Furthermore, Sheho had only one three-block long cement sidewalk, which we called a "street," and hardly anyone ever crossed it because there was nothing on the other side except four grain elevators, a tennis court, and the railway station. I quickly came to the conclusion that I would have to be creative if I wanted to do a good turn for somebody every day.

I thought of trying to avoid arguing or fighting with Sylvia, but she always started the argument first and if I didn't respond, it would take all the fun out of life. I thought of pleasing my sister Merle, my piano teacher, by practicing my piano lessons for at least ten minutes every day, but my fingers were growing so fast, it didn't make any difference if I practiced or not. I always hit the wrong keys.

It was really hard trying to do a good turn for somebody every day. Then I thought of my parents. Why not help them, thereby fulfilling my promise? Either Dad or Mom would get up a half-hour earlier than the rest of us every morning in order to start the fire in our kitchen stove. I would do my good deed for them by starting the fire myself, so they could stay in bed longer.

But if I had only known all the work involved in starting the fire, I would have practiced my piano lessons and made peace with Sylvia instead. Starting a fire depends upon many things, especially in winter. If the grates in the stove are first separated to drop the ashes into a bin, and if the ashes are emptied outside in the slop well near the back alley, and if the kindling wood is dry, and if it's brought into the house and cut into smaller pieces, and if the Jewish papers, the *Israelite Press* and the *Forward* arrive in time, and if my parents are through reading those papers and have accumulated a month's supply instead of taking them to the toilet, and if I crumple enough paper and put it below the kindling wood, and if there are enough matches so I can light the crumpled paper, and if the kindling wood is dry enough to ignite, and if I scrape the snow from the larger stick of wood outside so that it's dry enough to be placed on top of the kindling wood, and if all of this happens in its proper sequence, the fire will begin to burn long enough for me to add another larger stick of wood, and then close the top of the stove so that I can fill the large tea kettle with water from the pail nearby and place it on top of the stove, so that in twenty minutes it begins to whistle, waking up everyone in the house and providing us with boiling water for cocoa, then—when the fire has died down a bit—we can also make toast. If I had known all this before volunteering to start the fire, I would have done my good deed by pleasing both Merle and Sylvia instead.

Some day—perhaps even in my lifetime—it was prophesied that Sheho would have electricity. Someday, it was prophesied that Christ would return. I wasn't betting on either. So in spite of my misgivings about all the work I had to do to start the fire, I did my good turn for

Mom and Dad every morning thereafter, and I felt good knowing that I had made life just a little bit easier for those closest to me.

Every Tuesday evening at seven o'clock, we cubs gathered in the town hall and began our meeting with the Wolf Cub Howl and promise. Then Akela taught us many interesting and useful things, such as the history of our flag—The Union Jack—why it was called the Union Jack, which flags it was composed of, and the patron saints of each country: St. George of England, St. Patrick of Ireland, and St. Andrew of Scotland. St. George's flag was a red cross on a white background. I still remember that. St. Patrick's flag, as I recall, was a white diagonal flag on a red background. Or maybe it was a red diagonal cross on a white background. Or maybe it was a blue cross on a white background. Or it may have been a white diagonal cross on a blue background. Perhaps it was a blue cross on a red background. It might even have been a red diagonal cross on a blue background. I'm not quite sure. I get confused when I try to recall exactly which colors he chose for his flag and the exact colors St. Andrew also chose for his flag and how they were arranged. But after almost sixty years, I still remember the exact colors of the Union Jack: red, white, and blue. That's important. So what happened several years after I moved to the States? Canada got her own flag. And there's no blue in it. I learned all about the Union Jack for nothing.

We learned how to tie our shoe laces (I already knew that) and how to tie the reef knot and how to skip rope forwards and backwards and how to catch a ball and how to walk on a narrow plank above the ground like walking on a fence and how to build a fire using only two matches and all kinds of interesting and useful things. And after each meeting ended, at eight o'clock, Tracy and I were so excited we walked up and down the street discussing what we had learned and what we intended to learn and what we were going to do at our next meeting. We were planning strategy like two newly appointed field marshals.

Nobody in our pack had an official wolf cub's uniform except Ian Munro, Mr. Munro's younger son. He wore the complete cub's uniform—which included shorts, long woolen stockings, and a woolen jersey—at every meeting, no matter how cold it was in winter or how hot it might get in late spring.

You may wonder why we just wore our kerchiefs instead. If we had worn only those shorts, we would have frozen to death in the winter. And if we had worn those long-sleeved all wool jerseys and long woolen stockings, we would have roasted to death in the summer. The navy cap and brown wide belt would have been okay, but not the rest of the uniform. Our kerchiefs were just fine, thank you.

Seven months later, when I was twelve and joined the Boy Scouts, I ordered a green Official Boy Scout shirt from Toronto. The rest of the uniform might come later. But the shirt was important. I needed it for the badges I quickly earned.

I loved participating in our Boy Scout troop. In the fifteen months during which the troop was active, from 1939 through 1940, I quickly rose from tenderfoot through the ranks as far as one could go except for the highest rank, a king scout. I also earned a number of proficiency badges, including the astronomer's badge, all of which I proudly sewed on my shirt after Mom had shown me how. Of all the badges I earned, the one that gave me the most satisfaction was the astronomer's proficiency badge, for it involved many months of my favorite hobby—star gazing. I learned to identify about twenty constellations with their major stars, and eventually I could even tell time by the stars to within an hour, using as my guides Ursa Major (the Big Dipper) most of the year, and Sirus the Dog Star during the long winter nights.

When I first joined the Scouts, our troop was practicing certain skills for a competition to be held at a huge Boy Scout Jamboree in Yorkton during the long Queen Victoria Day weekend in May of 1940. Our team concentrated on seeing how fast we could put up a regulation size umbrella tent. Each team of scouts was assigned a particular duty, beginning with unrolling the tent, pounding wooden pegs into the ground— correctly—then opening the umbrella inside the tent, inserting the ends into the proper holes, tying the ropes down, and so on. At first it took us several minutes, but after repeating the process time and time again, we were able to pitch a tent in less than a minute. We knew we were good, but we didn't know how good. Finally, at the jamboree, surrounded by perhaps a thousand scouts from all over the area, we were ready to meet the challenge. The event was announced over a loudspeaker, a whistle blew, and we began. In a matter of seconds our tent was up. We stood by and waited for about ten minutes until the last troop had pitched its tent. Then the judges announced the winner. The Sheho Boy Scout Troop had set a record for pitching a tent.

Although there was a large A-frame tent which stood in Lys's yard every summer since I could remember, neither Tracy nor I ever slept in it until we became cubs. But sleeping in such a large tent wasn't as much fun as sleeping in a little pup tent. So the first summer after I had graduated from the cubs into the Boy Scouts, shortly after I had turned twelve, Tracy and I, with Mom's help, set up a little make-shift pup tent just outside the summer kitchen in our back yard. Mom donated an old gray woolen blanket and two fairly old brooms. Tracy and I began by sawing each broom handle off at its base, then pounding two of the handles with rounded edges into the ground. To complete the framework, Dad gave us a narrow board that we laid across the upright poles and secured it with the help of a hammer and nails. Then Mom lent us a small mattress, which we laid under this framework. Finally, we draped the blanket over the frame and stretched the sides of the blanket, pinning these sides into the ground at their edges with small staple nails. That was our official Jackie Katz-Walter Lys pup tent. It was about the same size as the official Boy Scout version, but much cheaper and a heck of a lot more fun because we had made it ourselves.

Practically every night during that summer of 1940, Tracy would come over to my home after we had finished our potato roasts under the Western bridge. We both would undress, lay our clothes just outside the tent, then one-by-one crawl inside. Although it was comfortable enough because of the mattress and pillows, it was really cramped inside. When I say there wasn't an inch to spare, I mean it. But it was exciting. We poked our heads outside the tent and for the longest time looked straight up at the Milky Way and a billion stars. And nobody in the whole world had a better view than we had of the most beautiful ballet imaginable— the Northern Lights. I thought there was only one thing missing— music.

Sometimes when Mom insisted, Tracy joined our family for breakfast. But usually he went straight home. Then, about an hour after our noon-day dinner, I rode my bike to his place, and we both pedaled the 1 1/2 miles over dirt roads to Maas's Lake. Someone had told us it was dangerous to swim immediately after eating, and that we should wait at least an hour before going into the water. Even though Maas's Lake was hardly more than five feet deep, except in the middle, where it was barely over our heads, we reluctantly waited for at least half an hour. An hour is a long time to waste when you're only twelve and you've got only three hours to spend at the lake before you have to go home for supper and there's only a month or so left before school starts. So, we made the most of it.

Although the lake was practically deserted every afternoon, we were occasionally joined by some of the other kids from town including girls. For this reason, we wore bathing suits. We had graduated from swimming bare naked in the old mud hole in the creek to respectability. Now we wore bathing suits while lounging on the shore or swimming in the almost half-mile long lake on Maas's farm.

Someone had built a log raft from poplar trees and left it floating near the shore. Tracy and I pushed it outward toward the deep water, then competed to see who could swim the fastest from the shore to the raft. I thought I was pretty fast, but no matter what stroke I used or how many times we raced, he always beat me. He beat me at practically every sport. A couple of years later, I bought an expensive tennis racket from Walter Woods and challenged him to a match. His racket had cost only $2.95 from Eaton's catalog, and I boasted that my $9.00 Walter Woods wholesale racket would beat his cheap Eaton's racket. He beat me in the first set, so I challenged him again. He beat me even worse. I never boasted again. I challenged him, but I never boasted.

When we got tired of swimming to and from the raft, we climbed aboard and simply lay down, sunning ourselves or looking up at the fleecy white clouds, with our feet dangling in the cool water, as the raft bobbed up and down and drifted along the shoreline. Then, for excitement, we used the two poles aboard the raft to push it along the lake. The poles, cut from young poplar trees, were about eight feet long, the same length as the raft, and barely slim enough to grip in our hands. Standing at opposite sides of the raft, we pushed the poles downward at an angle through the water until they stuck in the mud, thus propelling the raft forward. Then we tugged at the poles to pull them up from the mud and once more pushed them downward until we had reached full speed, maybe faster than a baby crawls before it learns to stand up. If we got bored with rafting, we simply lay our poles down and drifted, or else dived off the raft and swam around until we got tired. Then we resumed our adventure.

Early one afternoon while rafting about a hundred yards off shore, we spotted some girls in the water at the other end of the lake. "Look Tracy, let's go over there and say hello."

"Why not? I'll bet they're not wearing any bathing suits."

"I'll bet you're right."

We pushed and tugged on our poles as fast as we could, and the raft picked up speed, moving through the water faster than a baby walking. In less than an hour, we were almost half way across the lake. "Look, Tracy, you're right. They're bare naked."

"I told you so."

"Do you think they'll wait for us?"

"Why not? As long as we get there before the sun sets."

"Wouldn't it be something if we could surprise them before they were able to put their clothes on?"

"That would be something," Tracy replied, "but don't count on it."

"Yeah, but wouldn't it be something? I've never seen a naked girl. Have you?"

"No, just a naked baby."

"Me too. Maybe we'll get lucky."

So we pushed and tugged and pushed and tugged until we were past the point of no return. We had wondered how deep the middle of the lake was, so we dipped our poles straight down in the water until they barely touched the bottom, then pulled them up and held them straight up next to us. The waterline was over our heads by less than a foot. We thus calculated that the depth was almost six feet at the deepest point.

As we slowly approached the shore, about two hundred yards away, the girls appeared to notice us. "Look, Tracy, I think they've seen us. And they're still naked."

"Yeah, but wait. Look, they're getting dressed. Just like I said."

"Darn it! Do you think they'll wait for us."

"Why not? They don't have anything else to do."

"What should we say to them?"

"I don't know. What do you think?"

"I don't know. May be we'll figure it out when we get there."

Minute-by-minute the shoreline and the girls came closer into view. We recognized some of the girls—the Brozowskis and Slowskis. At last we reached the shore. Tracy and I got off the raft, walked toward them and blushed as we said, "Hello." That was all we said.

They blushed and replied, "Hello."

Then we turned around and headed back to the other shore.

Disgusted with ourselves for having missed the greatest opportunity of our lives, neither one of us had much to say on the way back. And that was the closest Tracy and I ever came to seeing a naked girl during our entire life in Sheho.

Tracy and I took turns sleeping in each other's tent. His tent was much larger, of course, so we could stretch our arms without bothering the other. We continued to sleep in our tents for the first few weeks after school started. Tracy, one grade behind me, was now in the seventh grade, so we had the same teacher, Mr. Fred Kindrachuk.

Mr. Kindrachuk lived in the hotel, right across the street from Lys's store. He was on very close terms with Mr. Lys and usually visited him a few times a day—often just before school started, at noon, and again after school. One morning, just after the bell rang, Mr. Kindrachuk made this announcement to his classes: "Jackie Katz and Walter Lys spent the summer sleeping together in their tents. Last night they slept in Walter's tent, and sometime during the night they had unexpected company that stayed all night. Anyone want to guess?"

The class buzzed with excitement. "Who? Who? Who?" They sounded like owls.

"You'll never guess. They slept with a muskrat."

"You're kidding," I said. "Your making it up." I knew I was Mr. Kindrachuk's pet, and I thought he was trying to make me the center of attention.

"No, honest! Mr. Lys found a muskrat in the tent this morning. He put it in a box with holes so it can breathe. It's still there."

Neither Walter nor I knew anything about that muskrat; so as soon as we went home at noon, we checked with Mr. Lys. The story was true. The muskrat had entered the tent while we were asleep. Immediately after school was out, Walter and I fastened the box tightly to his bike. As soon as I returned with my bike, we pedaled to Maas's Lake. We unfastened the box, then carefully carried it to the shore, right at the edge of the water, so that when we opened the box, the muskrat would be facing the water. Then we slit the strands of rope surrounding the box. It took at least four or five seconds before the muskrat realized it was free. Then it scrambled out of the box and immediately ran into the water and swam away.

For the next year, Tracy and I rode our bikes all over the place, including foot paths and trails through the woods where I'm sure nobody had ever ridden before. We made our own paths as we rode time and again, around clusters of poplar, willow, and birch trees. Our favorite trail, however, was the one north of the town well, through the open prairie, then through the woods toward the barbed wire fence at the edge of Wunder's field. It was here, at a clearing on the prairie, alongside a growth of poplar trees, that we studied for our final exams to be taken in the middle of June 1941.

That year, beginning in late May and culminating in the last two weeks of June, an infestation of billions and billions of caterpillars invaded Saskatchewan. So numerous were they in parts of the province, that on some railway lines they squirmed over every inch of the rails, piled one upon the other inches deep. When the railway engine ran over them, squashing this mass of worms into a slippery goo, the wheels simply spun around and around because the goo was so wet it prevented the wheels from gripping the rails to gain enough traction to move. In some cases train schedules were delayed by hours because of this infestation.

The main food source of these furry, one-inch long, orange and black squiggly caterpillars was the bark of poplar trees. They would crawl along the ground toward the very bottom of the tree, then squiggle their way upward, thousands of them, devouring the bark as they went along. Within four hours the entire tree and its branches would be completely covered with this mass of orange and black squiggling caterpillars. Hours later, the caterpillars would be gone from that particular tree, the bark having been completely stripped clean, with not even a tiny speck visible.

Because of this infestation, Tracy and I no longer rode our bikes through the woods. We did, however, continue to ride on our favorite trail but stopped at the clearing near the trees. It was here that we laid our bikes on the ground shortly after supper to study for our final exams. Being out in the open relieved the boredom of having to study.

We opened our notebooks and began studying. But looking at the caterpillars was more interesting. So we studied the caterpillars. I don't know who thought of it, but we decided to call them by another name—"McDoogals."

"Get away from me, you McDoogals," I said, as I flipped them off our blanket.

"Here's another one," Tracy said. "I hate them. Let's build a fire and toss them in."

We had long ago mastered the art of building a campfire. Within minutes, besides listening to the crackling of burning branches, we heard a new sound altogether—the faint sizzle of burning fat. "That's one way of getting rid of McDoogles," he said.

"It's better than squashing them," I said, as I pulled one off my pant leg and flipped it into the fire.

As the evening wore on, fading into twilight and eventually darkness, we continued to feed the fire with branches and large tree stumps until it became a roaring bonfire, vanquishing the darkness. The heat kept the McDoogels away, so we were able to study without interruption. Gradually the flickering flames cast shadows onto our notebooks. We waited until the flames died down; then we scraped dirt over the embers and left. It was late when we got home. But we had accomplished our goal. We had studied all our notes for one entire subject. We were now ready for that exam. We had only five more subjects to go. Tomorrow night we would cover another.

My final eighth grade examinations began during the third week of June. The only subject I had not reviewed was the section on grammar dealing with parts of speech. It bored me. I was a good writer, but I hated studying the parts of speech. I hoped that section would not be on the exam. Then I walked into the room to take my first exam—English. Mr. Kindrachuk showed us the sealed envelope containing the printed examinations from the Saskatchewan Department of Education. He broke the seal and took out the bundle of sheets—the grade eight English examinations. He handed them, one-by-one, to the entire class. I glanced at mine. Then I stared at it in horror. The first question required the writer to define adverbs and, as I recall, adverbial phrases and clauses. I didn't have a clue. I didn't know what to write. I was lost. I thought of praying to God for help, as Walter and I had done two years earlier, when a mean-looking, snarling dog had barked at us, blocking our way home from Paul's Lake. God had answered our prayers then.

At that *exact moment*, while I was thinking about how the Almighty had answered our prayers and had even anticipated my prayer to be spared from stinking like a skunk when it too had blocked our way —at that very moment our principal, Mr. Louis Tomaschuk, walked into the room and said, "Excuse me, class. I have an important announcement to make. Two students in grade eight have done so well throughout the year that they have been recommended. Congratulations to Annie Homeniuk and Jackie Katz. You will not have to take your exams."

"Thank God," I whispered. Then I thought to myself, "How did He know?"

I knew I was the luckiest guy in school, and I'm sure He did, too. Apparently it was the first time that anyone in our school had been recommended to pass on to the next grade without taking the final exams.

I immediately left my printed exam sheet on my desk, thanked Mr. Kindrachuk and Mr. Tomaschuk, said good-bye to the class and hurried out of the room. I had now completed public school. And I had the whole summer ahead of me.

When I returned from my holidays in Inglis later that summer, Dad had a surprise for me. " I bought for you from Mr. Darling his tent. He never uses it, so I gave him ten dollars. You and Walter should enjoy it."

That was my dad. Six years earlier when I had asked him to buy me a twenty-five cent hockey stick his immediate reply was: "My grandfather never had a hockey stick," and so on. We had been in the depths of the Depression then. Now, times were different. With farmers getting higher prices for grain and livestock, and with mail order houses unable to fill their orders because of wartime shortages, merchants were able to sell goods that in many cases had gathered dust over the years. And so my father, knowing how much I enjoyed sleeping outside in my make-shift tent, simply surprised me with a wonderful gift that I had never dreamed of getting: Mr. Darling's old but rarely used seven-foot umbrella tent. I pitched it, myself, in our yard that very day. Now Walter and I could sleep under the stars in luxurious comfort, thanks to Dad's generosity and to Mom's contribution of a large mattress.

For the remainder of that summer and the following one, Tracy and I slept in my tent practically every night. The most exciting event we experienced was a total eclipse of the moon. We watched the full moon slowly begin to disappear, as though it were being slowly bitten off, tiny bite by bite, as one might bite off one's finger nails until there is nothing left. My science textbook explained that this phenomenon was caused by the encroaching earth's shadow, since the sun and the moon were at virtually opposite sides of the earth. After about an hour and forty-five minutes, the bright moon had disappeared. It was now but a shadow. Then a few minutes later, it slowly began to reappear, first as a minute crescent, like the clipping of a finger nail, gradually getting bigger and bigger. Finally, the full moon was again visible; the eclipse was over.

Not every night was perfectly clear. Or perfectly calm. The weather on the Canadian Prairies is often unpredictable. Many a night after turning in, we were awakened by sudden gusts of wind that shook the top of our tent back and forth. Fortunately, because of my training in the Boy Scouts, I had learned how to pound in the pegs at the correct angle to prevent them from being torn loose by the wind, thereby ensuring that the tent secured by the ropes would hold.

But rainstorms were another matter. Although the canvas was virtually waterproof, the openings into which the prongs of the umbrella fit were not air tight, thus allowing a little rain to drip into the tent. We didn't mind a few drops or even a few more drops. But we had not planned for a downpour. Because the ground was not perfectly level, water could seep into the tent's floor if the ground became flooded. One night about 2:00 a.m. during an unexpected heavy downpour, water began pouring through the doorway into the tent. There was only one solution. Abandon ship. Tracy and I rolled up our clothes and tried to roll up the mattress as best we could, then ran outside and into our house. We slept in my room. The next morning we inspected the tent. The mattress was soaked in a foot of water that covered the floor of the tent. We swept most of the water out of the tent and left the flap open to air. But we knew it would be a long time before the mattress would dry out. So we decided to put our camping experience on hold. In time, we decided it was simply more comfortable sleeping in our own beds. Eventually, I took down my tent, rolled it up, and never pitched it again.

When I entered the tenth grade at the age of fourteen, I began to work in our store after school hours and all day Saturday. Ten months later, at the age of fifteen, when school was out, I did not take a vacation, but instead continued to work full time in the store, from 9:00 a.m. until 6:00 P.M. Although the store remained open for another hour, Dad gave me permission to leave so that Walter and I could bike to the lake.

Maas's Lake, which had begun drying up the previous year, was no longer much fun. We therefore decided to pedal nine miles north over a dirt road, halfway to the next village, Invermay. After an hour's ride, we turned off the road to our left, where we parked our bikes. We had reached our destination—Newburn Lake.

Over the years we had graduated from the mud hole in the Creek that flowed through Wunder's field to the almost half-mile long Maas's Lake, to a much larger, deeper and cleaner lake. Hot and sweaty after our ride, we agreed there was nothing more refreshing than taking a swim in the cool waters of our newly discovered lake. On our first trip, we entered the foreign waters apprehensively since we didn't know if there were rocks below the surface. Fortunately, there were none. Although we could wade out for a long distance before the water came up to our chins, it eventually became much deeper, presenting us with an exciting challenge to dive and reach the bottom.

Our new lake was much more popular than the old one. Although we were usually the only ones there from Sheho, every night we met several people from Invermay, including the odd girl who was not afraid to say more than "hello." One night we got into a conversation with a girl whose skin tight bathing suit accentuated every curve underneath. She told us she had won an essay contest sponsored by the Saskatchewan Cooperative Elevators and was about to go to Regina as a reward. Tracy and I wished we were all back in the mud swimming hole where bathing suits were not allowed, but we were afraid to tell her. Then we thought of making up a story to impress her, but changed our minds. We weren't creative enough and were afraid of telling fibs on such short notice. So we just listened to her. At the age of fifteen, Tracy and I both needed all the help we could get to perfect our social skills. As for any sexual exploits, fantasizing about what was underneath her bathing suit was as close as we ever got.

Throughout that summer and the following one, in 1944, when at the age of sixteen I was about to enter my final year of high school, we continued to pedal to Newburn Lake every evening just as soon as I got off work. At six o'clock I would leave the store, quickly grab a bite, then pedal to Walter's home, and off we would go. Exactly one hour later we would arrive at the lake. We would swim for an hour, then return, getting home at nine. Though it was still daylight at that hour in July, by the end of August it was dark by the time we reached home.

One evening in late August, just before I began grade twelve, Tracy took out his pocket knife and said, "I'm going to carve our names and this date on some trees. When we come back here next year, we'll see if our names are still there. And when we come back years from now, we'll try to find the these trees."

Perhaps he knew that this night would be the last one we would ever spend at Newburn Lake. And it would the last night we brothers would share our boyhood dreams.

Shortly afterward, Mr. Lys sold his store to Mr. Kuproski, and Walter and Jenny moved to Yorkton. Walter and his sister returned to Sheho on weekends occasionally to visit their parents who had remained behind. Walter, Jenny, and I talked about school—Yorkton Collegiate and Sheho High School— and about Frank Sinatra and the Hit Parade and the latest songs, including "Paper Doll," and what we were going to do when we finished high school. I missed Walter, but I was too busy with school and with working in the store to dwell on it.

In 1947 the Lys family moved to Saskatoon. I never saw Walter again until 1950, when I visited him briefly at his new home. Then in 1952, two years after he had graduated in pharmacy, he dropped in on me unexpectedly early one morning, in my one-room apartment in downtown Edmonton. He had had a quarrel with his dad and had left in haste. By the time I returned from work later that day, he felt bad and decided to return. We corresponded with each other during his pharmacy internship in Leask, Saskatchewan, and for the remainder of my years in Edmonton. In 1953 his dad bought a drug store for him in Norquay, Saskatchewan.

When I left Edmonton for Winnipeg in June of 1955, before moving to the United States, I wrote to Walter, telling him that I would be stopping overnight at Yorkton to visit my dear friends, Mr. and Mrs. Harry Ferman. Since Norquay was only about a half-hour drive away, I asked Walter to pick me up the following evening. He drove me to his cabin at a nearby lake, and over more than a few drinks of Seagram's V.O. in front of the fire, we reminisced about our youth. I rarely drank, but this was a very special occasion. Unfortunately, I could not hold my liquor well, and on our way back to the hotel, I threw up all over my clothes. When we got to the Blackstone Hotel and asked for a room, the night clerk took one look at me and said, "We have no vacancies."

"Give him a room," said Walter, "or I'll tell, the owner, Mr. Borkman." The clerk immediately gave me a key.

Walter accompanied me to my room. We said good-bye and shook hands. That was the last time I saw my brother.

After I moved to California, we corresponded from time to time. In 1958 he sent me a picture of himself and his dog, along with a picture of a hospital nurse he had been dating, Cornelia Grywascwchesk. Later that year he sent me a wedding invitation. I sent them a deluxe Sunbeam electric mixmaster with all the attachments. The gift plus duty cost me what would have been a week's pay. But since I was unemployed at the time, I dug into my savings. I wished I could have sent more.

In the summer of 1960, my sister Sylvia showed me a Canadian newspaper clipping. In May of that year, while his wife, pregnant with their child, was out of town, Walter had fallen asleep while smoking a cigarette which ignited the mattress and set fire to the building in which he was sleeping. Walter had died in the fire. He was only thirty-two years old.

In the fall of that year, his widow gave birth to their daughter—Waltra. I hope to meet her someday. After all, she is my niece.

CHAPTER SIXTEEN
My Ribbons, The Elocution Contest, And Mr. Kindrachuk

As I mentioned in an earlier chapter, whenever my father got disgusted with me, which was more often than you can imagine, he used to say, "*Foon deer vil zien a richh ahz foon myna twerizena schich.*" That high-and-lofty praise translates literally into English as "You will amount to as much as my torn shoes." What it really means, however, is "You will amount to as much as the torn soles of my shoes." There is a difference in meaning between the two versions. What can one do with the torn *soles* of a pair of shoes? They really aren't worth very much, even in a depressed economy. To him, my first place field-and-track ribbons were worth only slightly more than the torn soles of his shoes. But not much more. He didn't understand very much about the younger generation.

My track career began out of necessity. Whenever my sister Sylvia got mad at me, she would tell Papa some ridiculous story, accusing me of hitting her. That was all Papa needed. He never even thought of questioning me to find the truth. He didn't believe in finding out what really happened. Two sides to a story? What two sides? Evidence? Who needs evidence? He believed her every time. Immediately—and without warning—he would pull the belt off his size 44 pants and lash me on my seat with that belt several times until his anger had abated and he felt justice had been handed out. He never swatted me with his hand. Only with the belt. He sincerely believed that a strapping from his belt was less painful than a swatting by hand. Maybe it was less painful for him, but I never knew the difference. So whenever I saw him unbuckle his belt, I never stayed around long enough to ask why. I immediately ran out of the house and around our engine house as fast as I could, around and around, with Papa in hot pursuit. He was an excellent sprinter, but because I had at least a three or four second start on him and was at least 150 pounds lighter and forty years younger, with a lot more stamina, he never caught me.

Three times around the Sheho Royal Museum of Canada at full speed was all Papa could manage. Then he collapsed on the ground and watched his worthless son just keep on running. Believe me, I was fast. I mean really fast. It was no contest. Year in and year out he never even came close to catching his worthless son. He should have known that he was my coach and I was in training to become a track star.

My first red ribbon, signifying first-place in the fifty yard dash, was awarded to me in the fourth or fifth grade, only months after I had been forced into retirement from a less than promising pee-wee hockey career because I had outgrown my one-and-only piece of hockey equipment— my twenty-five cent hockey stick. And since Papa would never dream of throwing away fifty cents to buy me a bigger hockey stick, I knew that my chances of being drafted first overall in the National Hockey League were even less than the chances of Eaton's catalog selling worn out soles from torn shoes. So I never asked Papa for a fifty cent hockey stick because I knew what his answer would be: "Fifty cents for a hockey stick! Are you crazy?"

But canvas running shoes were a different matter. During the spring and summer, Papa stocked rubber-soled canvas shoes, also called tennis shoes or running shoes. Practically everyone—boys and girls alike — wore running shoes to school. They cost seventy-five cents wholesale, and Papa sold them for ninety cents, with discounts on quantity purchases. So I didn't have to ask him to buy me a pair of running shoes.

In early April, just after the crows and robins returned, his order for running shoes arrived, but there was still too much snow on the ground to wear them. A couple of weeks later—when we heard the meadowlarks sing their cheery refrain, "I was here a year ago, I was here a year ago," and the days grew longer and the snow began to melt, giving way to slush and mud everywhere, and Johnny Drobot challenged everyone to a game of marbles at school in the moist clay on the school-ground and won—I knew it wouldn't be much longer before the ground was dry enough to play softball. Then in early May, when the wild crocuses and buttercups and daisies and tulips carpeted the fields at the fairgrounds across the tracks, and the lean and hungry gophers came out of their burrows with their tiny young, and everyone began digging a vegetable garden in the back yard (and the front yard too), and the ground was now dry enough to play softball, then—in early May—I was furnished with a brand new pair of running shoes. I didn't have to worry about getting them dirty or scuffing them or getting them wet. They were all purpose shoes meant to last me at least through the summer and possibly through the fall if I didn't outgrow them. I was now ready to run.

And did I run! I ran everywhere: to and from school, from our store to the Elite cafe every afternoon when Papa gave me a nickel to buy an ice cream cone, to Mr. Leckie's store every Monday to read the weekly funny papers (then put them back on the newsstand afterward), to the Western bridge, to the creek that flowed through Wunder's field, to Walter Lys's home, and to-and-from the store to our house. I did not like standing still. Even Papa remarked to Mama, " *Keek auf dien zeen. Er fleet.*" [Look at your son. He flies.]

I was not consciously practicing for the Sheho sports event which was held annually at the fair grounds every Victoria Day, usually on the last Monday preceding May 24th. I just liked to run. So every afternoon in early May, when our school had practice tryouts to pick the winners who would represent the school for the big event, I was delighted.

I remember the first tryout for the fifty yard dash. All the boys in the fourth and fifth grades lined up at the starting line, at the east end of the school ground. We all crouched slightly forward with our hands on our knees and our left foot in front of the right. I was the shortest one in line by far. There was Johnny Fosti who could really run, and Eddie Grumetza who towered above me, and Boris Moroz who was the best stick handler on our hockey team, and George Homeniuk who was the fastest skater and all the other kids much bigger than I. What was I doing here? I didn't think I had a chance.

Mr. Black, our principal, said, "Get in line everyone. Don't step over that line. Your toe must not be over that line." We all moved our toes back—just to the very edge of the line. Then he said, "I'm going to count to three and then shout 'go.' Get ready now. One, two, three, GO!"

I leaped forward at the sound of "Go!" But I was behind some of the kids who had cheated. Even some who had not cheated, like Boris Moroz and George Homeniuk, were ahead of me. But not for long. It took me about two seconds, maybe three at the most, and I was even with the leaders. Another two seconds and there was nobody ahead of me except the vice principal standing at the finish line. I flew past him as he raised his arm and pointed to me. Then I gradually stopped and walked back to the finish line. "Jackie Katz came in first," he announced. I strutted past the others and all I could hear from them was "Little Jackie Katz came in first."

I was proud to realize I would be representing our school for our grade levels at the big event to be held at the fair grounds on Victoria Day. All the one-room country schools in our entire municipality would be participating. The closest one was Fosti school, three miles south of town; the farthest was Newburn, nine miles north. And then there was Dunrobin, six miles west; and then schools east and south of us: Runneymeade and Pohorlowitz and Deer Creek and Krasney — and every school in the entire area. It would be a huge event. Nobody stuck up his nose at these country schools. Although they rarely had more than a total enrollment of fifteen or twenty students in all grade levels, from one through eight and sometimes nine, most of their students were excellent athletes. I had seen them challenge our own softball team and almost win. Their best players were usually as good or better than our best, but they lacked depth. Otherwise they could have beaten our teams. But a track event was a different story. They could all run. And they needed only one participant to win.

We all hoped the weather would be good. Very often it rained on the Victoria Day holiday. Sometimes it even snowed. One could never predict what the weather would be like on the Prairies in May. So we hoped and prayed for good weather. And we were lucky on this day.

Once again I was the shortest one by far at the starting line. And I was nervous. These boys were bigger than my own classmates whom I had beaten. And I was sure they were older. They looked tough. They looked down at me, sneering as if they had discovered a stray cat that had mistakenly wandered into their midst. Some wore heavy work boots, others wore running shoes like mine, but most of them had nothing to cover their feet. They would run the race in their bare feet.

A length of binder twine indicated the starting line. Once again the instructions were shouted at us. " Your toes must not go over this piece of twine. They can touch it, but they cannot go over." We all pulled our left foot back, then slowly inched it forward. My left foot barely touched the line, but some of the others cheated. Then I heard the whistle. "Get ready. One, two, three, GO!"

This time I was behind for only a second, maybe two at the most. Then I was gone. Nobody even came close to me. I was now the fastest sprinter of anyone my age not only in Sheho but in our entire area —the whole municipality. And I had a red first-place ribbon pinned to my shirt to prove it.

I proudly wore the ribbon around the fair ground for a few hours, but after everyone stared at me, I took it off. The next day after school I thought I'd show it to Papa. I went into the store and waited until there were no customers. Then I pinned the ribbon on my shirt and went up to Papa. "See! I got this for running the fastest race in Sheho."He stared at it incredulously, then said, *"Maschigana kynd. Dee dahf loywfin for a ribbon. Veer hobin all kinds ribbons do for finif cents a yard. Dee volst a ribbon. Ich can gibben deer ribbons."* ["Crazy child. You have to run for a ribbon. We have all kinds of ribbons here for five cents a yard. You want ribbons. I can give you ribbons.] Then he paused and said *"Loz mir zayen dyne ribbon."* [Let me see your ribbon.] He lifted it from my hand and held it up to his glasses. "First Place." He paused. I waited for him to hand it back. *"Ah, es is tahka a shayna ribbon. I'ch vil hobben dyne ribbon."* [Ah, it is really a pretty ribbon. I would like to have your ribbon.] Before I could protest, he took my ribbon and pinned it to a box of lemons, just below the yellow and black boxes of Quaker corn flakes, in full view of anyone near the grocery counter.

For the next few days he proudly pointed out my ribbon to anyone who came into the store. "See, mine Jackie won this. He's the fastest runner in the whole Sheho country."

On Saturday afternoon when I happened to be in the store, Mrs. Annie Hanson came into town on her buggy, pulled by her old and faithful horse Nellie. While she waited behind the counter for Papa to fill her weekly order, which included a new horse collar, three boxes of Quaker corn flakes, a pound of coffee, and four lemons, she stared at the ribbon and finally said, "Louis, that sure is a pretty ribbon. Lemmie see it. First Place! Ain't that somethin."

"Mine Jackie won it for running. He's the fastest runner in the whole Sheho country."

Then she turned to me. "First place for runin. Ain't that somethin. You know, Jackie, My Nellie's gettin kinda old. She's slowin up a bit. Maybe that ribbon would pick her up a bit. Whataya think? And it would sure look good on her. Whataya think? I'd sure like to have that ribbon for Nellie."

"My ribbon on a horse!"

"She's not just a horse. She's my horse. My Nellie. She's been with me a long time. I know that ribbon would perk her up. And it would sure look good on her. Whataya say?"

What could I say? I wouldn't wear that ribbon any more, and I hadn't even thought of collecting trophies. "Okay, you can give my ribbon to Nellie."

Annie Hanson thanked me and secured the ribbon onto the new horse collar by tying string around it several times. Then she took off Nellie's old collar and put the brand new one—with my first-place red ribbon— around Nellie's neck. As I waved good-bye to them, it seemed to me that her horse lifted its tail and swished it back and forth, as if to say, "Thank you for awarding me your first place ribbon." And Mrs. Hanson swore that Nellie trotted home faster than ever, with her head held high and as proud as a horse could be, for the first time in years.

I owned the fifty yard dash for several years afterward, not only on Victoria day, but also on July 12th, Sheho's biggest event—its annual Sports Day. Practically every town on the Prairies sponsored a "Sports

Day," usually held on July 1st, Dominion Day (now called Canada Day). July 1st was Canada's equivalent of July 4th, except that Canada—instead of celebrating its independence from England—celebrated its confederation with other provinces to become a new country, a "dominion" belonging to the British Empire.

So as not to compete with other nearby towns which sponsored their Sports Day on July 1st, Sheho held its annual sports day on a Ukrainian holiday, July 12th, when it was sure to draw the largest crowd of the year. That day the population of the village swelled from about three hundred and fifty to perhaps a thousand. Entire families came from not only the village itself and from every farm in the whole municipality and also from neighboring towns like Foam Lake, eighteen miles away; Theodore, twenty-four miles away; and even as far away as Wynyard, fifty miles distant.

Every town, every village, and every farm school in the entire area had a softball team. And they all came to the Sheho Sports Day to compete for prize money amounting to as much as $25 for first prize, $15 for second, and $10 for third. Every town and every village had a baseball team, and many came to compete for big prize money amounting to as much as $100 for first place, $50 for second, and $30 for third. Every farmer had a horse, not like Nellie but a horse that could gallop around the half-mile race track, not once but even twice, for enough prize money to buy a new horse collar, a new curry comb for its mane, and enough blocks of salt to last the horse for an entire year and even longer. Every family had at least four children—boys and girls—who could run and leap and jump, and hop-skip-and-jump, and compete in every event offered for prize money as high as twenty-five cents for first place, fifteen cents second, ten cents third, and a nickel for everyone who competed. Everyone was a winner. It was a sure bet.

I lined up with my age group for the fifty yard dash. There must have been at least twenty of us jostling for position. I knew that some of the kids were older than they pretended to be. They were much bigger and taller than I. (Everyone was taller than I.) They were cheating. We were supposed to keep our feet back of the binder twine, the starting line. But everyone cheated. Some put their entire foot over the starting line. It wasn't fair. So I cheated too. Soon came the warning whistle, followed by the starting judge waving his arms as he shouted,

> "One for the money,
>
> Two for the show,
>
> Three to get ready,
>
> And four to GO!"

A few kids had cheated by leaping forward just before "Go!"

But it took me only a second to catch up with them. Then I was gone. I easily came in first. The judges at the finish line congratulated me; then one of them handed me a quarter. All the rest of the kids got money too. I felt proud to have won first place again, but I was not about to keep my quarter. I passed the stand where Cecil Wunder was shouting, "Come and win a prize playing housey, housey." It was a game like bingo, and people were putting down nickels and even dimes and shouting "Housey, housey" when they won. I walked over to the stand where the United Church of Canada was selling slices of watermelons and gave Mrs. Tansley my quarter. She gave me back 15 cents and a huge slice of watermelon. After I finished eating it, I walked over to another stand, like the first, built with wooden boards as counters, and nailed to poplar logs pounded into the ground and covered by a roof of small poplar trees and branches. I bought an ice cream cone for a dime. It was twice as much as I always paid at the Elite Cafe. But I still had a nickel left. So after I finished my ice cream, I moved over to the next stand and bought a bottle of coca- cola with the nickel. I was now full and I suddenly realized that I had no money left. It was really easy to spend twenty-five cents in no time at all on July 12th.

I went over to the baseball diamond to watch Sheho play Foam Lake. I sat down on the grass outside the fence that was about twenty feet behind the catcher. That fence had been built to stop any baseballs the catcher missed, including the ones which had been batted foul and flew backward high in the air. However, the fence was not high enough to trap all the foul balls. Not nearly high enough. So in order to retrieve these baseballs, the club offered young kids like me a dollar for the entire day if we would run back and retrieve the ball. As I watched Bud Curry, Sheho's pitcher, wind up and hurl his fast ball over the plate, striking out batter after batter, with more than the occasional fly ball sailing over the fence, I couldn't help but think back to the previous year, when instead of watching the ball game, I had participated.

After winning a nickel in the race, I had been offered a whole dollar in advance to retrieve baseballs that had been batted foul and had sailed over the fence behind the catcher. There were three of us—Walter Harris, another kid, and I. Every time a ball sailed over the fence, one of us would run to find it and then bring it back. Because there were several games played on this tournament day, we were kept busy all day. One game followed the other, and I just kept running back, picking up one baseball after the other. I wasn't hungry, I didn't have a watch, and I didn't know what time it was, although I suspected it might have been near supper time. But the sun was still high in the southwest sky. Gradually the crowds began to thin, and even the other kid left. Only Walter Harris remained with me now to pick up the foul balls. The sun was now slightly lower in the west. I hadn't even thought of going home for supper because I was working—fulfilling my obligation. Suddenly I noticed Papa coming toward me, sternly waving a switch from a poplar branch. "Go home!" he shouted. "Bum. *Foon deer vil zyen a richh as foon myna twerizena schich.*" [You will amount to as much as the torn soles of my shoes.]

I dropped the ball and ran home, crying all the way from embarrassment and humiliation as Papa continued to chase me with that switch.

I have thought about that incident many, many times during my lifetime. I never did understand some of Papa's motivations, and I know he didn't understand mine. He belonged to the old generation from the old country with old fashioned ideas and old fashioned ways of doing things. I was his opposite. I belonged completely to the new generation. I was a Canadian and proud of it. I spoke to him in English almost all the time, but he continued to speak to me in Jewish, rarely in English. And when he did speak English to my friends, I was ashamed of his accent and grammar. I was not very tolerant. But neither was he. I was interested in sports; he thought they were a complete waste of time. He had worked too hard in his childhood helping to support his father's large family to understand why playing at a sport was both enjoyable and healthy. He didn't believe in play; he had never played in his life. The gulf between us was impossible to bridge. On occasion we came close. But during my childhood, we just could not bridge it. As I grew older, I believe I may have become slightly more understanding. And so did he. In retrospect, I wish I could have been more understanding. I wish I would have had more empathy for him. We might have had a better relationship then. But might-have-beens don't count. Perhaps that's why I have always considered *King Lear* to be William Shakespeare's greatest masterpiece. I can empathize with the old king because by the time I studied *King Lear*, I could empathize with my father, and at times felt sorry for him. The Bard spoke for all of us. He certainly spoke for me.

I continued to win ribbons on Victoria Day for a long time, not only for the fifty yard dash but also for the high jump and long jump events. But they weren't always red ribbons. Sometimes I won a second-place blue ribbon for the high jump and a white third-place ribbon for the long jump. But the fifty yard dash was mine. First-place red all the time.

When I was twelve, in grade seven, I could no longer compete in the fifty yard dash. The challenge was now one hundred yards. I welcomed it. Once more, I felt it was made for me. And once more I won a red ribbon to prove it. I even won the red for both high jump and long jump that year. But that was as good as I got. I never won the hop, skip—and-jump or the shot put. Those events were out of my league and didn't really interest me. The following year, I still won the red for the hundred yard dash, and the blue and the white for the others. But by now, many of my classmates, a year or two older than I, were really starting to grow as fifteen-year olds do, while I was still a little scrawny kind of thirteen. But I still held onto the hundred yard dash.

In 1942, two months after I had turned fourteen and had reached the height of five feet and two inches, I had to compete in the sixteen- year-old and under category. That proved to be my Waterloo—the end of my field-and-track career. Although I ran faster than ever at the tryouts, I could not keep up with Walter Wolkowski. Not only was he two years older, but he was much bigger, heavier, taller, and—I must sadly ad-mit—much faster than I. We broke from the starting line, head-to-head, and for a while I kept up with him. But after fifty yards, he pulled away and I just could not keep up. It was no contest. For the first time since I had entered the tryouts, I came in second. But that was not good enough to represent our school. I was out.

He beat me in the high jump event. I cleared the bar at four feet eleven inches, just three inches short of my height. But that was as high as I could jump. He easily cleared it at five feet. Finally, even though I jumped thirteen feet and two inches in the long jump event, he beat me. I was through. At first I felt sad. But I realized I was cleanly and decisively beaten by a better athlete. He proved his worth on Victoria day, winning the first-place red ribbon for all five events, and earning the coveted first-place medal.

I consoled myself with the thought that since someone finally beat me, I was glad it was a Wolkowski. Mr. Wolkowski, our section foreman on the Canadian Pacific Railway, worked hard to provide for his large family of five boys and three girls. None of his children ever got into trouble or ever caused anyone any harm. On the contrary, they were all friendly and likable and worked hard to better their lives. And they were all good athletes. Walter wasn't the only one to win ribbons. His younger brothers Henry and Ludwig not only captured a number of red and blue ribbons, but kept them as trophies. Imagine my surprise fifty-two years later, at our Sheho mini-reunion at Calgary in 1994, when I saw these two brothers proudly wearing their red and blue ribbons. They had saved them all those years. I was astounded. I have no idea what happened to mine. I never showed them to anyone after I won them. Never. I didn't like showing off. I guess that's why I gave my first red ribbon to Mrs. Annie Hanson for her trusty, old horse Nellie. I hoped it would make Nellie feel younger. Besides, it looked better on her than it did on me.

MR. KINDRACHUK

In 1939, the year I entered the seventh grade, the overwhelming number of Sheho school trustees were Ukrainian; and for the first time in the history of Sheho Public School, two Ukrainian teachers were hired: the principal, Louis Tomaschuk, and the seventh and eighth grade teacher, Fred Kindrachuk. Fifty-three years later while visiting my old teacher Mr. Kindrachuk, I learned that some of the prominent members of the English power structure in town had tried desperately to prevent Mr.

Tomaschuk and him from being hired, going so far as trying to persuade the Yorkton area Inspector of Schools and even the Provincial Department of Education. But to no avail. The province would not interfere in local affairs. The ethnic barrier had been broken. It was time to acknowledge that the offspring of Ukrainian immigrants had every right to be hired as educators if they met the proper qualifications. And both Mr. Tomaschuk and Mr. Kindrachuk were highly qualified.

Mr. Fred Kindrachuk was young, witty, easy going, and had a wonderful sense of humor. Best of all, though, he was a man. I had had my fill of lady teachers. As good as they could be, they could not control the class without shouting. Mr. Kindrachuk was different. He told stories and jokes and played his mandolin and brought his portable radio to class and made learning fun. I took an immediate liking to him. I was the first to raise my hand to answer his questions and the first to volunteer for anything. I must have been a ham because I was forever talking out of turn; yet he never reprimanded me and always laughed at my stupid jokes. As mentioned previously, it was the first time I felt that I was teacher's pet.

Several weeks after school had begun, he announced there would be an elocution contest to be held in the town hall on November 10th. The contest would be sponsored by Sheho Teachers Local, whose president was our principal, Mr. Tomaschuk. Six schools in our area would participate, with each school sending a total of three representatives, one from each of these grade levels: first through second grade, third through sixth grade, and finally seventh through eighth grade. It would be the first elocution contest of its kind.

Mr. Kindrachuk invited everyone in our classroom to prepare a speech to be delivered orally in front of the class. He would then pick the winner, who would represent our classroom. Naturally, since I was not exactly the shyest student in class, I welcomed the challenge. I wrote an essay titled, "Why I'm Glad I am a Canadian."

Since I was only eleven at the time and had virtually no knowledge of world political economy and very limited knowledge of world geography except that the sun never set on the mighty British Empire, and our rich neighbor to the south was the United States, which didn't even have a king—only a President— and whose people all spoke perfect English (except for my aunt and uncle in Boston), and since I had never been farther south than Fosti School, three miles away, nor farther west than Wynyard, fifty miles away, nor farther east than Winnipeg, 350 miles away, you may wonder what made me especially glad to be a Canadian. That's a good question.

I knew that life in Canada had always been better than in Europe because whenever I left any food on my plate, Mama always scolded me with "Eat! The children in Europe are starving." Furthermore, both Mama and Papa had told me stories about the horrible *pogroms* in Russia, when Jews had been hunted and killed for sport by the Cossacks for no reason at all except that they were Jewish. I also knew that our public education through the twelfth grade was free and that all citizens had a right to vote for anyone who ran for public office, no matter how ignorant, stupid, dishonest or crooked the candidate was. Finally, I knew that Canada was an independent, democratic country even though it was part of the huge, mighty British Empire, upon which the sun never set, an empire that was colored red on the large roll-up maps of the world that we had studied in our geography classes every year since grade one. And I was glad, also, that we had a wonderful, exemplary royal family, headed by His Majesty King George VI—long may he reign! He was the highest ranking officer of the Royal Navy, outranking even the Admiral of the Fleet. Anyone could see that because he was always impeccably dressed in his elegant uniform reflecting that rank, with all kinds of medals and fancy ribbons on his chest whenever his handsome portrait appeared on the movie screen immediately after the end of every movie, accompanied by the first few strains of "God Save the King." That music forced anyone who had not run out of the theater beforehand to stand at attention. I always stayed to stand at attention because I honored my king and his beautiful queen, Elizabeth, and their beautiful young daughters, Elizabeth (who would someday become our queen) and her younger sister Margaret. So as you can readily see, I had many reasons to be glad I was a Canadian.

But the main reason I was glad to be a Canadian was patriotism. Canada had just entered the war, and it now involved one of our men from Sheho. Within weeks of Canada's declaration of war, John Brozoski, married and the father of a school age daughter, was the first Shehoite to enlist. He joined the Royal Canadian Army. I remember how proud he was in his brand new heavy woolen khaki uniform and polished black army boots as he strutted up and down the railway platform, waiting for the train to take him to training camp. Several others from town were talking about enlisting. Mr. Leckie had said it would be a long war and boys still in school would be involved before it was over.

So I wrote the essay. To be perfectly honest, I don't remember exactly what I wrote except that it was patriotic. But I certainly do remember the title and this exact quotation: "Canada is a democracy. A democracy is a government of the people, for the people and by the people." You will notice that I have underscored the word by. It's important. It's for emphasis. That's the word I emphasized in my speech.

I memorized the speech immediately. That was easy because I had written it. Then I practiced it at home in front of the mirror when everyone was out of the house except Sylvia, who thought I was crazy. I asked her to go outside and leave me alone because I was practicing an important speech that would make me famous. I will never forget the exact words she used as she left. "You're crazy."

Then I practiced the speech again, clenching my right hand into a fist and banging it down into the palm of my left hand as I shouted the word *by*. That was for emphasis— "*by* the people." I practiced it again and again until I knew I had the right emphasis on the word *by*.

The next day when Mr. Kindrachuk asked our class if there were any volunteers to deliver a speech, my hand shot up immediately—I mean before he had even finished his question. I was ready. The whole class snickered. But I didn't care. I was ready.

I got up in front of the class, looked around, took a deep breath, then began. "Why I am Glad I'm a Canadian." I have no recollection of what I said next, but I sure remember that somewhere in that speech, I shouted these exact words: "Canada is a democracy. A democracy is a government of the people, for the people, and BY the people." And did I ever shout the word BY! At that exact moment, I bent down and slammed my right fist into my left hand so hard it hurt. Everyone clapped. It was no contest. I was the one chosen from the grade seven and eight group to represent Sheho School at the elocution contest.

Mr. Kindrahuk suggested that I give him my speech so that he might make some slight improvements. In a few days he returned his improved version to me, every so neatly re-written in his own beautiful handwriting. The only original words left were these: "Canada is a democracy. A democracy is a government of the people, for the people, and *by* the people." You will notice there was still emphasis on the word *by*.

I memorized my new improved version that night. The next day I asked him what some of the words meant. I also learned how to pronounce them. So I practiced my speech again and again, not only emphasizing the word *by* but really dramatizing it as well. I also dramatized the definition of a democracy. In fact, I dramatized the entire speech. By the time the elocution contest was held on Friday night, November 10, I was ready for Hollywood.

I had never heard the expression "stage fright," and I could not understand why anyone could become frightened by standing in front of an audience of a couple hundred strangers who had come to see you perform. Besides, they weren't all strangers. I knew half of them—kids from school, their parents, and even some of our customers from the farm. All my sisters were there, too. Mama and Papa, however, had stayed home to read the weekly Jewish newspapers which had just arrived that day, the *Forward* from New York, and the *Israelite Press* from Winnipeg.

I didn't know any of the contestants who sat with me up front near the stage that night except Betty Finley, who represented the first two grades, and Marguerite Scott, who was chosen for grades three, four, and five. Everyone seemed nervous. Even I was beginning to get that feeling. We sang our national anthem, "O Canada." Then the curtain slowly rose and our principal, Mr. Tomaschuk, appeared on stage to welcome the competing speakers from the various schools, their teachers, and the audience. I don't remember which school representative went first or which went last, but I believe that I was somewhere in the middle of the final speeches. I don't remember any of the speeches, either, but I thought some of them were very good. I suspected that more than one teacher had offered his student "suggestions" to help his student as Mr. Kindrachuk had done for me.

Suddenly I heard Mr. Tomaschuk make the announcement. "Our next speaker is Jackie Katz from Sheho Public School." It was now my turn, and I was the one who was nervous. I climbed the steps to the stage, walked to the center and looked down at the packed audience. I suddenly realized that I didn't know half of them. I was really nervous now, but I told myself it didn't matter. I had practiced all these weeks, I knew my speech, and I knew how to deliver it. I took a deep breath, and began. "Why I'm Glad I am a Canadian." After the first sentence or two, I was no longer nervous. I forgot about the audience. I was now in complete command. I dramatically delivered an impassioned speech with enough dramatic gestures to impress upon everyone in no uncertain terms that I was glad I was a Canadian. And when I bent away down, almost to the floor, and hammered my right clenched fist into the palm of my left hand with a thud at the exact moment that I shouted "*BY* the people" everyone in the audience gasped. They all knew I meant business. And when I finished my speech, they applauded and shouted and whistled and stomped their feet and made so much noise it was deafening. I had brought down the house.

The contest eventually ended and the three judges began their deliberation. Chosen from outside the greater Sheho area, they included Mr. K.T. Killum from Foam Lake, and Miss Archer and Miss Muir, both from Theodore. I had thought it would take a long time. But suddenly Miss Muir mounted the steps and walked to the front of the stage. She was holding a small card. She glanced at it for just a moment, then made the announcement. "The winner of the Elocution Contest for grades seven and eight is Jackie Katz.

The audience clapped as I walked toward her to receive her congratulations and my winning certificate.

Mr. Kindrachuk beamed with pride as she congratulated me. I was glad I had won, not entirely for myself, but for him. I wanted him to be proud of me. That's how much I respected him.

When I got home that night, I mentioned to Mama and Papa that I had won the elocution contest. They looked up from their papers momentarily and said in English, " You won?"

"Yes, I won."

"Good. It's good to win." Then they resumed reading.

I never showed them the certificate. I don't believe I ever showed it to anyone except Mr. Kindrachuk. I was not a collector then. I did not collect ribbons or certificates. I didn't collect anything. Not even stamps. And I didn't think it was nice to brag about winning. So I hardly mentioned it to anyone until now. As Miss Muir said that night, "Not everybody can win, but everyone can try." That's what I think is important. Besides, somebody has to lose.

Mr. Kindrachuk and Mr. Tomaschuk took turns ringing the school bell. But Mr. Kindrachuk often gave me the pleasure and the distinct honor of ringing that hand-held school bell housed on his desk. He picked his favorite students for this honor, usually every week, and I was honored at least as much as anyone else, if not more. When my turn came, I rang it eight times a day: at nine o'clock in the morning, an hour-and-a-half later for recess, ten minutes later to end recess, at noon, at 1:30 P.M., at 2:50 P.M. for afternoon recess, ten minutes later, and at four. I loved to ring that bell. He would say, "Jackie Katz, you may ring the bell." I would pick it up, go outside the room to the hallway and clang that bell up and down as hard as I could with mischievous glee for almost a minute. I hate to brag, but it takes a certain skill to ring a bell properly, and when I rang that bell, everyone in school and everyone who lived anywhere near the school, as far away as the railway station, could hear that bell loud and clear. They all knew something was happening. Maybe what was happening wasn't too important, but it sure sounded important when I rang the bell. I still think ringing that bell was probably one of my major lifetime accomplishments.

Like the other single teachers, Mr. Kindrachuk stayed at the hotel, where he also ate his meals. On weekends, however, he would occasionally take the evening train to Yorkton to visit his girl friend and return by bus on Sunday night. Beginning in September of the following year, I would follow that same schedule—regularly—in order to be tutored for my bar mitzvah by Rabbi Joseph Eisenstein. I would stay with the Eisenstein family and return by bus on Sunday night. Whenever Mr. Kindrachuk went to Yorkton, then, I would have the pleasure of his company. I never thought of him as being away above me because he was my teacher. I just liked him because he was a likable guy. The fact that he was my teacher was an added bonus.

Mr. Kindrachuk rarely lost his temper; but when he did, it was usually for a good reason. He face would then turn beet-red and he would let everyone in the class know how angry he was. On occasion, when someone near his desk was disturbing the class by talking too loudly, he would grab a stack of books from his desk and hurl them at the guilty student. That worked better than the strap. It was called classroom control. It woke up the class and we all paid attention. But it didn't take long for most of us to learn how to duck whenever we saws a stack of books hurtling though the air. His aim wasn't very good.

During the entire year that I was in his class, he refused the principal's suggestion to use the strap. Except once. Once-and-only once. And I'm sorry to say that I was indirectly responsible.

Although I had been tormented and beaten up by bullies every once-in-a-while since starting school, for no reason except that I was Jewish and smaller than the bullies, I never told my teachers or my parents. I was not a tattle tale. Furthermore, I thought that by not making an issue of the incident, the bully would leave me alone. And he usually did. One day in late May, during morning recess, Tarres Koropatniski got into a fight with me, beat me up and tore my shirt. I didn't tell anyone. But when I got home at noon for dinner and Papa saw my torn shirt, he asked me what had happened. I broke down and told him.

I suppose Papa could have gone across the road to the Federal Grain Company elevator, operated by John Koropatniski, Tarres's father, and told John about the incident. But Papa remembered what John had done some years earlier. He had stood up in front of a crowd at the Ukrainian Hall and told everyone that the Jews had killed Christ; therefore, everybody should boycott the Jewish storekeepers in town. Papa learned about the speech from one of his customers the following morning. But instead of getting mad, Papa just laughed. "He's a fool," he said. Some weeks later, John came into the store and sheepishly asked Papa if he could buy a pair of rubbers on credit. Papa laughed, reminded him of the foolish speech and said, "Of course."

But Papa did not laugh this time. He got up immediately from his dinner and went to see Arthur Merritt, the postmaster, a British veteran of the Great War and one of Sheho's leading citizens, who had frequently served on the Sheho School Board. The post office was three buildings away from the hotel.

When I returned to Mr. Kindrachuk's room that afternoon immediately after the bell rang, he announced to the class what Tarres had done. Then Mr. Kindrachuk's face turned red. He pulled out a chair alongside the desk. He glared at Tarres, and in a voice filled with rage, commanded, "Come on up here! Now bend over!"

Tarres bent over. Mr. Kindrachuk took a wooden yardstick and swatted him over the rump as hard as he could—twice. "Crack! Crack!" The yardstick broke. Then—for the first and *only* time—he took out the strap from his desk, gripped it firmly, held it high in the air and brought it down with all his might on Tarres's rump." WHACK! WHACK! WHACK! WHACK!" He strapped him again and again, about four or five times. Tarres did not flinch. But his face was white. Finally, both Mr. Kindrachuk and Tarres had had enough. Mr. Kindrachuk put his strap away and, almost out of breath, said, "Let that be a lesson for you. And for everyone. No more fights." And from that time on, nobody in his room ever got into a fight. And from that time on, Tarres became one of my very best friends. We never even got into an argument.

CHAPTER SEVENTEEN
Journeys Toward My Rite Of Passage

If you have never been to a bar mitzvah or a bat mitzvah, I strongly suggest that you become close friends with Jewish parents who have either a twelve year old son studying for his bar mitzvah (on his thirteenth birthday), or a twelve year old girl studying for her bat mitzvah, also on her thirteenth birthday. Make sure the parents intend to impress their invited guests with the importance of the affair and with their status in the Jewish community. But equally important, make sure they have enough money, or can borrow enough, to do so. I promise you will not be disappointed.

My three sisters spent a considerable amount of money on each of their children's religious celebrations. I was impressed with my nieces' and nephews' confidence and the ease with which they performed their individual ceremonies. What impressed me most, however, was the expense my sisters incurred for the celebration that followed. But that was small change compared to the money spent many years later by one of my nieces and her husband on both of their children's religious celebrations. Yet even that amount, which I considered to be obscene, pales in comparison to some of the lavish affairs my sisters have told me about— formal, glittering affairs in a stately ballroom of a famous hotel, filled to capacity by several hundred guests —including friends and relatives from all over the United States, Canada, and even England. What a contrast from my Shnider cousins' bar mitzvahs, and my own one in particular which was held in the Yorkton Synagogue on a spring day of March 1941.

I don't think I had ever heard the word bar mitzvah until the summer of 1935 when, at the age of seven, I was spending my summer holidays with my cousins in Inglis, Manitoba. That was the first time I met Leon Leckie, the younger of Mr. Leckie's two sons. After losing his mother at an early age, Leon had been brought up in Winnipeg's Jewish Orphanage, where he had received a thorough Jewish and Hebrew education, as well as an excellent education from the Winnipeg Public School system. He had just graduated from the eleventh grade, the final year of high school in Manitoba. In need of a job, he readily accepted an offer from Uncle Abe to live with the family, work in the store, and tutor both Maurice and Charlie for their bar mitzvahs.

Maurice, after playing with me in the morning, excused himself because he had to study for his bar mitzvah, nine months away.

"What's a bar mitzvah?" I asked.

"It's a religious celebration that takes place when you turn thirteen. You have to be able to dahven. [read Hebrew prayers] and know a lot of other stuff in Hebrew. Then there's a party for you and you get lots of presents. I'm having mine next April."

"Will I have a bar mitzvah?"

"I suppose so. Almost all Jewish boys have one."

When I got home later that summer, I asked Papa if I would someday have a bar mitzvah.

"Noo, vooden!" he replied.[Well, of course!] "Bis dee nicht a yeed? Mine ayne-ohn -ayntzika zeen mist hooben a bar mitzvah." [Are you not a Jew? My one-and-only son must have a bar mitzvah.]

A few months later, while sitting with my Shnider cousins in the Yorkton synagogue during Rosh Hashanah services, when we were all supposed to be dahvening [praying], the conversation turned to bar mitzvahs. "Have you had yours, yet?" Kenny Kroll asked Maurice.

"No, not yet. I'm having mine in April."

"I had mine a couple of years ago, Kenny said proudly." Then he turned to Shimon Laskin. "How about you?"

"No I'm not going to have one. I know a few kids who didn't have a bar mitzvah. I don't have to have one. "

We all stared at Shimon as though he had just shouted an obscenity.

"I'm going to have mine in a couple of years," Charlie Shnider said with pride.

"And I'll have mine in another three years," his cousin Mervin said, with almost as much pride in his voice.

The bar mitzvah signified the rite of passage from innocent boyhood into responsible manhood; it meant that one now assumed the religious responsibilities of an adult. A bar mitzvah, therefore, was a badge of honor, entitling anyone who had already had one to proudly boast about it, because he was no longer a boy. He was now a man! And the closer the boy came to being "bar mitzvahed," the closer he came to becoming a man; therefore, the closer he came to boasting about it.

Maurice Shnider's bar mitzvah —the religious ceremony, not the celebration—took place at the Yorkton synagogue on a Saturday morning in April following his thirteenth birthday. He told me about it later. Because somebody had to look after the store, his tutor was left behind. Maurice traveled to Yorkton with his father, mother, and younger brother. Unfortunately, Leon could not share the joy of his accomplishment— watching his protege perform.

On Saturday morning, Uncle Abe, who was well known in Yorkton, used his influence to round up a *minyan* [quorum] of at least ten Jewish adult males required for a religious service. Saturday was always the busiest day of the week for any merchant, but especially so in Yorkton. To be gone for the "entire" morning and leave the store in somebody else's hands was completely out of the question. "*Maschiga darf mir zyeen!*" [One must be crazy!] " For an hour or hour-and a-half, yes. I could manage it. Two, maybe. But no more. Make it short!"

That was the understanding. A gentleman's agreement. Two hours at the most.

And so the Sabbath morning service began. Although Maurice had never been to a bar mitzvah in his entire life, or even to a Saturday morning service, he was not intimidated. And he certainly wasn't bashful. He had always been an outstanding student. Moreover, he had been so thoroughly educated by his tutor— beyond the customary demands of the bar mitzvah candidate—that he began leading the congregation, *dahvening* the entire service. He even chanted the parts usually reserved for the rabbi or cantor. He was doing everything a rabbi or cantor normally does. Right from the beginning. The whole *geshichta*. [story] All by himself. Just thirteen years old. Amazing!

There was only one thing wrong. He was a perfectionist. He was meticulously trying to clearly enunciate every single word in Hebrew, letter by letter, with exactly the right inflection. And since he had never been to a Sabbath morning service before, he had no concept of how much time it normally took for the service. He was much too slow. At this rate he would certainly not get through in two hours. He would be lucky to finish by noon. And it was already 10:30.

One-by-one the men looked at their wrist watches and pointed to them. Then they motioned to the Cantor, Mr. Rosenblattt the dry cleaner and tailor, who was supposed to be leading the service. Then they poked him and pointed to their watches. Twice. "*Giech!*" [Fast!] "*Giech!*" [Hurry up!] It was urgent. He nodded his head.

Cantor Rosenblattt patted Maurice on the shoulder. "Nice boy," he said, as he proceed to shoulder Maurice aside before taking over the service himself.

All the men nodded and smiled with glee as Cantor Rosenblattt began *dahvening* faster than the sing-song chant of the world famous Lucky Strike tobacco auctioneer in Goldsboro, North Carolina, broadcast by radio every Saturday night on *Your Hit Parade*. The pages turned as if swept up by a tornado. The bar mitzvah service was now well ahead of schedule.

Cantor Rosenblattt turned the service over to Maurice again when it was his time to perform his ritual for his bar mitzvah. Maurice made the appropriate blessings on the Torah, then chanted the *Maftir*, a passage from the Torah, then read the *Haftarah*, a passage from the Book of Prophets, then completed whatever he had to complete for his bar mitzvah—all in Hebrew—and on time. He was now a man.

"*Mazltov!*" [Congratulations!] "*Mazltov! Mazltov!*" Everyone in the synagogue congratulated him and his father and mother, then adjourned to the hall for a bite of pastry and a sip of Manischewitz kosher wine or Crown Royal rye whiskey, distilled and blended by the Seagram Company, owned by Harry and Sam Bronfman, formerly of Yorkton, one-time close personal friends of Uncle Abe. Although they could not be there in person, their "spirits" were literally part of the celebration.

The real bar mitzvah celebration, however, at Shnider's store in Inglis, was held the next day, when everyone could attend. That's what I remember. How can I ever forget it? To me, *that* was Maurice's bar mitzvah. It was the first one I had ever attended. To an eight-year old, it was "something else."

Papa hired Frank Norris to drive us to Inglis early that Sunday morning. I don't think Papa wanted to go through the same ordeal he had gone through three years before with Mr. Darling's 1922 Dodge. Besides, that Dodge had never been driven since then and its driver was aging along with the car. Mr. Norris was a small bent -over man who had lost one finger while servicing the huge steam-driven locomotives in Sheho for the C.P.R. He was always dressed in overalls that had been colored coal black from countless hours of crawling in and around the coal dust to service the locomotives. His hands and face were almost always smeared black as well. He was always in a hurry wherever he went, as if he could not wait to get back to his locomotives. He spoke rapidly with a slight nasal quality in his voice. He got along well with everyone I knew, and Papa had the highest regard for him. Since Mr. Norris owned a fairly new black Chevrolet and indicated that he would be interested in driving us to Inglis, Papa hired him. When he drove up to our home, it was the first time I had seen him all cleaned up. His face was clean, his hands were clean, his white shirt was clean, and his pants were clean; and he was wearing the new dress shoes he had just bought from our store. I hardly recognized him.

We climbed into his car—all eight of us, including Mr. Leckie and Mr. Norris. Sylvia sat on Papa's knee, with Mama and my two sisters in the back, while I sat up front on Mr. Leckie's knee, along with the driver. There wasn't much room to spare.

Unlike our trip three years before, Mr. Norris did not have to crank up the engine to get it started. Nor did we have to roll down the leather flaps to keep the dust and wind out. This car had real windows that could be rolled up and down. And Mr. Norris drove faster than thirty-five miles an hour top speed. We passed other cars; they didn't pass us. And the weather was clear. No rain. Instead of taking us six hours to travel the 150 miles to Inglis, this time we made it without incident in less than four. We arrived half-an-hour before noon—about an hour later than the Bill Laskin family. They had stopped at our home earlier that morning after driving almost four hours over the quagmire country road from Rose Valley to Highway 14, then almost another hour to Sheho. The Laskins were gluttons for punishment. But this was a very special occasion —a bar mitzvah celebration for a very special family. Next to a wedding, or a silver wedding anniversary celebration (if the couple lived that long), nothing equaled the celebration of a bar mitzvah.

For his *oldest* son's bar mitzvah—a *very* special occasion, Uncle Abe had invited all the Jewish storekeepers and their wives within a fifty mile radius, as well as all the Jewish adults in Yorkton, ninety miles away, as well as the entire Katz family and Mr. Leckie from Sheho, 150 miles away, and even the entire Laskin family from Rose Valley, over 230 miles away—a round-trip journey of more than sixteen hours. The Jewish guests numbered over sixty. The Shnider family numbered five. And, as I found out the during the speeches after dinner, there was one guest who was "not Jewish."

All the counters in Uncle Abe's store had been pushed back to the rear and jammed together tightly so that enough tables and chairs could be brought in to accommodate this huge crowd that equaled a quarter of the entire population of Inglis. The store was jam-packed. There was barely enough room for the tubs of ice-covered soda pop and beer, and the case of Seagram's rye whiskey.

Johnny Zrudlo, Uncle Abe's hired man, who was considered one of the family, was the waiter for soda pop and beer as well as bartender. Although most Jews are not known as heavy drinkers, Uncle Abe was not taking any chances.

Aunt Bessie, with help only from her teen-age daughter, Myra, and her hired girl, Vera, had prepared the kosher feast. And what a feast! Chopped liver, cucumbers and tomatoes for an appetizer; roast chicken, knishes, two kinds of keegle, and varnichkas for the main course; and for dessert—two kinds of mouth watering strudel, apple and cherry. Almost everyone drank pop. But there was enough beer and Seagrams whiskey left over for at least another bar mitzvah.

After dinner came the speeches. Uncle Abe was greeted with applause. He thanked the guests for coming, then spoke briefly before turning the affair over to Mr. Rothstein from Yorkton, the master of ceremonies. Mr. Rothstein thanked Uncle Abe and Aunt Bessie on behalf of the guests for this wonderful celebration, and then delivered a speech. Not too long, and not too short, it was a good speech. Then he called up the bar mitzvah *boocher* [graduate] himself to deliver a speech. Maurice was up to the occasion. He had written his own speech in English, with the help of his tutor. In addition, his Uncle Moishe in Boston, Aunt Bessie's brother-in-law, who had visited the family the previous summer, had ghost written a bar mitzvah speech— in Jewish —for his nephew. Maurice was now ready to deliver not one but two speeches. It's not every bar mitzvah who can deliver a speech both in English and Jewish. [Bar mitzvah translates into "Son of good deeds" or "Son of the commandment" depending on the translator.]

He spoke first in English. I don't remember his exact words, but they went something like this: "First of all, I'd like to thank my devoted parents for their loving care and for educating and clothing me and bringing me up in the Jewish tradition. And I'd especially like to thank them for giving me this bar mitzvah. I'd also like to thank my Jewish and Hebrew teacher, Leo Leckie, for his patience and dedication over the past few years in preparing me for my bar mitzvah. And I'd like to also thank my sister Myra and my brother Charlie for their love and encouragement while I was studying for my bar mitzvah. Last, but not least, I'd like to thank all you guests who have traveled so far to come to this celebration.

"Today is the day I assume my religious responsibility as a Jew. It is a great responsibility, but I accept it." And so it went—on and on. When he was through everyone clapped and clapped.

After the applause had ended, he took out another piece of paper, unfolded it and said, "Thank you. I would now like to give a speech in Jewish."

A few people uttered an almost inaudible "oh" under their breath.

But Uncle Abe and Aunt Bessie and Papa and Mama and most of the audience clapped. A bar mitzvah who knew enough Jewish already to give a Jewish speech!

Once again, I don't remember the exact words since they were in Jewish; but the translation began something like this: "Today is the day I assume my religious responsibilities." And on and on. When he had finished, everybody clapped. His parents and Mama and Papa beamed with joy. They were really proud of him. The rest of us thought it was a good Jewish speech, but a little long. We were glad he was through.

The master of ceremonies now called upon every adult guest to give a speech—or "at least come up and say a few words." I mean every adult guest. I don't mean every other one. I mean EVERY SINGLE ONE!

And so it went—on and on and on. Some of the speeches were rather long; others not too long; and some, thank God, very brief. I don't remember any of them. But I distinctly remember that at the very end, the master of ceremonies uttered these exact words: "There is one person here today who is not Jewish. Mr. Frank Norris. We'd like you come up now and say a few words."

I blushed with embarrassment. I thought it was shameful for anyone to single out an individual like that. I had been singled out altogether too many times because I was Jewish—because I was different. Now somebody else was being singled out because he, too, was different. I thought it was in extremely bad taste. I wondered why Mr. Rothstein had not mentioned the other gentile, Uncle Abe's hired man, Johnny Zrudlo. But I guess that since Johnny was treated as one of the family, he was considered to be an "insider," not a gentile.

In retrospect, after many years, I now think that what the master of ceremonies had really *meant* to say was that *although* Mr. Norris was not Jewish, he was most welcome at this Jewish gathering, and we did not want to discriminate by failing to call upon him for a speech. We wanted him to feel as though he were indeed a welcomed guest.

Mr. Norris smiled as he came up and said a few words, thanking Uncle Abe and Aunt Bessie for making him feel welcome at their son's bar mitzvah, and congratulating Maurice on this festive occasion. I was relieved. Perhaps Mr. Norris had not felt slighted after all. I hoped not.

And that was how I remember Maurice's bar mitzvah ending.

Someday, too, I would have a bar mitzvah. But it certainly wouldn't be as big as this one. We were not rich like the Shniders. And I really didn't like being the center of attention. But I would still have a bar mitzvah. Not because I particularly wanted one. But I knew Papa wanted me to have one. He had made it quite clear to me. I was Jewish. I was his one-and-only son. It was mandatory. That's all there was to it. But it was a long way off. Five years is a long time. And I wasn't holding my breath.

Charlie Shnider's bar mitzvah was an entirely different affair. He was not the intensely dedicated and zealous student that his older brother had been. He just wanted to get the darn thing over to please his parents. Besides, he was the second son. And just as the second son of the King or Queen of England does not have the same privileges and prestige and the same honors as the oldest one (the Prince of Wales), the second son in the Shnider family likewise did not have the same honor at his bar mitzvah as his older brother did. For one thing, on Saturday, Charlie did not have his bar mitzvah in the Yorkton Synagogue. Instead it was held in a private home in the neighboring town of Roblin, with a *minyan* comprised of Uncle Abe, Maurice, seven Jewish storekeepers from surrounding towns, Jack and Louis Malinsky, the delicatessen owners from Russell who had given me my first ham sandwich, and Dr. Hershfield.

Also, instead of a huge celebration the following day, there was a much smaller one. We attended, along with Mr. Leckie. But *not every* Jewish storekeeper in the whole area was there, nor was every Jewish businessman from Yorkton. His father had blown his money on this first son. That was it!

I didn't think about bar mitzvahs for several years afterward because I hadn't attended any. I was too busy having a good time.

Then one day in mid August of 1939, two weeks before the outbreak of war, Papa told all of us that since my bar mitzvah was only a year-and-a-half away, he had made arrangements with the Winnipeg Jewish Orphanage to send us a girl who could tutor me, as well as my sisters, in Jewish and Hebrew after school hours, and work in the store during the rest of day.

Bernice Shatsky, a pretty young brunette, about a year older than my sister Merle, had just graduated from high school and the Orphanage's Hebrew and Jewish school. She was very friendly and a natural born teacher. She started with the Hebrew alphabet and explained the pronunciation of the different diacritical marks which appeared below the letters to indicate the exact vowel sounds. Within a couple of weeks, my older sisters and I could all read Hebrew. We didn't know the meaning of the words, but we could read them.

A few weeks later, we learned how to read Jewish; only this time we knew what we were reading. By the end of the month, we could also write in Jewish.

I found it rather humorous reading Jewish sentences from Bernice's primary level reader. *"Beryl est da epple foon da teppl"* translates into English as " Beryl eats the apple from the pot." The only time we used the word teppl in our home was when referring to one of our two *pisch teppls*—[pee pots] —the white enamel one with a handle and the gray one without a handle. We used them in the house every night to save us the long trip to the outhouse. Who would eat an apple from a pee pot?

Coming from the big city of Winnipeg to the tiny village of Sheho must have been quite a shock for Bernice. There wasn't much to do in town, and Papa ran a tight ship with curfew hours strictly enforced. The arrangement didn't work out. After three months, Bernice returned to Winnipeg. In the meantime, I was not learning any Hebrew for my bar mitzvah, which was now less than two years away. That didn't bother me in the least, so I never gave it a second thought. But not so with Papa. His one-and-only son would have a bar mitzvah, no matter what.

The following summer, shortly after his hernia operation, performed in Yorkton by Dr. Harry Portnuff, Papa unceremoniously informed me that he had already made arrangements with Rabbi Eisenstein in Yorkton to teach me for my bar mitzvah, now only six months away. Just in case I couldn't understand Jewish—after twelve years of listening to it— he spoke in English. " Next week you'll start. On Friday night you'll take the train to Yorkton and stay at Eisensteins. There you will learn from the rabbi for your bar mitzvah. On Sunday you'll take the bus back. Be good and learn."

Mama also spoke in English, just to be on the safe side—just in the unlikely event that I had suddenly suffered amnesia and had forgotten all the Jewish I had ever learned. You never know. "This new blue suit we just got you from Kays Limited size thirteen for *Yon Tiff* [the holidays] you'll wear. And your new shoes from Patricks Limited size five and your new cap. For the rabbi, you shouldn't look like a *schlepper*. [beggar] And I'll pack for you in this little suit case from Great West Saddlery some everyday clothes you should wear when you play so you don't get your suit *shmutzig*." [dirty]

At first I was apprehensive about staying for a weekend with a family whom I hardly knew. I had met the rabbi's son during the Jewish high holy days of 1937, shortly after the rabbi and his family had moved to Yorkton. Barney was about a year younger than I and about the same height, but much thinner. If I was skinny, he was emaciated. He wore rimless glasses and hardly ever smiled. I thought he looked like "one of the children in Europe who were starving." Sometimes he joined us kids in the upstairs hall of the synagogue when he was not dahvening alongside his father. But he never played pranks on anyone like some of the other kids. He made friends fairly easily, and I thought it amazing how well he had picked up English in just a few months since emigrating from Poland. And each year I noticed how much his command over the English language had improved and how little remained of his Polish and Jewish accents.

What made me nervous about the prospect of studying with the rabbi was his appearance and demeanor. He never smiled. He was almost always immaculately dressed in a navy blue serge or black mohair suit, a white shirt and dark tie. He was a handsome, rather short and slim man, with piercing clear blue eyes that looked at you sternly and demanded attention. He wore a mustache and a very small, neatly trimmed black beard, the only beard in his entire congregation. And when he spoke, there was no misunderstanding about his intentions. He meant business. The total effect of his appearance, his manner and his voice upon me could be summed up in these words —fear and respect.

Although I had seen them in the synagogue, I had never met his wife nor their daughter, a couple of years younger than Barney, nor their young son. I therefore felt uneasy about staying with a strange family, even though it would be for only a weekend.

At the age of twelve, however, anything out of the ordinary was an adventure for me. Consequently, although I barely knew the rabbi and knew almost nothing about his family, I looked forward to my new experience in Yorkton with the Eisensteins.

For me, it was an adventure. It was the first time I would be going away from home by myself. Late in the afternoon, on the first Friday after Sheho School had started, just after Mama had bencht lecht [blessed the Sabbath candles], she fed me her Sabbath supper, which I nibbled and pecked at, and finally finished without leaving any food on my plate. She then gave me a new small change purse into which she had folded two dollar bills plus change. "Here's for your ticket. And extra. Just in case. Careful. Keep it in your pocket. Don't lose." Then she handed me my brand new shirt and my teal blue suit and packed up my little suit case. "Be a good boy and listen to the rabbi."

I kissed her good-bye, waved at my sisters, and walked to the station. Although the train was not due to arrive until seven, when the store closed, both Papa and Mama had insisted that I leave half-an-hour earlier just in case. Just in case meant anything could happen. Instead of it taking me five minutes to walk three blocks to the station, it could take me half-an-hour—just in case I sprained my ankle and forgot the way. Instead of it taking Mr. Curry two minutes to write up my train ticket, it might take him half-an-hour—just in case he had broken his hand and the waiting room was packed with passengers going away somewhere. Instead of the train arriving and leaving exactly on schedule—to within a minute—it might bypass every town on the line and arrive half-an-hour earlier and leave right away—just in case Jessie James and his gang were hijacking the train. You never know. So I left half-an-hour early. Just in case. And I got to the station twenty-five minutes before the train was due to arrive. Just in case.

Mr. Curry was seated at his desk behind the steel caged wicket, tapping on the telegraph key. I was glad I had arrived ahead of schedule. Just in case. Someday, I thought, maybe even within my lifetime, everyone will have a telephone, and the telegraph will go the way of the ox cart. But in the meantime, sending a telegram was usually the most effective way to send an urgent message, as long as there was a station agent at the other end to receive it and the person for whom it was intended was at home. I wondered who had sent the telegram. I wondered whom it was intended for. Perhaps Mr. Curry was sending an urgent telegram to Jessie James and his gang, warning them not to hijack the train because Jackie Katz had to board that train so he could go to Yorkton for the weekend to begin learning whatever there was to learn for his bar mitzvah.

I waited at the wicket. I was the only one in line. I was the only one in the station. I wanted to make sure I got my ticket before the line got any longer —just in case everyone in Sheho decided to leave on the evening train. You never know.

I stared at the large oak wood clock on the wall. It was much bigger than our big kitchen wall-clock. It was also much more accurate because our clock often stopped when one forgot to wind it. Then the job of winding it and setting it to the correct time was usually given to me because I was very good at climbing. First, I had to move a kitchen chair close enough to the wall so that I could get up on the chair and insert the large key into the slot at the center of the clock and turn the key clockwise again and again until it was so tight I couldn't turn it any more. Then I had to push the pendulum which started swinging back and forth, and the clock started ticking again—tick tock, tick tock—every second, as the pendulum swung back and forth. Then I had to move both hands of the clock to the correct Roman numerals so that the clock indicated the right time. But I didn't have a wrist watch. I didn't even have a pocket watch. Papa had the only watch in our family. It was a silver colored pocket watch which he wound at least twice a day so that it would keep exact time—to within five minutes. That was close enough. So immediately after I had climbed up on the kitchen chair and turned the key as tight as I could to wind up our big old kitchen clock, I had to go to the store to ask Papa what time it was. If he was busy with a customer, I had to wait until he was through. Sometimes it took a long time. Exactly how long I don't know. I didn't have a watch. But it could take a very long time. Then he would pull out his pocket watch, wind it just in case it needed winding, stare at it, and finally tell me the time. Then I would go back to the house—if I wasn't distracted. But I usually got distracted for some reason or other, especially in mid winter when the horses' droppings became flash-frozen as soon as they hit the hard snow-covered road. We could then use them to play soccer or hockey. Either way, they came in handy. So I would usually join a game already in progress, right outside the store or in front of our home. By the time the horse droppings had disintegrated, signaling the end of the game, I suddenly remembered that I was supposed to set the time on our kitchen clock. But I didn't know how long we had been playing. So I had one of two choices. Choice number one: Guess the time. I was pretty good at that. I probably wouldn't be off by more than fifteen or twenty minutes. Choice number two: Go back to the store and again ask Papa what time it was.

Choice number two was not a good choice. If he was busy with a customer, I would have to wait until he was through. Then when I asked him the time, he would stare at me and say, "*Grobba khop.*" [Thick head] I just told you the time. *Host dee forgessen?*" [Have you forgotten?] He often spoke in Jenglish—a mixture of Jewish and English. But I knew that if I told him what I'd been doing, his immediately reply would be, "Bum. *Foon deer vil zien a richh ahz foon myna tzerisena schich.*" [You will amount to as much as the torn soles of my shoes.] So I would just nod my head and say, "I forgot." And that would be almost the truth because although I remembered what time it was when I had first asked him, I didn't 't know how long I'd been stick handling those horse droppings and therefore had no idea of the correct time this very minute. Choice number two, therefore, was not a good idea. I had used it before. It was too complicated with too many risks.

So I usually went for choice number one. It was easier that way and it saved time. That's what I had gone to the store in the first place—to find the correct time. So I just guessed at the time. Actually, I calculated it to within twenty minutes. I remembered what time it was when I had asked Papa. Then I guessed at how many horse droppings we had used during the game and multiplied that by two minutes each, thus giving me the approximate number of minutes I had spent playing with those droppings. I added those minutes to the original time. Finally, in case I had forgotten some horse droppings, I added five extra minutes to be safe. I thus calculated what the approximate time should be on our kitchen clock when I got back to the house. Of course, it wasn't the exact time; it might have been off by ten or twenty minutes, or maybe more. But that was close enough. It wasn't a matter of life or death. So I went back into the house and climbed up on that kitchen chair and moved the hands of the clock to my estimated correct time. Then I would climb down and set our Westclox alarm clock to the exact time indicated on our kitchen clock. That way everyone in the family knew what time it was.

But my older sisters did not leave well enough alone. Etta was afraid of getting to school late, so without telling anyone, she would set the alarm clock ahead by ten minutes. And because Merle wanted to make sure she got enough piano practicing time before going to school, she also set the alarm clock ahead by at least ten minutes. (They were never late for school.) Our alarm clock, therefore, which originally had been set to the kitchen clock's time was now keeping its own time. Everyone kept saying, " That alarm clock is always fast." But nobody confessed. So for the exact time, everyone looked up at the kitchen clock—my time. And that made me proud. To this very day, I can usually estimate the time fairly accurately. To within half an hour. I've had a lot of practice.

When our kitchen clock was running, it would chime every hour on the hour. Actually, it sounded like a gong. And on Sunday when Mr. Leckie and the Teskey family were visiting us and Papa was telling them a story and the clock struck the hour, Papa would say, "*Clinked the zeygar.*" [The clock chimes.] That meant, "As sure as the clock chimes, I am telling you the truth." Nobody ever challenged him. The clock knew the truth—even though it might have been off by twenty or thirty minutes or more. Who cared? When he was talking and the clock happened to strike the hour—any hour——it meant he was telling the truth.

I watched the large minute hand on the big C. P. R. oak clock move ever so slowly as the pendulum swung back-and-forth, back- and-forth, making a loud tick-tock sound every second. Finally, Mr. Curry finished tapping on the telegraph key. He placed the message on top of his desk, then walked up to wicket. "Hello, Jackie. Where you going?"

"Yorkton. One way." I took out my purse and handed him a dollar bill.

"Yorkton, " he said, as he handed me some change. Then he picked up a quill pen, dipped the nib into a bottle of blue-black Quink ink, the same kind we sold in our store, and began writing "Yorkton" on the ticket. "I got a letter from Bud a couple of weeks ago. He's now stationed at Air Force Headquarters in Ottawa. He told me the R.A. F. is going to build a large service flying training school in Yorkton for fighter pilots. They'll be coming there from all over the British Empire for advanced training."

"Really! An advanced training school for fighter pilots from all over the Empire. That's great. We sure need them now. In a hurry. It's pretty grim over there."

"Sure is," said Mr. Curry. "They pounded the heck out of Dover and Portsmouth a few weeks ago. We shot down almost six hundred planes, but it cost us 265 fighters."

"Those are huge losses," I said.

"They're enormous. Looks like Hitler is gambling. Looks like he's trying to wipe out the R.A. F. so he can invade England."

"Do you think he'll invade?"

"Not if we keep shooting down their bombers." he said.

"I wonder how many Hurricanes and Spitfires we have left? And how many pilots? "

" That's a good question," said Mr. Curry. " I'm sure Hitler would like to know."

"I sure hope we get a lot more Spitfires in a hurry. They're the best fighter planes in the world. And I'm glad Yorkton is getting a fighter pilot school."

"They can't build it fast enough to suit me," said Mr. Curry. He put away his quill pen and gently placed an ink blotter over the ticket, then rubbed his hand back and forth over the blotter. When the ink was dry, he stamped the ticket and handed it to me. "One way to Yorkton. Have a good time."

I sat down on the long oakwood curved-back bench and waited for the big event. Sheho's most exciting event in the evening—by far—was going to the station to watch the train arrive. Unless a cataclysmic meteor struck the town, every evening without fail just about everyone in town would slowly walk down the hill to the station just before seven o'clock to watch the train come in. One-by-one they came, until the town was empty except for the postmaster, the businessmen, the teachers, and their families. They had already seen the train arrive at least once, and they knew it wouldn't look any different this time. But not so with the rest of Sheho's residents. This was big time excitement. What else was there to do in town? Meet the train, see who's going away, who's arriving, how many small packages are on the baggage wagons, how many big packages are on the larger red express wagons, how many passengers are in each railway coach, how much steam comes out of the engine, and how much coal is left. Then—after making sure that the mail addressed for Sheho had been placed directly into the hand-pulled canvas cart to be taken to the Post office—then the crowd would very slowly begin to leave the station's platform, but only after making sure the Saskatoon Star Phoenix newspapers were safely in the hands of Henry Walkowski and his younger brother Ludwig, to be delivered to their customers. Finally, as if leading a funeral procession, the postmaster's brother-in-law began pulling the canvas cart slowly up the hill, followed by the crowd three paces behind, out of respect for the mail inside the canvas cart . When the canvas bag reached the post office, it was rushed inside the back door while the crowd outside anxiously watched for at least five minutes to make sure it stayed there. Then, like a swarm of bees, the sound of the crowd intensified as everyone filed into the post office and waited for the evening's second biggest event—the delivery of the mail.

Behind the closed wicket, the postmaster, Arthur Merritt, one of Sheho's three British veterans from the Great War, first emptied the precious contents of the canvas bag onto a table. Then aided by his wife, they quickly began sorting the letters and parcels, first placing those with post office box numbers into one pile and the rest into the general delivery pile. Next, they shoved the box-numbered mail into the appropriate boxes and sorted the larger pile of general delivery mail alphabetically to expedite the final process.

Meanwhile, inside the post office, the crowd buzzed with excitement. It wouldn't be long now. Maybe fifteen minutes at the most before the mail was all sorted and the wicket opened. The buzzing increased. The frosted glass door was shoved upward and the wicket was finally open.

Those who had rented post office boxes dialed the secret combinations and opened their boxes, while the others huddled around the wicket and asked for their mail. That was the nightly ritual. What else could be so exciting?

So I sat on the hard oakwood curved bench waiting for the train while just about everyone in Sheho filed into the station, one-by-one. I hoped nobody would ask me where I was going. Or why I was going. I really didn't know how I would answer.

"Oh look, there's little Jackie Katz. He's all dressed up. Where you going, Jackie?"

"Yorkton."

"Yorkton. Why?"

"To study Hebrew."

"What's Hebrew?"

"A foreign language."

"Like French."

"Not exactly."

"Why are you studying Hebrew?"

"Because I'm Jewish."

"What's Hebrew got to do with being Jewish?"

"I don't know. The letters look the same, I guess."

" You mean like English and French."

"Yeah, I guess so."

"But I'm English and I don't have to study French."

"You will when you're in high school. You'll learn how to read and write in French so you can understand what's on the back of corn flakes boxes."

"Do Jews have corn flakes boxes with Hebrew on the back?"

"Not in Canada."

"So why are you studying Hebrew?"

"It's a long story. Forget it." I didn't want to tell him I was studying for my bar mitzvah because he would then ask me what a bar mitzvah was and why I had to have one, and I really didn't know the answers except that I had to have a bar mitzvah because I would soon be thirteen and every Jewish boy had a bar mitzvah as soon as he reached that age— every single one except Shimon Laskin. And I wondered how he got away so easily.

"TOOT—TOOT." The excitement mounted when we heard the two long warning blasts from the train's engine as it crossed Highway 14, only one mile away. I picked up my suit case, walked outside, and stood on the wooden platform, looking at the huge black steam-driven mon- ster gliding nearer and nearer, its huge fly wheels grinding along the steel rails slower and slower, and finally screeching as it came to a stop, with steam hissing from its head and from all sides. No matter how many times I had seen the locomotive arrive, the effect was always the same. It was frightening.

I waited until all the passengers from the train had stepped onto the platform—all three of them. Then I climbed the steps into the coach, entered, and looked around for a seat. Practically every seat was taken by young men dressed in khaki or air force blue. How exciting it was to see all the ranks and insignias on real soldiers and airmen in person! Although some of the men looked to be in their mid twenties, about the same age as Norman Leckie, most looked as if they belonged in grade twelve, like Walter Fedorchuk in Mr. Tomaschuk's room, or my cousin Maurice Shnider. They were a loud bunch of fellows and seemed to be having a good time.

Even though I had never seen any officer higher than a single V- striped lance corporal before, I recognized all their ranks and insignias because I studied the monthly brochure our store received from a coal company in Drumheller, Alberta. The brochure also illustrated the different aircraft of the Royal Air Force, the United States Army Air Corps, and the German *Luftwaffe*. It also contained a stupid joke of the month. The brochure was my favorite reading material. It was much more interesting than any of our reading assignments in school.

Most of the soldiers were army privates or lance corporals, but a few wore the double stripe of a corporal or the triple stripe of a sergeant. There were also a few commissioned army officers: second lieutenants wearing a single pip on their shoulder straps, and the odd first lieutenant with double pips. That was the highest ranking army officer on the train.

Among the youngsters in air force blue, however, I noticed more officers, both non-commissioned and commissioned. What I found most conspicuous was that most of these officers had earned their wings, indicating that they had graduated from their respective training schools. The wireless air gunner wore his single "W" wing embroidered with an electric design. The air observer, commissioned as a Pilot Officer, also wore a single wing with but an "O" for air observer—a carry over from the Great War when he was actually the observer and machine gunner, but not the navigator and bombardier, as he was now. Only the pilot, also commissioned, wore the complete wings. I thought this was insulting to the wireless air gunner and the air observer, both of whom had graduated from an equally rigorous course and were equally at risk of being shot down or blown up in the air. But the Marshall of the Royal Air Force had not asked me for my opinion. Otherwise, the wings might have been different.

I found a seat only partially occupied. The blond-haired, blue-eyed boy who was sitting in it appeared to be about my age, maybe a year or two older. I placed my suit case in the overhead rack and sat down. "Hi, where you going?"

"Toronto."

"What's Toronto like?"

"You've never been to Toronto?"

"No. I've never been past Winnipeg."

"Toronto is much bigger than Winnipeg. It's real big. It's the second biggest city in Canada. It's a nice city, but it has too many Jews. They have all the money."

"Really. *All* the money?"

"Well, maybe not all the money. But most of it. That's what I don't like about Toronto. Otherwise, it's great. I go to military school there."

"Military School! That must be fun." I said.

"It sure is. We wear uniforms all the time and we learn how to march and drill. We do a lot of exciting things."

"How did you get into military school?"

"My parents sent me. I've been home for the summer holidays. Now I'm going back to school there."

"I'll bet it's expensive."

"Yeah, it costs a lot of money. But that's what they want."

I liked the idea of going to military school, especially since I would wear a uniform and march in parades. It sounded exciting. But I knew Papa and Mama couldn't afford it. And I certainly knew exactly what they would say if I ever brought up the idea. "*Bist dee maschiga?*" [Are you crazy?] So, reluctantly, I gave up the idea of ever attending military school in Toronto, where there were too many Jews who had most of the money. I wondered what else this cadet had learned about Jews—or about anything else. Yet he seemed friendly enough, especially since he didn't know I was Jewish. And I wasn't about to embarrass him or get into an argument with him. We were getting along too well.

The train was halfway to Yorkton when he said, "Have you ever been in the observation car?"

"No."

"Come on. I'll show you." He led the way down the aisle, balancing as the train rocked from side to side. We carefully stepped onto the bridge outside which connected our car to the next, then proceeded through it, again from one car to the another, through the dining car, and finally to the last car on the train—the observation car. We held the guard rail and in the faint light spreading outward from the car, we stared at the railroad ties and telegraph poles quickly flashing backward and disappearing into the darkness, one after another. The clickity-clickty noise of the wheels rolling over the spaces between connecting rails dulled our hearing and held us entranced. How long we stood there, I have no idea. But it must have been at least twenty minutes, for we had traveled from one town to another, from one set of grain elevators to another—a total of ten miles. The train was slowing down. We wobbled carefully along through the aisle, back to our seats.

"Thank you," I said. "That was a lot of fun."

He nodded." That's what I like about traveling. It's a long ride to Toronto. Two nights and three days. And there aren't many people I can talk to except soldiers and airmen and the odd sailor."

"You know where they're going?" I said.

"To be stationed somewhere or home on leave, I suppose."

"Maybe. But I'll bet most of them are on their way overseas."

He looked at me skeptically. "How do you know?"

"Look at their ranks," I said. "The airmen have just graduated.

They're either going home on embarkation leave or they're going to Halifax. I think they're on their way to England. In a couple of weeks they'll be flying Hurricanes or Spitfires, shooting down Messerschmitts or German bombers. Some will be flying our own bombers—Blenheims or Hudsons or maybe even Halifaxes."

"How do you know so much about the war?" he asked.

"I follow it. I listen to Lorne Green on the C.B. C. news from Toronto every night, and my buddy listens to the American stations. We study it. Hitler is trying to knock out the R.A F. before invading. But he won't succeed. You know why?"

"Why?"

" Our pilots are better than his. And our Spitfires are better than their Messerschmitts. He'll never win the battle in the air. And if he can't beat us in the air, he can't invade. That gives us time. It's going to be a long war."

"I'll probably be in it. I hope so."

"Me too."

I liked him, even though he didn't like Jews. But I was sure he liked me. I wondered what he would have said if I had told him I was Jewish. He probably would have said, "Oh, I didn't mean you." I assumed that he had learned anti- Semitism from his parents. I wondered what it would be like in the world if there were no organized religions. Maybe that would eliminate prejudice and we'd all be a lot better off. Also, there wouldn't be any need for a bar mitzvah, and I wouldn't have to come to Yorkton every Friday night and stay with a strange family, so that the rabbi could teach me everything I had to know for my bar mitzvah to please my parents. But I wanted to please my parents. So I had better keep these thoughts to myself.

We shook hands and said good-bye as the train pulled into Yorkton.

CHAPTER EIGHTEEN
Son Of Good Deeds

I got off the train and was surprised to see Barney Eisenstein waiting for me. "That's very nice of you to meet me." I said as we shook hands.

"We thought maybe you forgot where we lived."

"No, I remember. Just a few houses from Irwin Schwartz. Across the street from Mervin Shnider." He nodded and we began walking along Broadway to Betts Avenue.

"So you're coming to learn for your bar mitzvah?"

"Yeah. Every weekend from now 'til March 26th."

"That's nice. It's not hard. So how many Jewish families are there in Sheho?"

"Just us and Mr. Leckie and his son.

"That's all?"

"That's all." We crossed Betts Avenue and stopped to look at the window display of E.B. Smith men's wear. " Most small towns usually have only one or two Jewish families. Storekeepers. Bigger towns might have a doctor and dentist. Five families would be a lot. Not like Yorkton. I hear Yorkton is getting an air force training school for fighter pilots."

He nodded and we turned north along Betts Avenue. "That's right. There's a big write-up about it in the Yorkton Enterprise this week. Pilots will be coming here from all over the British Empire. It's a huge project. They're starting construction in a few weeks. Just as soon as they take the crops off the field. There'll be all kinds of construction jobs then. With good pay, too."

"That's great. But they'll have to stop construction during winter and won't be able to continue 'til the snow melts in spring. When do they think it will be finished?"

"Maybe in April. Depends on the weather."

"Then it won't be finished 'till after my bar mitzvah?"

"Maybe not. Depends on the weather. Maybe before."

"I hope it's finished before," I said as we reached the two-storied house with the verandah. I followed Barney through the back door and into the kitchen.

Rabbi Eisenstein and his wife and Hannah were waiting for us.

The rabbi was the first to greet me. "*Geet Shabbas*!" [Good Sabbath] He shook hands with me. I returned the greeting. We all said "*Geet Shabbas*!"

I had started to take off my cap when I noticed that the rabbi was wearing a *yarmulke* [skull cap] and Barney, who had already taken his cap off, had replaced it with a *yarmulke*. I felt embarrassed. Should I leave my cap on or should I take it off? I immediately thought back to that day during my first week in school when I had sat down at my desk and had kept my cap on in Miss Griffiths's classroom. "TAKE YOUR CAP OFF!" she had shouted. "WHERE DO YOU THINK YOU ARE? YOU NEVER WEAR YOUR CAP WHEN YOU'RE INSIDE A ROOM!" From that day on, I had always taken my cap off inside a room except in a synagogue. But the rabbi's home was not exactly like Miss Griffith's classroom. Nobody shouted here, and the rules were different. One's head must be kept covered out of respect for the Almighty; or if not the Almighty, out of respect for the rabbi. So I kept my cap on. I think Barney sensed my uneasiness. He handed me a *yarmulke*. Everyone seemed relieved.

Mrs. Eisenstein was wearing a kerchief over her head. "Here *zitz* [sit down], she said, as she pulled out a chair. "*Kenst dee farshtayne Yiddish*? [Can you understand Jewish?]

I nodded my head. "Of course," I replied."*Ich ken farshtayne but Ich kennisht reden geet*." [I can understand but I cannot speak well.]

She seemed pleased. Then she spoke in English. "You're hungry, maybe? Here. Taste my sponge cake. *Ess.*" [Eat] She placed a large piece of cake on a plate and handed it to me. "*Dee glachts tay?*" [You like tea?]

I nodded. She poured a tenth of a cup of tea from her teapot into a cup, then filled it with hot water. Then she placed the cup on a saucer and added a slice of lemon. That was good Jewish tea, I thought. Just like Mama makes.

"How's your family?" asked the rabbi.

"They're fine, thank you."

"How's your father?" he added.

"He's fine, thank you."

"How's your mother?" asked Mrs. Eisenstein.

"She's fine, thank you."

"How's your sisters?" she added.

"Fine."

"How many sisters do you have?" asked Hannah in a timid voice, as if she was almost afraid to ask. It was the first time she had spoken.

"Three. Merle, Etta, and Sylvia."

Hanna's face lit up and her voice seemed more confident. "Sylvia is the youngest, isn't she?"

"That's right."

"I think I know her. She was here for Rosh Hashanah and Yom Kippur last year, wasn't she?"

"That's right."

"It's late," said the rabbi. "To bed. Hannah, turn out the lights."

We all filed upstairs to bed, leaving Hannah behind to turn out the lights. It was *Shabbas*, the Sabbath, the day of rest. Work was forbidden. Turning out lights was work; therefore, it was forbidden. But Hanna was not yet old enough to assume her religious responsibilities. Therefore she could work. And so it was her job to turn out the lights. I was getting an education about the ten commandments.

When I got up and walked down stairs the next morning, the rabbi wrapped in his *talis* [prayer shawl] was standing in a corner, facing the east, *dahvening*. He reminded me of Uncle Leachman who used to *dahven* beside our piano when he visited us. I was just a child then. The rabbi eventually finished and we all sat down to breakfast. Because this was a super orthodox family, I assumed we would not be eating bacon and eggs. My assumption was correct. Instead, we had Quaker corn flakes with milk. And cocoa. I preferred the slightly larger flakes that came out of the white and red Kellogg's box. But since I wasn't home, I didn't complain about such a hardship. We all have to make sacrifices in our lifetime. So I ate Quaker Corn Flakes.

After breakfast, I sat down with the rabbi at the dining room table to begin my studies. He asked me if I knew my *aleph, baze* [a, b, c's]. I said yes. He asked me if I could read Hebrew. I said "*Ah bissel.*" [A little bit.] He opened a book, pointed to a line, and asked me to begin. And so I began my bar mitzvah studies, mumbling and stumbling and getting up off the canvas and plowing straight ahead, at least two miles an hour. I was making progress.

"*Geet,*" [Good] said the rabbi. I knew he was lying. And on the Sabbath, yet. But he was using psychology. He was raising my self- esteem so that I would gain confidence.

"*Noch a mool,*" he said. [Once more]

So I took my time and pointed at each word, and little by little the correct pronunciation came to me, and the rabbi nodded his head.

"*Geet,*" he said. "*Noch a mool.*"

This time I didn't need my finger and hardly stumbled at all. What I had forgotten since Bernice Shatsky had first taught me two years before was now rapidly coming back. By the time I had finished my first session with the rabbi, I could read Hebrew almost as well as I could when she had been my tutor. And I was sure God would forgive the rabbi for lying, even on the Sabbath. After all, it was just a little white lie. In fact, it wasn't even a lie. Just a slight exaggeration. Besides, it was for the greater "good" that the rabbi had exaggerated. He was preparing me for the day when I would assume my religious responsibilities as a good Jew.

Then he had me read the blessing one should make before eating bread. I read it a few times until I memorized it as he requested. *"Borooch Ato Adoyna Eloyhaynoo Melech Haoylom Hamoytze Lechem Meen Haoretz."* [Blessed art Thou O Lord our God, King of the universe, Who brings forth the wheat from the ground.] Then he asked me to read and memorize the blessing for wine. *"Borooch Ato Adoyna Eloyhaynoo Melech Haoylom Boyrey Pree Hagoffen."* [Blessed art Thou O Lord our God, King of the universe, Who brings forth the fruit from the vine.] I felt good realizing that I had already memorized two major blessings which I would soon be using. Furthermore, I knew what the words meant.

It felt strange to me when we all sat down to dinner together, exactly at noon. At home, especially on Saturday, Papa would rush in to eat while Mama or my older sisters looked after the store. And every evening we often ate before Papa did because the store was open until seven during weekdays and until ten on Saturdays. But here, everyone sat down together except Mrs. Eisenstein, who waited on us. The first thing the rabbi did was to pour water over his hands, even though he had washed them just moments before. Then he wiped them, tore off a piece of bread, and made the *Hamoytze*, the blessing for bread. He asked me to do the same. I felt good when I rattled off the words almost as fast as he did. Everyone first looked at me in awe, then at the rabbi. He beamed with pride. He had performed a small miracle, yet the day had barely begun.

Mrs. Eisenstein was a good cook, about as good as Mama, and she cooked the same kind of food, including keegle. She also pronounced it "keegle"—the proper way, as Mama did—not "koogle," the way some other Jewish people did. And she said *sheel* for synagogue, not *shule*. I was beginning to feel at home.

After dinner the rabbi brought out his *Chumash*, the Jewish translation of the first Five Books of Moses. The outside cover was blue and looked like some of the textbooks we had in school, nothing fancy. It didn't look at all like my impressive black grained-leather bound copy of the Holy Scriptures that I had bought the year before. My copy was printed in small type with two columns on each very thin page with pink edges, so that when you closed the book, the pink edges stood out in sharp contrast to the black cover and gold engraved lettering which read:

"THE HOLY SCRIPTURES." Even though my Bible was small enough to be easily held in my hand, it looked much more impressive than the rabbi's blue *Chumash*. But I guess the stories were the same, except that mine was printed in English and his in Jewish. I had already read the first three books of Moses. That's as far as I had got. Someday I would get around to reading the rest of it. In the meantime, I was starting at the beginning again. I mean the very beginning. "*Tsum ershten*," which translates as "To begin with," or " First of all," or "In the beginning."

I mumbled and stumbled at first, but I actually understood the words. That's because they were in Jewish, not Hebrew. But the stories sounded different—not like the same passage I had read the year before. At first I thought that perhaps the Jewish translation was wrong. But then I quickly realized that the Jewish translation was from the original Hebrew, the same language from which the English translation originated. I thought that if I had translated the Bible into English, I might have done a better job. But then I would have had to know Hebrew, and that would have been next to impossible; so I forgot about that idea.

Every now and then the rabbi would ask me questions about what I had read. He asked me in Jewish, but I answered in English. We were a good bilingual team. I was learning Jewish and he was learning English. Sometimes he'd ask me the meaning of a certain English word, and I'd try to explain it in Jewish. But my Jewish vocabulary was limited, so I had to try to explain the meaning in English. That's when he got confused. I got frustrated and he got confused. I don't know which was worse.

Our sessions lasted about two hours each. Maybe a little longer. I didn't have a watch and I didn't pay much attention to the time; but I was good at guessing the time, so I figured they were about two hours. I wasn't tired and I could have gone on a little longer. Maybe an hour longer. But I think the rabbi was tired. I felt a little sorry for him. How would you like to spend at least two hours at a stretch sitting on a chair, listening to somebody learning to read, mumbling and stumbling in low gear? Rabbi Eisenstein was a patient man. I think he was glad when he heard the interruption.

His back was toward the verandah. He was patiently listening to me. God was just about to finish creating the sixth day and was admiring His own "very good" handiwork. I thought the translation —or perhaps the creation—left something to be desired. "Very good" would be equivalent to the letter grade of B- or at the most a B. Certainly God could have done better than that. At least an A- or even a solid A. If I had been present, I would have told Him so. "Very good is not outstanding. And it is not perfect. You should always strive for perfection." That's what I would have said. But since I had not been available on the sixth day, I wished I had been present when the Holy Torah was written. I would have told the scribe what I thought.

That's when I, too, noticed the interruption. Molly and Reva Levinson were walking up and down the verandah, as if to politely let the rabbi know it was time to let Barney come outside and join them. The footsteps were getting louder.

Instead of turning around, the rabbi looked at Barney who was nearby, reading, and said, "Who's that?"

Without looking up, Barney replied, "It's the lemons." He kept on reading.

The rabbi had hoped that the heaven and the earth would be finished by the time he dismissed me, but that would be on the beginning of the seventh day, and I was still on the sixth. I think he was silently praying, asking God to make me hurry up so we could get to the seventh day— the day of rest.

Just about then Irwin Schwartz walked onto the verandah, patted the girls on their heads, and began showing them some dance steps he had seen in the latest Fred Astaire movie. He danced toward the kitchen door, then without knocking, entered. He was the same age as I, but about ten feet taller. "Mrs. Eisentstein," he said in a voice happy and loud enough to let everyone know he was here and it was time to liven up, " How are you?"

"*Geet Shabbas*, Shruleck. I'm fine, daenk you." She seemed delighted.

"Hannah, *zug* [say] *Geet Shabbas*."

Hannah, barely audible, obeyed her mother.

"Hello, Hannah. Where's baby Eisenstein?"

"In the next room with Barney."

Oblivious to my Jewish rendition of the creation of the universe, now almost about to begin the seventh day, Irwin greeted Barney, who was sitting on the chesterfield near the radio, then bent down and patted Barney's three-year-old brother on his head. "Hello Baby Eisenstein. How's Baby Eisenstein today?"

"My name is Avrum. I'm not a baby. Don't call me baby."

Irwin patted him again. "Okay, I won't call you baby anymore."

"You always call me Baby Eisenstein. My name is Avrum."

"Ssch," said the rabbi, turning to the three seated on the chesterfield. "Geneeg!" [Enough!] Then he turned to me and asked me to read the sentence instructing us that "on the seventh day God finished His work which He had made; and he rested on the seventh day from all his work which he had made."

And when I finally finished reading the sentence—thank God!— Rabbi Eisenstein said, "*Geet! Geneeg!*" [Good! Enough already!] And he closed the book, took out a handkerchief, and wiped his brow. That was the end of my first day's instruction. Like God, I, too, felt proud of my accomplishment, even though His was slightly more complex. And like God, I also felt it was time to take a break.

Barney, Irwin, and I joined the Levinson sisters, who were now at the end of their patience. I was sorry I had taken so long between the end of the sixth day and the beginning of the seventh. Fifteen minutes is a long time to wait when you're only thirteen years old and your sister is only eleven. Both were pretty brunettes, but Molly had acne and was considerably taller and thinner than her younger sister. Reva was even shorter than I. She was pleasantly plump, with a round, full face and big, beautiful brown eyes. I thought she was one of the prettiest girls I had ever seen. I was glad I had come to Yorkton.

We walked across Betts Avenue to the east side of the street and continued south, past the Jewish stores— Belles's, Levinson's, Rosenblatt's Dry Cleaners, and Maerovich's, where Molly Maerovich joined us. She was about thirteen. All six of us now continued past the New York Cafe, and turned east at the corner onto Broadway, stopping momentarily to stare at the window display of E. B. Smith's Ladies'

Wear. Then we continued east, past Woolworth's and again stopped for at least five minutes to stare at the two crowded windows of Croll's Broadway Store. The first displayed men's suits, topcoats, overcoats, sheepskin coats, leather jackets, Stetson hats, dress shirts, neckties, flannel shirts, Stanfield's woolen underwear, Penman's cotton underwear, and dress shoes. The ladies' window on our right was just as crowded. It revealed fur coats, cloth coats with and without fur collars, woolen suits, dresses, blouses, skirts, slips, brassieres, bloomers, panties, rayon stockings, and shoes. Kenny Croll, who dressed the windows, did not believe in any space between any of the items. He did not believe in leaving anything to the imagination. He was a natural born artist.

We continued east for a couple of blocks to the drug store that had a glass enclosed booth where one could listen to the latest 78 R.P.M. records before making a purchase. We listened to Glenn Miller and his orchestra play "In the Mood" and "Blueberry Hill." We listened to the foghorn voice of Vaughn Monroe sing "There I Go." We listened to Bing Crosby warble "Only Forever" and the Inkspots harmonize "Maybe" and "We Three—My Echo, My Shadow, and Me." Then we put all the records back and walked out without buying anything.

We continued along Broadway and turned left on Fourth Avenue to the big white house with wide walk-up steps at 65 Fourth Avenue, the home of the Fermans. Irwin led the way. He knocked on the door twice, then without waiting for an answer walked in, the rest of us following. Gloria, eleven, a pretty rather slim girl with sparkling brown eyes, who looked a little bit like Barbara Stanwyck, greeted us, then invited us into the den (as if we needed an invitation). Bookshelves full of Jewish and English books, including a set of encyclopedias, lined two of the walls; a piano was placed against another wall, and a couch against the remaining one. Some of us had to sit on the floor.

Her younger brother, Avrohom, about seven, joined us and kept interrupting our conversation, while her brother Malcolm, a year older than I, virtually ignored us. He was practicing "I'll Never Smile Again" on his clarinet. It wasn't going too well, so he began to improvise. Then he mumbled some explanation about what he was trying to do. Finally, he put the clarinet down and began playing the same piece on the piano.

It went a little better. It sounded more like the original piece. I was quite impressed with his accomplishment. I could barely play a simple piece like "The Jolly Roger," using two hands. One hand always got in the way of the other. But Malcolm could play two instruments. I didn't know anyone else who could play two instruments except Abe Katz, my cousin in Guernsey, who was an excellent musician. Eventually, Malcom put down his sheet music and quit playing. Then he mumbled something about the time and left the room. The rest of us stayed a little longer, the girls gossiping about whom Valli Jean Portnuff had gone out with two weeks ago and whom she was going with tonight. Eventually, Barney reminded us it was time to go home.

Shortly before sunset, Rabbi Eisenstein began *dahvening Mincha*, the pre-evening prayer. After he had finished, he waited for a few minutes, looked at his watch, looked out of the window to make sure the sun had set, and then began *dahvening Mariff*, the evening prayer. Both prayers went on for quite a while. I'm sure God was impressed. But I didn't think God needed two long prayers just before nightfall, especially since they both meant practically the same thing. But then, nobody had asked for my advice. Not even my opinion. And I certainly wasn't about to express it here—of all places. But someday!

We all sat down to supper together—everyone except Mrs. Eisenstein. I thought she walked and looked like a queen, even in a cotton dress. I thought we should have been waiting on her instead of the other way around. But it wasn't my home and I wasn't about to open my mouth.

The next day the sessions got a little longer. I think the rabbi must have gotten his second wind. I could now read a little faster, both in Hebrew and Jewish. We were moving right along. Adam was now 930 years old. That's what the book said. Then he died.

I had hoped we would again be interrupted in the afternoon by the Levinson sisters stomping on the verandah, but I guess they had different plans. I missed them, especially Reva. She was cute. However, the Eisensteins did not lack for company. Irwin Schwartz again came over and this time showed his dance steps to Hannah and Mrs. Eisenstein. Her face lit up and she laughed, the only time I had seen her laugh. It's not easy to be a rabbi's wife. The rabbi, hearing the commotion and afraid of burning out his star pupil, decided to conclude my session. "*Geet*, mine student. *Dee host geet gelernt*." [You have learned well.]

As the rabbi brought out another book, the Talmud, for a slightly more advanced course, Barney now replaced me as his star pupil. I joined Irwin, now on the chesterfield with "Baby Eisenstein." Barney began reading, constantly interrupted by his father who would question him in Jewish, point-by-point, on what the passage said and what it might mean and what it could mean and how else it could be interpreted or might be interpreted or should be interpreted. I thought the rabbi was preparing his son to follow in his father's footsteps.

The Socratic study lasted about an hour. Suddenly we heard stomping on the verandah, as if someone was shaking wet snow off his boots. But it wasn't even fall. "Who's that?" shouted the rabbi.

"The lemons," said Barney without even looking up.

The rabbi looked at his watch, waited for Barney to finish reading the sentence, then said, "*Geet! Geneeg*."

I wondered how in the world the Levinson sisters knew exactly—to the minute—when Rabbi Eisenstein would dismiss his students. I think they were afraid of the rabbi. That's why they never knocked on the door.

During my bus ride home, I felt good realizing that I now had a new group of friends, Jewish friends. Although I had a few friends at home, it wasn't the same. I had something special in common with my Jewish friends. I couldn't pinpoint it, but I knew it was something special. Perhaps it was acceptance. Perhaps it was a feeling of belonging to the same tribe. Whatever it was, it made me feel good. My weekend trip to Yorkton wasn't too bad after all.

Every weekend, except for the high Holy Days, the routine was practically the same. But one Saturday, shortly before Christmas, I became very ill with the measles. Papa was notified and he hired Bill Finley to drive him to Yorkton to take me home. It was late at night when they arrived. I felt horrible. I was glad they had come.

I did not return until early January. By then, since the bus no longer ran because the highway was blocked, I would remain at the Eisensteins until eight o'clock Monday morning when I would take the train back home, arriving just after ten. I would go directly to school dressed in my holiday best. Some of the kids made fun of me. But I tried not to let it bother me. Sometimes that's the price one pays for being different or even wearing something different.

The rabbi now had an additional student, Kippy Lertzman. His father owned a general store in Canora, a town of just over a thousand population, about thirty miles north of Yorkton. Although his son was only ten years old, three years away from being bar mitzvahed, he believed it was never too early to start preparing him for the big day. So in early January, I had a roommate.

Although Kippy, who had a slight lisp, was a clever ten-year old, I thought he sometimes acted like a six-year old. He was full of energy, never still, always talking, often interrupting, and never afraid to give an opinion on any subject whether asked for or not. Some of his opinions were so far out, I felt sorry for the rabbi. But I guess he was used to all kinds of kids by now. He taught a classroom of at least twenty every weekday afternoon in the synagogue.

Even though I was sometimes irritated by Kippy's behavior, I got along well with him. We slept in the same bed, for which I was glad because our room was not the warmest one in Saskatchewan when the outside temperature fell to forty and even fifty degrees below zero.

On some Saturday afternoons, we would all go to watch the Yorkton Terriers practice hockey in Yorkton's large indoor skating arena. The Terriers belonged to a professional league that included Moose Jaw, Regina, Saskatoon, and Flin Flon. This was the closest I had ever come to watching a professional hockey game. They skated much faster than anyone in Sheho, and they could cut to the right as well as to the left. I never thought I would ever get the chance to see a professional game, and certainly never one in the National Hockey League. So I appreciated watching this professional workout.

On Sunday afternoons, since I had brought my skates along, we often went skating. Just about everybody skated. I liked skating hand-in-hand with Gloria Ferman. We kept our woolen lined leather mittens on, though, because it was too cold to take them off. She was about as good a skater as I, and she looked really cute when her cheeks got flushed as we skated around and around to the music. Kippy used to call her Floria Gherman, just to irritate her. I never did that, even though I liked the way her brown eyes sparkled when she got mad.

One Saturday morning toward the end of January, we all joined Irwin Schwartz at *sheel* [the synagogue] for his bar mitzvah. Practically all the Jewish families in Yorkton were there. They had come to honor one of their own—the Schwartz family— pillars of Yorkton's Jewish community. Mr. Schwartz owned Yorkton Bottling Works, a soda pop factory that made every imaginable flavor of soda pop except Coca -Cola. He was a friendly, honest hard-working businessman who attended *sheel* whenever it was required, his wife was a member of the Hadassah sisterhood, and he and his family were long-time residents of Yorkton. They were well liked by everyone. It came as no surprise, then, that on this Saturday morning the *sheel* was full. Even Irwin's sister from North Dakota was present.

I was quite excited. Not only was this the first bar mitzvah ceremony I had ever attended, but I thought it might be a preview of my own bar mitzvah now only two months away. I sat in the first seat on the right-hand side, in the very front row, where I would get the best overall view of the performance.

Irwin, for the first time, had a *talis* draped around his neck. He wore a new green suit and a gray hat with a medium sized brim and a wide black band. He mounted the steps to the *bimah*, a platform on which stood the table for reading the Torah and the Book of Prophets. Then he sat down, flanked by his father and Rabbi Eisenstein. He looked nervous. I didn't blame him. I would have been nervous, too.

Soon Rabbi Eisenstein, on the *bimah* facing the congregation, began *dahvening*. This service was much like any Saturday morning service on Rosh Hashanah—only it wasn't as long and not nearly as boring. I guess the reason was that by now I knew how to read Hebrew; so I *dahvened* out loud along with everyone else, and almost as fast. Occasionally, the rabbi faced the Ark of the Covenant, on the east wall. That's when we all stood up, continuing to *dahven*. I was proud of myself. We were moving right along. Irwin was still up front, in his new hat, towering above everyone else in Yorkton.

Eventually, Rabbi Eisenstein drew back the curtains covering the Ark and opened it. That's when *everyone* stood up. He placed the frilled ends of his *talis* on the Torah then quickly withdrew and kissed them, all the while uttering a Hebrew blessing on the Torah. Next, he took out the sacred Torah, carefully pulled off the royal purple velvet covering, and placed the Torah on the table. Then he began to unroll the scrolls. When he came to a particular passage he stopped, then gingerly placed a metal pointer on the words and began to chant. He soon stopped and asked for a *kohayn* to make the first *aliyah*— that is, to "ascend" and make a blessing on the Torah.

[The first honor of making an *aliyah* goes to the *Kohayn* because he belongs to the highest ranking tribe whose members are considered to be descendants of the Priest Aaron, the brother of Moses. The second tribe to be honored is the *Levi*, representing the Priest's assistant, and the third honor goes to the Yisraelite, who represents the remaining Jews, the *Yisraelim.*]

Norman Croll climbed the steps to the *bimah*, kissed the Torah with his talis as the rabbi had done, and uttered the Hebrew blessing on the Torah. Then the rabbi read a short passage from the Torah, after which Norman Croll again made a blessing. Then he descended and walked back to his seat. The rabbi read a little more, then asked for a *Levi* to make the second *aliyah*. The process was repeated. Next he asked for a *Yisrael*.

Although the minimum requirement for *aliyahs* had been fulfilled, with one from each tribe, the rabbi continued asking for *aliyahs* until the maximum of seven was completed.

Finally, the moment of truth had arrived for Irwin Schwartz—bar mitzvah— "Son of good deeds." He stood up, towering above the table on which the Torah lay, towering above Rabbi Eisenstein, who stood alongside him, and towering above everyone on the Canadian Prairies. He kissed the Torah and blessed it as the others had done. Then he bent down, almost to his waist, while the rabbi held the metal pointer below the first word of the particular passage for this particular week—the passage Irwin had practiced again and again—his *Maftir*. And Irwin began chanting his *Maftir*. It was a long passage, but he never faltered and his voice hardly ever cracked. After he finished, he made another blessing for the Torah. The Torah was then put away. I could see the smile on his face. He had rounded second base and was now almost at third. Now he began to read the *Haftarah*—a particular passage from the Book of Prophets. He read smoothly without mumbling or stuttering. He had rounded third and was now on his way to home plate. Nothing could stop him now. And finally he finished. He grinned. He had hit a grand slam home run.

At that very instant, a hail of peanuts hurled from the balcony pelted his hat. Every Jewish kid in Yorkton was leaning over the balcony, aiming handfuls of peanuts right at his head below. They couldn't miss. But this was just the first barrage. He grinned and draped his talis over his head and face as salvo after salvo of peanuts rained down upon him. It was a peanut storm. Finally, the storm ended. Irwin descended the steps to join the rest of us who shook his hand and wished him "*Mazltov.*" [congratulations and best wishes.]

All the women and kids from the balcony descended to the hallway, where they began to hug him and wish him "*Mazltov.*" And all the adults shook hands with Mr. and Mrs. Schwartz and wished them "*Mazltov.*" Then all the kids made a bee line for the pastry table and picked up handfuls of sweets. Finally, they made a bee line for Schwartz's soft drink table filled with bottles of cream soda, vanilla, chocolate, orange, lemon, lime, raspberry, strawberry, cherry, and every imaginable flavor except cola.

I don't know what kinds of gifts he received or how many, but I know he was never in need of a fountain pen for years afterward. I also don't know if his parents threw a big celebration for him the following day. If they did, it must have been for adults only because Barney and I were not invited, and Barney was his closest friend. Their nicknames were Mutt and Jeff, after the funny paper characters, one of whom towered above the other.

My own day of reckoning was fast approaching. Although I could now read Hebrew fairly well as long as the diacritical marks appeared with the letters to indicate the vowel sounds, I was almost lost when the letters were bare. And that is how the Torah is written. There were no helping signs for reading my passage from the Torah, my *Maftir*. But that was not all. Now I had to learn how to chant, and I don't mean mumble. There were little tiny marks by the letters, primitive musical notes for chanting, indicating a rise or fall in pitch, equal to about three notes on the scale. I could read real musical notes, but these marks were something else. They weren't invented for the piano. And they weren't invented for singing. They looked like tiny grains of sand that had stuck to the scrolls during a sandstorm, when Moses and the Children of Israel left Egypt and got lost and wandered around in the desert for forty years.

In spite of these obstacles, I learned how to chant my *Maftir* and Rabbi Eisenstein had me practice it again and again until I sounded like a eunuch. And I practiced reading my *Haftarah* until the rabbi was proud of me.

On the Saturday before my bar mitzvah, I went to the Hudson's Bay Company to find a hat that would go well with my teal blue suit. I bought a dark green one for $2.95 plus tax. The salesman inserted a beautiful orange and yellow feather in the band, slanting the feather at a slight angle so that the feather brought out just the right contrast to compliment my new felt hat. It was the first hat I had ever worn, and I felt distinguished—like a grown up.

The calendar indicated that winter had just turned to spring. The long nights had grown shorter and the days longer; they were both now equal. But the snows had not yet begun to melt. Winter does not give way easily on the Canadian Prairies.

A few days before my big event, Mama's aunt from Winnipeg, whom we all called Auntie Leachman, came to our home to help Mama prepare sweets for my bar mitzvah. They spent days mixing the batter and shaping it and putting it in the oven, time and again, baking batch after batch of corn starch cookies and strudel and other pastries. It was a happy time. Auntie Leachman was the matriarch of her family. Her niece's one-and-only son was about to be bar mitzvahed. She would share in the celebration.

On the Friday night nearest to March 26th, 1941, leaving my sisters in charge of the store, Papa, Mama, Auntie Leachman and I boarded the train for Yorkton. As soon as we arrived, we went directly to the Yorkton

Hotel, where they registered and took their suit cases up to their rooms. (I kept my suit case because I would not be staying there.) Then, about nine-thirty, we all went directly to the Eisensteins.

Although Auntie Leachman and Rabbi and Mrs. Eisenstein had never seen one another before, they might as well have been long lost relatives. They all had come from Poland and each asked the other a dozen questions about their homeland and about their life in Canada. Their conversation continued long after Mrs. Eisenstein had served sponge cake and tea with lemon. Rabbi Eisenstein told Papa he was proud of me. Papa thanked him for his patience in preparing me for my bar mitzvah and for teaching me Jewish and Hebrew so "I would know who I am." Papa and Mama thanked Mrs. Eisenstien for looking after me. Finally, Auntie Leachman, Papa and Mama went back to the hotel. Tomorrow would be their big day. I stayed at the Eisensteins. It had become my second home.

The rabbi had informed Yorkton's Jewish families that his student, Katz's son from Sheho, was going to be bar mitzvahed next Saturday morning. But since Papa had not sent out invitations, he had to make sure there would be at least ten men present for the minyan, which was supposed to begin at nine-thirty. At nine o'clock sharp he hurriedly began going from one Jewish businessman to another with his urgent request. "*Mine ayne oun aynzticke zeen gate bar mitzvahd zyen. Veer dauf hooben deer fur a minyan. Kim.*" [My one-and-only son is going to be bar mitzvahed. We must have you for a quorum. Come.]

He did not waste time.

Although he had been a regular at Yorkton for High Holy day services since 1913 and knew everybody, not everyone was available. Saturday was the busiest day of the week. All he needed, though, were eight men, since he plus the rabbi would equal ten. That would be enough for the *minyan*. If he got more, so much the better. But if not, the ten would do. A *minyan* is a *minyan*, and he was not trying to impress the world. He would round up a *minyan* by nine-thirty.

So he started making his rounds, first calling on his old friend Ben Glass, who had sold his failing store in Insinger (twelve miles east of Sheho), and was now in Yorkton, where Sam, his oldest son, had become a successful wholesale jobber. Yes, of course, Glass would be there. Good. Next on Broadway, he called on Harry Ferman from Regal Ladies' Wear, Segal from Sally's Style Shop, and Norman Croll from Croll's Broadway Store. Norman Croll had salesmen and saleswomen who could look after the store. He would be there for sure. Then on to Betts Avenue: Rothstein, Belles, Levinson, Maerovich, Rosenblatt the Dry Cleaner and Tailor, and Schmidt Brothers fur traders. Finally, across the street to Burt Lexier from the Pool Hall and Bowling Avenue. That was enough. He hurried north up Betts Avenue, past Eisensteins, to *sheel*.

By the time he got to the synagogue, Mama and Auntie Leachman were already there with their pastry and with Papa's bottle of brandy and his bottle of Manischewitz Kosher Concord Grape wine. They had brought everything they needed for the celebration and were setting it up on the table in the hallway.

When the Eisensteins and I arrived, everything had already been set up. Soon the men began arriving, one-by-one, and eventually there were at least ten or maybe even twelve; that was more than enough for a *minyan*.

Only twice in my life during a personal celebration have I been so excited and so nervous that I was hardly aware of what was happening. The first was my bar mitzvah; the last was my 25th wedding anniversary celebration. Both times, after months and months of planning and preparation, everything went by so fast it seemed like a blur. When Marilyn and I celebrated our 25th anniversary, we hosted an elegant dinner party in the evening at a fine hotel for over 125 guests from California and Canada. The party included an open cocktail bar and dancing to a live band afterward. It was some contrast from my bar mitzvah.

All I remember about my bar mitzvah was that Papa was on the *bimah* with me, as proud as anyone could possibly be; and when for the first time I looked at the beautiful hand-printed lettering on the open scroll of the Torah, just before I began to chant my *Maftir*, I couldn't help but think of the thousands and thousands of hours of painstaking work some devoted scribe had done to accomplish such artistry. Every letter was perfect. Every line as straight as a ruler. It looked as if it had been printed. I was in awe. I was in awe for another reason. This was the Holy Torah—the revealed word of God—handed down from Moses to his followers, generation after generation, for thousands of years. It was sacred.

With my rabbi holding the pointer on the words, I nervously chanted my *Maftir*. I don't remember whether or not my voice cracked. I don't think it did. Then I read the *Haftarah*. It went well. And then it was over. I was out of breath. That's when the hail of peanuts hit me. Not as many as Irwin Schwartz had received. Not as many kids from Yorkton were there. And there was only one salvo. So I didn't have to put my brand new little *talis* over my new hat to protect my face. I was glad there was only one salvo of peanuts. And I was glad it was all over.

Papa kissed me and said "*Mazltov!*" Then the rabbi hugged me and said "*Mazltov*, mine student!" That made me really proud. And when I descended the steps everyone shook my hand and said "*Mazltov.*" And when I entered the hallway, Mama and Auntie Leachman hugged me and kissed me and said "*Mazltov!*" And I felt proud. And Mrs. Eisenstein hugged me and said "*Mazltov!*"— right in front of Mama and Auntie Leachman. And that made me really proud. I was particularly happy that I had made Mama and Papa proud of me. It had all been worth while. Then all the kids wished me "*Mazltov*" before racing over to the pastry table, where I soon joined them.

Norman Croll and Ben Glass and his son Sam, and Bert Lexier and the rabbi and Mrs. Eisenstein and a few others whom I don't remember wished Papa and Mama "*Mazltov.*" Then everyone sipped a tiny glass of brandy or wine and picked up a piece of strudel and a corn starch cookie and chatted for a while. Then Norman Croll and the others left. And that is all I remember about my bar mitzvah.

That evening Barney paid for my movie ticket at the Roxy theater. It was my bar mitzvah gift from the Eisensteins. I also got a little toy car from Mr. Glass and his family. It was one of the very few toys I ever received in my life. I could wind it up and it would run straight ahead and bump into anything in its way. It lasted a month. Those are the only presents I remember getting; although Merle, my oldest sister, insists that I got a fountain pen from Bert Lexier. If I did, I made good use of it.

But I was kind of disappointed. I had hoped to receive at least a few more presents. But that's life.

I realized there is more to a bar mitzvah than presents. I had made Papa and Mama happy, and they were proud of me. I had given them *nachas*—that is, "a joyous blessing." And that was the most precious gift I could possibly have given them. I realized that with the exception of their wedding and the birth of their children, this was the most joyous event of their lives. I was proud that I had given them *nachas*.

CHAPTER NINETEEN
Katz General Store: The Depression Years

The last time I was in Sheho, for the Sheho School Reunion in 1998, I was curious about what had become of the six general stores in operation when I had moved away fifty-one years earlier. What a disappointment! There were no general stores left. The two remaining stores carried a complete line of groceries, but that was all. There was not a single item of hardware to be found, nor a single item of footwear, clothing, or accessories. Both stores were self-serve, modern grocery stores. The customers helped themselves, brought the groceries to the front counter, behind which the owner stood and rang up the total on an electric cash register. The owner then collected the money and packaged the order, all in a matter of minutes. No charge accounts, at least none that I saw. The customer was then on his way. No gossip. No idle chit chat. No prolonged visits. To merely use the word *contrast* to describe the difference between these two remaining stores and Katz General Store would be a vast understatement.

From my earliest recollections until I moved away from Sheho in the winter of 1947, everyday life for me revolved around our store. The store was actually a complex of two wooden buildings, both painted white with black trim, and with black lettering on the second story of the main building that read KATZ GENERAL STORE. The main building was the store; the small shed on its right was the flour house. The main building contained two warehouses—a small, narrow one for grocery supplies on the left— and a separate large warehouse at the back for storing farm produce like horsehair, hides, eggs, and seneca root.

The flour shed housed not only fifty and hundred-pound sacks of flour, but hundred-pound sacks of sugar, fifty-pound sacks of granulated salt, blocks of salt for cattle, sacks of oyster shells for chickens, feed for cattle, and dozens of mice which I regularly caught as soon as I was old enough to set the mouse traps.

Mr. Darling, one of Sheho's oldest pioneers, had earlier built his own home where the sidewalk ended—at the western end of the village, right next to the town well. Some years later, he had built the store, a two-story structure with two large windows on each side of the door, two smaller slanting windows adjoining the door, and two windows upstairs, where my father and his older brother Maurice lived after opening their store in Sheho in 1914. A year later they were joined by their younger sister Bessie, who kept house for them. My father had worked in Mr. Dashefsky's store in Theodore, two villages east of Sheho, after arriving in Canada in 1912; and two years later he and his older brother pooled their savings of $600.00 to open their own store.

My father's brother Maurice died during the influenza epidemic of 1918. A year later, a handsome Jewish cowboy, Abe Shnider, who was managing a local ranch owned by Mr. Dachas in Yorkton, began courting my father's sister and married her shortly afterward. As a wedding gift, my father made his new brother-in-law, Abe Shnider, a partner in the business, known for nine years afterward as "Shnider and Katz." My father, along with the Shnider family, continued to live upstairs until 1922, when he married Rose Izen, a newly arrived immigrant from Poland. He then built a home to the right of the flour- house, leaving just enough space for the first of two vegetable gardens that would produce not only lettuce, tomatoes, radishes, green onions, but weeds of every known variety.

In 1928, the same year that I was born, my father and his brother-in-law dissolved their partnership, and the Shnider family moved away to Inglis, Manitoba. From then on my father's business was known as "Katz General Store."

From my earliest recollection until I remodeled the store at the age of sixteen, its general layout remained virtually unchanged. The slanted showcase containing candy and cookies was on the left as I entered the store, and then the long grocery counter with a big bronze colored scale in the middle, and next to it a wire dispenser holding several sizes of brown paper bags. Laying alongside the front of the counter were blocks of cube-shaped salt, about eighteen inches on all sides, both white (untreated) and red (iodine added), for cattle and horses to lick. The red was my favorite. It tasted better. Since there was only one chair (with no back) in the store, these salt blocks, piled about two high, served a dual purpose, as did the cases of Macintosh apples or Sunkist oranges across the aisle from the salt. A large sack of oyster shells for chickens, and chop (feed for cattle) also lay outside the counter. Finally, a large barrel of herring in brine stood next to the oyster shells. At the end of this counter was an entrance for my father, who stood behind it and waited on customers, one at a time.

Inside the counter were pull-out bins containing white sugar, brown sugar, navy beans, raisins, prunes, dried apricots, and dried apples. The rest of the groceries were in shelves directly behind the counter. The middle shelf included four-pound cans of Empress Pure Strawberry Jam and the less expensive mixture of Cottage Strawberry and Apple Jam, pails of Rogers Golden Corn Syrup, as well as the brand supposedly used by the Dionne quintuplets— Karo Golden Corn Syrup. When empty, these pails were used by the farmers' children to carry their lunch to school. Next were four bins, each three shelves high: one for Sunkist oranges from Riverside, California; one for Sunkist lemons, also from California; one for Macintosh applies from the Okanagan Valley in British Columbia; and the last one for unsalted, unshelled peanuts. Finally, along the bottom shelf, lay four-pound cans of peanut butter, boxes of Rinso, Oxydol, Lux flakes, and P-and -G white naphtha laundry soap, as well as bars of beauty and bathing soap including, Lux toilet soap, Ivory, Lifebuoy, and Palmolive.

A separate shelf contained tobacco products and during spring and summer, cans of gopher poison. Attached to the tobacco shelf was a dispenser for the small cans of Copenhagen snuff, as well as two other dispensers for the tiny packets of Chantecleer and Zig-Zag cigarette papers. Inside the shelf were small packages of Zig-Zag, Ogden, and Sweet Caporal cigarette tobacco, and Ogden pipe tobacco; large cans of both

Ogden and Prince Albert pipe tobacco, and "tailor-made" Sweet Caporal cigarettes. Cigarettes were quite a luxury; most of the smokers rolled their own. Finally, for the odd cigar smoker, there was also a box of cigars, which sold for a nickel apiece.

At the age of ten or eleven, I was curious about a lot of things, including cigars. I wondered what it was like to smoke a cigar. I had already tried to make a cigar by rolling up some brown kraft paper. When I put a lighted match to it behind our chicken coop, the paper caught fire immediately, and as I puffed, it burned so rapidly I thought my nose would catch fire before I even inhaled. Somebody had told me that you're not really smoking unless you inhale. So I tried to inhale and started coughing immediately. I threw down my homemade cigar and stomped on it until the fire was out. But I still wondered what it was like smoking a "real" cigar. So one day when nobody was looking, I took a real cigar from the box, hid it in my pants pocket, and hid behind the chicken coop. I lit a match, held it up to the cigar and began to puff. Puff, puff, puff. I puffed really hard. Then I tried to inhale. I felt sick immediately and vomited so hard my dinner came up. I could see what I had eaten and it looked ugly and smelled worse. That was the last time I ever tried to smoke a cigar. And I did not even try to smoke a cigarette until several years later.

Except for breakfast cereals along the top shelf, the rest of the groceries in the easy-to-reach lower shelves included coffee, tea, cocoa, lard, jelly powder, yeast cakes, spices, canned extracts of vanilla and lemon, canned fish and canned vegetables. [11]

Like almost all general storekeepers, my father never stocked more than one size of any grocery product because that was the size the wholesaler sold. Since the wholesaler sold jam in four-pound cans, that was the size my father stocked, and that was the size the customer bought. There was no such thing as small, medium, large, or economy size. There was only one size and it was the right size because "one size fits all."

As my father faced his customers, to his left on another counter was the National Cash register, whose door sprang open with a bang whenever he punched a key and pressed down on the handle. The cash register, which could record individual sales and even total them, was never used for that purpose. Instead, it was used mainly to deposit money when the village customers paid their monthly bill, when farmers paid something on their annual bill after shipping cream to the creamery in Foam Lake or selling cattle, or when they paid in full after selling their crops in the fall. Whenever we needed to open the register, we merely punched "0" and pulled down on the handle. At the end of the day, it was very easy to calculate how much money had been taken in, especially during the Depression. We didn't need an adding machine. Grade one arithmetic would do fine.

The cash register lay on top of a long counter that extended all the way to the back of the store. Behind this counter was the hardware section whose shelves were filled with mouse traps, steel-jawed gopher traps, rat poison, Whiz- Bang .22 bullets, shot gun shells, hammers, screw drivers, screws, nuts and bolts and paint brushes and cans of paint and enamel in various sizes, as well as pots and pans and stainless steel flatware and butcher knives and cups and saucers and glasses and plates and bowls and all kinds of kitchenware and modern state-of the-art conveniences— like candles—and even coal oil lamps, glass lamp chimneys and lanterns. Sheho was well into the 20th century. No doubt about it. Someday, it was rumored, we would all have electricity. Someday pigs would fly.

Also behind the counter, not visible to the customer, stood a large metal container of sulfur, another metal container filled with boxes of Eddy's "Strike Anywhere" matches, and a large container of mixed spices that I loved to smell even though I sneezed every time I opened the lid. The top of the counter was cluttered with jars of chicory (used to enhance the flavor of coffee) and sour rock salt that I liked to suck on, and curry combs for grooming horses. In front of this hardware counter, open to the public, stood a large metal container of lime, a wooden crate full of plate glass, and wooden kegs of nails, staples and spikes. Atop the counter, at the very end, lay a small manually operated scale with a metal scoop on top, used for weighing horsehair and nails. Also at the back of the store was a door that opened into the big warehouse. Inside this warehouse was a pump for pumping coal oil housed in a large tank beneath the black oiled wooden floor. Next to the pump was a large upright scale for weighing hides and other produce. Also along the floor lay a drum of thick axle grease, hides, boxes of horsehair, crates of eggs, and other produce. And standing upright was the huge coffee grinder in which I almost lost my finger at the age of five.

Inside the store at the back, on the other side of the warehouse door, were shelves filled with men's black ankle-high work boots and black dress shoes, ladies', children's, and babies' shoes and house slippers. At the very top of these shelves lay various sizes of horse collars and, in the winter, knee length felt socks. Next to this was the dry goods section. [12]

Between the grocery counter and the drygoods section were small counters on which were displayed rubber-soled running shoes, as well as rubbers and rubber boots in the spring and summer—and in the fall and winter—overshoes and felt boots. These items were not easy to steal.

In the middle of the store was a large cast-iron, coal-burning potbellied stove that glowed red in the winter. Contrary to popular lore, nobody ever sat around this stove. And for a good reason. It gave off more heat than a blast furnace and would have seared anyone who stood within four feet of it.

One of my earliest recollections is that of climbing the cement step from the sidewalk onto the oiled black wooden floor of the store and seeing Papa standing behind the grocery counter. He was always standing behind that grocery counter. This time he was waiting on Mr. and Mrs. Slowski, pouring a scoop of white sugar from a bin into a large paper bag which lay on the scale, in the middle of the counter. When the needle on the scale stopped moving, Papa poured the remainder of the sugar back into the bin, closed it, then folded the top of the paper bag and sealed it by winding string around it a few times, first one way then another, knotting the string, and breaking it off with his thumb. Meanwhile, he kept carrying on a conversation in Ukrainian with the Slowskis and another family, all of whom stood patiently waiting for Papa to fill the first order. (They weren't going anywhere for a long time.)

I crept behind Papa to another bin, my favorite. It was full of brown sugar. Brown sugar was thicker than white sugar and it tasted better, even though it was kind of sticky. Papa never scolded me if I opened the bin of brown sugar or dried apples or apricots or prunes or raisins. But he didn't like it when I opened the showcase full of chocolate bars. He never let me eat chocolate bars. But he let me eat brown sugar. And he gave me a nickel every afternoon to buy an ice cream cone from the Chinaman in the Elite Cafe. That's why I liked coming to the store. Besides, it was too quiet in the house except when my baby sister cried and there was nothing to do there except get into trouble.

"*Die mineh rrizha.*" [Give me rice.] said Mr. Slowski. I understood a little Ukrainian, but I never spoke it. I hardly ever spoke Jewish either. Nor did my sisters. We were living in Canada—not the old country. Everybody should speak English here, especially those born in Canada.

"*Die mineh rrizhinkee.*" [Give me raisins.]

"*Die mineh slovok.*" [Give me prunes.]

After Papa had finished filling and tying bag after bag with rice and prunes and raisins and dried apples and beans, he led Mr. and Mrs. Slowski to another row of long counters at the opposite end of the store. The shelves behind these counters were stacked with all kinds of dry goods (bolts of cloth) in every color I knew. Some of these dry goods had dots and circles and all kinds of patterns in all kinds of colors. Papa called them cotton prints. Mrs. Slowski wanted one for a house dress. Papa told her he would give her a "bargain." He said the word *bargain* in English, just in case Mrs. Slowski (who, like Papa, was born in the Ukraine) didn't understand Ukrainian, or in case there was no such word as *bargain* in the Ukrainian language. Papa was always giving everyone a bargain, and every customer understood what the word *bargain* meant. It didn't matter if the customer was Ukrainian or Polish or German or Norwegian or Swedish or even English. *Everyone* knew what the word *bargain* meant. It meant Papa was going to save the customer money. So, instead of charging Mrs. Slowski twenty cents a yard, he would sell her four yards for only seventy-five cents. And even though I was not yet in school, I knew that was a "bargain."

He pulled out the bolt of print and began to unwind it, again and again. Then he held the edge of the print against a bronze colored yardstick attached to the counter, spreading the cloth until it was flush with the yardstick, and measured off one yard at a time, counting in Ukrainian: "*Rahz, dvah, trri, schterra.*" He then held his thumb down at the edge of the cloth he had just measured and moved his thumb over to his right to make sure Mrs. Slowski would have more than enough cloth for her dress. Finally, nicking the cloth with a large pair of sheers and following a pattern, he cut the cloth off from the bolt, folded it neatly, and then put the large bolt of cloth back in the shelves.

Mrs. Slowski pointed to some other yard goods which she needed to make shirts for her sons. Just then another family came into the store, and the man walked up to Papa. "*Die Bozha,*" Louis." [Give God]

"*Die Bozha*, Mr. Turnavertski."

Papa asked me to run to the house and tell Mama there were customers in the store. I liked that. It made me feel important. So I ran next door and told Mama to hurry up and go to the store because it was full of customers. She took off her apron and hurriedly followed me back to the store. She took over from Papa and sold Mrs. Slowski all kinds of different dry goods to make shirts and blouses and even another dress—a fancy one— from red satin. She also sold her a spool of white thread and black thread and red thread and needles and ribbon and yarn and a pair of bloomers and ladies' stockings and all kinds of stuff. Mama then took everything over to the grocery counter, where Papa wrote up the order in a little book.

Mr. Slowski said "*Pachih!*" [Charge it] Papa tore out a sheet from the order book and handed it to Mr. Slowski. [My father, as I mentioned previously, would never—ever—insult a customer by asking him to sign a bill.] Then Papa went to the warehouse and brought back a large cardboard box. He then tore off a large piece of brown kraft paper from its roller, located right next to the cash register, wrapped and tied all the packages carefully, and put them into the box. He carried the box outside and put it into the horse-drawn wagon. As the Slowskis were climbing into the wagon, Papa unlocked the flour warehouse, picked up a large bag of "Foam Lake" flour, and carried it to the wagon. Then Mr. Slowski said, "Giddyup," and as the horses began pulling the wagon, they lifted their tails and began leaving a pile of steamy, fresh droppings behind.

A year or two later Papa showed me how to pull the eggs out of the pails filled with grain when the farmers brought them in for trade. Eggs were worth twenty cents a dozen, and there were usually twelve eggs in a pail. That's a dozen. For a pailfull of eggs, the farmer could get two pounds of sugar or a package of tobacco. So I had an important job to do—searching for eggs in all that wheat. The wheat felt good as I sifted through it in search of an egg. But when the pail was full of oats, it wasn't fun because oats had sharp, pointed edges and they hurt. So I usually left the pail when it was full of oats. But I was glad when the pail was full of wheat because it didn't hurt my fingers. I had to be careful, though, because I could break the eggs if I pressed too hard looking for them. So I pushed the wheat aside until I found an egg. Then I gently pulled it out and put it into the cardboard space where each egg is supposed to go in the flat layer of the egg crate. By the time I had pulled out twelve eggs, I had filled two rows in that layer. That was a dozen eggs. I figured it would take one chicken twelve days to lay all those eggs. Or it would take twelve chickens only one day to lay those eggs. I was learning arithmetic. I'm sure my first grade teacher, Miss Griffiths, would have been proud of me. But each layer in the crate could hold three dozen eggs. And there were five layers in one side of the crate and five in the other because the crate had two sides. Now that's a lot of eggs. It would take me all day to count that many eggs, so I would have to wait until I got into grade two or three to figure out how many chickens it would take to lay all those eggs in one day. I knew for sure it was a lot more chickens than we had fenced off in our yard.

We had about fifteen chickens and one rooster. The chickens were gray with white flecks and the rooster was brown. I thought he was mean. He liked to chase one chicken at a time around the chicken coop, around and around until he caught her. Then he would jump on top of her for a few seconds, rapidly fluttering his wings and shaking before letting her go. An hour or so later, he would run after another chicken and do the same thing. He did that all day long. I mean *all day long*. I didn't like him. But Papa never got rid of him. Other chickens came and went. But not that rooster. I asked Papa why he kept that mean old rooster that was always chasing chickens and jumping on them. But Papa never answered my question. All he said was, "It's not your business. You shouldn't know from such things." That's what he said. In English. Just to make sure I understood that he and the rooster were keeping a secret.

We always had fresh eggs. Not like the eggs the farmers brought in for trade. They might have been stored for a week or more. But not our own eggs, because our chickens laid eggs every day. And every day Papa or our hired girl would go into the chicken coop to collect the eggs. But I never went into the chicken coop because the first time I went inside, the chickens fluttered their wings and flew all over the place and frightened me. So I never went back. Besides, I never ate eggs unless Mama hard boiled them for at least half-an-hour.

But Harry Soifer, a produce buyer from Melville, ninety miles away, loved eggs. I hated to watch Harry Soifer squash his fried eggs all over his plate and dip his bread into that yellow goo and open his mouth to chew all that ugly, messy goo, while showing a mouth full of gold fillings as he carried on a conversation with Mama and Papa. Whenever he came to town, Mama insisted that he stay for dinner or supper.

About once a month he came to the store to buy the produce my father had taken in for trade. Besides the crates of eggs, some of which I had helped pack, Dad's produce also included seneca root, furs, hides, and horse hair.

Seneca root was a type of wild plant whose root was dug up by the farmers, then brought in for trade. It had to be dried before my father would buy it; otherwise, it would weigh less when he sold it to produce dealers and he would lose money. Eventually it was resold and processed for medicine. It might take a farmer a day to dig up a pound, for which he would receive about fifty cents in trade. Each root looked like a small, narrow, dirty brown crooked finger, still attached to its clump of earth. I remember Dad putting it into a large burlap bag, then pounding it down with a wooden pole about five inches in diameter, again and again, then repeating the process, as clouds of dust poured out from the bag choking us each time he pounded that seneca root tighter and tighter, until the bag was full. The dust was so bad that he had to stop after about five minutes. It took several days before he managed to fill a single bag. For all this work, he made about three dollars per bag.

In the winter, farmers brought in the tiny hides of weasels they had snared or caught in a steel trap. The hides, scraped clean and turned inside-out, looked like a piece of brown kraft paper about the size of a narrow necktie folded in thirds. The only fur visible was the tail. When unfolded however, these beautiful black and white furs were eventually sown together to make expensive ladies' coats called Ermine. Occasionally, a few muskrat furs were also brought in. But my father did not buy them. They were much bigger and harder to hide than the tiny weasels; and since a license was required to deal in furs, he felt it was too dangerous to bother with them and too costly for the license, considering that there weren't that many muskrats anyway. With the tiny, easily hidden weasels, however, it was different matter. They were more plentiful and he did not want his customers to take their weasels elsewhere for trade. So even though he did not have a fur-buyer's license, he took weasels in trade from his customers for about seventy-five cents each, and sold them as soon as he could for about eighty-five cents cash, to Harry Soifer or any other produce dealer who called on him.

No license, however was required to deal in horsehides or cowhides. These hides were the biggest and messiest of all the produce he bought. They were so big and messy that no other storekeeper in town except George Lys bothered to buy them. As soon as a farmer felt his horse or cow had outlived its usefulness, he dispatched his animal from this world to the next, then salvaged what he could, including its hide. After skinning the animal and cutting off the head and legs, he would usually fold the hide in quarters, with the fur outside and blood still dripping, tie it up, and bring it into our store, where my father would weigh it on the big scale in the warehouse. Sometimes a farmer would put the hooves and rocks inside the hide before folding it, so that it would weigh more and he could collect more money. However, my father was not exactly new at the game, nor was he stupid. He knew how much a horse or cow usually weighed—dead or alive—with or without hooves and rocks. Yet there was always some farmer who thought he could put one over on Louis Katz. Once, when the hide weighed too much and my father told the farmer he was not about to pay for rocks, the farmer challenged my father to a fight. But my father replied, "Go take your hide to somebody else. Or take the rocks out." A few days later the farmer brought back the same hide, much lighter than before.

"I see you took the rocks out," said my father.

"No, I never had rocks. This is a different horse. It just died. Don't look at me like that. I swear I'm telling the truth."

After untying the heavy hide, spreading it out and turning it over on the warehouse floor, my father would pour coarse salt all over the bloody skin to prevent it from rotting, then leave it open to dry for a few days before refolding it and tying it up again, ready to be picked up by a produce dealer. During the Depression, he bought hides for about one or two cents a pound, then resold them —just above cost—for about fifty cents per hide. In the 1940s, when tractors and trucks began to replace horses, the price of horsehides went up to about three dollars each. But that was long after the Depression. I don't know exactly how much money he made on a hide, but how much money can you make on a fifty cent transaction? However, money was so scarce then that working for a dime or even a nickel was necessary. Besides, I think my father liked farm animals—alive or dead.

He also bought horse hair, the long, silky thick hairs from the tail, used for making brushes, and the cheaper shorter hairs from the neck, the mane, used to stuff sofas. In the late 1940s, nylon replaced horse hair, putting an end to the entire horse hair industry.

Another responsibility I had as a child was to be on the lookout for shoplifters. Papa would say *"Zie royah."* He told me that was Hebrew for "Watch that the customers don't steal." He was afraid that if he spoke Jewish, his customers would understand him and they would suddenly stop stealing. But if he spoke in Hebrew, they wouldn't understand what he was saying and they could go about their business stealing to their heart's content, thus giving me a chance to catch them in the act. So, as a child of five or six, I crept around the store, like clumsy Inspector Kluso looking for clues to an unsolved murder. I felt important. But I never caught anyone even attempting to steal, though Papa told me that one customer in particular was stealing us blind.

He was big, tall man, whom I shall call Mr. Shefchuk. In the winter he walked around the store in his huge full-length buffalo coat. I mean it was really huge. Much bigger than the three-quarter length buffalo coats the Mounties wore. He could have hidden a piano underneath it. His breath stunk from garlic, especially when he used to hold me up and say,

"*Te zhid*." ["Thou Jew" is a Ukrainian pejorative for "Jew."] I didn't like that expression. It was like calling me a "dirty Jew."

Although Papa had caught him stealing more than once, he joked about it to Mr. Shefchuk because he didn't want Mr. Shefchuk to get mad. Mr. Shefchuk was such a big man he could have killed my father with one blow. Besides, Mr. Shefchuk was a good customer. He was always buying hundred-pound sacks of sugar. Everyone knew he used the sugar to make to make home brew (vodka). But the Mounties never bothered him. They were probably afraid of him. Besides, he could have hidden a dozen barrels of home brew under his buffalo coat, so they never would have found it.

Early one evening in June when I was about seven, I was with Papa as he was filling grocery shelves just before closing the store. It was a hot sunny day, and sunlight had been pouring through the glass window-pane at the top of the grocery warehouse. That's where Papa kept grocery supplies like rolls of kraft paper and paper bags. His grocery warehouse was a narrow separate room right next to the grocery section. I was helping him fill the rack which held different sizes of paper bags, so I accompanied him to the warehouse door. Just as he opened it, a blast of smoke poured through the door and flames leaped at us. He immediately slammed the door shut and began shouting "FIRE, FIRE!" as we both ran outside. We stood in the middle of the road and he kept waving his arms and shouting as loud as he could, "FIRE, FIRE! HELP! HELP! MY STORE'S ON FIRE! PLEASE HELP! MY STORE'S ON FIRE! EVERYBODY COME AND HELP! FIRE! FIRE, FIRE, FIRE, FIRE, FIRE!"

At first only John Koropatniski, Bill Finley, and the two other elevator agents across the road ran out to see what was happening. But soon just about everyone in town came running up to the store to watch the excitement. Soon the town's fire bell began to ring. It sounded like the fire bell in the school basement, only not quite as loud because this bell was on top of the fire hall next to Grumetza's store, about three blocks away. Unlike the school bell, this bell kept ringing again and again, and it just kept on ringing. And the more it rang, the more people came. Before I had time to think about what would happen if the whole store caught fire, I saw Maurice Peters and Tommy Merritt and Cecil Scott and Bulba Koropatniski and Norman Leckie and about four other men slowly pulling the town's fire engine toward the store. It took them forever to reach us. They pulled the engine right up to the sidewalk, then put a ladder up to reach the window pane through which we could see the flames. Then they climbed the ladder and pulled a hose right up to the window pane and smashed it. Clouds of black smoke poured out as they began pumping water right into the warehouse. As soon as the water hit the flames, I could hear a loud "HISS." Soon the smoke turned gray as they continued to pull the pump handle up and down and up and down, until finally the smoke turned white, and soon there was no smoke at all. Only steam. And finally the hissing noise stopped and the steam stopped coming out of that window.

All the volunteer firemen and Papa and I went into the store and opened the door to the warehouse. The fire had been completely put out. But there was nothing left inside except ashes and black cans of groceries and a few broken panes of glass. Everything else was black. I mean black. The floor was black and wet. All the walls were black and wet and they smelled from smoke. It penetrated my nostrils and all I could smell was smoke. Not like tobacco smoke or bonfire smoke. This was a pungent sickly sweet odor that filled the warehouse and clung to my clothes and hair. The entire warehouse smelled from smoke and ashes. It was a real mess. But as Papa said, " Thank God for all those firemen. They saved my store."

The next day he cleaned out that warehouse and nailed boards over the space where the window pane had been. Someone had said the fire had started because of "spontaneous combustion." That meant the glass pane had acted as a magnifying glass, super heating the paper bags inside the warehouse until they got so hot they ignited. The glass pane had acted like Johnny Drobot's magic glass lens, when he focused the sun's rays onto a piece of paper until it caught fire. I wish Johnny Drobot had shown Papa what he could do with his magic lens a year earlier. I'm sure Papa would have learned enough about spontaneous combustion then to prevent the fire. All I can say is "thank you" to those wonderful volunteers who put out that fire. Without them, Papa's store would have burned to the ground.

For a few years afterward, our class clown, Boris Moroz, who was two years older than I and who would do anything for a laugh, used to mock Papa by shouting "Help, Help! Fire, Fire, Help! All the people in the people in the village, come and help. My store's on fire." I suppose he thought he was funny, but I didn't think so. I never said anything because if I did, that would give him an excuse for beating up on me. I had learned that whenever the older kids teased me, if I kept my mouth shut they would eventually stop and go away instead of beating me up. Sometimes kids can be awfully cruel.

I never made a fuss over being teased and taunted by some of the older kids, nor did I ever tell my parents or teachers. To this day, I cannot understand what pleasure they got from trying to humiliate me because I was small and Jewish. One winter night while I was sitting on the bench in the skating rink, taking off my skates, Boris's older brother Miros kept insulting me. I ignored him. Suddenly he picked up the ax near the wood pile, put it over his shoulder as if to strike, and jokingly said, "I'm going to kill you." I just looked at him but kept quiet. All of a sudden he swung the ax and drove it deep into the wooden wall. The ax had missed my head by only a foot. He laughed nervously but his face turned pale. I finished taking off my skates and walked away without saying a word. That was the last time he bothered me.

Although our warehouse fire was the most frightening event to occur in our store, there were other occurrences that caused some excitement. Early one morning in summer when I was about nine, Papa came running back to our house from the store, more excited than I had ever seen him except for the evening when we had discovered the warehouse fire. "Somebody broke into the store last night and robbed us," he shouted. "Go get Bill Filney! Tell him to phone the police."

I hurried across the road to McCabe Brothers grain elevator where Bill Finley was doing some paper work. "Papa just found out our store was robbed last night," I blurted out. " He wants you to phone the Mounties." I knew when Papa said "police" he certainly didn't mean Ed Howe, our village constable, who hung up the four gas burning Coleman lanterns every night on telephone poles one block apart on our main street, to provide the only outside light for our entire village. His other constable duties included using his horse and a crude snow plough to clear the waist high snow from the four-block long sidewalk after a blizzard. He also shot stray dogs. No! That was not who Papa meant when he said "police." Everybody knew the " police" meant the Royal Canadian Mounted Police, the R.C.M.P. in Foam Lake—all two of them. These were our Mounties who maintained law and order in their entire territory, all the way from their headquarters in Foam Lake eighteen miles away from us on the west, to Insinger, twelve miles to the east of us, plus an equal distance west of Foam Lake and north and south as well. The Mounties were the very best police force in the whole world. Everybody knew that. They always caught their man.

I had hoped that when they arrived they would be wearing their official dress uniform—wide brimmed hats and scarlet red coats and black breeches with yellow stripes running down the sides to their high top boots that had spurs jangling on the back. What an impressive uniform! No wonder it was reserved for National Holidays or official parades or special events. Unfortunately, the day Katz General Store was broken into was not a national holiday, and worse, nobody in town had scheduled a parade. The Mounties were merely on everyday duty, even though investigating a break-in was not an everyday occurrence. So when they pulled up to the store in their black Ford V-8, they were dressed in their everyday brown uniforms and regulation caps. Right then and there I wondered if they would catch their man.

After shaking hands with Papa and asking him a few questions like "When did you discover the break in?" and "How did you discover it?" and "What was stolen?" they assured us they would make a thorough investigation. The first thing they did was to go outside to determine how the burglar had gained entrance. That wasn't hard. Even I could see how it was done. But when they explained it to Papa and Bill Finley and me, it sounded like an official discovery. "I can see how they broke in. Look!" The corporal pointed to the row of two-foot wide iron bars attached to the outside narrow window, which was attached at an angle to the door on its left. "See! These bars are on the outside window and they lead all the way up to the top window which has no bars. All he had to do was to climb them up to the top, then break the window and jump down. It was real easy. That top window should have had iron bars, too, Mr. Katz. Or all the bars should have been on the inside. It was real easy for him to break in."

Papa nodded. "I'll put bars on top."

I wondered why whoever installed those bars was stupid enough not to have put bars on the top window. And I also wondered why the burglar hadn't just broken the large glass plate of the display window and climbed in. It would have been simple— much easier than climbing up all those iron bars, then breaking the glass on the small window and squiggling to get through, then jumping down to the floor, then climbing up again and squiggling out and finally climbing down. I thought he was even dumber than the man who put up the bars. Maybe he liked climbing? Maybe he was training to become a telegraph line repair man for the Canadian Pacific Railroad? Maybe he was training for the circus? Or the Olympics? Maybe he was training to climb Mt. Everest? Why else would he have done such a stupid thing? Some people just don't think. But I never said anything. Not a single word. I was just a little kid. Who cared what I thought?

We all went inside and the Mounties poked around the store as if they were hunting for the burglar. But he wasn't there. Then they stood at the grocery counter, and as they questioned Papa for the second time, they began to write their official report in their official book. "So what did he take, Mr. Katz?"

"He took all the money in my register from yesterday."

"How much was that?"

"Forty dollars. That's all I took in yesterday. I should have put the money somewhere else."

The Mounties nodded. "What else did he take?"

"Three pairs of overalls."

"And what else?"

"Some work shirts and socks."

"Anything else?"

"A whole box of chocolate bars and a two pounds of tobacco and a whole box of cigarette papers."

The Mounties suddenly looked at each other and nodded their heads. "Sounds like it was Krafchuk," the corporal blurted out. "He has a farm near Tuffnell. That's the kind of stuff he takes. We'll get him." He closed his notebook. The Mounties shook hands with Papa and left.

Thus ended the official R.C.M. P. investigation of one of the worst crimes ever committed in Sheho while I was there—the break in and burglary of Katz General Store.

I don't know if the Mounties ever charged Mr. Krafchuk or anyone else with that notorious, horrible, unspeakable crime, let alone convict him. If they did, I never heard about it. Nor did anyone else. But the crime left an indelible impression in my father's memory. He would make sure that nobody ever broke into his store again.

Late at night, he would unlock the small drawer in the dining room buffet closet, where he kept his loaded .32 caliber revolver that had been licensed by and registered with the Royal Canadian Mounted Police. Carefully taking it out of the drawer, he would cradle it in his hand as he went back to the store, unlock the door, enter, and lock it again before climbing up on the long, hard dry goods counter, on top of which he had spread out some overalls before lying down. There he would spend the night. These were hard times and many people were desperate.

Jobs were so scarce that young men rode the rails from one end of the country to the other and back, looking for work. Any kind of work. But there was no work. On top of practically every box car on every freight train throughout Canada and the United States were young men in dirty clothes, unshaven, unkempt, carrying their entire possessions wrapped inside a cotton bandanna. Some people called them bums or tramps. Others called them hoboes, out for adventure. But they all had at least one thing in common. They were poor. They were broke. They were destitute. And they were hungry. When the freight train stopped at any town, several of them would climb down from the roof of the box car and go from house to house looking for work and for food. But there was no work.

With food, however, it was a different matter. There was usually something to eat. Whenever they came to our home, they did not go away hungry. Usually they were loners and came to the house, one at a time. If one or two of them came by and my mother was in the house, she made sandwiches for them. Peanut butter or jam sandwiches. If she was extremely busy or if there were more than two, she would slice a loaf of homemade bread and give each one of them each a few slices. Our hired girls did the same. Never—ever—was even one of these men turned away from our home empty handed. That would have been unthinkable.

One summer afternoon, a long freight train came to a stop, and instead of just a few getting off, there were probably twenty or more. They were coming across the railway tracks toward the store. My parents and I were alone in the store at that time. "Hurry! Let's lock up before they get here," shouted my father. "We could have a holdup." So he locked the store and we all went into the back, out of sight of this crowd. He waited until they had left with the freight train before opening the store. I felt sorry for those men, but perhaps my father had good reason to fear a holdup or worse—a killing.

During the spring and summer of 1932, a rash of store break-ins occurred along Highway 14. In an attempt to prevent them, the Mounties would stop suspicious cars late at night to investigate. At 1:40 a.m. on Tuesday, July 5, Constable M.V. Novakowski from Yorkton attempted to pull over a stolen blue Plymouth inside of which were three occupants. But the car sped away. He pursued them for sixty miles to Sheho, where he stopped and telephoned ahead to Corporal Leonard Ralls, eighteen miles away in Foam Lake. Ralls used his police car to set up a road block on Highway 14 near the creamery at Milligan Creek Bridge, which had been completed just the year before. When the Plymouth stopped there in the darkness, one of the fugitives slid out of the car and hid behind the creamery building. As Ralls walked toward the Plymouth to apprehend its occupants, two of the fugitives—Bill Miller and Bill Kurulak—circled him and opened fire from different directions. Retreating, he fired back. But he had already been shot twice; once above the heart and once in the ribs. As he lay on the ground, the three then tore the ignition wires out of the police car, pushed it into the ditch, and drove away. Although Sandy Baird heard Corporal Ralls' cries for help and rushed him to Dr. Somers, Ralls died at 4:30 a.m., leaving behind his wife of eighteen years and four children, ages seven to twelve.

Within two hours, radio station CKCK Regina broadcast the tragedy and word spread throughout the province. A few hours later, Inspector W. J. Moorehead arrived from Yorkton to organize the manhunt. By 1:00 P.M. fifty Mounties from throughout Saskatchewan converged at Foam Lake, joined by three airplanes and seventy local farmers and towns-people. The airplanes spotted the abandoned Plymouth in the bush near Lintlaw, north of Foam Lake. On Thursday morning the killers stole three horses near Kelvington. Hours later, the posse discovered the horses tied to a tree on a farm near Kinloch, and when seventeen year old Mike Kurulak approached, he was captured without a struggle. The other two killers, however, when ordered to surrender as they came out of the farm-house, shot their way into the bush and ran away in different directions. Bill Kurulak, Mike's twenty-four year old brother, escaped to the Adams farm near Green Water Lake and asked for a place to sleep. Mr. Adams complied, then went to a neighbor's house and phoned the police. As Bill Kurulak lay sleeping with a loaded revolver nearby, he was cap-tured on Friday, July 8, at 4:00 a.m. without a struggle. However, Bill Miller, thirty-seven, was more elusive. Although spotted by the airplane several times on Friday morning, he escaped the posse each time in an exchange of gunfire. Late Friday afternoon, northeast of Kelvington, after a heavy exchange of gunfire, he was seriously wounded with a shattered leg and hole in the abdomen. When the Mounties found him, with his revolver still in his hand, he was dead from his own gunshot to the head. William Kurulak was tried, convicted of murder, and hanged on December 29. His brother was convicted of manslaughter and sen-tenced to fifteen years in prison. [13]

My father never got over the loss of his very dear friend Leonard Ralls. It scarred him forever. Although the murderer was executed, it offered my father little solace. And even though he had enormous re-spect for the Mounties, he kept his distance. He never became friends with any one of them afterward, because he was leery of what might happen again. And he was always afraid of a robbery or a holdup. So he continued to sleep on top of the overalls on the hard counter in the store every night, with his loaded revolver right next to him.

One night after he had fallen into a deep sleep, he was suddenly awakened by a noise. The window was rattling. It sounded as if somebody was trying to break in. He was terrified. "STOP!" he shouted, "Or I'll shoot." Then without waiting for an answer, he reached for his revolver, cocked it, and aimed toward the ceiling. He pulled the trigger. "BANG!" The explosion not only hurled the bullet deep into the ceiling, where it probably remains to this very day, but almost shattered the window panes and shook the tiny bottles of vanilla extract so violently they fell to the floor and smashed. That was enough excitement for one night. My father returned to the house, a shaken man. And that was the last time he slept in the store overnight.

However, it was not the last time he slept on that counter.

Some years later, he would wake up about six o'clock and retreat to the store for two hours of badly needed sleep as soon as he heard my oldest sister, Merle, begin practicing her piano lessons. She had been taking piano lessons for about ten years, and now in grade twelve, at the age of 15 1/2, was preparing for her degree—Associate Toronto Conservatory of Music (A.T.C.M.)— from the Toronto Royal Conservatory of Music. It had been a long grind, and the hardest part was still ahead.

In order to get at least four hours of practicing in every day while still taking one class in high school, she had to get up at six, so that she could practice two hours before going to school. After school, she practiced at least another two hours before supper, after which she would do her school homework. My sister Etta, two years younger than Merle, was also preparing for her A.T.C.M. and she too practiced the piano every day, although not quite as long. In addition, my young sister, Sylvia, took piano lessons from Merle, and she, too, practiced. That poor piano was going all the time.

Even though my father would rather have slept in his comfortable bed for the two remaining hours before getting up, he took the hardship of sleeping on the hard counter philosophically. The money he had invested in that piano and the music lessons for his two oldest daughters was finally paying off.

Although we did not have a piano in 1929 when Merle was six, my mother, especially, felt that music was so important, she sent her oldest daughter to Mrs. Harold Black, the school principal's wife, who had an A.T.C.M. and gave piano lessons. The cost was fifty cents for a half-hour lesson, an astronomical price at that time. At first, Merle practiced next door on Mrs. Darling's organ. When that didn't work out, she began practicing on a real piano, at the home of her class mate, Pola Zoski, whose father ran a blacksmith shop on a side street, in the next block from us. But that, too, didn't work out; so my parents decided to buy Merle a piano.

Since they knew nothing about pianos, which were sold only in the big cities, they asked Mrs. Darling for help. She showed them an adver-tisement in the Regina Leader Post for a Heintzman upright piano that cost $150, payable in thirty monthly installments of five dollars each. That seemed affordable, so my father ordered the piano—sight unseen—in Merle's name. When it arrived, they were shocked to see it was not a regular upright piano, but a player piano that had been rebuilt and con-verted into an upright. Nevertheless, as disappointed as they were, they decided to keep the piano. Every month without fail, they sent a five dollar postal money order to the Heintzman Piano Company. One day the sales representative found out that the person in whose name the piano had been ordered was only six at the time, and at the age of seven was obviously still a minor. He wanted to repossess it. My parents— and Mrs. Darling in particular— were adamant. "How can you do that when she's making the payments you agreed upon?" And that ended the argu-ment. Finally, after thirty months, that mahogany upright Heintzman piano legally belonged to my sister. It was the most expensive piece of furniture in our home. But as far as my parents were concerned, it was well worth their struggle to pay for it.

In the depths of the Depression, my father was paying Mrs. Black one dollar every week for his two daughters' piano lessons. That was an enormous amount of money. (Years later, it was all I could do to get a twenty-five cent hockey stick.) Although he didn't begrudge the money for the lessons, he was irritated that neither she nor her husband ever spent a nickel in our store. My father thought that was extremely unfair.

" It wouldn't hurt them to walk an extra block from the Red and White Store to buy even a pound of sugar from me. Fair is fair." But not everybody is fair.

Nevertheless, Merle and Etta continued taking piano lessons from Mrs. Black, eventually paying seventy-five cents each for the hour-long advanced lesson. They practiced the piano for a total of at least six hours a day until the Blacks moved to Theodore in 1938, one year before the outbreak of war. To accommodate my older sisters and another student, a piano teacher from Foam Lake, Miss Pomroy, would visit us every week.

And so, with Merle now practicing for her A.T.C. M., Dad continued to get up at 6:00 a.m. and go to the store for some badly needed sleep as soon as he heard Merle warm up with finger exercises, which included scales and triads and octaves and arpeggios and chords. Then she would practice the great etudes and sonatas of Chopin, Beethoven, Brahams, Schubert, and Schumann. But by then, my father was fast asleep on the hard counter.

My sisters were not the only ones in our family to take piano lessons. Every once in a while if there was not a pick-up hockey game on the road, using flash-frozen horse droppings for pucks, I would please my older sisters and Mom by putting in some hard time at that piano. I had to take piano lessons. With a Jewish mother from Poland who thought the sun rose and set on the great Polish pianist Paderewski, and with two sisters already giving piano lessons to Mrs. Black's former students, I had no choice. So I began with the scale of C major—the white keys— played with only one hand—my right one. I was pretty good. I hit every key in order—all eight of them— mainly because they were all in order, all eight of them. I eventually graduated from kindergarten and may even have completed grade one or the first book. Take your pick. I was still using only my right hand, and only the white keys. That's why the notes were all in the treble clef—for the right hand.

Then one day I passed into grade two and was introduced to the bass clef—for the left hand. That was hard enough. But when I had to learn sharps and flats—the black keys—and had to play with both hands at the same time, that was away beyond my capability. To make matters worse,

I was twelve and my fingers had started to grow. I mean really grow, from one week to the next. If I reached for an octave, I usually hit nine notes instead of eight. And when I tried it again, I would hit only seven, or sometimes only six. But that didn't bother Merle. She was determined to teach me. And she did. She taught me how to play the first two chords of "God Save the King" and "The Jolly Roger."

One evening she held a recital in our home for all eight piano students in town. They included retarded learners like me and more proficient students like Walter Lys and Murray Wunder, and more advanced students like Jenny Lys, my sister Etta, and Etta's own student Mickey Haluke. We all had to perform a piece we had mastered. That was the program. And after each solo, we all clapped because each performance was flawless. Everyone hit the right keys. My sister beamed with pride. Then it was my turn.

I had chosen "The Jolly Roger" because I had mastered it long before the recital and I believed I could make my sister proud. So I began to play. But that week my fingers had suddenly sprouted wings. They wanted their independence. Only they had not consulted me. So somewhere near the end of that piece, they rebelled and I hit the wrong note. One note. With the last finger in my right hand. That's all I had missed. I should have left well enough alone. One note more or less shouldn't make too much difference to the Jolly Roger. But I was a perfectionist. And I was determined to find that note. The lost note. Not the lost chord. I had already found part of the lost chord. All I needed now to complete that chord was one note. One lousy note. With the fifth finger. So I began my search for the lost note. Since there are only eighty-eight white keys on the piano, half of them for the right hand, it shouldn't be too hard for me to find that note. That's what I thought. So I hit every one of them. But I couldn't find the note. It was still lost. It must be hiding somewhere among the black keys. So I began another search.

In the meantime, all the guests had been trying desperately to smother their laughter. But when I began my search for that lost note among the black keys, they could no longer restrain themselves. And so, amidst bursts of laughter, I continued my search, hitting every black key until at last, I found that note. Everyone applauded. But I did not take a bow. And that was the last time I ever played the piano in public.

After the recital Merle served the tiny checkerboard sandwiches she and Etta had made for the evening's event. They had attended a cooking school in Sheho and had learned how to use both brown and white bread to make tiny sandwiches which when arranged on a plate looked like a checkerboard. Alongside the plate were tiny pickles. Murray Wunder and I admired the artwork so much we decided to use another plate to make a checkerboard with our sandwiches and play checkers, using the pickles as checkers. That was the last recital Merle ever hosted.

CHAPTER TWENTY
Sheho Goes To War

On September 10, 1939, one week after Great Britain and France declared war on Germany, the Dominion of Canada joined her mother country by also declaring war. Shortly afterward, during the Jewish High Holy Days, I remember standing in the hall of the Yorkton Synagogue listening to a Jewish discussion about the war.

A Jewish discussion can be carried on in any language, so long as there are at least two Jewish participants called *mavens*, but the more the better, since each *maven* has at least three different opinions on any subject. [*Mavens* are self-proclaimed experts.] Also, in a Jewish discussion, nothing is ever resolved.

"England and France will beat Germany within a year."

"I don't know about that. Germany has more troops and planes."

"But we're also in the war now."

"So with ten million population, how may troops can we send?

"Enough. Besides, we've got the entire British Empire."

Someone else said, "Now you're talking. That means India, too."

"But they've got the Siegfried Line."

"So what? We've got the Maginot Line."

"He's right. Don't forget, we've also got the strongest navy."

"Now you're talking. England rules the seas."

And on and on it went, as more men took a recess from *dahvening* [praying] and joined the lively discussion. Barely audible, Mr. Leckie said, "It's going to be a long war. Young boys just entering high school will be fighting and dying before it's over."

But not many men paid attention to his prophecy. They were all busy with their own opinions. Besides, most of the *mavens* believed the might of England and France and now Canada would certainly overwhelm Germany. The United States wasn't even mentioned because the United States was not a player. She was invisible. We would take care of Germany by ourselves. It was just a matter of time. But the war was really a long way off. It was away "over there" —somewhere in Poland and France. It was a long way off.

I don't remember whether it was just before the High Holidays or immediately afterward, but it seemed to me that we were either going to Yorkton or just coming back when I saw John Brozowski strutting up and down the railway platform, as proud as he could be, in his new shiny black boots and khaki wool flannel uniform of the Royal Canadian Army. He lived in a very small house on the eastern outskirts of town with his wife and daughter, Mildred, and had been a laborer doing farm work and odd jobs for a living. Although he would have had no trouble getting work during the harvest season, he answered his country's call to arms immediately. The son of Ukrainian immigrants was Sheho's first volunteer, our first living example of Canadian patriotism. We were all proud of him.

At the age of eleven, I thought every able-bodied man should follow John Brozowski's lead and rush out immediately to join one of the three branches of the armed forces. I was disappointed because it took over three months until I saw another khaki uniform. From then on, however, the list of volunteers grew longer and longer until toward the end of the war, by February of 1944, there were no more able bodied young men left in Sheho except me; and at the age of sixteen, I was too young to enlist.

In January of 1940, Jack Holmes, whose English father had been gassed in the Great War only twenty-two years before, left his job as locomotive fireman on the Canadian Pacific Railway to enlist. About the same time Steve Giverego, my former teacher—the first Ukrainian teacher ever hired by the Sheho District— also enlisted. So did Ross

Grumetza, whose father had also fought in the Great War. Mr. Grumetza owned the small general store which also housed the provincial telephone. Then Tommy Merritt, son of our British postmaster who had also fought in the Great War, joined up. So did Charlie Howe, the son of our drayman, and Joe Hoffman, whose German parents, good customers of ours, owned a large farm a mile south of town. Then a number of other fellows joined up. The list was growing. Suddenly, in the spring of 1940, with Germany's capture of Holland and Belgium, followed by the collapse of France in June and the last-minute evacuation of British troops from Dunkirk, the war didn't seem so far away.

For the graduating students in my sister Merle's twelfth grade class, the war was now closer than ever. Normally, their senior year would probably have been the highlight of their lives. They were all completing their final year of high school and, with no plans to go on to college, they normally would count the weeks or even days until they were through with their final exams. Then they could eagerly look forward to the prospect of going out into the world and beginning a new career. But Merle, like the rest of her classmates, did not count the weeks or days until they were through with school. Instead, she felt sad. For she realized most of the boys in her class would be joining the service. She knew that as soon as school ended, many of them would be going overseas, some never to return. She especially thought about Hector Munro, her first boyfriend.

Hector, a tall red head, was the older son of Reverend Munro, the pastor of the local United Church of Canada, as well as our Scout Master. Hector had been the Assistant Scout Master and was one of fifteen students in Merle's twelfth grade class. He sat a few desks behind her and they passed notes to each other. He used to come over to our home, where they studied trigonometry together. In winter, he walked her home from the skating rink. In spring, they went cycling together. And during an amateur night contest, she played "The Barcarole," from Offenbach's opera *Tales of Hoffmann*, while he accompanied her on the violin. But when Hector asked her to go to a movie with him in Foam Lake, eighteen miles away, my father was incensed. His daughter was not going to get involved with a *shaygetz* [gentile boy]. He forbade her to go. Hector took one of Etta's classmates, Elane Finley, to the movie instead. Hector and Merle broke up. And that was that. Thus ended any possible romance between a gentile boy and my sister.

But Merle knew that Hector would be joining the Royal Canadian Air Force as a pilot just as soon as school ended. She also knew how dangerous that was. And she remembered Mr. Leckie's prophecy. So when Hector, at the age of eighteen, became the first from Sheho to join the air crew of the R.C.A.F. she was saddened by the prospect that he, along with some of her other classmates, might never return.

By now many of our boys who had been shipped overseas and were stationed "somewhere" in England were writing letters home. The letters were written on small light-weight onion skin paper that probably weighed less than a feather. The lighter the paper, the more airmail letters could be sent home. The letters were opened and censored in England before being resealed. The censor's job was to make sure the letter did not contain military secrets. If he thought a word or passage might possibly be of use to an enemy spy, he blackened or cut out that part of the letter. After the wives, sweethearts, or parents had received and read their letters—and if the letters were not too personal—they usually handed them to our postmaster who tacked them on the wall for all to read. I remember reading some of the letters which mentioned whom the writer had seen while on leave in London and what sights he had taken in. In late summer and fall, the letters also described the dogfights—Hurricanes and Spitfires shooting down Messerschmitts and the other way around.

Besides the posted letters, a large conspicuous poster warned, "A slip of the lip might sink a ship."

The list of volunteers continued to grow, and their letters continued to be posted and read. There were no casualties or fatalities. Not yet.

In May of 1940, shortly before Merle's class graduated, Dr. Rubin, the only doctor in our area, from Foam Lake to Insinger, left his practice to join the Army's medical corps. Dr. Somers, much older than Dr. Rubin, returned to resume the practice he had left years before because of ill health. We were now beginning to witness manpower shortages on the home front.

In November of 1940, four months after Hector Munro (our Assistant Scout Master) enlisted in the R.C.A. F. as a fighter pilot, Mr.Leckie's twenty-four year old son Norman (who had been my Cub Master a year earlier) also joined the R.C.A.F. as a Wireless Air Gunner. His job entailed sending and receiving Morse coded messages and firing machine guns at attacking German fighter planes. He was the second serviceman from Sheho who was actually in the air crew. We all knew that being in the air crew was more dangerous than being on the ground, but we were optimistic. Other airmen would be killed in action, but somehow *our* boys would survive. And I'm sure Mr. Leckie felt the same way. I'll never forget the day Sam Glass, a wholesale jobber from Yorkton, visited us and told us confidentially how dangerous Norman's job was. "He's an air gunner. You know what that is. He sits in the back of the plane and tries to protect it from German fighters with his machine gun. But that's the first place the fighters aim at. He's their most important target. Their job is to kill him first. And their fighters are much faster than bombers. It's the most dangerous job of all." We promised not to tell Mr. Leckie.

Several months later, toward the end of 1941, Norman was home on embarkation leave, proudly wearing the Flight Sergeant's three stripes and single wing with the lightning insignia of the Wireless Air Gunner. In November of 1941 he arrived overseas for operational training in Northern Ireland and Northern Scotland. That was all we knew about him at the time. The war was getting closer.

That same year, in June of 1941, just two months after reaching the age of eighteen, my cousin Maurice Shnider in Inglis, Manitoba, joined the air crew of the Royal Canadian Air Force. When I was visiting there during my summer holidays, he explained that an Air Observer had the dual role on a bomber of not only being its navigator but also the bombardier. He was responsible for guiding the bomber to the target, then aiming and dropping the bombs. In the fall of that year he began his training as an Air Observer. After graduating as a commissioned officer and buying his own uniform on which the single Pilot Officer's stripe circled the sleeve, and the single "O" wing of an Air Observer was sewn on the chest, he came home in December of 1942. He was on embarkation leave and had come to visit us and to say good bye. He was the third young man very close to me who was now in the air crew of the Royal Canadian Air Force and who would soon be seeing action in the skies over Europe.

The war had started three years before, when I was in the seventh grade. My teacher loved joking about anything and he referred to a newspaper quote which stated that Hitler said he was putting on his uniform and would not take it off until he had won the war. Mr. Kindrachuk paused, then said, "Isn't he going to take a bath?" Mr. Kindrachuk often brought his portable radio to school and sometimes tuned on the news to keep us informed about the progress of the war. The following year, in 1940, I sat up front in a row of desks right next to the window. At 10:15 when the morning recess began, I used to look out the window and watch the train pull into the station. The train had barely come to a stop when I could see about ten airmen jump off the observation platform and run up and down the platform, then across the railway tracks, playing games with each other, showing off and acting like a bunch of kids. They looked as if they should still be in high school. I realized they were still a bunch of kids, even though they were now in uniform. But now they were on their way to training camps. Within a year they would be sent overseas. I wished I could have been one of them. But then I realized some would never return.

The following year, in 1941, at the age of thirteen, I entered high school. Entering high school actually meant that instead of walking into Mr. Kindrachuk's room as I had done for the previous two years, I now entered the adjoining class room—our principal's room. This was our high school, where all subjects in grades nine, ten, eleven, and twelve were taught by Mr. Tomaschuk, who held a Bachelor of Science degree from the University of Saskatchewan. He was the only teacher in our school who held a degree, and I was proud to be in his classroom. I felt that I was no longer a kid; I was now a high school student--in the same room as my sixteen year old sister Etta, who was in grade eleven. For the first time that I could remember, we shared the same room with the same teacher. That meant I was growing up, even if I was only thirteen.

I felt grown up for another reason: school was no longer compulsory. Public education in Saskatchewan was compulsory until the student completed eighth grade or the age of fifteen, which ever came first. Although I was not yet fifteen, I had completed the eighth grade. Therefore, theoretically, I no longer had to attend school. I say "theoretically," because even if I had jokingly said to my parents, "I've completed grade eight, so I don't have to go school any more," my mother would have fainted immediately and my father would have killed me on the spot. There would have been no argument. None! I would be dead. "A Jewish boy who quits school!" That would be worse than a major sin. It would be much worse than disobeying the kosher food laws, such as eating a chocolate bar during Passover or even pork, or even pork on Yom Kipper when good Jews are supposed to fast. It would be almost as bad as marrying a *shiksa*. It would also have been unthinkable for me. Although five out of my fifteen previous classmates had quit, I had never entertained such thoughts. Education was free and we were expected to take advantage of this opportunity.

High school, however, wasn't exactly free. High school meant that for the first time I had to buy my own textbooks. That was also exciting. Up until now, the school had furnished all our books at the beginning of the year-not that there were that many. We got a reader and a speller and that was it. Then at the end of the year when we passed into the next grade, we got new books. But now we had to order our own from Regina. So I ordered one for every subject including English, history, geography, math, science, and Latin. Although Latin was not compulsory, Mervin Laskin, who would be studying premed in another year, told me I needed Latin to become a doctor. So I ordered the big red Latin book. I loved studying Latin because I believed the subject was actually required for medicine.

Mr. Tomaschuk's room was quite different in other respects from any of my previous classrooms. For one thing, there were no discipline problems. Everyone in his room was there by choice. There was no time to waste by playing games because there was too much school work to be done, and Mr. Tomaschuk ran a tight ship. Unlike easy-going, humorous Mr. Kindrachuk, my new teacher was all business and had no time for jokes, classroom clowns, or nonsense. Whereas I knew I had been the teacher's pet for two years in Mr. Kindrachuk's room, I wouldn't dare show off now in front of the principal, who was lean and looked mean, especially when he got excited and his straight hair fell all over his stern face. He was forever sweeping it back. I thought he should have cut it shorter or used Vaseline hair tonic. But he never asked me, so I never offered any suggestions. Anyway, he never had to shout at anyone. His straight hair forever sweeping his face and his commanding voice were enough.

Another difference was that instead of listening to my teacher instruct only one-or two other grade levels at the most-I could now overhear his instruction for grades ten, eleven, and twelve. So when he taught Shakespeare, I, too, listened intently to his lessons on *Julius Caesar*, *Macbeth*, and *Hamlet*. I found those plays far more interesting than our play, *A Midsummer Night's Dream*. I even memorized some of the required speeches and soliloquies, even though I didn't know what some of the words meant. But I loved the sound of the words and their rhythm. Shakespeare sure had a way with words. Anyway, when I passed into the next grade, I knew everything about the play that we were supposed to know, especially the famous speeches and soliloquies. By the time I got into grade eleven and had to study *Macbeth*, I had memorized almost the entire play verbatim. I wish Shakespeare had written a play about anatomy and organic chemistry and physics. It would have made my studies in premed so much easier, and I might have become a doctor. Even if he had written a play about French or German or political economy, it might have helped. If I had been alive then, I would have advised him what to write, even if scientists had never heard of molecules, let alone atoms. But forgive me. I was talking about Mr. Tomaschuk, not Shakespeare. There is a difference.

As much as I would have liked to listen to Mr. Tomaschuk's other class lectures, I didn't have that much time because I had plenty of my own work to do. His instruction for each subject lasted no more than fifteen minutes, after which he went on to another grade level, leaving us alone to complete our assignment. An hour or so later, he returned for another fifteen minutes to write notes on the blackboard and instruct us in another subject. Then he was off again. And so it went in my ninth grade. For the first time I had homework. And I mean in more than one subject. Especially in Latin. But I loved learning Latin, even though I did more homework in it than in any other subject. I realized it was one of the main roots from which the English language had evolved. So I memorized my vocabulary and declensions and conjugations and everything else. And it paid off. On the final exam I received 92%—the highest mark I got in the ninth grade.

On December 5, 1941, Mom traveled to Winnipeg to attend the wedding of her cousin Harry Leachman and his bride Sue Shapiro. Mom used to go to Winnipeg twice a year on buying trips for the store. This time she combined her buying trip with the wedding. She had prepared part of the Sunday dinner ahead of time and left my sisters Etta and Merle, ages sixteen and eighteen, to complete and serve the feast. Sunday dinner, served promptly at 1:00 P.M., was a regular special event. Mr. Leckie never missed a Sunday; and for the past few years, the Teskey family from Wynyard, fifty miles away, were also regular guests.

It was Sunday morning, December 7, 1941. The Teskeys had driven over the hard, snow- packed highway in their green 1939 Chevrolet and had arrived at their usual time, 11:30 a.m. Mr. Leckie was sitting on a kitchen chair, carrying on a conversation with Dad and me, while my older sisters were preparing dinner. Mrs. Teskey remained with my older sisters, while Sylvia and their daughter, Helen, went into another room to play. They were both about the same age—ten. Mr. Teskey, Mr. Leckie, Dad, and I went into the sitting room to talk and listen to the New York Philharmonic Symphony Orchestra, conducted by Sir John Barbirolli, while waiting for dinner. Listening to the Sunday symphony was a regular event. We never missed it. Suddenly the music stopped and an announcer broke in, shouting, **"We interrupt this program to bring you a special news bulletin. Japanese planes have just bombed Pearl Harbor. The surprise attack came about one hour ago, at 7:a.m. Honolulu time. First reports indicate there was heavy damage. Keep tuned to this station**. We will bring you more news as it develops. We now return you to your regularly scheduled program."

We were all stunned. "Where's Pearl Harbor?" I asked.

Nobody had ever heard of it. But we soon knew because every few minutes the symphony broadcast was interrupted by another news bulletin giving us more details about the attack.

We kept the radio on during dinner, while Mr. Leckie tried to explain what would happen now. "The United States and Japan are now at war."

"Will the United States enter the war against Germany?"

"Looks like it. Japan and Germany are allies. I don't think she'll have a choice."

"But why did Japan attack the United States?"

Mr. Leckie mentioned something about an embargo against Japan. But nobody really knew. It didn't make sense. A tiny country that made cheap toys and silk stockings had attacked an enormous country so potentially powerful that it could eat tiny Japan for lunch. How could Japan possibly hope to win? The United States was an elephant. A house cat should not attack an elephant. But as each news bulletin kept coming in, hour after hour until late at night, we learned a little more about the horrible damage Japan had inflicted at Pear Harbor. We also learned that Japan had attacked the Philippines. Japan was no longer a house cat. She was a tiger. She had caught the elephant fast asleep. And she had seriously bloodied the huge beast.

We listened to all kinds of news bulletins and rumors about Japan possibly invading Hawaii and Japanese planes possibly attacking targets in California, and even a blackout being ordered along the Pacific Coast. Who knew what to believe? We stayed up until almost midnight. These were exciting times—history in the making.

The next day Mr. Tomaschuk brought a portable radio to school and we listened to President Roosevelt's famous speech: "Yesterday, December 7, 1941, a day that will live in infamy." We all felt better. Our big neighbor to the south was no longer invisible. The United States had entered the war.

Eleven months later, in November of 1942, when I had been in grade ten for only about three months, my classmate George Homeniuk told our principal he was quitting school because of an offer to play hockey in Regina. Mr. Tomaschuk scolded him. "You'll never be able to earn a living playing hockey. It's more important for you to learn algebra and geometry and everything else. You've got to get an education." But George had already made up his mind.

I'll never forget the day George came to say good bye to us. It was a bitterly cold day and the howling wind blew gusts of snow all over the place, chilling one to the bone. George was wearing a blue suit. It was the first time I had seen him in a suit. That was all he had on. I felt sorry for him. I thought he would freeze to death before he got to the train station at ten in the morning. He said good-bye. Then he was off.

A month later, in December of 1942, Mr. Tomaschuk also left school, but for another reason. He was going away to join the Royal Canadian Air Force. But not the air crew. He was a married man with a daughter. And he knew he would be safe as a wireless technician--on the ground.

A few months later in early April of 1942, just before supper, I had been helping Dad unpack a soft goods order from Winnipeg. The store was still open. Mr. Curry, the station agent, came into the store, a telegram in his hand. He asked Dad to step outside. He knew how close Dad and Mr. Leckie were, and he wanted Dad to be the one to break the news. The telegram read, "The Minister of National Defense regrets to inform you that your son Flight Sergeant Wireless Operator Airgunner Norman Abraham Leckie is missing after air operations."

Dad closed the store and went to see Mr. Leckie. When he returned, he told us that after reading the telegram, Mr. Leckie had gone into his warehouse to cry. Dad said it was the first time anyone had seen him cry.

Mr. Leckie knew the odds. When a bomber was shot down over the North Sea, almost none of its crew ever survived. He knew he had lost his oldest son. In the days that followed we tried to comfort him with the hope that Norman might still be alive. But it was extremely awkward. He had accepted the inevitability. Six months later, another telegram arrived. "The Minister of National Defense regrets to inform you that your son Flight Sergeant Wireless Operator Airgunner Norman Abraham Leckie, who has been missing after air operations, must now be presumed dead."

Norman Leckie was the first air fatality from Sheho, as well as Sheho's first fatality from all branches of the service in World War II.

We wondered about the air operations that had claimed his life. We knew that he had been required to maintain radio silence and assumed that his plane had been shot down over the North Sea. Then, fifty-four years later, while I was visiting Sheho in 1996, a dear friend of mine, Clara Hoffman Holmes, whose own brothers Joe and Henry, as well as her brother-in-law Jack, had served in the war, gave me a special gift: *Lest We Forget: Royal Canadian Legion History of Sheho Branch # 356.* The book contained a brief write-up on most of the local servicemen who had served in the war. The book stated that Norman had arrived overseas in November 1941, and "after some operational training at Londonderry in Northern Ireland and Northern Scotland he was posted to Canadian Squadron 407—known as the 'Demon' squadron about April 1, 1942. They belonged to Coastal Command and engaged in anti-shipping strikes from the coast of France up to Norway."

Although "he served with an all Canadian crew and his pilot had already flown 26 successful missions. . . the average life span for crew in the 'Demon Squadron' was 5 missions." He "went missing on his second mission in a Hudson Aircraft on the morning of April 6, 1942 over the island of Sylt just off the Norwegian coast. None of the four member crew (Pilot, Observer, and two Wireless Airgunners) were ever found and it is assumed that either anti aircraft gunners or German fighter planes (109's or 110's) got them." (Pages 51-52.)

We wondered about Sheho's other airman, Hector Munro, who had enlisted in 1940, just months before Norman. The Munro family had moved away in 1941, after which we lost all contact with Hector.

And we also wondered about another classmate of Merle's who was one year behind her. Walter Fedorchuk, a very quiet and likable boy had come to Sheho from Insinger to complete high school. He enrolled in grade eleven in 1939, one year behind Hector Munro, and enlisted in the R.C.A.F. in November 1942 as a Flight Engineer. In May 1944, after being promoted to Flight Sergeant, he was sent to England, where he received his commission as a Pilot Officer and served as the flight engineer on a Halifax bomber.

Toward the end of 1943, we got the second bad news. We heard that Flying Officer Hector Munro had been killed in a training accident in

England. The fatality rate for Sheho's aircrew was now two out of two. One hundred percent.

Then in February of 1945, we received the third bad news about Sheho's young airmen. Pilot Officer Walter Fedorchuk had been killed in action. Three out of three. The fatality rate was still 100 percent.

But my cousin Maurice Shnider was still alive. We prayed that he would survive.

As was the case with Norman, I did not learn any details about the death of Hector Munro and Walter Fedorchuk until more than fifty-four years later when I read the Canadian Legion book.

"Hector William Munro was a Flying Officer Pilot serving with the R.A.F. Squadron No. 170 and was killed on November 24, 1943, at the age of 21 years in a flying accident on a Mustang aircraft just outside the village of Bishops Stratford, Hertfordshire County, England. Cause unknown." (Page 62)

Pilot Officer Flight Engineer Walter Fedorchuk "was killed in action February 15, 1945- #429 Bison Squadron (Fortunae Nihil) Halifax aircraft # MZ 865 went down in the sea off Sweden during a night mine-laying operation in the Western Baltic south of Copenhagen." (Page 25)

In June of 1943, Canadian troops, including some from Sheho, who joined the British and Americans landing in Sicily, distinguished themselves in the Italian campaign.

Sheho's other young men in air force blue who were not in the air crew were safe. And—for the time being— so were our young men in khaki, now training in England for the invasion of the continent which would come. Nobody knew when. But it would come. Maybe in three months; maybe in six months; certainly within a year. It was only a matter of time. And when our troops scaled the cliffs in France or hit the beaches, there would be heavy casualties. And death. But for now they were safe.

Early in the morning of June 6, 1944— D-Day— Canadian troops stormed the beaches of Normandy and advanced toward Caen. A month later the First Canadian Army, along with British and Polish troops, captured Caen. Then they fought their way north and east across France, Belgium, and the Netherlands, and into Germany. They took heavy casualties and losses. By the time the war ended, many of our boys had been wounded—some for life. And thirteen of our boys from the tiny village of Sheho and its immediate surrounding area had paid the ultimate price for victory with their lives. The war had permanently scarred our small, tightly knit community. It would never be the same.

CHAPTER TWENTY-ONE
Shortages

How can I illustrate the law of supply and demand? I remember sitting in my car behind a long line waiting to buy gasoline in 1975 during the first oil crunch. The OPEC countries had put the squeeze on the United States not only for political reasons, but for economic ones as well. They had cut back on their production and export of crude oil and had tripled the price almost overnight. The pumps were open for only a few hours a day, and the price for a gallon of gas had gone up from twenty-five cents to seventy-five. I got out of my car to stretch, as did almost everyone in line. "When do you think this shortage will end?" I asked another motorist.

"As soon as the price reaches a dollar a gallon."

"That's four times what it used to be. Four hundred per cent. It's gouging. It's legalized robbery by the oil companies and OPEC."

"It's a seller's market right now. When the companies get the highest price the traffic will bear, the shortage will end."

A month or so later, the price reached ninety-five cents a gallon and the shortage ended. A few years later, in 1979, there was another squeeze, another shortage, and the price went up to $1.50 a gallon. It stayed there for a long time—until the oil producing countries cheated on their mutual production agreement and began exporting more oil, thereby eliminating the shortage. This was another lesson in the unfettered law of supply and demand—charging whatever the traffic can bear. It was a far cry from the prices we charged during the worst shortages of World War Two.

By 1943, the war had brought many changes to our daily lives throughout Canada. For one thing, with so many young men and even young women in the armed forces, the whole country began experiencing labor shortages. University students were sent home for a week in the fall to help farmers with their harvests. Mervin Laskin, now in his third year of premed at the University of Saskatchewan, along with Lyonel Israels, another premed student, returned to the Rose Valley area to help the farmers. Jewish premed students working on the farm! This was something even the *mavens* in Yorkton at the outbreak of war had not predicted.

The shortages also included teachers. Grade twelve plus a year of normal school was all the preparation required to become a teacher in Saskatchewan for any grade level, even high school. But Sheho's principals from as far back as I could remember always had a university degree. Not now! Almost anyone who could stand in front of the class might qualify. Even though the Saskatchewan Department of Education set the rigid curriculum and final examinations for all schools throughout the province, and even graded the examinations for all schools in the smaller districts like ours, it did not require a university degree for certification as a high school teacher. There simply weren't that many university graduates available. Now with the war on, their numbers in the teaching profession declined rapidly, leaving a scarcity of qualified high school teachers.

Early in 1943, while I was in grade ten, just after our teaching principal Mr. Tomaschuk left school to join the Royal Canadian Air Force as a wireless technician, we got a new teacher, Mr. William Suschinsky. Poor Mr. Suschinsky! Spectacled, tall and thin, he stood in front of the class confused and totally bewildered. I felt sorry for him. I'm sure he had never taught high school before, certainly not the eleventh or twelfth grade. "I don't know why I'm here," he said to my sister Etta's twelfth grade class one day as he was trying to figure out the answer to an algebra question. "I don't understand any of this." Etta helped him with the answer.

Whereas our previous teachers used to read a particular chapter at home, then summarize the major points and write them on the blackboard for us to copy into our notebooks, and sometimes discuss the material, he simply opened the book and read the material aloud. Etta's class used to write letters to their friends or servicemen while he read. She studied her musical theory and harmony lessons, preparing for her Associate degree in music from the Toronto Conservatory of Music. She did that practically all day long.

I don't remember what I did, but it couldn't have been very much. I think I spent my time memorizing just about all the poetry in our reader as well as most of the speeches in Shakespeare's *Julius Caesar*, and also studying pictures of the native African women with big bare breasts in the *National Geographic* magazine. I even had a lot of time to daydream and think. I don't remember what I was thinking about. Maybe Africa. I would have liked to visit Africa. Those women sure had big breasts. Poor Mr. Suschinsky! I sure learned a lot about Africa in his class.

A few months after our "standby"—Mr. Suschinsky—succeeded Mr. Tomaschuk, we got another standby. Mr. Stan Gorchinsky was tall and slim with rosy cheeks, deep blue eyes, and wavy hair. He was extremely handsome, to say the least, probably the most handsome man we had ever seen. And he was extremely shy. He was happily married and all he wanted to do was to avoid looking at star-struck girls who simply could not take their eyes off him— not even when he held a book in front of his face and read. That was all he did. They loved to watch him blush when they asked him a question, forcing him to look at them. Unfortunately, he, too, was not prepared to teach the upper grades in high school.

Fortunately for Etta, she was able to use the notes Merle had taken while in Mr. Tomaschuk's class three years earlier. Thus she was able to do very well on her final examinations.

Unfortunately for me, I had no such notes. Furthermore, by the time Mr. Stan Gorchinsky arrived, I had gotten into the habit of doing only enough homework to satisfy the teacher. And not a minute more. Nevertheless, I did pass grade ten, but only with slightly above average marks. My interests lay elsewhere. I was now spending most of my time in the store.

I had started to work in the store during the summer holidays of 1942, just before entering the tenth grade. I had already celebrated my bar mitzvah the year before. That meant I was a man. Now, at the advanced age of fourteen, I was old enough to work in the store. The first thing I did was to learn the most important thing about managing a general store—how to sweep the oiled wooden floor. "You don't hold the broom that way," my father explained. " You hold it this way. Then you push the *schmutz* [dirt] and peanut shells this way. Ahead of you—not behind." He spoke mostly in English, just in case I had suddenly forgotten Jewish. Besides, how do you say "peanut shells" in Jewish? Schmutz, however, included not only dust, dirt, and peanut shells, but sunflower seeds and cigarette butts and burnt matches and empty packages of tobacco and chocolate bar wrappers and chewing gum wrappers, and chokecherry pits and everything else that lay on the floor. This was not the floor of the House of Commons in the Canadian Parliament in Ottawa, often known as the House of Comics, whose elected representatives sometimes made outrageous speeches. And it was not the Yorkton synagogue where we Jews went to celebrate the High Holy Days. No siree! Our customers from the farm did not come here to make fools of themselves or to pray. They came to Katz General Store to socialize before being waited upon, while being waited upon, and after being waited upon, by Louis Katz and his wife Rose. They felt more at home here than at their real home. That meant they could throw anything they wanted to on the oiled wooden floor—at any time. They knew that Louis Katz wouldn't dare say anything since that's what his floor was for. Discarding things when you were through with them. Besides, Louis Katz would sweep up all the mess after he closed the store. "If they had to sweep up this mess, they would be more careful," I said to my father. His reply was, "If the hen had testicles it would be a rooster."

So it was now up to me to sweep all the *schmutz* into one big pile—Katz's big pile. Then he demonstrated how to slant the dustpan at the exact angle with his right hand so that he could finish the job by holding the broom near its base with his left hand. But he was left -handed. So we got into an argument before he realized that I was right-handed. Then I showed him how to do it the right way. That's important. Sweeping the trash into the dustpan with the right hand if your right-handed. Finally, he showed me how to carefully empty the trash without spilling it, one dustpanful at a time, into the empty, huge potbellied stove. Eventually, he would burn it, after the store closed. That was the only time he lit a fire in that stove during the summer. It was plenty hot outside—and inside, too. We had never heard of air conditioning. And even if we had, there was no electricity in Sheho. So we just kept the door open to let the warm breeze and dust and flies and mosquitoes circulate. As for the industry now known as "garbage or trash collection," I emptied our garbage into the slop well at the back of our yard. And I carefully burned our trash. I was making progress. Who could tell what the future held in store for me?

The next thing I learned about managing a store was how to cover up the items displayed on the counter, as well as those in the ladies' wear section, just before we closed the store. My father had carefully cut white cotton sheets to just the right size in order to cover the counters displaying merchandise such as overalls and canvas running shoes, as well as the racks of ladies' wear. The next morning, just before the store opened, I removed the covers, neatly folded them, and put them away until we again closed the store. I was learning fast.

I did not care to work behind the grocery counter because I found that too boring. There was no challenge. If a customer wanted his usual weekly or monthly supply of groceries, it would be silly for me to convince him to double his order. "Why don't you buy two bags of flour instead of one? That way you won't have to come to town for another two months."

Besides, there wasn't much profit in groceries. The other stores also sold groceries and competition did not allow for a profit of more than a few cents per item. Our average markup ranged from 15% to 25% above cost. If corn flakes cost us 7 1/2 cents a box, we couldn't sell it for more than 10 cents or three boxes for a quarter. On a five dollar weekly grocery order, we would be lucky to average 75 cents profit, or a dollar at the most. Even though certain items such as sugar, chocolate bars, butter, and meat were now rationed because of wartime shortages and required coupons, which we tore off from the customer's ration book so that we could reorder these items, it was illegal to raise prices. The Wartime Prices and Trade Board clamped a lid on prices in an attempt to hold down inflation. For the most part the policy was successful. And even if we had raised prices by a nickel here and a dime there, how much money can you make on a five or ten dollar grocery order? Besides, every storekeeper in town had his own customers. They didn't run from one store to the next to buy sugar or chocolate bars. Not without coupons.

However, with ladies' and men's wear and shoes, it was a different matter. They didn't require coupons and the markup was considerably higher. Although George Lys also carried some soft goods similar to ours, he was not our main competitor. Our major competition had always been the mail order catalogs—Eaton's and Simpson's. But now there were shortages.

The soft goods shortages had started about a year after the outbreak of war, when the mills and factories began sending much of their production to the armed forces and instituting a quota policy for their other customers—the mail order houses, department stores, and wholesalers. The wholesalers who supplied the general stores followed suit by also instituting a quota system for their customers. But the department stores and mail order houses could not possibly maintain such a policy because they had no personal relationships with their customers who were too numerous to count. So they sold everything on a first-come basis. And when they ran out of certain items, that was it.

We first noticed the effect of some of these shortages gradually, then more and more. At first some people we knew who had memorized both the Eaton's and Simpson's catalogues and had always sent away for anything they needed except groceries began coming into our store. Their catalog orders had not been completely filled. Both Eaton's and Simpson's began substituting items, hoping that their customers would keep them. But not everyone was satisfied, and more and more customers began returning the merchandise for refunds, and buying from us, even though our prices may have been somewhat higher. The catalog customers were now ours. So they came into our store and paid cash for dry goods (fabrics), men's and ladies' wear, footwear, and just about everything we stocked in the way of soft goods that had lain in the shelves for a year or more. The hard times were gone.

One of the first shortages was Penman's cotton fleece- lined underwear for boys and men, as well as cotton bloomers for girls and women. Men's combination (one-piece) underwear cost us $1.50 each from both of our major soft goods suppliers—Kay's and Karasick's Limited in Winnipeg. To compete with the mail order houses, we had always sold them for $1.75 each, a razor thin markup of only 16.6%. But now, we also felt the shortages. Our suppliers, the wholesalers, had been placed on a quota direct from the mills; and in turn, our quota from the wholesalers was based upon a certain percentage of what we had ordered the previous year. So, unable to buy as much underwear as we would have liked, we reserved it for our best, long-standing customers, like the Hoffman family, who had always bought most of their clothing needs from us.

After our "regular" customers had been serviced, we kept the remainder of short-supply items for other "new" customers; and after they had been serviced, I suggested raising the price of the remaining underwear by twenty cents to $ 1.95 for Penman's combination underwear, giving us a profit of 45 cents for a whooping, unheard of 23% markup. Unbelievable! After ten years of eking out profits of nickels and dimes and sometimes even quarters, this was big time business, and my father felt guilty. He thought we were robbing the customers.

Although my father did business as he had always done, since opening the store in 1914, when Sheho was a booming village on the frontier, he never kept up with the changing times. To his credit, his heart was as big as the Canadian Prairies, and he was the most honest man I have ever known. But, coming from a tiny hamlet in the Ukraine, he lacked the business sophistication of my mother. He thought of profit in terms of nickels, dimes, and quarters. To make a dollar or more on any item—except for a pair of shoes—was beyond his comprehension.

My mother, on the other hand, was born and reared in Lutzk, a large "beautiful" city in Poland, as she described it, near the border with Russia. Her parents had owned a small beer tavern, and she had acquired a knack for business. When she began working in the store during the Depression and learned that the total profit on a pair of overalls was only twenty-five cents—and sometimes even less—she began to take an interest in buying when the traveling representative from Kay's or Karasick's came to town. Twice a year Mr. Epstein, a heavy, pompous and sometimes arrogant man, who represented Kay's Limited, one of the largest wholesalers in Winnipeg, would visit us. His competitor, Mr. Frankel, a small, quiet, pleasant man, who represented Karasick's Limited, a much smaller wholesaler, also visited us in the spring and fall, but often on a different month. When the morning train arrived, each got off and waited for his numerous large trunks to be unloaded, then hauled by the drayman on duty to Katz General Store. The trunks contained samples of almost everything in the line of soft goods that a general storekeeper might want to stock. Each traveler spent the entire day at our store, waiting for it to close so that he could display his goods. In the meantime he was our guest. It would have been unthinkable for my mother not to invite *any* Jewish traveler to our home for both dinner and supper. After my father had closed the store for business, he and Mom and the traveler would return to the store, where the traveler would open his trunks, one at a time, displaying every item he had, hoping for a big order. Since we were his only customer in town and his company was one of our major suppliers, he was not disappointed. The next day the traveler went on to another town. By the time I got into high school, I was included on the buying team.

The trunks contained not only soft goods but some notions like buttons, needles, and bobby pins. Mom did most of the buying.

One evening shortly after I had begun grade ten, we were unpacking an order from Kay's Limited. "See this bobby pins," she said to me, as she pulled out a packet from the box. "They cost ten cents. A *gantza tzen cent*. [An entire 10 cents.] We sell them for twenty-five cents. I make as much on two bobby pins like a pair of overalls. Sometimes more. I make as much as Papa *schlepping* [lifting] that big sack of flour giving him a rupture for Dr. Portnuff to operate last year. *Schlepping* flour give you ruptures. From bobby pins or combs you don't get ruptures. Your father's not a good business man. Sometimes he's a *nahr*. [fool]

"Horsehair and hides! How much can you make on horsehair and hides? A quarter. Fifty cents. For fifty cents he *schleps* [drags] that hide from the horse the farmers bring him that died all with blood inside to make him *schmootzick* [dirty] to untie. Then to put salt inside and tie up again and *schlep* in the warehouse and wait for Harry Soifer to come from Melville and pay for all that *schlepping* and blood and *schmutz* for a quarter. Maybe fifty cents. A *gantza fiftzick cent*! [An entire fifty cents] *Kim. Ich vil deer vazen fiftzick cent.*" [Come. I will show you fifty cents.]

We walked toward the back of the store where linoleum had been laid over the wooden floor. Ladies' cotton house dresses hung on a moveable chromium rack underneath which lay the linoleum floor. Next to it stood two smaller wooden racks with cast-iron bars at the top. On one hung ladies' skirts; on the other, ladies long sleeve blouses. "Dee zeyst. [You see.] Nice house dresses from Kays Limited I bought when Mr. Epstein was here for spring with his trunks. I buy house dresses from Kays and Karasicks and Nozick's. For twelve dollars a dozen they cost. I sell them for $1.50 and $1.75. Just like Eaton's. I make fifty cents profit a house dress. Even seventy-five cents. I have to sell three pair overalls for seventy-five cents. Papa didn't know from house dresses. He didn't want house dresses. He knows to sell dry goods. Cotton prints for twenty-five cents a yard. We make a *gantza* [entire] five cents profit a yard. Even fancy angelskin and rayon prints. We make a gantza ten cents profit. Three yards for a dress, we make a *gantza* thirty cents. So three years ago in Winnipeg, I go to Nozick Commission. I buy skirts and blouses and nice dresses. *Dee zeyst*? [Do you see?] Nobody in Sheho has skirts and blouses and nice dresses. Maybe Lys, one or two. That's all. But I buy size fourteen to twenty, good sizes, and one size twelve. Nice skirts and blouses." She picked up a skirt from the rack and held it up proudly for me to examine. " A dollar I make on this skirt. The same on blouses. Nice dresses I bought also from Nozick's. *Kim. Ich vil deer vazen.*" [Come. I will show you.]

She took me over to the section of ladies' fancy dresses. A six -foot long row of shelves from top to bottom which had previously held bolts of dry goods had been cut away and replaced with a metal bar at the top from which hung ladies' fancy dresses. To the left of the section was a small dressing room, inside of which hung a mirror. "I tell Papa, 'Lebca, give me this dry goods shelves for dresses. Good dresses. Give me this shelves for dressing room with a curtain to try on dresses. We can make

$1.50 a dress, sometimes even two dollars.' So now we have ladies' good dresses for customers to try on and see in the looking glass before buying. See this nice rayon dress with flowers from Nozick Commission. " She held it up proudly and smiled. "It cost $3.75. We sell it for $5.50. A dollar and seventy five cents profit. Almost two dollars! That's as much like Papa makes *schlepping* ten sacks flour to give him a rupture for Dr. Portnuff in Yorkton to operate from the flour house to the farmer's wagon."

She had a point.

About once a week in the fall, a huge veneer crate arrived from Winnipeg containing the goods that Mom had ordered from Kay's, Karasick's, Nozick's, or from one of several smaller jobbers she had visited while on a buying trip in Winnipeg. The demand for scarce merchandise exceeded the supply. So the small jobbers bought whatever they could from the mills, factories, and larger wholesalers; and they marked up their merchandise to get whatever the traffic could bear. They sold Penman's underwear and other merchandise for more than we did. But at least they had some to sell. Mom paid them two dollars cash under the table for Penman's combination underwear, and we sold it for $2.25. Although this price exceeded the one established by the bureaucrats in the Wartime Prices and Trade Board, who had never been in a general store, our "new" customers didn't complain. They were glad to buy it at any price because they couldn't get it anywhere else.

These veneer packing crates, especially those containing our orders from Kay's and Karaskick's, were huge. They were nailed shut both at the top and bottom, and Dad had to use a crowbar to pry the top open. Then I began pulling out each item and checking it against the packing slip and the invoice. Then Dad, Mom, and I held a conference to decide how much we should charge for the item. Gone were the days of bargaining with the customer for fifteen cents profit on a pair of men's woolen lumbermen's socks. Gone were the days of struggling for twenty cents profit on a man's donegal tweed cap or plaid flannel shirt or a pair of lady's silk stockings. Gone were the days of hoping for fifty cents profit on a sweater. Dad no longer felt we were robbing the customers blind, just overcharging them. Mom was more practical. She knew how scarce merchandise was. And I knew the main reason our "new" customers bought from us was that they couldn't buy these items anywhere else. Besides, the farmers could sell all the produce they could raise at prices they had never dreamed of. They now had more money than ever. So I didn't think we were taking advantage of them. But that's not what my dad thought. So we got into an argument.

"You've struggled all your life to make a living," I said. " Now you have a chance to make a little money. The customers can't get these goods at Eaton's, and we can't get them any time we want. The customers have money. If these socks don't sell right away, we'll lower the price." Reluctantly, he agreed. So he sewed men's woolen dress socks and lumbermen's socks into parachute like bundles and tied them to the rod suspended from the ceiling. Then I raised the price by twenty cents and printed 95c on a sign, which I attached it to the rod. We never lowered the price.

I cleared one of the counters on which Dad had displayed knee-length felt socks and rubber -soled canvas covered overshoes. There was very little profit in these items which were not yet in short supply. I replaced the display with a stack of flannel shirts, sweaters, and caps, all neatly ticketed by me with the new selling price. Although I still followed the regulations of the Wartime Prices and Trade Board, the maximum markup of fifty percent was by far the most we had ever taken. But nobody complained. My displays were working.

Later, toward springtime, while still in the tenth grade, I began removing men's black denim and blue drill pants from the shelves behind the glass counter and putting them on top of that counter for the customer to help himself. Now, because of our improved cash flow, we were able to pay our bills within thirty days, thus enabling us to buy these pants direct from the factory. Instead of twenty-five cents profit a pair, we now made fifty cents. And when Mom bought rayon sharkskin dress pants for three dollars a pair, I piled them on top the glass top counter and sold them for four dollars a pair, giving us an unheard of profit of one dollar on a pair of pants. Mom bought men's fedora style green felt hats for two dollars and we sold them for three. We reordered again and again. My father was amazed. But he no longer felt we were overcharging the customer. We were simply making better buys and selling better merchandise. And he no longer had to offer his customers a special "bargain," or to haggle with them over the price of an item. For the first time since he had gone into business, Katz General Store had a "set price." It was a fair price, and the customers knew it. Equally important, they could see and try on the merchandise before buying it, then take it with them. The fancy pictures and slightly lower prices in Eaton's catalog didn't mean a thing because most of the time they couldn't get what they wanted from the catalog anyway. It was just easier to buy what they needed from Katz's.

During our summer holidays of 1943, after completing grade ten, I worked in the store full time, from nine in the morning until six in the evening, after which Walter Lys and I would cycle to Newburn Lake for our daily swim. Although the store didn't close until seven, Dad did not begrudge letting me off work an hour earlier. All the stores in town could have closed at six without missing any business to speak of, but somehow it just didn't seem right to close the store before the train arrived at seven. Who knows? Maybe somebody will need a package of tobacco or a chocolate bar before going down to the station to watch the train come in. Maybe somebody will need a bar of Lifebuoy soap "to stop B.O." as the radio commercials promised, or a box of Rinso "to get your clothes Rinso White," or a box of Kotex "to keep you safe and confident" before the store closes. You never know. Business is business. One could lose a customer by closing early. So everyone kept his store open until seven.

From nine in the morning until seven at night, five days a week, except for Saturday, when we stayed open until ten— those were our hours. Dad usually opened the store at 9:00 a.m. and as soon as I arrived, about five minutes later, he would walk three blocks down the street to the barber shop, where Mike Lazatsky, the owner, would give him a shave. During the hard times, he used to get a shave every other day for ten cents; but now, with our new-found wealth, it became a morning ritual, even though the cost had gone up by 50% to fifteen cents, for a grand total of ninety cents a week. He was now living it up in the lap of luxury.

As a child growing up and then as a youngster, I had accompanied him many times to the barber shop and watched as first Mr. Hesper, and later Mike Lazatski, would perform the ritual. After seating him in the barber's chair and covering his shirt with a large towel, Mike would slowly lower the chair backwards until Dad was comfortably lying almost supine. Then, from the copper boiler, Mike pulled out a steamy towel and draped it over Dad's face. For my dad, this was the best part of all—the hot wet towel. It was a *mechieya*. [wonderful] Soon he heard the razor rubbing against the leather strap, back and forth, slap, slap. Nothing would be sharper than Mike's straight razor after he had stroked it in long swipes against the leather strap, back and forth. Dad liked the sound and the rhythm. Slap, slap. He was almost asleep when Mike removed the towel and began plastering thick lather all over his face with a soft bristled shaving brush. Next came the shave. With a steady right hand, Mike slanted the razor-sharp steel against the face and began to scrape upward, from the chin to the short sideburns at the ear lobe. One small stroke at a time. With each stroke, a small patch of lather and whiskers clung to the steel, underneath which was now visible a strip of clean white skin. After each swipe, Mike wiped the lather-covered blade against a strip of tissue paper until the blade was clean. He shaved one side of the face, then the other; then the neck, and finally he pinched the nose with his left hand, and with his right, completed shaving underneath the nose. Next, he poured after shave lotion generously into his cupped hands and rubbed the lotion all over the face. Finally, he twirled a towel around and around, just over the face, blowing over it like a cool refreshing breeze on a hot summer's day. It was invigorating. Dad felt refreshed, he smelled good, and he was ready for business.

Business, however, was not necessarily ready for him. Except for Saturdays, the lazy days of summer are far from the busiest of the year. Sometimes two or three hours could go by before anyone would come into the store. Occasionally it might be a customer. More often than not, however, it would be Gree-gor—ee, the obese three hundred pound Doukhobor, who waddled into the store, sat down on the broken chair and began chewing sunflower seeds and spitting the shells on the floor. Then slowly, very, very slowly, he would again begin to narrate in

Ukrainian his epic tale to Dad about another heroic personal experience as a sailor in Tsar Nicolai's Imperial Russian Navy, shoveling coal into the furnaces of a battleship during the Russian-Japanese War of 1904. Slower and slower and on and on it went, longer than the war itself. Gree-gor-ee's epic went on forever. I mean forever. Finally, after Gree-gor—ee had left (thank God!), Mr. Biskewhyna, the school's elderly janitor, would come in and sit on the same broken chair and slowly kill the rest of the afternoon talking in Ukrainian with Dad. Then, just before leaving, he would curve his thumb and middle finger until they almost met, making the largest claw you ever saw. This human claw was a signal for me to bring him free matches. If I brought him a few matches, he would shake his head. He wanted to help himself from the box. Dad would say, "Bring him the box." So I would bring him a large box of Eddy's strike anywhere matches that sold for ten cents. He would open the box, then extend his enormous claw, clamp it around the matches, and lift out at least half a box of matches all at once. If one or two dropped to the floor, that was my problem. Or if only a quarter of a box was left, that was also my problem. He never paid for matches. Not even once. But he bought tobacco and cigarette papers from us. That was all he bought. But as far as Dad was concerned he was a "regular" customer. Fortunately, there was never a shortage of matches. And almost every day it was all I could do to restrain myself from this excitement.

But there was more. Never a dull moment. How can I describe it? Every week the three grocery travelers from whom we bought all our groceries visited us for their weekly order. Now that's what I call real excitement. All three lived in Yorkton, which was also the shipping point for two of the companies, Macleans and Smith Fruit. The travelers worked their routes in a circle from Yorkton west to their farthest point, then returned east on another highway to their home for the weekend. On Monday it was Alan Maclean of George Maclean Limited in Yorkton, our biggest supplier. He was a short, balding, middle-aged, friendly man who eventually ran for Parliament on the Liberal ticket and won. Then came the tall, strictly business traveler from McDonald's Consolidated, headquartered in Winnipeg. Finally on Friday, the young traveler from

Smith Fruit called on us in the morning on his way back to Yorkton. "How's your apples?"

"Gimmie a box." Dad did not mince words.

"What about oranges?"

"One box."

"What about lemons."

"No. I'm okay."

"Tobacco?"

"Let me check. Yeah. Same as last week."

I didn't know how much longer I could take all this excitement. It wasn't easy.

Week in and week out, no matter how hot it was, each traveler was always neatly dressed in a wool suit, a long-sleeved white or striped dress shirt, a conservative looking tie, black or dark brown shoes, and a gray or tan colored felt hat. Although I never paid much attention to the dark colored suits worn by most of the travelers, including the ones representing the dry goods companies in Winnipeg, I couldn't help but notice the suit worn by the Smith Fruit traveler. It was a single breasted medium brown suit with white chalk stripes. I thought it was the sharpest looking suit I had ever seen. It looked even nicer than the ones worn by the movie gangsters Edward G. Robinson, James Cagney, and Humphrey Bogart, especially since most of the movies I had seen them in were in black and white. And now, at the age of fifteen, having suddenly outgrown all my "boys" clothes, including my bar mitzvah suit, I wanted a Smith Fruit Company suit—brown with white chalk stripes. It would make me look grown up and important—like Humphrey Bogart.

Even though I knew my size, men's 36 regular, I didn't ask Mom to get me one from Kay's Limited because I wasn't sure Kay's stocked that particular suit. Besides, I was now ready to buy my own clothes. And since the High Holy Days were only about a month away, I persuaded Mom and Dad to let me go to Yorkton on Friday with the Smith Fruit traveler to buy my new suit for *Yon Tif.* [Jewish Holidays] I would then return later that evening on the bus.

"Don't lose this *gelt* [money]," she said nervously, as she folded four ten-dollar bills into a small change purse, closed the purse, then shoved it deep into my pants pocket on my right side. "*Gib achtick.*" [Guard it] Then she took a large safety pin and fastened my pocket shut. It was the most money I had ever carried on me. I never carried money in my pants except for a nickel to buy an ice cream, or ten cents to go to the odd movie that came to town, or twenty-five cents to go to the odd dance in the Town Hall. But that wasn't real money. It was change. The only folding money I had ever carried before was two dollars during my trips to Yorkton while preparing for my bar mitzvah and one dollar during our family trips there for the High Holy Days. I never needed money because I never spent any. But now I was going on a long, dangerous, costly expedition to the unknown and I needed a huge amount of money— forty dollars. A king's ransom. I would guard it with my life. I put my handkerchief in my left pocket and kept my right hand pressed tightly over the other one—the Royal Bank of Canada.

We left shortly after twelve noon. Our first stop was Insinger, twelve miles away, population just over one hundred. Nine years before, two Jewish storekeepers, Ben Glass and Itzick Shnider, had tried to eke out a living in this one-block-long all Ukrainian hamlet. They had since gone on to bigger and better things. Itzick Shnider had his own one-truck delivery business in Winnipeg; and Ben Glass, who had lost his wife to cancer, had moved to Yorkton, where his older son Sam (also known as Mel) was now a jobber and also a representative for the American Pad and Textile Company of Chatham, Ontario, which manufactured Walkers overalls and pants.

If Sheho was small, Insinger was microscopic. I followed Smith Fruit into the store. We waited for the storekeeper to finish talking to a customer. Suddenly a man burst in and, almost out of breath, shouted, "The Mountie's in town." Everyone froze. Within minutes, half of Insinger rushed into the store. There was standing room only. The room buzzed like a swarm of mosquitoes. This was the most exciting event in the history of Insinger. Waiting for the Mountie. It was just like a cowboy movie, waiting for the shootout. We could now hear the sidewalk's wooden steps creak louder and louder as the Mountie approached. The buzzing stopped. The breathing stopped. The only sound was the loud creak of wooden steps just outside the store. Then we heard a louder creak of wooden steps leading from the sidewalk into the store. Finally, the creaking gave way to a loud stomp as the Mountie, towering above everyone, set foot on the wooden floor and slowly stomped toward the counter. Everyone strained to hear why the Mountie had come. Had there been a bank robbery in Yorkton? Were the robbers heading this way? Were there hostages? We held our breath.

"Do you know if anyone has seen Kowalchuk's cow?" asked the Mountie.

"Which one?" replied the storekeeper.

"The Holstein."

"You mean the black and white one."

"Yeah. It's black and white."

The storekeeper shook his head. Then he turned to the crowd and shouted, "Has anyone seen Kolwachuk's black and white cow?"

Twenty individual heads shook in unison and replied "NO!"

"If anyone finds it, let me know," said the Mountie. Then he turned around, proudly stomped out of the store, and was gone. The store emptied except for the customer, the Smith Fruit traveler and me. As soon as the traveler had written down the order for apples, oranges, lemons, tobacco, and cigarette papers, we were on our way.

Theodore was about three times the size of Insinger, but not quite as exciting. No Mounties. Then came Springside, just eighteen miles from Yorkton. The only exciting thing I saw in Springside was the cute redhead who worked in Mr. Stitz's store. Before I had time to talk to her, Smith Fruit and I were on our way. I wished I lived in Springside. But now we were finally in Yorkton.

"Thanks for the ride," I said.

"You're welcome. Good luck in finding a suit."

I paused to look at the crowded men's window display at Croll's Broadway Store. Conspicuous among the suits, overcoats, leather jackets furnishings and shoes was a mannequin clothed in the official Pilot Officer's uniform of the Royal Canadian Air Force, complete with regulation cap and double wings. Overhead, the drone of Harvard training planes making sharp climbing turns was another reminder that Yorkton's advanced training school for fighter pilots from all over the British Empire was now fully operational.

Although I had often looked at Kenny Croll's overcrowded artistic window display masterpiece, this was the first time I had ever gone into his father's store. Inside, it was more crowded than the window display. I was amazed. Tables were stacked high with shirts, socks, underwear and ties. I walked toward the back where the walls held racks stacked three high, each one packed with hundreds of men's suits. Mickey Nathenson was waiting for me. He reminded me of Wunder's dog during my early days when we would drown gophers just above the creek that ran through Wunder's field. As we poured pailfuls of water down the gopher hole, Wunder's dog was barely able to restrain himself, waiting for the gopher to come up so he could grab it in his mouth and yank it out of the hole. I thought of turning back and running away. But it was already too late. Mickey's stare had hypnotized me.

"Hi. Looking for a nice suit?"

"Yeah."

"Do you know what size?"

"Yeah. 36." We walked over to a rack which held about two hundred suits. He waved his hand over a few suits, eight or nine at the most. "These are 36s. Here's a sharp looking herringbone tweed. Just right for a young man like you." He pulled it out and held it up admiringly. "Real sharp looking, isn't it? Why don't you try it on?"

"No. I'm looking for a brown suit with white chalk stripes."

"A chalk striped suit for a young man like you?" He shook his head and put the suit back. "We don't have any. A striped suit is nice for someone about thirty-five or forty years old. When you get to be thirty-five or forty, that would be a nice suit to wear. But not now."

"Thank you. I think I'll look around."

I left hurriedly and turned west on Broadway, crossed Betts Avenue, and entered the men's store of E.B. Smith, Yorkton's second largest clothing store. Once more I asked to see size 36s. Again, there were only a few my size, mostly dark colors including ugly browns with shadow stripes—old men's suits. No medium browns with white chalk stripes. I felt as though I had been disqualified from the hundred yard dash—for life. I went back to Croll's.

Wunder's dog was waiting with a big grin on his face. He could see the gopher coming out of its hole, its head in full view. Now came the fun. Grabbing the gopher's head and viciously shaking the drenched animal to death. "Hi!" He grabbed the herringbone tweed suit from the rack, took the coat off, and held it out. "Here! Try it on!"

What could I do? I extended my arms.

He pulled the coat collar up to my neck, smoothed the shoulders, then buttoned the middle button. Then he pulled the coat downward. The coat felt comfortable, especially at the shoulders, but it was a little loose around the waist.

"Fits perfect. Just like made-to-measure. Look in the mirror!" He pushed me toward the three-way mirror. " See! Just like tailor made. It couldn't fit any better."

"It's a little loose at the waist."

"Just a tiny bit. Size 36 is the smallest size made for men. You'll grow into it in no time. Here! Try the pants on!"

"They're a little loose at the waist."

"Don't worry. You're a young man and you're growing fast. You'll grow into them. Here! Hold them up at your hips and I'll measure your inseam." He bent down, held his tape measure up to my crotch, then extended the tape downward until it reached almost to my heel. "Twenty-nine inches."

"I usually wear 28."

"Don't worry. I'm making them a little longer because you're growing. You're growing so fast, in another year this suit will be too small for you. Trust me. I know. You're Louis Katz's son from Sheho, aren't you?

I nodded and shook hands with him. "Jack Katz."

"How long are you going to be in town?"

"I'm going back on the bus at six o'clock. How much is the suit?"

"Twenty-five dollars."

It was considerably less than I had planned to spend. But the suit wasn't what I had really wanted. However—I told myself— that's life. You can't always get what you want. Besides, it wasn't a bad looking suit.

"I'll get the cuffs put on the pants right away." He scribbled on a paper tag, then looped its string through the belt loops. "Mary, come here! Take these pants to Rosenblattt the dry cleaner for cuffs and wait for them. Tell him to hurry. I need them right away." Then he turned to me. "What else do you need, Jack? A nice hat?"

"Yeah, I'd like a nice hat. How much are the Stetsons?

"They start at seven dollars.

Do you have anything a little less?"

"Sure. We carry Kensingtons. They're made by Stetson. They look just like Stetsons. They're only five dollars. What size do you wear?"

He pulled out a tan colored hat from the box and blocked it, then handed it to me. A narrow band circled the wider brim. It looked just like a Stetson. It was the softest hat I had ever touched and the sharpest look-ing one, too. I thought it looked even better than the ones I had seen George Raft or Edward G. Robinson or Humphrey Bogart wear in the movies. Now I felt grown up. "It's beautiful," I said."

"What about a tie?" He pointed to three different racks on top of which were three printed signs: $1.50, $2.00, and $2.50. These signs were not printed with black crayon like the ones I hurriedly made at our store. They were printed by an artist. Anyone could see that. I glanced at the flashy, expensive silk neckties on the racks. Some were so gaudy they looked like the ones worn by my gangster movie heroes. Some day when I could afford to, I would buy one. But for now, I settled for a $1.50 pretty blue paisley tie that contrasted with my black and gray her-ringbone suit.

I accompanied Mickey to the wrapping counter where he handed my suit, hat, and tie to the cashier and wrote up the order. The bill, including tax, came to just under $32. I unfastened the large safety pin from my pants pocket and pulled out my change purse containing the forty dollars Mom had given me. I knew she would be glad I had not spent it all.

Norman Croll and Kenny were standing on the opposite side of the counter. Mr. Croll, chewing on an unlighted cigar, was wearing a tan camel hair sport coat with brown gabardine slacks, and Kenny was wearing an old man's dark brown shadow striped suit. "Mr. Croll," said Mickey, "This is Jack Katz, Louis Katz's son from Sheho."

Mr. Croll glanced at the suit, the hat, and the tie, and then at me and said, "Nice looking suit. Nice hat. Nice tie. How are you?"

"Fine, thank you."

"How's your fadder?"

"Fine, thank you."

"How's your mudder?"

"Fine, thank you."

"Nice young man's suit." Then he walked away.

Several weeks later during Rosh Hashanah, as I entered the Yorkton Synagogue, I felt almost six feet tall in my new suit and hat. I was now a man—not because I had already had my bar mitzvah two years before, but because for the first time in my life, I was wearing a real man's suit—not a boy's suit from Kay's Limited. And I was also wearing a real man's hat, made by Stetson. I felt I had grown up. Almost.

But this Rosh Hashanah was not like the ones in the past. My sisters Merle and Etta had moved to Winnipeg, and at times I felt a little lonely. My cousin Maurice Shnider had long since gone overseas. He was now in Ceylon, in the Japanese theater of war. Yorkton's Service Flying Training School was now host to young airmen from throughout the British Empire, and some of them were part of our congregation. There were also a few young men in khaki and navy blue. But the predominant color by far in the synagogue was air force blue. The servicemen felt at home here. Practically every Jewish family in Yorkton had taken these young men into their homes—not only for the High Holidays but whenever they had a weekend leave—and made them feel as if they were special. And when the young men in air force blue got their wings and left for overseas, the families scanned the daily casualty lists in the newspapers, hoping against hope that nobody they knew was on that list. But all-too-often they recognized the name of the young man just out of high school who had been their guest only months before.

Times had changed. Molly and Reva Levinson were gone. The family had sold the store and moved to Vancouver. But the Fermans were still here. Gloria had blossomed into a beautiful girl. For the first time in my life, I had a real crush on a girl. I knew I was growing up.

CHAPTER TWENTY-TWO
The Exodus Begins

Because we had always been a closely knit family, our lives underwent a major change when my older sisters, Merle and Etta, moved to Winnipeg in the late summer of 1943. I had always felt close to them as far back as I could remember. Even before I started school, I was included in some of their games, despite our age differences. While still a child, they taught me how to kick a huge rubber ball along the ground, then later how to bounce a worn-out old tennis ball on the sidewalk. Next came "Hide -and-Seek" and more sophisticated running games including "Anti-Anti I Over" and "Hit the Can."

Since the roof of our vacant engine house —the Sheho Royal Museum of Canada—had a thirty degree slope, which made it higher at one end of the building than at the other, it was perfect for Anti-Anti-I Over. It wasn't too hard, then, for the person who was "It" to throw our only tennis ball over (or lob it on top of) the roof so that whoever was on the other side could catch it. Then that person would run around the building and try to hit "It" with the ball. To start the game, I would stand at one end of the building while my sisters stood under the roof at the other end and wait for me to shout "Anti-Anti-I Over." I would then lob the ball over the roof and wait for one of them to catch it. Then I would start running around the building, attempting to avoid being hit by the ball as my sister raced around the building to catch me. However, since I didn't know whether she was coming from my left or right, and she didn't know in which direction I was headed, we both might continue to run around and around like our rooster chasing a chicken. Or we might run into each other. Either way, when she spotted me, she would throw the ball at me and if she connected, she changed places with me and became "It." The only danger we faced was if one of us slipped, one might fall into the large manure pile between the barn and the Sheho Royal Museum of Canada.

We also played "Hit the Can." The only equipment required was an empty can and a heavy stick to hit the can far enough so the rest of us could run and hide before being caught by "It"—the person who retrieved the can. In late summer our big yard provided plenty of places to hide, including the tall rows of corn in our garden.

Another reason I missed my older sisters was that I rarely got into arguments with them and looked up to each as an older friend and adviser in whom I could confide. Although I felt close to Merle, five years older than I, she was always busy. After completing grade eleven, she had stayed home from school (except for taking one class) in order to devote full time to her music studies. The following year, in 1939, after receiving her Associate degree from the Toronto Conservatory of Music, she returned to complete high school. After graduating, she began a career as a traveling music teacher, giving piano lessons in four neighboring villages.

With Etta, though, my relationship was different. I felt closer to her since she was only three years older than I, and we had shared the same classroom for the past two years. Even before then, she seemed to take more interest in me and often gave me suggestions about what I should or shouldn't do. Once she handed me a book she had bought—*Peter Pan*—and said, "I think you'll enjoy reading this book." She was right. I wished I could fly like Peter Pan. Then she handed me another one she had bought. I enjoyed that one too. But I felt sorry for Pinochio who suffered from a common addiction—telling lies. It's a disease.

Those were the only two books we had in the house. Our home was not exactly the Library of Congress. So I never read any more books (other than school books) until I was ten or eleven. Then one day, Mr. Leckie, who had an extensive library in his home, above his store, said, "Here's a book about the Crusades. I think you'll enjoy reading it." He was right. It took me only a few months to read that book, and I wished that I had been alive then to join all those knights on their crusades. But since I was Jewish, I don't think Dad would have allowed me to go. Then Mr. Leckie said, "Here's a good book you'll enjoy reading." It was The Universe Around Us by Sir James Jeans. I was fascinated by the author's description of the universe. I learned it was much larger than I had thought. I knew immediately that I wanted to become an astronomer. The only problems were that I was only in grade eight , and it would be a few years before I took algebra or physics and, therefore, I did not understand the equations in the book. Nevertheless, although it took me six months, I finally read the entire book.

Then Mr. Leckie handed me another book and said, "Here's a good book you'll enjoy reading by Sigmund Freud. His *Introductory Lectures on Psychoanalysis*. Once more I was captivated. I learned that my mind was composed of a conscious, unconscious, ego, super ego, and id, and that if I psychoanalyzed myself, I would learn that I had an Oedipus complex and wanted to kill my father so that I could sleep with my mother. Even though I questioned Freud's theory, I decided to become a psychoanalyst. I would specialize in psychoanalyzing astronomers.

Then I had to study for my bar mitzvah, so I never read any more books except part of the Bible. I did that on my own. The truth is, I never read any books unless someone said, "Here's a good book you should read." Even in high school, unless my teacher said, "You *must* read this book," or "You *should* read this," I never read it. In our twelfth grade English literature class, for supplemental reading we were supposed to read Thomas Hardy's novel *Far From the Madding Crowd*. Our teacher did not say, " You *should* buy this book because we don't have it in the library, since we don't even have a school library." He thought I was smart enough to know that since we didn't have a library and nobody else had a copy of that book, I should order it. So I never read it. But the day before I took the final examination, I looked in the cupboard which contained copies of old magazines and old examination questions, and lo and behold, I saw a picture of the heroine, Bathsheba, and a two sentence summary of her conflict. Would you believe that one of the questions on the final examination required a pen portrait of the heroine? That's the truth. Did I ever write a pen portrait? I really piled it on. Thomas Hardy must have turned over in his grave. I got a B on that exam. But forgive me. I was talking about my sister Etta.

Once when Mom was away on a buying trip, Etta assumed responsibility for preparing the meals. She made what she called a "Waldorf salad" containing apples, celery, and walnuts. "That's a good salad," I said after our noon day meal.

"You really like it?"

"Yes, it's delicious."

So guess what she served for dinner and supper, every day until Mom returned? And that was the last time I ate Waldorf Salad. Even after all these years, whenever she serves Waldorf Salad at her home and says, "Won't you have some," I reply, "No thank you. I'm just too full."

I felt comfortable asking Etta for answers to sensitive questions. When I was about fifteen, Milo Harris, three years older than I, told me that many girls over seventeen were no longer virgins, and by the time all girls got married, most had long ago lost their virginity. I was shocked and wondered if he was telling me the truth. I had always believed that all girls preserved their virginity until their wedding night. So I asked Etta what she thought. She thought Milo was probably right. I was crushed. It was worse than the day Johnny Drobot told me Miss Griffiths was lying about storks bringing babies into the world. Then he explained how I was born. Two shocking disillusionments already in my life—storks and virgins. Now virgins were also an endangered species. What next?

About the time I got into high school Etta taught me how to dance. Almost everybody in Sheho knew how to dance. We all knew how to skate and how to dance. Our outdoor ice skating season lasted only four months and sometimes even less, depending on the weather. When the ice turned to slush, that was the end of the season. But with dancing, it didn't matter if it was forty degrees below zero or eighty above. It was open season twelve months of the year. That's because we danced in the town hall or Ukrainian hall, both of which were not affected by the weather.

Whenever somebody wanted to put on a dance, hopefully to raise money for a worthwhile cause or simply because there hadn't been a dance in over a month, he simply persuaded anyone who owned a violin or an accordion or both, that it was high time to play for a dance. If he could persuade someone to the play the piano, he had a full orchestra. But usually he settled for a squeaky, out-of-tune fiddle—I mean *really* out of tune— and an accordion. Next, he rented one of the halls and finally put up a cardboard sign in the post office and at the town well. The sponsor didn't have to go to the trouble or expense of printing flyers or putting an ad in the newspaper or broadcasting announcements over the radio. A simple crayon sign on a piece of cardboard tacked to the post office wall, as well as another sign on the wooden fence enclosing the town pump would do. A week's notice would ensure a crowd be-cause every week the farmers came into town to pick up their mail, and someone from every family in town not only went to the post office every day, but also to the town well to pump water at least once a day, 365 days a year. So everybody at the post office and at the well saw the sign. "DANCE! FRIDAY NIGHT, TOWN HALL. Music by the Toe Ticklers. Admission 35 cents. Come one, come all."

The Toe Ticklers, a group of professional musicians headed by Mr. Mercer from Theodore, two villages east of Sheho, was the best dance band in the entire area. In contrast to most local groups consisting of two so- called musicians who rarely played in tune because they couldn't tell C sharp from Z flat, the Toe Ticklers included a saxophone, violin, pi-ano, and drums. Not only could they all read music and play in tune, but their repertoire included "The Beer Barrel Polka."

Preparing for the big dance was like preparing for the World Series; and waiting for the Toe Ticklers to arrive was at least as exciting as waiting for the World Series to begin. First, the wooden folding chairs in the hall had to be unstacked, then opened and placed along the west side of the long hall, all the way from the cast-iron potbelly stove to the stage. The chairs were for the ladies to sit on while they waited for the men to ask them to dance. If nobody asked them to dance, they were called "wallflowers" and they sat on the chairs all night. You didn't need a neon sign reading, "For Ladies only." Everybody knew the chairs were for the ladies and the wallflowers. The heck with the men. They could stand.

Next, the hardwood floors were swept clean, at least twice—not by a corn broom that cost fifty cents from Katz General Store, but by an expensive long- handled horsehair push broom, the same kind that our school janitor, Mr. Biskewhyna, used every day after class. Finally, the promoter-custodian began walking up and down the hall while vigorously shaking a container of granulated wax until it covered the entire dance floor. It looked as if there had been a snowstorm inside.

Although the ticket window didn't open until 8:30 P.M. and the dance was not supposed to begin until nine, like every other event in Sheho, nobody was about to take a chance on missing the dance. Who knows what could happen? The Toe Ticklers might arrive ahead of time. They might start the dance without us. So one-by-one, people began crowding around the ticket window shortly after eight. They didn't line up. That type of organized grouping was much too advanced for Sheho. Nobody had ever heard of it. Instead, people just pushed and shoved and herded together like cattle, only without mooing. Finally, the window opened and the herd pressed together even tighter, like the cattle in the stockyard being loaded into a boxcar for shipment to Winnipeg.

All the young ladies and wallflowers sat down along the western wall, powdering their noses and retouching their lips. They appeared not to notice the young men combing their hair, standing at the opposite end facing them, sizing them up, deciding whom they would ask for a dance.

Soon the crowd buzzed with excitement as the Toe Ticklers arrived and climbed the steps to the stage, lugging their instruments. They were taking forever to unpack. They were taking forever to rearrange the chairs. They were taking forever to warm up. Finally, the music began. "The Beer Barrel Polka."

The young men who began stampeding across the wax-covered slippery floor would often slip and lose their balance, then slide the rest of the way to the western wall, almost crashing into it before they stopped, just as ladies stood up to meet them. If the lady did not stand up, the young man might say, "May I have this dance with you?"— or "Care to dance?" But more often than not, he simply stopped in front of his chosen partner and bowed slightly or held his hand out, and they began dancing. If the young lady didn't like the young man or was waiting for some other partner to ask her to dance, she might say, "No thanks." The young man then asked the next lady or the next or the next until someone said "Yes." It was a sure bet. But not so with the wallflower. If nobody asked her for a dance, she would warm the chair all night.

We all dressed up in our Sunday best for the dance. Men wore woolen suits from the Eaton's or Simpson's catalogue, or dress slacks with shirt and tie. When our store stocked men's rayon sharkskin slacks and matching jackets—all in blue—half the crowd was dressed in blue. Nobody ever came to a dance in blue denim jeans, even if they were washed. That would be unthinkable. Jeans were designed strictly for rough work, like shoveling manure. And that's why they were worn. The ladies wore fancy dresses or skirts and white blouses, either from Eaton's or Katz General Store. "Casual" clothes were for everyday wear, not for dances. We all wore black or brown leather dress shoes with leather soles. And we danced close together, not like the kids today—with somebody at the other end of the hall.

After dancing a lively polka or two, while dressed in our Sunday best, in a packed hall without air conditioning, we began to sweat. I didn't say "perspire." I said "sweat." I mean really sweat. Now I don't care what the Lever Brothers ads used to say about Lifebuoy soap. " He bought the most expensive suits but his tailor hated to fit him. He had B.O. He should have used Lifebuoy soap. It stops B.O." When you sweat—the good old fashioned way—no matter how much Lifebuoy soap you've used before going to the dance, it doesn't help. Unless you use a strong underarm deodorant, like Arrid or Mum. But when I first began going to dances, I'm sure nobody in the hall had ever heard of underarm deodorants except our family, because we were probably the only ones in town who read the ads in *Look* Magazine. That's when we began ordering Arrid and Mum from the mail order catalog. Now when the dance really got into high gear and my sisters and I were the only ones who used a deodorant, we could smell B.O. all the way from the town hall to the stockyards. In fact, it smelled worse than the stockyards. I almost gagged. Realizing there was an untapped market for underarm deodorants, I ordered the little jars of white sticky cream called Mum and Arrid from our notions wholesaler and sold them in our store. We made twenty-five cents profit on a jar. It took years, long after I had moved away, but in time Sheho became educated about underarm deodorants. Yet even now, after all these years, whenever I watch a movie about the "good old days" (B.D.—before deodorants), all I can think of is the B.O. in our town hall during a dance.

Etta (pronounced Eeta) was quite plump. She was also good-natured. I think most plump people are good-natured. The plumper they are, the better-natured they seem to be. My parents used to call her Etta the *geeta*, which translates into Etta the "good one." She was also quiet. I mean she wasn't always blabbing or voicing her opinion about anything and everything like some people. The only time I recall her having a strong opinion about anything was the day she finished her last exam in grade twelve—her last day of school. I had finished my exam a little earlier and was in the store when she rushed in about five minutes after twelve. "Well, I just finished my last exam. I'm finally through with school. I'm going to play tennis to celebrate." That's exactly what she said. And that was exactly the way she celebrated her graduation from high school. A month later she moved away.

Since there were no prospective Jewish husbands anywhere near Sheho, plans for the future of my older sisters had been made and approved years in advance. After Merle graduated from high school, she would continue to live at home until Etta also graduated. In the meantime, Merle would teach piano lessons in neighboring towns, occasionally staying overnight before going on to the next town or returning home. She would also help out in the store on Saturdays. In three years, after Etta completed high school, both would move to Winnipeg to begin secretarial careers and meet nice Jewish boys, some of whom they would date while seeking a prospective husband who would support them in the manner to which they were accustomed. (And having lived in Sheho, that "manner" was not exactly unattainable.)

One evening toward the end of July in 1943, our family accompanied Merle and Etta to the station. After they boarded the train for Winnipeg, we returned home. For the first time in my life, it seemed empty. There were still four of us living in that house, but it just wasn't the same. I realized that all my life I had taken my older sisters for granted because they were always there. Now they were gone. I felt lonely and I knew Sylvia felt the same. I looked at Mom and Dad who kept taking off their glasses to wipe their eyes. I didn't say anything. What could I say? Sometimes it's just better to keep quiet. Besides, in two years I would also be gone. Then there would be only three left in our home. The exodus had begun.

CHAPTER TWENTY-THREE
Loneliness

I had always wanted a dog for a pet. In fact, my first memory is the morning Sylvia was born. When the nurse told me the doctor had brought me a baby sister, I angrily replied, "I'd rather have a dog." A couple of years later I thought my wish had been fulfilled when I adopted a long-haired black dog that a farmer had left behind. I quickly named my pet Blackie. When its master returned a few weeks later, the dog followed the team of horses back to the farm and I was left crying. Although I could always pet Walter Lys's dog, Tootsie, then later Bonnie, it wasn't the same. Then while in the seventh grade, I came close to sort of adopting another pet. After a deer hunting trip, Frank Wunder brought home a fawn after its mother had been shot. The fawn used to walk along the snow covered highway every day, all the way into town. I would meet it on the road and hold out a slice of bread, which it grabbed and ate. In time it would eat out of my hands and eventually I could even pet it before it would scamper off, its white under tail waving good-bye. Then one day I missed my fawn. Some dogs had killed it.

A few years later, when I was in grade ten, a small, skinny female black-and-white dog wandered into our yard. I wasn't about to ask questions. I fed her and petted her and named her Lupa, which I remembered from my ninth grade Latin meant "she wolf." Now I had a dog I could pet and play with. I quickly fell in love with Lupa.

Our town constable, Ed Howe, whose duties besides hanging up the four gas burning lanterns every night included shooting stray dogs, was not happy about my Lupa. He knew it had been a stray, and more than once he demanded that he be allowed to shoot it. "Not my dog!" I replied. Then one day Lupa began running around in circles, foaming at the mouth. Shocked and frightened, I quickly ran to tell Mr. Howe. Within minutes he was in our yard with his loaded .22 rifle. I watched as he carefully aimed his rifle at Lupa. Holding back my tears, I watched Lupa standing still, her mouth covered with white foam.

"BANG." Lupa keeled over.

"I told you before to let me shoot her," he shouted as he picked up the limp corpse and walked away. I hid behind the chicken coop. I did not want anyone to see me cry.

A few weeks before I entered grade eleven, Mrs. Illchuk, who lived on a small farm about half a mile beyond the Western bridge, came into the store as she did almost every day, to chat with Mom and occasionally buy some dry goods. Her husband was Ukrainian and she was German. I thought that was an odd match. He always spoke Ukrainian and she spoke German or broken English. On her way out she told me her dog just had puppies and asked me if I'd care to come over some time and take a look at them. She was going to give them away. Without hesitation I said, "I'll be over tomorrow afternoon. "

Now at last, I would have my own pet dog. A real pet—not a stray. Nobody could take it away from me. That's what I told myself as I passed the railway crossing on the highway and walked up the road to Illchuk's cabin. I hadn't told anyone else, though, not even Mom and Dad. I suppose I was afraid of what they might say. Besides, it would be my dog. I would be the one who would take care of it. Why would they object?

Both Mr. and Mrs. Illchuk showed me the litter. They were all sand-colored, short-haired puppies, all five of them, the cutest puppies I had ever seen. They looked like a cross between a Pomeranian and a Boxer— a tiny boxer. "I'd like to see that one." Mrs.Illchuk pushed their mother aside. I picked up the cutest one and held him in my cupped hands. He squirmed for a few seconds. Then his moist little black nose sniffed my hands, and he licked my fingers. "May I have him?" The Illchuks nodded. "Thank you very much." I would give him a royal name from Latin— Rex—meaning "King."

As I walked home along the railway tracks, I held him close to my chest and zipped up my leather jacket to protect him from the cool afternoon. He cried at first, but soon settled down and was sleeping under my jacket. Suddenly I realized that whenever I had asked Mom if I could keep a dog inside our home, her edict was, "*Ich vill nicht hoben kein hint in shteeb.* " Translated, the ultimatum was "I will not have a dog in the house." Well, I would simply surprise her. The worst that could happen to her would be a heart attack. When I got home I unzipped my jacket and said to Mom, "Look, isn't he cute?"

Instead of going into cardiac arrest, she smiled as I had never seen her smile before and almost childlike said, "*Er is a kleina.*" Then, to make sure I understood, "He's a little one."

I held him up to her. At first she barely touched him. Then, gingerly she began to pet him. " He's so small," she said. "You got him from Mrs. Illchuk?" I nodded. "You're going to keep him?" Then, without waiting for my reply, she said, "Come. The engine house. We'll make him in the engine house a nice place to sleep. He needs a blanket. And a box. Maybe he needs water. Maybe he's hungry. He needs milk. Bring him some milk in a saucer. *Er is a pitzel. Zere sheyne. A pitzel.* [He is a tiny one. Very beautiful. So tiny.]

That night we put him in a blanket-lined cardboard box, his bed that Mom had made after clearing out some clutter in the engine house. Poor Rex! It was dark inside and he was all alone. He cried all night, keeping us awake. I was afraid Dad would be so upset he would tell me to give him back. But all Dad said was "Did you hear him cry?"

"No! I didn't hear a thing."

"Your puppy cried all night. Maybe tonight he won't cry."

Dad was right. It took Rex only one night to get used to his new bed. In the morning he had the entire yard to explore. And when Mom was out of the house, I took him inside. Within weeks, I smuggled him inside my bedroom at night. I think Mom knew, but she didn't say anything.

Rex made friends with our chickens, which we sometimes allowed outside their pen. Occasionally they laid eggs in the tall grass. In the morning Rex would pick up an egg in his mouth and bring it to our back porch, where Mom or Dad would find it. At other times he dropped it at their feet. "Look what your Rex found in the grass from the chickens," they would say. "They hide in the grass their eggs. He knows we want the eggs. So he hunts in the grass for the eggs. Then brings them to us. He's such a smart dog."

Within a month he was no longer tiny, just small. I needed two hands to hold him, all three pounds of him. I was tired of people saying, "What a cute little puppy!" So one day when Renee Holmes asked me what breed he was, I replied, "He's a pure bred Siberian wolfhound."

"Oh, I didn't think they were that small," she said. Soon word got around town that I was raising a Siberian wolfhound.

One Sunday afternoon when our usual visitors were at our home, Mr. Leckie and Mr. Teskey asked me to get them something from our store. Both of them accompanied me, with Rex following behind. Just as I was about to unlock the door, I caught a glimpse of Rex running onto the highway. At that very moment a car came speeding by. In an instant the car was gone and Rex lay on the road—motionless.

"They ran over Rex, I cried. "They killed him. They didn't even stop. He's dead." I broke down and sobbed uncontrollably.

Mr. Leckie tried to console me. "I'm sorry," he said. "Get me a shovel. We'll take him out to the field and bury him."

I cradled his soft limp body in my arms as we walked toward the field. Mr. Leckie dug a deep hole and took the limp body from me. He placed the body inside the hole and covered it with earth. I sobbed all the way back to our house.

With the loss of Rex coupled with my older sisters' departure to Winnipeg earlier that month, I felt more lonely than I had ever felt before. I spent most of my time in the store until school started, as it always did, on August 26th. Now I was in grade eleven, with only two more years of high school left before I would go away to university.

Bashful, blushing, handsome Stan Gorchinsky, who had been our principal for the last half of the previous year, had moved to the next room where he obviously was now more comfortable teaching the lower grades of seven through nine. Sylvia adored him, not as she might a movie star, but as a wonderful, gentle, caring teacher. When she learned that he was leaving Sheho at the beginning of the new year for another teaching position, she brought him a gift as she said good-bye and broke down crying.

Stan's older brother John was our new principal. He was a tall, husky, huge man with a big head and sparkling eyes that looked squarely at you when he lectured or slowly answered your questions in a friendly, self-assured, resonant baritone voice. Although he spoke with a slight Ukrainian accent, it did not distract from his position. His very appearance and stature commanded authority. I don't think anyone in our class ever dreamed of irritating him let alone disobeying him. Yet in spite of his size, he reminded me of a big friendly dog. I liked him immediately.

I also took a liking to his son, Walter, a twelfth grader, who sat directly across the aisle from me in the row of seats next to the window. There were seven in grade twelve, seven in grade eleven—only four of whom were from my original first grade class —and four in grade ten. Our ranks were thinning every year. If it weren't for the students who had transferred in from their one-room farm schools, our room would be practically empty.

Wally Gorchinsky told me that his dad had a reason for never losing his temper. Some years before, while teaching high school in a rough-and tumble village, Mr. Gorchinsky had lost his temper when an unruly student, the town bully, had challenged him to a fight. "Dad just picked up that guy with one hand and threw him out the window. Just like that. Dad has never lost his temper since then."

Wally wore a dress shirt and tie and a brown porcupine-blocked felt hat to school every day. He also wore a red pony-horsehide leather jacket that sold for $12.50 in Eaton's catalog, subject to supplies on hand. Walter Lys wore a green one that his dad had ordered for him from their wholesaler. Leather jackets were now in style. Amidst protests from Dad, I went out on a limb and ordered eight from our wholesaler in assorted colors. The wholesaler was in collusion with Henry Ford, who once said, "We can build your car in any color you want, as long as it's black." Guess what color we got? The jackets cost us $11.00 each. It was the most expensive item in men's clothing that we had ever carried. We sold them almost immediately for the same price as Eaton's. Dad was amazed. He now gave me virtually a free hand to do the buying for men's clothing, under the supervision of Mom and Henry Ford.

School was another matter. Mom and Henry Ford weren't there. Instead we were supervised by Big John Gorchinksy, who was not interested in what color leather jackets anyone wore or what kind of parkas Jackie Katz had ordered for Katz General Store or what kind of ladies' coats the store had recently bought from Continental Cloak for $18.00 each and sold for $25.00 plus one percent education tax. Big John was interested in only one thing: teaching.

Every night he carried home a catalog case full of textbooks that weighed almost as much as the fifty pound sack of Foam Lake flour that Jackie Katz could now lift with both hands and carry out to the farmer's wagon. And every morning Mr. Gorchinsky returned with the same catalog case full of books plus notebooks filled with hand-written notes that he would copy on the blackboard for each lesson in each subject in each grade, from ten through twelve. Big John may have been a friendly pussycat, but he had no time for jokes or stories, even from Jackie Katz. And he had absolutely no time for nonsense.

Unfortunately, I thought Euclid's plane geometry was sheer nonsense. But I never voiced my opinion. Far be it for me to tell Big John Gorchinsky what I thought of Euclid's theorems and corollaries. Who cared? That's why I never learned them. And that's why I could never answer the questions in the back of the book about proving one stupid angle inside a stupid triangle was equal to another. Once you've seen one triangle, you've seen them all, even if they're sideways or upside down. A triangle is a triangle —no matter what kind of angles they contain. That's Katz's theorem. But don't ask me to prove it.

I never asked Mr. Gorchinsky for help in geometry. I didn't want him to think I was stupid. I may have been ignorant but I wasn't stupid. That's why I became friends with Walter Hudyma, one of four transfer students in our class who had taken correspondence courses on the farm for their first two years of high school but had now come to town to complete the last two years. He tried to help me understand geometry. It was like trying to help me understand hieroglyphics.

Both he and his classmate Johnny Shewchuk, lived in a little one-room unpainted wooden shack, right next to our yard. The shack had been built two years before by Mr. Joe Sebulski when his son decided to complete high school in Sheho. Now it provided low income housing for two needy students. Walter Hudyma had very poor eyesight but his parents never bought him glasses. Although he held the book right up to his eyes when he read, that did not hinder him from studying. He studied all the time and answered all the geometry problems in the back of the book. By contrast, Johnny had excellent eyesight, especially when he played pool, which was most of the time. He learned all there was to know about angles the easy way—at the pool table. He knew more than Euclid. He answered all the questions with ease.

Whenever I took an interest in a subject, I did quite well. I liked chemistry. It made sense to me; so even though I was in the eleventh grade, I took grade twelve chemistry. We had no chemistry lab to speak of. Consequently, our class was unable to do the experiments. Fortunately, the final exam was not based on experiments, and I received 92% as my final mark. I also did well in English, partly because I loved Shakespeare and partly because Mr. Gorchinsky's strength was in teaching the liberal arts. As for Euclid's geometry, I won't tell you exactly what I received on my final geometry exam, except to say that I did not fail that course. I'm sure the reader in Regina who graded my paper apparently believed there was a fine line between 49% (a failing mark) and 50% (the lowest possible passing mark). I'm also sure he was much too kind and much too generous. But I never complained. I believe in the old saying, "Never look a gift horse in the mouth."

The loneliness I had felt at the beginning of the school term gradually disappeared as the school year progressed and I became engrossed in school work and helping out in the store. I would usually stay in the classroom for an hour after school to do some of my homework and then help out in the store until it closed. After supper I went back to the store to unpack any orders we had received that day and then finish my homework under the dazzling white light of the Coleman compressed air gasoline burning lamp. I liked the solitude of the night; there were no interruptions. The only sound was the continuous hiss from the jet of forced air being thrust from the tiny valve of the Coleman lamp as it illuminated the darkness. I lost track of time, and since I had no watch, I stayed until I had finished my work or was too tired to do any more. As I turned the black knob which shut off the air, the hissing instantly stopped, the white glow from the mantles began to fade, then sputtered into shades of orange, purple, and blue, before finally fading into darkness, a darkness that matched the color of the sky on a moonless night. And as I locked the door and looked up into southeast sky, Orion the Hunter with his sword pointing to Sirus the dog star—the brightest star in the heavens— reminded me of the season, the month, and the hour. It was late.

Late in the fall on the Canadian Prairies, the weather turns cold at night and white frost covers the roofs, while thin layers of ice form along the ponds and lakes. Overhead, dark clouds drift in ominously from the northwest, gathering together, threatening the earth below with freezing weather, snow, and eventually winter. Below, the ground lies barren, waiting, waiting for the white blanket to cover its nakedness. It won't be long now. It's freezing cold.

You go to bed at night and throw on an extra blanket. During the night a miracle occurs. When you wake up in the morning, all you see is white. The earth has been transformed. It is now covered with a blanket of pure white snow. I cannot remember exactly how old I was when I awoke in the morning to my first snowfall. I was probably three—about the time Sylvia was born. But each year afterward, I marveled at the first snowfall of the season. It seemed miraculous. A pure white blanket on the ground! It cleanses the soul.

That winter—when I was in grade eleven—time passed quickly. Every Sunday, as long as the highway remained open, the Teskey family from Wynyard continued to visit us around noon. One Sunday they were joined by the Orloffs from Foam Lake, who brought along the new doctor in town.

Dr. Irving Miller was a handsome young man of twenty-four, with black hair and dark brown eyes. He had graduated from medical college at the University of Manitoba the year before and had just completed his internship. He had just taken over the practice of Dr. Rubin who was now with the Canadian Army Medical Corps. We had seen Dr. Miller drive through Sheho on special house calls, including some as far away as thirty miles from his Foam Lake office. He was bright, friendly, full of energy, talkative, Jewish, and engaged. What more could we ask for in our doctor? We liked him immediately.

I'm sure he felt at home with us, especially after Mom's Sunday dinner. In fact, he became a regular visitor on Sundays, even after he married his sweetheart from Winnipeg, Rita Shenkarow. We embraced the Millers as family and were thrilled when they brought their newly born infant, Marilyn, along for Sunday dinner. I had just bought a baby brownie Kodak camera and took a snapshot of them holding little Marilyn. All one can see in that little Kodak brownie snapshot, which I still have, is Dr. Miller and Rita holding a bundle, inside of which is a tiny face. It was the first snapshot, I believe, of their first born child.

My little camera must have been designed especially for me because it was so simple to operate. No light meter, no focusing, nothing. All I had to do was to squint through a tiny view finder opening until I saw whatever I wanted to photograph, click a tiny spring, and that was it. A perfect, tiny, black-and-white snapshot. The only problem was I didn't know how to load the film. But that didn't bother me. I always found somebody who knew how.

In late spring of that year, Sylvia took a snapshot of Dad, Mom, and me. I still have that snapshot. Dad is dressed in his one -and-only suit, Mom is in her fur coat, and in the middle, wearing my tweed suit, which by now was almost too small, I tower above both of them. I was now almost five feet five inches tall. But alongside them, I felt like a giant.

I told Dr. Miller about my plans to become a doctor and asked him about the rigors of the course. "It's hard," he said; then added, "I remember smoking cigarette after cigarette well into the night." Although I didn't smoke and never studied well into the night, I thought I could do both if I had to. Then I asked him about the University's discrimination policy against Jewish students applying for medical college. "It's getting better," he replied. "They let in eight this year." Eight out of a few hundred, I thought. Those odds weren't too encouraging. Perhaps I had better find out about the University of Saskatchewan. But I still had another year of high school left before I made my decision.

On June 6th of that year, less than two weeks before our grade eleven final exams began, I turned on the radio while I was eating breakfast.

Every station carried the news flash. D-Day had arrived. General Eisenhower announced that allied troops had landed on the coast of Normandy. The First Canadian Army was part of the invasion force. At school, that's all we could talk about. Everyone in town was excited. It won't be long now until we win the war. That's what we all thought. But in the back of our minds we knew there would be heavy casualties, and death. And some of our boys would never make it home.

CHAPTER TWENTY-FOUR
Major Changes

The summer of 1944 brought major changes into my life. Before joining the service, my buddy Howard Tansley had been advised by Mr. Curry, our station agent, to submit an application for a job with the Canadian Pacific Railway so that when he got out of the service, he would receive seniority with the company. Exactly one day after completing his final grade twelve exams, Howard submitted the application, then immediately joined the Canadian Army. Shortly afterward, I learned that Walter Lys's father had sold his store to Bill Kuproski, a country-school teacher, and that Walter and Jenny would be moving to Yorkton to complete high school. Although Mr. and Mrs. Lys would remain in town, my very closest buddy would be gone. Furthermore, with Jenny's departure, there would be only two of us left from my original first grade class. As for the change of ownership in Lys's store, since Bill Kuproski was a novice in retailing and obviously knew very little about the soft goods business, we were bound to gain those customers who had previously bought their clothing and footwear from Mr. Lys. This assumption influenced Mom's decision to take me to Winnipeg for a buying trip later in the summer. Besides, it had been almost a year since I had seen my older sisters, Merle and Etta.

I had not traveled to Winnipeg since I had gone with Mom ten years before, when her brother Dave Izen had gotten married. I was only a little boy then, in Miss Griffiths's second grade class. Now, at the age of sixteen, about to enter my final year of high school, and going on a buying trip with Mom, I thought I was a young man—almost grown up. That's what I told myself. But the truth is I was just as excited as the first time. The only difference is that Mom and I had separate sleepers this time and, therefore, I could not keep asking her questions every time the train stopped.

When we got off the train in Winnipeg and walked downstairs into the huge station, I was almost as amazed and bewildered by the crowds as before; and when we got outside and I saw signal lights and all the traffic—cars, busses and clanging street cars —I once more felt like a six-year-old. Thank goodness I'm with Mom, I told myself; otherwise I'd be lost. Winnipeg is not Yorkton. Three hundred thousand population is not five thousand. And a taxi ride from the Canadian Pacific Railway station to the seven hundred block of Pritchard Avenue is not like walking a few blocks from the Yorkton Hotel to the synagogue.

Mom's father's sister, whom we all called "Auntie Leachman," had lost her husband since I had last been in Winnipeg, when they had lived at 713 Selkirk Avenue. Auntie Leachman now lived in a house around the corner on Pritchard Avenue, along with her daughter Mabel (Mom's first cousin, who was actually my second cousin), and Mabel's husband Bill Cutler and their young daughter Jackie (Mom's second cousin, who was actually my third cousin.). It gets worse.

Now, during the summer holidays, besides having Mom and me as house guests, they had one extra member of this extended family— the eighteen year old son of Auntie Leachman's oldest daughter Bessie and her husband Sam Lackman, from Long Beach, California. Since Larry Lackman was Mom's cousin's son, he was actually her second cousin and, therefore, my third cousin. And since he was my third cousin, he was also the third cousin of all my sisters, including Etta. Far be it for me to leave any doubt in one's mind about the relationship and courtship of any members of this extended family. But that comes later. In the meantime, we all felt as if we were one big happy family.

Ever since Merle and Etta had moved to Winnipeg, they had looked forward to Friday night, when they had gone to Bill and Mable's home for Friday night supper, their one good meal of the week. At first they had made arrangements with the Goldbergs on Manitoba Avenue for room and board; but after tasting Mrs. Goldberg's meals, they decided to take up light-housekeeping and prepare their own meals—except for

Friday night. Mabel's delicious meals were the highlight of their week. Besides dating.

They had both graduated from Success Business College and had taken office jobs—Merle with Crosstown Motors, and Etta with Dominion Furs. But their long term goal was to meet and eventually marry a nice Jewish young man. And how do you find a nice Jewish young man? Simple. By attending different affairs at the "Y" as in Young Men's Hebrew Association. And by dating.

Winnipeg did not suffer from a shortage of young Jewish men, even though most of the healthy ones were now in the armed forces. But the city did suffer from a shortage of gasoline, which was rationed. Besides, not every Jewish bachelor had a car. However, even though Winnipeg was considerably larger than Yorkton, its streetcars and buses were more than adequate to transport a couple from Manitoba Avenue to the movie theaters or the Roseland Dance Gardens on Portage Avenue for their Saturday night date. Every Saturday night Merle, as well as Etta, would each go out on the town with her date and another couple. It was called "double dating." Double dating was the first stage in dating. If a particular couple liked each other, they would eventually go on a date by themselves, even if they had to take the streetcar— which was most of the time. If they didn't particularly care for each other, they would go back to double dating. That way they could play the field until they found the right one.

By the time I visited them, they had both double dated numerous times and had even gone out on more than a few single dates, but that was all. Although Merle was dating Saul, a nice young Jewish man rather regularly, she was far from getting serious about him. And Etta had barely passed the preliminary stage of double dating. So when "our" (third) cousin Larry Lackman at first began spending a little more time with Etta than with the rest of us, we hardly noticed. Everyone has preferences. Besides, he was closer to her age than to Merle's and he made a convenient double date with Etta whenever Merle asked them to join her and Saul for a movie or dance. However, when I accompanied the four of them on an all day riverboat cruise down the Red River to Lockport, I began having second thoughts about my "third" cousin and Etta. He seemed to be hugging her awfully close when I took snapshots of them with my little Kodak Baby Brownie. [I still have those snaps.]

Larry, who had just graduated from high school in Long Beach, California, was no stranger to Winnipeg. In previous years, whenever his mother took her vacation in Winnipeg, he often accompanied her on the three-day bus trip from Long Beach. This time he had come alone to spend the entire summer with his grandmother and cousins before returning to join the United States Navy. Although he was only 1 1/2 years older than I, he spoke as if he were a man of the world, all wise and all knowing, especially about men's clothing. And since I had outgrown my size 36 suit, I was glad when he agreed to help me look for a new one.

I still thought about a brown suit with white chalk stripes, but Larry insisted that I did not fit the gangster image. " A solid color will look best on you, " he said. " Tan or brown wool gabardine. That's what you should get if we can find it." So we started looking for a gabardine suit in Winnipeg's largest department stores, but we couldn't find a single one.

Then we hurriedly went from one men's clothing store to another on Portage Avenue, sliding in and out of those spit-and-polished hardwood floors on which I almost fell until I realized that Louis Katz did not oil these wooden floors with thick black machine oil to keep the dust down. Nor did the farmers spit sunflower seeds and throw peanut shells and chocolate bar wrappers and all kinds of other refuse on them, as they did on the oiled softwood floors of Katz General Store. No siree. These were the smoothest, most slippery hardwood floors in the most fashionable men's ready-to-wear stores in Winnipeg, right on Portage Avenue, no less. Gregoree the Doukhobor did not come here to sit on a broken chair and spend the entire morning telling tall tales about his heroic adventures shoveling coal into the furnaces of the Tsar's battleship during the Russo-Japanese War of 1904-1905, all the while chewing sunflower seeds and spitting their husks on the floor as he reminisced. Not on this floor on Portage Avenue. No siree. If your shoes didn't have rubber heels, you could slide from the west end of Portage Avenue all the way east to Main street if the hardwood floors were that long. I was glad I had learned how to skate. But without rubber heels, it was hard to stop.

"Do you have any wool gabardine suits?"

"No."

I slid right around the salesman and back out the door.

And so it went, from store to store, every one of them. "Do you have any gabardine suits?"

The salesman stared at me, then slowly began to answer. "There's none to be had." But it was too late to stop. I grabbed the showcase, then turned around and slid out the door.

We slid in and out of every men's clothing store on both sides of Portage Avenue, with the answer always the same. "No," or "Sorry." Even the stores with carpeted floors had no gabardine suits, not in my size anyway. Why should a scrawny kid who wears only size 37 be entitled to a gabardine suit? That's what the salesmen might just as well have said.

Finally, just as I was about to give up hope, we walked into a store in which a salesman was about to finish vacuuming the thickly piled carpet on the floor. We waited. He nodded at us, then put down the vacuum cleaner. "Hi. May I help you?"

I might as well blurt it out. "Do you have any gabardine suits?"

He nodded. " We just got in a few. What size?"

"37"

"I think we have one left." I could hardly believe his answer. He led me toward the rack. "Yes. Here's one." He pulled it off the rack and held it out. Medium brown, it looked stunning. I tried on the coat. It fit. I took the coat off and tried on the vest. It was loose. "You won't wear the vest," said Larry. "Nobody wears a vest in California." If nobody wears a vest in California where all the movie stars live, why should I wear one in Saskatchewan? We left the vest alone. Then I tried on the pants. They were a little loose at the waist and the tailor wanted to take them in. But I told him exactly what Mickey Nathenson had said less than a year before when my suit pants had been a little loose: "You'll grow into them." Now they were too small. So all the tailor did was sew the cuffs. The salesman packed the suit in a cardboard box and handed me back two singles from my forty dollars. As I left the store, carrying the box under my arm, I felt as if I were now an adult, the owner of a fine, expensive suit, as good as any on display at Crolls in Yorkton, or any store in Winnipeg. For the first time in my life, I really felt grown up.

I spent almost two weeks in Winnipeg, the first accompanying Mom on her rounds to the different wholesalers and factories, after I had bought my suit. I was surprised to learn that she not only knew which streetcar to take to the garment district, but how well she knew her way around that entire area. She introduced me to the Brotman brothers who owned Canadian Garment Limited, and she gave me a free hand when I ordered men's parkas and club jackets and wool tweed pants for the store. From there we went to Continental Cloak where we bought ladies' fall and winter coats, and then to Nozick Commission for ladies' dresses, blouses and skirts. On my own, I went to Peerless Garments, owned by Ronnie Glassman, to whom Merle had introduced me. His factory manufactured leather jackets. Although they were in very short supply, I could now buy all we needed and save money, since I was buying them direct from the maker instead of from Kays Limited. Even after paying Ronnie one dollar under the table for each jacket, I still saved almost two dollars per jacket.

The next stops were with Mom accompanying me: Patrick's Limited for shoes, Karaskick's Limited for soft goods, and on to Kays Limited, where I ordered men's brown melton overcoats—the most expensive item we had ever ordered for the store—as well as flannel shirts, under-wear, woolen stockings and everything else we normally ordered from that wholesale house. I also bought a wool gabardine topcoat and a black wool Elysian winter overcoat for myself, and three beautiful silk ties. I would be going away to university the following year and now was as good a time as ever to begin getting my wardrobe.

With her buying for the store completed, Mom returned home alone, while I stayed in Winnipeg for another week. By now, having learned what streetcars went downtown, I bravely ventured out on my own every afternoon to the movie theaters on Main Street and Portage Avenue. I felt as if I were an explorer who had suddenly discovered the North-west Passage. But instead of leading to the Pacific, it led to Dreamland direct from Hollywood. What better way to spend an entire afternoon than sitting in a plush-lined armchair in the cool comfort of a darkened movie theater, watching John Wayne and other Hollywood heroes sweating in the sultry jungles of the South Pacific as they heroically battled the Japanese, sometimes man-to-man, suffering heavy losses, but finally winning. Japanese, Germans, or Indians—the outcome was guaranteed when they encountered John Wayne. When the battle ended, I awoke to reality, only to leave one theater and enter another. All afternoon. It was pure escape. I saw more movies in one week than I had seen in the previous ten years. By the time I left Winnipeg, I didn't care if I never saw another John Wayne movie for the rest of my life. Some hero? I wondered why *he* wasn't in the service.

After returning home, I told my parents I would like to visit Laskins in Rose Valley to learn all I could from Shimon about making merchandise more visible to the customer in order to increase sales. They knew that for the past year he had been my mentor, giving me tips on merchandising, including what he bought from specific clothing factories and why he chose one over another. They also knew that he was largely responsible for the success of his father's store, and whatever advice I had received from Shimon had proved to be beneficial. Both Mom and Dad agreed with my plan. Shortly before school started, I took the train north to Rose Valley. I was now almost eighty miles north of Sheho, away up in northern Saskatchewan, only a few thousand miles from the Arctic Circle. The daytime temperature was still eighty degrees Fahrenheit, the same as in Sheho. Only there weren't as many flies here as at home. Laskins didn't have a cow and, therefore, they didn't have a manure pile.

Both Mr. and Mrs. Laskin fussed over me as though they hadn't seen me for a decade and I had been starving all that time. "Here, have some more," they said, as they shoveled more food onto my plate which was almost empty. I realized now why Mr. Laskin was fatter than my dad. He was not shy about taking seconds.

Shimon pointed out how the layout of their store differed from most general stores. Instead of having the grocery section visible immediately to the customers as soon as they entered, with clothing and footwear hidden at the back of the store, Laskin's layout was the exact opposite. All the clothing—both men's and women's—as well as the footwear section, was up front; and the groceries were at the back. "When customers come into the store for groceries," he said, "they'll have to walk through the store to get to them. In the meantime, they're forced to see our clothing section. That way they know we stock clothing. And when they know we have certain items, it leaves an impression in their mind, so the next time they need clothing or shoes, they'll remember where to buy them, instead of the catalog."

His younger brother Mervin had received his Bachelor of Science Degree from the University of Saskatchewan a few months earlier and had recently been accepted into its School of Medicine. He had been doing research with Dr. Altschul of the histology department during the summer but was now home for a brief vacation before going back to Saskatoon to begin his first year of medical studies. I told him I was planning to go to Winnipeg the following year to study premedicine and asked him which university he thought had a more lenient policy toward accepting Jewish applicants into medical college. His reply shocked me. "They both have very strict quotas," he said, "but the only university that's more anti-Semitic than the University of Manitoba is the University of Berlin." I felt an immediate lump in my throat. My mouth was suddenly dry. My plans had taken an abrupt 180 degree turn. Instead of joining my sisters in Winnipeg, where my parents would also eventually move, probably in a couple of years, I would now be going to Saskatoon, a strange city, where the only person I knew besides Merv was my cousin Rachel Katz. Well, at least I had another year at home before going away.

As soon as I returned home, I explained the layout of Laskin's Store to Dad and Mom and told them why I thought we would benefit from remodeling our store. "You mean you want to move the groceries to the back?" asked Dad.

"Yes, that's the idea. Everyone knows we carry groceries. But not everyone knows we carry parkas and leather jackets and club jackets and overcoats. That's what I want them to see as soon as they come in. We make a hell of a lot more money on clothing than on groceries. And I want a deck built over our counters so we can put flannel shirts and caps and sweaters on top for the customers to see and help themselves. I want to put everything out in the open so they can see it. When they see what we have, they'll buy. And if they don't buy the first time, at least they'll know where to come when they're ready to buy."

I had thought Dad would resist such a drastic remodeling of our store, but he had seen our sales increase dramatically during the past two years due to the more expensive clothing items we now stocked. Within a week he hired a carpenter to build a deck over the counters I indicated. Then just before school started, he hired some other help to move the entire grocery section, heavy counters and all the groceries, to the back of the store. In their place was the shoe section. And, at the very front, was the men's clothing section, including a rack of overcoats. When customers walked in, they were aghast at the change. Where were the groceries? What were men's overcoats doing here? Katz General Store had been transformed into a clothing store.

When school started, I ordered the required textbooks from Regina; but since I didn't think I would miss instruction until they arrived, I stayed home for a few days to work in the store because farmers needed extra groceries to feed their harvesting crews.

During harvest time the farmers would hire extra help, first of all, to stack the sheaves of grain that had been cut and tied by the binder into larger bundles called "stooks." Then, after all the grain had been stooked, the workers pitched the heavy stooks into a wagon which the horses then pulled toward the steam-driven threshing machine. Finally, the threshing crew pitched the stooks into the threshing machine which poured out a stream of grain into another wagon that was then pulled toward the granary to be unloaded. Depending on the size of the farm and the size of the work crew, the harvest could last anywhere from one to three weeks. During this time the main course for the lunches between the main meals was invariably bologna or ringed garlic sausage known as "kielbasa." And since hard outdoor work contributes to hearty appetites, there was always a great demand for both garlic sausage and kielbasa during the last week of August and first two weeks of September.

The problem with stocking these hardy cold cuts is that without refrigeration, they don't stay fresh very long in the open air grocery shelves, especially when the weather is hot. And since one can usually count on a heat wave just when the harvest season is about to begin, and since

Sheho did not have electricity, let alone refrigerators, Dad was afraid to stock bologna and kielbasa lest he throw out more than he would sell.

Someone—I believe it was a grocery traveler—had told me that these meats would be as fresh as the day they were made if they could be kept covered in a salty brine solution. In the little room inside our warehouse stood a large empty crock that Dad had once used for making pickles and also Concord wine for Passover. It was perfect. I told him about my discovery—homemade refrigeration. We could now order all the bologna and kielbasa we wanted and none of it would spoil. During the next month we sold more "fresh" bologna and kielbasa than anyone in town. It always looked as fresh as on the day it was made. I never realized, however, that it absorbed all that extra salt. But I guess the farmers and their work crews loved the flavor. They always came back for more. And so did other customers. Although the other storekeepers stocked these perishable meats, Katz's kielbasa was always fresh. Besides, it had a special flavor of its own. One of the storekeepers once asked me where we got our sausage from. "I'm afraid I can't tell you," I said. " It's a trade secret."

When I returned to school, I was elated that big John Gorchinsky was still our principal. I had grown very fond of him. He was glad to learn that I would be going on to the University of Saskatchewan after completing grade twelve. That's where he had received his Bachelor of Arts degree. He spoke lovingly of one of his English professors. That was the first time I had ever heard a teacher compliment any professor. It was obvious that Professor Matheson had left quite an impression on my principal. Perhaps I, too, would be lucky to take a class from Professor Matheson.

This year, instead of sitting in the back of the classroom, I took a seat up front, in the first desk. Right behind me was Walter Hudyma, still without eye glasses, and still my next door neighbor at Sebulsky's shack. The builder and owner of the "Sheho Hilton," Mr. Sebulsky, had not yet painted his wooden one-room shack, right next to our yard. It was the only unpainted building on our street. I once thought of asking Dad to donate a quart of paint to Mr. Sebulsky to spruce up the outside of the

Hilton, but since he was not our regular customer, I knew what Dad's reply would be; so I dropped the idea. In addition to Walter Hudyma, who had been with me the previous year after transferring from his one-room farm school, we were now joined by a new transfer student—Martha Kulak, the only girl in our class. She was rather reserved. She sat at the very back of the room, almost out of sight, and hardly ever said a word unless someone spoke to her. I spoke to her once. I said "How are you?" She replied, "Okay." That's all she said. And that was all I said. It was the shortest conversation I ever had. I think she occasionally spoke to Johnny Koropatniski, who sat right in front of her. I think he felt sorry for her. So did I. But Johnny sat closer to her than I did. Besides, he was a better conversationalist.

I was saddened to see that Johnny Koropatniski was my only class-mate remaining from my original first grade class of twenty-nine. Most of the boys were now in the army or air force. Others had gone away to work in war plant factories in Hamilton or Windsor, Ontario. Not only were Johnny Koropatniski and I the only survivors from the first year when we had started school in Miss Griffiths's class, but we were now the oldest boys in town who were actually from the village of Sheho. He was seventeen; I was a year younger. Then one day, shortly after he turned eighteen, he left school to join the army. Now, at the age of six-teen, or barely seventeen, I was the oldest Sheho boy left in the entire village.

A few weeks after school started and the crops had been harvested, I wrote a letter to the weekly newspaper in Foam Lake, the only printer in our entire area. I ordered a few hundred flyers to be printed and speci-fied what I wanted advertised and the prices : For ladies— winter coats, dresses, blouses, skirts and ski suits. For men: overcoats, parkas, leather jackets, club jackets, tweed pants, and flannel shirts. When the flyers arrived, I took about a hundred to our postmaster, Arthur Merritt, and asked him to distribute them in all the mail boxes in town, as well as to all the families who picked up their general delivery mail at the wicket. I then mailed packages containing the rest of the flyers to the postmas-ters in our neighboring villages with the same request. I was following the advice Shimon Laskin had given me. Within weeks—and throughout that fall—new customers began coming in not only from Sheho but from villages as far away as twenty-five miles. Our business boomed. From yearly sales of only $12,000 to $14,000 a year during the Depression, the annual sales in our store now exceeded $22,000. Dad had never dreamed that such business was possible in Sheho.

As I had done the year before, I stayed after school to do my homework. Only this time I did not have to worry about Euclid's theorems. Instead, we had a different kind of geometry—analytical geometry, the geometry of spheres and cubes. I loved it. I also loved trigonometry. And I was even beginning to like algebra. In fact, I liked most of my subjects except French. So, like a bad dream which I hoped would disappear in time if I left it alone, I tried to forget my French lessons and did an excellent job at it. It's easy to forget something you hate, especially if you try hard enough.

A couple of weeks before the start of the Jewish High Holy Days, Dad enclosed train tickets in his letter to my sisters in Winnipeg, asking them to come home for the Holidays, so that we could all celebrate them together in Yorkton. It had been over a year since he had last seen them. I would be going away to Saskatoon the following year, and he probably sensed that this might be the last time we would all be together for the Jewish holidays.

In Yorkton, he took us to Russell Studios, where we had a black-and-white family portrait taken. Mom, in a new black dress, was seated on Dad's left. She had a slight smile and looked as young and pretty as ever. Dad, dressed in his latest three-piece suit that he had bought only three years before and wearing one of the three silk ties I had recently bought in Winnipeg, looked sternly ahead at the photographer as if to say, "This is costing me plenty, so you better take a good picture of my beautiful wife, my three beautiful daughters, and my one-and-only son who did me proud by learning what he had to know for his bar mitzvah and also gave me this new silk tie and might yet amount to more than the torn soles of my shoes if he works hard and doesn't marry a *shiksa*."

My sister Merle, wearing a corsage in her neatly upswept hair, had a slight smile and looked happy to be with her family again. Wearing my new gabardine suit, a new white shirt, and new silk tie, I stood between

Merle and Etta, my smile showing more than a hint of pride to be the tallest one in the family, even without a heavy head of curly dark hair. To my right stood Etta, also with a heavy head of curly hair that swept around her full face, her eyes looking into space or at the photographer or at the door, as if in a daze trying to solve the answer to an illogical algebra question that poor Mr. Suschinsky had mistakenly scribbled on the blackboard. Finally, Sylvia, now thirteen, skinny, with long, curly hair, stood with slumping shoulders, looking curiously at the photographer as if to say, "Why are you staring at me like that? Why don't you stare at Jackie? He insisted on getting a boy's bike. There are three girls in the family and only one boy. But he never thought of that when he ordered a man's bike. And the only way I can reach the pedals is to stick my leg under the crossbar. But he doesn't care. He never thought of that. He never thought of anyone but himself. So why don't you stare at him?"

The photograph was only the second one taken of our complete family. The first one had been shot about eight years before, when a traveling photographer had stopped at our home unexpectedly on a Sunday afternoon and had photographed our family in front of our home. I was just a little kid then, staring off into space, as though I had just awoke. My sisters all smiled, as sisters are supposed to do when a traveling photographer suddenly appears. But my parents looked serious—and bored, as though irritated at being interrupted from eating their family dinner served promptly at noon. This photograph in Yorkton, however, was the only one taken in a real photography studio. It proved to be a wonderful family portrait. Our last one.

As I entered the synagogue, I felt as if I were now really grown up, proud to be wearing my new gabardine suit, which was as fine a suit as any in the building. I had grown a couple of inches in the past year and several people stared at me for a few seconds before they recognized me. Barney Dachis, who worked at Crolls, came up to me and said, "My you've grown. You look so handsome in that suit. You dress so well." I suddenly felt over six feet tall.

We all stayed at the Yorkton Hotel; but instead of eating my meals with the rest of our family, at the home of Mrs. Dachas, I was invited to the home of Mr. and Mrs. Harry Ferman, Gloria's parents. I suppose that the look in my eyes and the attention I paid her clearly indicated that I had a crush on her—the first one I had ever had. I just kept staring at her. I couldn't help it. She was absolutely gorgeous. She looked like a younger version of Barbara Stanwyck, only much more shapely and far more beautiful. Her nose was a little bit on the large size, but I liked that. Her lips were now a sensuous bright red, the latest shade. I liked that too. The lines of her bustline showed beneath her dress and even beneath her brown houndstooth check coat. I liked those lines even more. But most of all, I loved to see the sparkle in her eyes. Whenever she smiled or laughed, her hazel-brown eyes sparkled like none I had ever seen before, and it made me feel warm, even flushed, and sort of dizzy. What can I say? I was in love.

I was glad the Fermans had also invited a few airmen stationed at the Air Force training base to join us for the holiday feast. I was rather shy and afraid of being embarrassed by my obvious crush on Gloria. I certainly didn't want to be the center of attention. Fortunately, her parents, sensing my uneasiness, made me feel right at home. I guess my hearty appetite also helped. Mrs. Ferman was a wonderful cook.

After dinner several other kids came over and we all went out on the verandah, where I took snapshots of Gloria and the others with my little baby Kodak camera. I had hoped to think of a pretext which would allow me to spend some time alone with her, hopefully to kiss her, but both cruel Fate and Destiny conspired against me. It's not easy when you're sixteen and very shy, and you'd like to kiss a girl but you've never kissed one before, and there are a whole bunch of other kids around. Even if you're wearing a brand new wool gabardine suit, the best that money can buy, it doesn't help. You feel cheated.

For almost three months afterward, I felt cheated. And deprived. What had I missed? I thought about her incessantly. I mean all the time. Would I ever have an opportunity to kiss her? It's unbearable when you're sixteen and you have a terrible crush on a beautiful girl whom you'd like to kiss, but she lives sixty miles away. That's a long way to travel to kiss a girl, especially if you don't have a car; and even if you did, the roads in winter are blocked with snow and won't be opened until spring. But there's always the train, even if it runs three or four hours late in December when the temperature dips to forty degrees below zero Fahrenheit. Yes, there's always the train unless a blizzard blocks the railway tracks between Edmonton and Sheho, and you have to wait for the snow plough to come from Edmonton (600 miles away), or if you're lucky Saskatoon (only 200 miles away), to clear the drifts so that the trains can run, even if they're only six hours late. But what pretext can you use to travel all that distance—and if all goes well and you're very lucky—get an opportunity to kiss her? That's a good question.

Fortunately, Fate or Destiny or both intervened. Someone invited me to a gathering of Young Judeans from all over Saskatchewan, to be held in the Yorkton Synagogue on Christmas Eve and the following day. After all these years, I would like to think I got the invitation from Gloria. That would be nice. And very romantic. That's what I would like to think. I might even be telling you the truth. So let's just leave it at that. As for the Young Judeans, I had never heard of them. I didn't know what they did or how they did it, or when they did it or where they did it, or what it was they did, or if they did anything at all. In other words, I was not exactly the world's leading authority on the Young Judeans, even the Young Judeans from all over Saskatchewan. But who cared? It could have been the Young Buddhists or Young Christians or Young Hindus. It wouldn't have made any difference. This was my golden opportunity, my pretext to go to Yorkton to see my sweetheart and, hopefully, to be alone with her, and—if the Almighty were on my side—to kiss her. I felt as if it were a once-in-a-lifetime opportunity, like viewing a total eclipse of the sun under clear skies, on the summit of Mt. Everest, during balmy weather, in the middle of June. My prayers had been answered.

Out of respect for Christians all over the world and Young Judeans from all over Saskatchewan, God Almighty in His infinite mercy did not allow the mercury to fall lower than twenty degrees below zero, and there were no storms or blizzards. As a result of this good fortune, the trains ran only two hours late. Not wanting to waste even an hour of my golden opportunity, I took advantage of the spur line train from Nipiwan to Yorkton, the "Peanut," which normally left Sheho at 4:30 P.M. and arrived in Yorkton about two hours later. However, because of the delay, I arrived in Yorkton around eight.

It was the first time I had been away from home on Christmas Eve. It felt weird. That's the only word I can think of to describe my sensation of walking up Betts Avenue, now completely deserted, listening to the hard snow crunching beneath my feet, instead of sitting around our radio at home, listening to Christmas carols, and the announcer telling us that it won't be long now before Santa comes down the chimney to deliver all his presents. In my mind's eye, I, too, was sitting around the brightly decorated Christmas tree, impatiently waiting for the big day to arrive. Christmas was a joyous time. I wished that I could have been part of that celebration, even though I was Jewish. That's how I had always felt through the magic of radio on Christmas Eve. Radio brought us together, especially on Christmas Eve. It didn't matter if we were Christians or Jews or agnostics or atheists or whatever. The only exception was Young Judeans, especially Young Judeans from all over Saskatchewan. They brought only a few of us together, but for a different reason. That's why I was now in Yorkton.

The hall of the synagogue was crowded with perhaps fifty or more boys and girls approximately my age, as well as a number of adults. Except for those from Yorkton, I didn't know a soul. Mr. Norman Croll greeted me in a hearty voice, "Merry Christmas." I was shocked. Jews did not celebrate Christmas. That was the first time any Jew had ever wished me a Merry Christmas. And in a synagogue, yet! Barely audible, I returned the greeting.

Yorkton's Jewish community had made arrangements to house their out-of-town young guests. I was to share a bedroom in the Wolinsky home with another boy whom I had never met. He was from Preeceville, about fifty miles north of Yorkton, and kept boasting about his sexual conquests. I didn't know if he was telling me the truth or not. I didn't tell him that I had never even kissed a girl.

I spotted Gloria among a group of boys and girls from Regina and Saskatoon who were discussing some problems about the Arabs in Palestine and Trans Jordan. I had no idea what they were talking about, so I kept my mouth shut. All I knew about Zionism was that the Jews hoped to have a homeland in Palestine someday, and there had been occasional conflicts between the Zionist settlers in Palestine and its Arab natives. I also knew that Dad sometimes donated money to the Zionist cause, in the hope that Palestine would someday become a national homeland for Jews. Perhaps I was being selfish, but at the moment I wasn't the least bit interested in Zionism. I had something else on my mind.

Gloria was glad I had come. She wasn't exactly elated to see me, but was glad I had come. There is a difference. I don't remember what we talked about, but I do remember asking her if I could walk her home. "May I walk you home tonight?" Those were my exact words. How can I ever forget them? She said "yes." That's exactly what she said. It was the most thrilling moment of my life. I could feel my heart pounding. At last I would be alone with her.

Although I had brought along a pair of earmuffs which I hid in my overcoat pocket, I wanted to show her that I was a real he-man, not the least bit afraid of getting cold ears. That was supposed to be a sure sign of bravery and more important, manhood. Not covering your ears. Even when it's twenty below zero. The colder it got, the braver you were and the more manhood you showed your girl if you didn't cover your ears. I would show her that I was not only man enough but brave enough *even* to win the most coveted medal for bravery in the entire British Empire— the Victoria Cross, awarded only rarely and usually posthumously to the most heroic of the Empire's wartime servicemen for "outstanding valor above and beyond the call of duty." That's why I never wore earmuffs under my hat the night I walked her home.

We had walked less than a block when my the tips of my ears began to sting. That's what they do when it's twenty below and they're not covered. Also, my nose was cold. But that was not yet an issue. I was now building up almost enough nerve to put my arm around her waist. Would she let me do it? That was the issue. By the time we got to the second block, I finally did it. I put my arm around her waist. Just her waist. That's all. And would you believe she didn't take my arm away? It was the biggest thrill of my life. I was almost in ecstasy. But not quite. My ears were freezing. And so was my nose. But I couldn't stop now. No matter how bad they hurt. I was out to win the Victoria Cross.

By the time we got to the third block, I began wondering about whether or not she would let me kiss her and if so, how I should kiss her.

I knew I was supposed to kiss her on the lips—I wasn't stupid—but where exactly should the noses go so they wouldn't get in the way? That was my dilemma. I had kissed my mother and my aunt and my cousins and my sisters. But those weren't real kisses. Not like kissing a girl. This was uncharted territory. Also, when we kissed, was I supposed to close my eyes or look into hers? Or was she supposed to close hers, like the movie stars? And what should I do with my hat? Would it get in the way? And if it did, should I take it off? I had never thought about how complicated it could be to kiss a girl. I wish I'd thought of it sooner. Somebody should write a manual about what you're supposed to do on your first kiss. Think of all the trouble it could save. It would easily outsell The Holy Bible.

By the time we reached the big white house at 65 Fourth Avenue, where she lived, the stinging pain in my ears and nose was so bad I knew they were frozen. But I had endured. I was sure I had left no doubt in her mind about my valor—and my manhood. Now came the payoff. The moment had finally arrived. The moment I had been dreaming about all these months. As I walked her up to the steps, I was sure she could hear my heart pounding. How could she miss it? This was absolutely the most exciting moment of my entire life. This was it! I thought about suddenly sweeping her up into my arms and kissing her. That's what I'd seen Clark Gable do in *Gone with the Wind*. But would that be too impulsive? What would she think about me? Suppose she wouldn't like that? No I couldn't take that chance. So, just as she was about to climb the steps, I blurted out, "May I kiss you goodnight?"

Now, at this very moment, fifty-four years after I froze not only my ears but also my nose, leaving it discolored for many years to come, I still blush with embarrassment at her answer. She didn't mince words. "No!"

And I didn't even win the Victoria Cross.

CHAPTER TWENTY-FIVE
High School Graduation

Highway 14, which was invariably blocked with snow during most of the winter, usually opened by early spring. With the melting snows came the end of our outdoor skating season, followed quickly by slush and mud covering not only our sidewalks but all trails and roads including Highway 14. But at least the highway was open. That meant we could again receive our regular Sunday visitors—the Teskeys from Wynyard; and now in 1945, Dr. Irving Miller, who had opened a practice in Foam Lake the previous year, and his wife, Rita, and their baby Marilyn.

Shortly after the highway opened, Dr. Miller made an emergency house call to our home. It was a couple of days after the beginning of Passover. Mom, as usual, had cleaned the house for Passover and taken away all the everyday *chametz* [non-Passover] dishes and pots and pans and silverware and packed them away for the eight days of Passover. Then, after I had climbed the stairs in the warehouse to the vacant second floor of the store, where the "Passover" dishes and pots and pans and silverware were stored and brought them down for her to unpack and wash and put in the cupboards for the eight days of Passover, she had prepared the special feast for the first two nights of that holiday. On the second night of Passover—or it may have been the third—she suddenly began to lose her balance. That's all I remember about her sudden attack that night. Apparently, I have blocked the details from my mind, except that someone telephoned Dr. Miller to come immediately. When he arrived and asked me what had happened, all I remember saying was that she often took sick right after "killing herself for Passover."

My mind is also blank about the rest of the details. Apparently Dr. Miller took her back to the hospital in Foam Lake, while Dad got Bill Finley to drive Sylvia and him to the hospital. That's all I remember about that night.

Early the next morning, I was awakened by Dad and Sylvia entering my room. They were both crying. In between sobs, Dad said, "Your mother had a stroke." Then, in between sobs, he added, "The doctor said if she has another one, she'll die."

It is impossible to describe how I felt at that exact moment. Disbelief! Shock! Fright! Perhaps a combination of all of these at once. I don't remember what I said or if I said anything at all. I do remember, however, asking God to spare her life so that I could love her as I had never loved her before. "If You grant me this one prayer, that's all I ask. Then You could take her away any time you want afterward. But please let her live this time!" That was my silent prayer to my personal God.

Mom had been ill for most of her life. She had told me that during the Great War she and her sister in Poland had been hidden by their parents in the cold, damp cellar of their beer tavern for long hours on end whenever soldiers entered the tavern. Although she had never mentioned the word "rape," the implication was clear. Her parents feared that their beautiful young daughters would be raped by the soldiers. She had become ill as a result of the cold and dampness and had contacted rheumatic fever, which had left her with a weakened heart. In later life she had been bothered with gallstones and other problems. But up until now, only her weakened heart had been life threatening. Now her condition was critical. So I prayed, asking God to spare her life. But I did not expect a miracle. I believed there was only so much God could do to prolong her life. And I would cherish every moment I could with her while she was still alive.

Dad telephoned my sister Etta at work in Winnipeg. She took the train back to Sheho that night.

Mom returned from the hospital in a few days and recuperated at home. We all helped her shuffle along, one tiny step at a time, and she slowly regained the use of her paralyzed arm and leg. Her contorted mouth slowly regained its normal shape and she began speaking normally without slurring her words. By the time all the snow had melted, she was walking from our house to the store, and even staying in the store for an hour or so at a time. Etta returned to Winnipeg.

As Mom regained her strength, she began talking longer walks with me. We liked to walk along the highway to the Western bridge, about a quarter of a mile away. We liked listening to the single bass-baritone note repeated from the chorus of bullfrogs in the water-filled ditches along the graveled highway. " Croak-croak, croak-croak." That was their entire repertoire and they knew it by heart.

I was amazed at how quickly Mom regained her strength. By early May, she was back working in the store and cooking Sunday dinners. She seemed to have completely recuperated.

That Mothers Day, for the first time in my life, I decided to surprise her with a special gift—flowers. As far as I knew, nobody had ever given her flowers, except for the odd bouquet from our garden. Because of the season, locally grown flowers would not be available for at least another month. Therefore, whatever flowers were available at the nearest florist shop in Yorkton would obviously be very expensive. Nevertheless, I ordered a mixed bouquet of flowers from Yorkton to be sent by Greyhound bus. When they arrived, I put them in a vase and presented it to Mom. At first she was speechless. Then, after thanking me, with tears in her eyes, she said, "You shouldn't have spent so much money." But I knew it was the best use I had ever made of money. For years afterward I always said, " Give flowers to the living." I'm glad I gave Mom flowers when she was alive.

The war in Europe was now nearing the end. On May 5, all German forces in the Netherlands and north-western Germany surrendered to the British. Two days later at Reims, General Alfred Jodl signed an unconditional surrender; and on May 8, Field Marshal William Keitel completed the signing at Berlin. After five long years and eight months of slaughter, the greatest and costliest war that Europe had ever suffered was finally over. V-E Day—victory in Europe—had arrived.

Oddly enough, there was no celebration of V-E Day in Sheho. All of us, in our own way, gave thanks, and we all talked about it. Otherwise, it was business as usual. That was not exactly the case, however, in Foam

Lake. A few days later, Dr. Miller and his wife and baby visited us in time for Sunday dinner. "We just got a new maid," he said. " I don't think she's too smart. On V-E day the bells started ringing and she said, 'Why are the bells ringing today?'

"I told her they're ringing because the war is over. She looked at me puzzled, then said 'Who won?' "

Dr. Miller told us they would be leaving Foam Lake within a year, so that he could do postgraduate work in internal medicine, probably in Europe. We had all grown fond of the Millers and were sorry they would soon be leaving our area. Mom and Dad especially would feel the loss of such friendly and compatible Jewish company.

Nor were the Millers the only Jewish family in our area to talk about moving away. The Orloffs, also from Foam Lake, were planning to sell their store and move to Winnipeg. And the Laskins from Rose Valley were talking about selling out and moving to Edmonton. With one family after another, their situation was almost the same. As soon as the kids are grown and finish high school, their parents send them to the city—Winnipeg, Edmonton, Vancouver—in order to pursue professional careers and to meet and marry within the Jewish faith. Eventually, the parents, who want to be with their kids, will follow. It's just a matter of time.

Even our family had talked about eventually selling the store and moving to Winnipeg. With my older sisters now living there, and with Sylvia just two years away from finishing high school, it would be only a matter of time before my parents, too, would move. That seemed to be the logical thing to do. But was it really logical? What would they do in Winnipeg? How could they earn a living in that city? In Sheho, their store was the biggest one in town and they were always able to make a living. They were the biggest fish in the pond. In Winnipeg, they would be minnows swimming in an ocean filled with sharks. We discussed these problems but never found a satisfactory answer. Mom was very hesitant about moving. Dad was even more so.

Another problem was that I was planning to go to university in Saskatoon instead of Winnipeg, where I might have lived with my sisters and saved money on board-and-room had I chosen to go there. But I had already made up my mind. Mervin Laskin had emphasized that the University of Saskatchewan was less anti-Semitic in its medical school admissions policy than the University of Manitoba. I had therefore chosen the University of Saskatchewan and would be leaving home in the fall for Saskatoon. As for the added cost of living there, I did have misgivings; but to tell you the truth, I never sat down with my parents to analyze the problem. Barely seventeen years old, I never bothered to analyze any problem except the odd one in algebra and trigonometry. I was in a big hurry to do what I wanted to do and never bothered to think very deeply about alternatives or consequences. I seemed to think that if I ignored the problem, it would eventually disappear. I'm ashamed to admit this, but at seventeen and even later at eighteen, I was too self-centered to seriously worry about anything else besides me. Perhaps my sister Sylvia is right when even today, fifty -three years later, she says, "You never thought about anyone except yourself."

About six weeks before I was scheduled to take my final exams, Sheho entered the twentieth century with real talking pictures shown in the town hall once a week. I mean these were real black-and-white movies made in Hollywood no less, not by Edison. And they starred actors who not only talked but were still alive, heroes like Lon Chaney in "The Wolf Man." Every Thursday evening, even though I was studying for my exams, Mr. Leckie would come by our home and say, "Come on Jack. I'll take you to the movie." Although I knew I should be putting in more time with my studies, I felt his offer was one I couldn't refuse. Besides, it's not everyday one gets a chance to see Lon Chaney grow so much hair on his legs in a matter of minutes that he suddenly turns into a wolf. I was now also growing hair on my legs, but not as fast as Lon Chaney, and my arms and chest were also hairy. I could even howl like a wolf. After the movie I wondered if I, too, would eventually turn into a wolf. When I showed Dad my hairy legs and chest, he was astounded and bewildered and tried to explain the phenomenon. "Your mother must have gazed upon a bear when she was pregnant," he said. There were no bears anywhere near Sheho, nor did the circus come to town in those early days. But as far as Dad was concerned, she had gazed upon a bear when she was pregnant with me, and the result was an offspring who resembled a boy but was also a cross between a wolf and an ape. Perhaps I should have been called Wolfman Jack or better still, Jack the Ape Man.

Early in June, Mr. Gorchinsky passed out the printed schedules from Regina for our final examinations which were to start in two weeks. Since I had already passed chemistry the previous year, I now had to write only eight exams instead of nine—a real snap: algebra, analytical geometry, trigonometry, physics, English, French, world history, and modern problems. Each exam had a time limit of three hours: from 9:00 a.m. to noon, or from 1:30 P.M. to 4:30 P.M., depending on the subject. On some days I was scheduled to take two exams, my only break being for lunch. While taking the exam, nobody was allowed to leave the room, even to go to the toilet without permission from the principal. Now, after twelve years of attending school, this was it—our final examinations— the completion of our high school education. From my beginning class of twenty-nine in Miss Griffiths' room, away back in 1933, I was now the only original survivor in 1945 to be taking the final examinations in Sheho School District number 953. My other two classmates were trans- fer students. But I did not dwell on that thought. One exam at a time. One day at a time. Then I would be through. Finished with high school. Ready to start a new life.

As I had done for several previous years, I studied hard for every subject the night before the exam. I also made sure that my fountain pen was working properly and the bottle of ink was full before each exam. But I was not especially nervous. Both of my older sisters had passed with flying colors—in the 90% plus range. Although I had never done as well as they had, except in chemistry and English, I wasn't stupid. So I never worried about my "finals."

Each morning, in front of the class, as Mr. Gorchinsky tore open the large brown manila envelope containing our departmental exams and passed them, one at a time, first to me, then to Walter Hudyma, and finally to Martha Kulak, one could hear a collective rustle of papers, followed immediately by a faint, almost inaudible sigh. Then, for the next three hours—except for the faint rhythm of breathing—the only sound in the room was the continuous scratch of fountain pen nibs rubbing against paper. Scratch, scratch, scratch. And in between—silence. And then, "You have fifteen minutes left."

One by one, we began handing in our papers. First Martha. I followed her, five minutes later. Finally, reluctantly, Walter Hudyma handed his in. Our first exam was over. Only seven more to go. Then six. Then five. Then four. Three. Two. And finally it was all over. Twelve noon. We had just written our last exam.

"Well, that's it," I said to Walter Hudyma, as we left the yellowish-brown brick school building, never expecting to ever return—not in a million years. "We're finally through."

"Yes, we're finally through," he echoed, as we walked down the cinder sidewalk, past the shoe repair shop, where the cement sidewalk began.

"We're finally through," I repeated, as we approached Mike Lazatsky's pool hall and barber shop. "You know what? We should really celebrate!" Suddenly, as we were about to pass the pool room, we both stopped dead in our tracks. At that *exact* moment—four minutes past twelve noon— he looked at me and I looked at him. He knew exactly what I was about to say. " Let's go in and play a game of pool to celebrate."

I had never played a game of pool in my life, and I'm sure he hadn't either. My father had no use for anyone who squandered his money and time in the pool hall. He looked upon such a person as a bum. Fifteen cents a game was just like gambling. I'm sure Walter's father felt exactly the same. But at this particular moment, we were elated to be through with school, and we were out to celebrate our graduation from high school as recklessly as we could. So we entered the pool hall.

Mike Lazatsky stared at us as though we were virgin boys who had entered a brothel for the first time. What was Louis Katz's son doing at a pool table? He knew what Louis Katz would do if he ever caught his son in such an act. But business was business. He kept his mouth shut, took the money, and set up the table.

Please believe me when I tell you that although we attracted quite a crowd of laughing onlookers, who eventually got tired and walked away, neither Walter nor I were ever a challenge to Minnesota Fats. I don't remember who won the game or if we ever finished it, or if we just got tired of missing all those shots. But eventually, at least an hour later, we both left the pool hall, having celebrated in grand fashion our graduation from high school.

When I got to the store, Dad said, "Where were you?"

"I just wrote my last exam. I'm through with school. Walter Hudyma and I played a game of pool to celebrate."

He glared at me and immediately uttered his famous prediction: "*Bum! Foon deer vil zeyen a rich as foon myna tzerisena shich.*" [Bum. You will amount to as much as the torn soles of my shoes.]

And that was exactly how I celebrated my high school graduation.

CHAPTER TWENTY-SIX
University Of Saskatchewan

The summer of 1945 passed quickly. Mom recovered completely from her stroke and I accompanied her to Winnipeg on a buying trip, as I had the previous year. This time she gave me virtually a free reign to do most of the buying. I added three new items: Sheepskin coats on which we could make eight dollars each; and extra heavy flannel shirts and heavy wool mackinaw pants, both of which could earn us a profit of $1.50 each. I also supplemented my college wardrobe with a corduroy bushcoat and a wool houndstooth check sportcoat.

Unlike the previous year, I did not stay in Winnipeg longer than necessary after completing my business. Merle, still unattached, was dating different boys. Etta, however, was now quite serious about our "third' cousin Larry Lackman. She had been corresponding with him ever since they had last seen each other a year ago.

After joining the United States Navy, Larry had shipped out on the aircraft carrier U.S.S. *Bunker Hill*, which had recently been in the thick of action in the South Pacific. In April, during the Battle of Okinawa, two Kamazkee planes had hit the carrier, setting the flight deck on fire and killing almost four hundred crewmen. Larry had been below on the hanger deck, where the aircraft were kept and, although badly shaken up, he had survived.

Because Larry was still on duty in the Pacific, Etta had decided to come home to work in the store when I went away to university. Her decision relieved my anxiety about leaving Mom and Dad alone in the store now that business had almost doubled from the desperate years of the Depression. I knew it was too much for them to handle alone; but being as self-centered as I was—I'm ashamed to admit—my main concern was my own future. I never for a moment thought that perhaps I should be the one to stay home and sacrifice a year or two by postponing my career. I was in a hurry. Yet I had mixed feelings about going away. I was concerned about all the responsibility of running the business now being placed upon Mom and Dad when I was gone. That's why I was grateful that Etta would be coming home.

On August 8, about an hour after the store had closed, I went cycling with Walter Lys, who had come from Yorkton to visit his parents. "You know what I'd like to do?" I said. "Let's do something daring."

He looked at me as if I had suddenly decided to hop aboard a freight train and leave the country. He knew the most daring thing I had ever done in my life was to steal a cigar from the store and throw up immediately after trying to inhale. But now the gleam in my eye indicated that I had a much more malicious and evil deed in mind.

"Like what?" he asked.

"You know that dugout behind the skating rink?"

"Yeah, the one that collects water from melted snow and rain, to flood the skating rink in the winter. What about it?"

"It's kind of deep and it's absolutely forbidden to swim there."

"You mean we should be the first ones to break that ordinance?"

"Why not?"

"What if we get caught?"

"We'll get Henry Walkowski to be the lookout. If Mr. Petroshak comes down to see who's swimming there, Henry will warn us and we'll ride away.

We picked up Henry, who had just finished delivering the Saskatoon *Star Phoenix.* "We're going to swim in the dugout," I said. "How about being our lookout?"

He stared at me with delight as if we were Jessie James recruiting a new member of that infamous gang about to rob a gold-laden train on the main line of the Canadian Pacific Railway.

"You're really going to swim in that dugout? Honest?"

"Yeah," said Walter. " We're going to be the outlaws."

"Boy oh boy, that's really something. What do you want me to do?"

"Just ride the bike up and down the dirt road and warn us if Mr. Petroshak or anyone else comes by. Whistle or yell, so we can get away."

"Boy, this is really exciting! " said Henry. Then he added, " The Americans just dropped a new bomb on Japan. It's called a- at- at- o-om."

"Atomic!" I interrupted.

"Yeah, that's it. How do you say it?"

"Atomic Atomic bomb!" Really? When?"

"Yesterday, I guess. It was in today's paper."

"Holy Moses! I wonder if they split the atom. But that's supposed to be impossible. That's what we learned in physics: 'The atom is the smallest indivisible particle.' Maybe they did something else. The explosion must have been enormous. Now the Japanese will have to surrender. Don't forget to let us know, Henry, if anyone comes by."

Walter and I undressed behind the wooden cabin and jumped into the muddy dugout. The water immediately turned to the exact color of Old Colony black house paint, the same brand we sold in the store; only the muddy water wasn't quite as thick. On top floated every dead insect ever classified by entomologists, as well as every prehistoric one that was long thought extinct. But it was too late to turn back. We had to finish the dirty deed. We dog- paddled across the dugout, careful not to swallow even a drop of the thick, black goo, now buzzing with angry mosquitoes and other disturbed inhabitants. Then without stopping, we continued on our way back. Suddenly we heard Henry shout, "Hurry up! Someone's coming!"

But Walter and I were too fast for Mr. Petroshak or whoever had decided to track down Sheho's notorious outlaws. Within minutes we had dressed, jumped on our bikes, and ridden away. We had committed the perfect crime, witnessed only by Henry Walkowski, our accomplice. Nobody else knew about it. And nobody else ever found out. Until now. I guess nobody else ever cared, even though that was the most serious crime I had ever committed with the exception of stealing a cigar from our store. Although we got away with that crime, Walter and I paid for it: We needed a thorough scrubbing that night.

On August 9, another atomic bomb was dropped on Nagasaki.

A day or two later, on a Sunday, our family and Mr. Leckie visited the Teskey family in Wynyard, who had also invited the Tobachnik family from nearby Wadena. I learned that Mr. Orloff had sold his store to a group of local farmers who renamed it "The Co-op." I was afraid that if such a cooperative venture came to Sheho, it would present fierce competition. Myer Tobachnik's reply reassured me. "What are they going to sell? Overalls?"

We then speculated on how long Japan could hold out after the dropping of the second atomic bomb. "If they don't surrender right away, I'd drop the bomb on every city until they do," he said.

On August 14, Japan surrendered , followed by her formal announcement the following day. The war was over.

Our family was elated. Maurice Shnider—by now Flight Lieutenant Maurice Shnider—had survived. He had been awarded the Distinguished Flying Cross while serving in India and Ceylon. We now knew that he would be coming home—alive. He had beaten the odds.

About a week later, with the beginning of university classes drawing near, I took the train to Saskatoon in order to find a home where I could have room and board. It was the first time I had ever been farther west than Guernsey, where my cousins Abe and Minnie Katz owned a general store. The only people I knew in this strange city were Merv Laskin, now in his second year of medicine, and my cousin Rachel Katz, about ten years older than I. She had moved from Guernsey and was now living in an apartment by herself. I looked her up immediately and asked her if she knew anyone who might take me in. "Why don't you stay with me?" she said. "You can do light housekeeping and we can share expenses." I thought the offer was too good to be true and took her up on it immediately.

I then visited Merv Laskin on the University campus. He had been assisting Dr. Altschul in the histology department during the summer, and he showed me around the laboratory. He kept reaching into a jar of the strongest formaldehyde solution I had ever smelled to pull out various parts of a dismembered cadaver and identify them for me. "This is the pelvis of a female, and here are the different parts." It looked awful. I thought of the gravedigger scene in Shakespeare's *Hamlet*, but Merv was not philosophizing over the previous life of the remains of this female. Maybe in another four years I would be doing the same. I returned home the following day.

For the next few weeks I unpacked, ticketed, and displayed the merchandise that arrived from Winnipeg, and I also ordered special flyers advertising our new fall line of clothing. With Etta now home, my mind was at ease, as I packed my clothes and got ready to move to Saskatoon for the beginning of my freshman year at university. Finally, the day arrived for me to board the train for Saskatoon. Both Mom and Dad had tears in their eyes as I kissed them good-bye. But I held back mine. I was all grown up now—a young man—on his way to university, to become a doctor. I was the first person from Sheho who had actually completed all twelve years at our local school and was now going on to the University of Saskatchewan.

When the train stopped at Wynyard, I got off to see Mr. Teskey, who had come to greet me. He was emotional. "What your mother and father are doing for you is wonderful. They're making a great sacrifice. A great sacrifice. Don't forget it. Work hard. Don't disappoint them. Make them proud." As we shook hands just before I boarded the train, he added, "Don't forget. Work hard."

After thinking it over, my cousin Rachel had decided not to share her apartment and had notified me only a few days before registration was to begin. She had suggested, however, that I temporarily stay with her relatives Sam and Minnie Cramer, since they had an extra room to rent.

The room was in the basement. It had a bed, a chair, a dresser, a small desk, and an electric light. Without the light it was cold, dark, damp, and dreary. When the light was on, however, it was only cold, damp, and dreary. It would have been an excellent room for a winery to store the oakwood casks of newly pressed grapes, allowing them to ferment and eventually turn into wine. It would even have been a better room to store the wine after fermentation, especially Cabernet Sauvignon, allowing it to age until it reached its peak, say in nine or ten years—or longer if necessary—because the temperature never varied between fifty-two degrees and fifty-five degrees, winter or summer, fall or spring, 365 days a year, even when the furnace was on. If the famous wineries in the Napa Valley had known about this room, they would have made a bid on Cramer's house so that they could store their wine in the room. However, since they didn't know about my cave, they had to settle for deep limestone caves in the Napa Valley, caves which despite every precaution taken, including the use of very low wattage electric light bulbs, were more brilliantly lit —and warmer— than my room in Cramer's basement. Since I knew nothing about the winery business at that time and had never even heard of the Napa Valley, I obviously missed out on the opportunity of a lifetime. Instead, I took the room. What can I say? The world is full of missed opportunities. And surprises.

I had no sooner settled into my room when I got another surprise—a visitor whose name was also Jack Katz. He was a close buddy of Murray Katzman, who had rented the upstairs room. Both were freshmen from Prince Albert, a city of about ten thousand population, ninety miles north of Saskatoon. Jack, grinning and sporting the brush-cut, a short athletic styled haircut, was about my height but much heavier. Built like a weight lifter, with very broad shoulders, thick arms and huge calves, he was a star athlete. Baseball, softball, football, hockey, track, and girls—he excelled in them all, especially girls. He sometimes went by his middle name— Sam—but had registered as Jack S. Katz. He was going to study pre dentistry. I didn't realize we would be taking some of the same classes.

Murray Katzman, shorter and much thinner than I, with black straight hair combed sideways, big front teeth and rather big ears, was sometimes called "gopher" by his buddy. He had a resonant voice and would have loved to be a radio announcer, but instead was going to major in commerce. His father owned a small clothing store in Prince Albert, and although part of Murray's extensive wardrobe was from that store, he had added to it with the latest styles from the better men's stores in Saskatoon. He knew the names of the better makers of clothes and which stores featured them. He also knew more about girls than I did. So I just kept my mouth shut. I didn't want them to know how naive I was.

I was also naive in another area. Instead of looking for another room immediately, I stayed in the cave almost a week, until I had registered for my classes. After registering, I went to the business office to hand in my registration form and pay my tuition. The girl at the wicket looked at the form and said, " Jack Katz, your name is Jack Katz? But you've already registered and paid."

"No, I haven't. That must be the other Jack Katz—Jack S. Katz, from Prince Albert."

"Oh, I see. There are two of you."

"No, just one. I'm Jack Katz from Sheho. He's Jack S. Katz from Prince Albert."

"Are you related?"

"No. I just met him. I'm the original Jack Katz."

Then I went to the chemistry lab supply store to buy a lab smock and pay for my locker. The man stared at me and said, "Jack Katz, weren't you just here?"

"No, that must be the "other" Jack Katz. Jack S. Katz."

"Oh, yes, now I see. Are you related?"

"No, I just met him."

And so it went for the next month. "I'm Jack Katz. He's the "other" Jack Katz—Jack S. Katz."

One Sunday morning I attended a brunch sponsored by the newly appointed rabbi, a young energetic man who eagerly wanted to form the city's first Hillel chapter. Among the gathering of Jewish university students were a few high school girls only a year away from entering university. Almost every one was friendly and eager to meet everyone else. I met most of the girls, including one of the prettiest ones, Kayla Wine, whose parents owned one of the better ladies' wear stores in the city. She reminded me somewhat of Gloria Ferman, whose father also owned a fine ladies' wear store. I must have been attracted to girls whose fathers owned ladies' wear stores. Maybe I would have better luck with this girl. But I didn't ask her out immediately. I was too shy. So I waited a few days, then telephoned her and said, "This is Jack Katz. I met you last

Sunday at the Hillel brunch and was wondering if I could take you to a movie tomorrow night." She accepted my invitation.

The next night, looking forward to my first date in Saskatoon, I rang the doorbell. She opened the door and stared at me. Then her jaw dropped and her mouth opened. I mean *really* opened. Not quite wide enough for a dentist to work on her molars, but only her front teeth. And since I wasn't a dentist, I said, "What's the matter?"

She exhaled, then said, "Oh, I thought you were the *other* Jack Katz."

"No, he's Jack S. Katz. I'm Jack Katz.

"Are you related?"

The evening went as well as could be expected. We both made the best of it, but I never dated her again. Nor did I date anyone else that year. I was much too serious to waste my time and money on dating.

On September 28, a day after classes began, I learned that the barracks at the Air Force training station were now to be used as dormitories for the hundreds of returning war veterans currently attending university, as well as for other varsity students who needed a place to stay. Eager to leave my cave, I packed my suit case and moved to the barracks on the former R.C.A.F. base. It was just like being in the Air Force, except that we weren't issued uniforms. We all retired early at the same time, in one huge room that was bigger than the Ukrainian hall in Sheho. It also housed more men than the entire population of Sheho. We all slept on our own little bunks, got up early together, showered, then shaved together in a huge bathroom, and ate a huge breakfast together, including all the grapefruit juice we wanted. We brushed our teeth together, then all boarded the bus together which took us to the campus together—in time for classes. In the late afternoon, we all took the bus back to the barracks—together. Then we all tried to study—together. But I couldn't concentrate amidst all the noise and commotion. So, after two days of togetherness, I had had enough. I returned to my cave below Cramer's house.

At least here I would be alone and could take the street car to university at my convenience. Furthermore, I could take short walks up and down the street whenever I wanted to, and drop into a coffee shop for a five cent cup of coffee and look at the waitresses at the same time. What a bargain! I could also take longer walks across the "overhead" pedestrian bridge which was built above the railway tracks and led to the downtown part of the city, where the movie theaters were located. Once I got out of my cave, I was back in civilization.

The west end was a middle class neighborhood, home to most of the Jewish families, as well as to Ukrainians and others. Many, if not most, of the Jewish varsity students, including out-of-towners, lived here. I had just taken a walk one evening when I saw two young men dressed in gabardine topcoats like mine, standing on the corner staring at me. The taller, thinner one abruptly shouted at me, "Hey, you!"

Frightened, I stopped dead in my tracks. Would they attack me? The hairs on the back of my neck stood up. I clenched my fist.

"Are you Jewish?" he shouted.

With my fists still clenched, I slowly replied, "Yes."

"So am I," they both replied, as they approached me and extended their arms to shake hands. "I'm Maurice Faigen, from Neudorf."

"And I'm Lou Kanee, from Melville."

"I'm Jack Katz, from Sheho."

"Any relation to the other Jack Katz?"

"No. That's Jack S. Katz from Prince Albert.

"Are you premed?" asked Maurice.

"Yes. First year."

"We're both in second year medicine," said Lou.

"Then you know Merv Laskin."

"Of course. And Lyonel Israels, too." he said.

"Are you a brain?" asked Maurice.

"I don't think so. But I didn't do too badly."

"It's very hard to get into medicine," said Maurice. "You've got to study hard. And you've got to be a brain."

His warning emphasized what I had learned after meeting a second year premed student just before registration. Sid Sharzer, a native of Saskatoon, not only knew every Jewish student on campus but more important, knew everything there was to know about the first year of premed and how difficult it was to get into medicine. "You need a minimum of twenty-one credits out of thirty," he explained." That's at least a "B" average. You get three for an A, two for a B, and one for a C." I got eleven last year, so I have a good chance of getting in."

Then he added, "I know what books you'll need. I kept some of mine from last year—the ones you'll need. They're in good condition. No sense paying extra money for the same books just because they're new. Besides, I've even marked the most important parts you should learn. That should help you a lot. And I can give you my notes from last year if you want."

I bought his books but decided to take my own notes. I still had to buy other books, though, including a huge book for English literature and another for botany. So, at the end of the street car line across from the university, I crowded into Bell's Drug Store, which housed not only a coffee shop and drug store but also the bookstore where we all lined up to be served—one-by-one—by the clerks behind the counter. Finally, with my arms full of books, I was ready for my classes: English, French, inorganic chemistry, botany, zoology, and political economy.

Every morning shortly after eight, I boarded the street car already crowded with students on their way to nine o'clock classes. Sometimes I sat with Maurice or Lou if seats were available; at other times with "Duchy" Drabinsky, "Eppy" or Sid Sharzer. All three were second year premeds or predent. I particularly liked Sid. I envied his witty remarks, laughed at his jokes, and looked up to him as though he were a helpful older brother. But my admiration for anyone now studying medicine was much greater. Dreaming of the day when I would be in medical school, I looked up to Maurice and Lou as my models. I envied them. And because of the morning ritual, as the street car clanged along the tracks and crossed the winding Saskatchewan River, I eventually felt a camaraderie with all five of them.

Occasionally, I saw the other two Jewish second year med students on campus, Merv Laskin and his buddy Lyonel Israels, as well as Lyonel's girlfriend, Esther Hornstein, from Prince Albert, now in her first year of medicine. But since they lived in the Nutana district, near the university, my association with them was neither as frequent nor as close as with the others.

All the buildings on campus —with the sole exception of the red brick engineering building—were constructed of a special gray stone meticulously cut and fit together so well by master masons that these castle-like fortresses would endure for a thousand years or more. To say the least, they looked most impressive. These classic looking buildings gave the campus, at the very eastern edge of the city, an air of isolation, tranquillity, permanence, and most of all—nobility. The University of Saskatchewan was a special place. It overpowered me with a special emotion—impossible to describe.

The chemistry building was especially impressive. It looked like a medieval castle. Over decades, the stone steps leading from the main floor up to the huge lecture theater on the second floor had been worn away at the edges from the millions of students stomping up and down these stairs in a hurry to get to chemistry class and then hurrying back to another class in another building five minutes away. It was a long way from the chemistry building to Convocation Hall, where both my English and French classes were held.

I took an immediate liking to Professor Murdock M. Matheson. He was a middle aged gentleman in black horn rimmed glasses whose voice resonated with emotion whenever he discussed the great works of English literature. And when he discussed the theme of compassion in Shakespeare's King Lear, compassion which King Lear's older daughters should have shown to their aging father, I immediately thought about my own father. Perhaps I should have been more understanding and should have shown him more compassion. I had always liked English literature, but in Professor Matheson's class I quickly learned to love it.

French, unfortunately, was another matter. I had always disliked French and had never done well in that subject even though I had managed to translate two books, *Seven With One Blow* and *The Three Musketeers*, with the help of my sisters' notes and my teachers. Now, however, I was on my own, and we were translating college-level literary works. Moreover, I had never bothered to learn the parts of speech, let alone French grammar. So when my professor mentioned that adverbs usually end in -ly, I said to myself, "Now I knew how to recognize one."

Our professor was a middle-aged short lady who sometimes actually kept her glasses on for as long as five minutes. The rest of the time she occasionally let them hang by their chain around her neck. But most of time she twirled them on her finger around and around and around and around, and my eyes went around and around and around and around, keeping time with her glasses, until I thought I might become cross-eyed. But I still wanted to focus on her glasses, so I used my head, which went around and around and around and around, until I eventually became dizzy and looked in another direction. Just then she would stare at me as if she wanted to wake me up and say, "It's too hot in here. Mr. Katz, get up and close the register." So I swayed from side to side like a drunken sailor whenever she commanded me to close the register. Exactly ten minutes later she would stare at me again and, absolutely certain that she had now had my full attention, say, "It's too cold in here. Mr. Katz, get up and open the register." That's what I did all year long in her class— get up every ten minutes to open or close the register.

One day she tried to teach us how to speak French. "When I ask you 'Where do you come from?' in French, ('*Ouez venez vous*?'), I want you to reply in French, '*Je vien de Saskatoon*,' or '*Je viens de Prince Albert*,' or wherever you're from." Everyone in class responded perfectly and all went well until it was Jack Bowman's turn.

Like half of the freshmen on campus, he was a returning veteran about ten years older than the rest of us and about a hundred times more worldly. At least that's how he sounded. He was also different. Instead of moving his head around and around whenever the professor twirled her glasses, he would stare at her and twist the ends of his long, thick, black waxed mustache back and forth, back and forth, until the points were as fine as the lead in a sharpened number two pencil, and he looked like the perfect field marshal in the British Army. Jet black hair, shiny jet black mustache, pearl white teeth, dark brown piercing eyes, Field Marshal Jack Bowman would have put Field Marshal Sir Bernard L. Montgomery, commander of Allied ground forces, to shame if both had been in our French class.

"Mr. Bowman, *Ouez venez vous?*"

Instead of replying "*Je viens de* Montreal," he used the actual French pronunciation for the city. "Madame Professor, *Je viens de Moryell.*"

"*Oh bien. Vouz venez de Moryell.*" [Oh good. You come from Montreal.] Surprised and absolutely delighted to have at last found someone in her freshman class after all these years who could actually speak French fluently with a French dialect no less, the professor began pouring her heart out to him in rapid fire French—as fast as the Lucky Strike tobacco auctioneer.

"Hey, wait a minute," shouted Jack. " Slow down there. I don't understand a word you're saying. I'm really not from Montreal. I just passed through that city on the train. I'm from Saskatoon."

That was the last oral lesson we ever had.

Jack Bowman and I also shared another class, botany, the study of plants, including wood. I'm glad somebody else thought the study of wood was interesting. I sure didn't. How would you like to spend three hours a week studying about wood? Wood comes from trees which have something shaped like tubes, and something else shaped like something else. They're called xylem and phloem. That's what I learned. Some trees are asexual. That means they're neither male nor female, but reproduce by themselves. Others are sexual—female and male—and need a partner tree to reproduce. I thought they should have really been called heterosexual, just to set the record straight. I wondered if any trees were bisexual or homosexual. I had heard that some people were bisexual and some homosexual. But since both bisexuality and homosexuality were outlawed in Canada, our professor never talked about bisexual or homosexual trees, and I couldn't even find anything about them in our textbook, which I couldn't understand anyway. That's why I asked Jack to help me understand what the professor was mumbling about when he turned his back to the class and began drawing all sorts of different circles and shapes on the blackboard that were supposed to represent the life cycle of spores in bread mold, and cones in heterosexual pine trees. Or maybe they were bisexual. Or homosexual. How could I ever forget such intimate details? Perhaps someday Hollywood would make an X-rated movie about the sex life of the lonesome pine. If the movie could get past the Hayes Office censorship on what the public was allowed to see, it would become a real block buster. [14]

Is it any wonder,then , why I soon became fast friends with Jack Bowman? Botany and French—they brought us together. I believed everything he told me about trees until we took our first test and we both got a "D." Or it might have been an "F" as in "fool." After that, I studied botany on my own. So did he. But that didn't end our friendship.

Three nights a week, even in the midst of winter, I left my cave and took the streetcar to the end of the line in the north end of the city, then walked (or trudged through the snow) several blocks to his house, where we cooperated in trying to translate our French assignment into English that would make sense to somebody besides us. Sometimes it didn't even make sense to us. In fact, most of the time it didn't make sense at all. That's why we never volunteered to read our translation in class. Not even once. Our version more often than not was weird. Sometimes, however, it was interesting. But it wasn't even close. The only thing I really learned from him came on the morning of our final exam. Frustrated, about ten minutes before we were to begin, I said, "I wish I knew how to swear in French."

"Oh, it's easy," he said. "The worst swearing you can say is '*Mon dieux et tabernackle.*' That literally means My God and the Church. But to the French, it's the worst curse you can utter."

I memorized it immediately. I felt good, but not completely vindicated. "What else can I say?"

"*L'enfant de la chien.* Son of a female dog."

I memorized that too. "Now I'm ready to take the exam."

My professor must have appreciated all the work I did during the year, opening and closing the register. I think she felt I deserved an "F" for French, but an "A" for opening and closing the register. She awarded me a "D."

If I hadn't studied with Jack Bowman, I am sure I wouldn't have done even that well because I found it impossible to study in my cave. My boarding arrangements included breakfast and supper, neither of which is worth commenting on. But food was the least of my worries. After supper I would return to my cave and try to study. However, the cave was so cold and dreary, and French was so difficult, that I was grateful when Jack Bowman invited me to come over to his home to work on our assignment together. But that was only three nights a week. That left four more nights on my own. I was so frustrated with my situation and so worried about what I should be doing and how hard it was to do, and how much money it was costing my parents every month for my room and board and spending money—which I would not spend unless I absolutely had to—that I was overwhelmed by it all. I decided that the only way to solve these problems was to escape occasionally and forget about them for a couple of hours by going to a movie.

Usually four nights a week, I would visit a neighborhood movie theater on 20th Street, or walk four blocks from Cramer's house on Avenue E to the overhead walkway bridge on Avenue A, climb the stairs, walk over the railway tracks, then down the stairs to downtown—Second Avenue—the movie theater district. Here, with only twenty-five cents for admission, I could see Gloria Swanson in *Sunset Boulevard,* or Jeannie Crain in *State Fair,* or Barbara Stanywck or Betty Davis or Tyrone Power or Errol Flynn or any number of beautiful and handsome movie stars who acted out make believe roles containing make believe problems. And so, for ninety minutes, I almost forgot my own problems. Almost forgot, but not quite. Not unless the drama was overwhelming, like a murder mystery or unless the conflict was so real that for ninety minutes my attention was completely focused on the movie. Only then could I escape. I felt guilty. But I kept on escaping. My problems felt so overwhelming, I thought it was impossible to solve them. It seemed so futile. That's why for the first two months, I went to the movies usually four nights a week.

By November I had discovered another way to avoid my cave. It was located inside Convocation Hall and was called the "library." From the floor reaching almost to the ceiling, bookshelves packed with stacks of books lined the walls, and ladders leaned against the uppermost shelves for students to reach the top. Oakwood chairs were arranged along large oakwood tables that filled the room except for the corners in which were placed newspapers, magazines, large references books, and one huge dictionary resting on a lectern. Immediately after supper, I would usually take the streetcar back to the university, where I would attempt to study in the warm, cozy library, which at this hour was not overly crowded. During the day, however, the library was usually so crowded that I found it impossible to concentrate, especially when there were girls sitting at the table across from me or sometimes even next to me. But I didn't move away. I would like to have talked to them, but that was forbidden. So was whispering. But somebody was always whispering. No matter where I sat, I could hear constant whispering. It annoyed me.

I never whispered except when I bumped into my former classmates Alice Curry and Jenny Lys, who were now also enrolled in university. Alice had graduated from high school in Regina, and Jenny had completed twelfth grade in Yorkton. But since all of us had spent most of our school years in Sheho, we considered it as our home town and realized that we were the first group of students from Sheho to ever attend a university.

I also whispered when I saw Maurice Faigen during the noon hour break for lunch. "I never eat lunch at noon," he whispered. "It makes me sleepy. Instead, I smoke a cigarette, then take a short nap, so I'm awake in the afternoon. Then, when I get home in the evening, I take another nap after supper so I can stay awake to study."

Maurice was always immaculately dressed in a suit, shirt and tie, as were almost all of the med students. The undergraduates, mostly young men and some veterans, usually wore sport coats and wool dress pants, white or striped dress shirts, and ties knotted with the wide Windsor knot, which I had just learned how to tie. Sometimes we wore jackets or sweaters, and wool dress pants; and we always wore shirts and ties, unless we wore sport shirts. Otherwise, the dress was shirt and tie. And we all wore well polished leather dress shoes and, of course, a hat—Biltmore, Stetson, or Kensington. In the fall, almost everyone wore a tweed or gabardine topcoat; in the winter, a brown, black, or gray heavy wool overcoat. Most of the girls and young ladies wore wool skirts with silk or rayon blouses or wool sweaters, and sometimes dresses. In the winter they wore fur-collar trimmed wool coats or ones made from the actual furs of muskrat, beaver, or Persian lamb. And we all wore fur lined flight boots. On more than one occasion in the chemistry building, when hundreds of us hurriedly hung our coats on the racks just before entering the huge lecture hall, we would return after the lecture to find somebody else wearing our coat. They all looked practically alike. That's why I had my name embroidered on the lining. Although there was no written dress code for university students, the code was understood. It was based on tradition. And nobody in his wildest dreams would ever think of changing it. I can't imagine what would have happened if a student would have dared to set foot on campus wearing blue denim jeans. It would have been almost as unthinkable as coming to class naked. At the very least, the student probably would have landed in jail. And for good reason. Some crimes are too horrible to even think about.

I thought about many things including finding another place to stay. About a month before our Christmas holiday vacation, I caught a bad cold. The only medication I had ever taken for colds was hot lemonade with honey—that, plus Mom's homemade chicken soup. And although my bedroom had never been too warm, it had never been kept as cold as an icebox, even in winter. Under such treatment at home, I usually recovered from a cold in about ten days. This time, however, I didn't have any chicken soup; and the temperature in my dark, dismal, dreary cave was constant at fifty-two degrees—perfect for storing cabernet Sauvignon, but not exactly helpful for overcoming my cold. It hung on and on. Finally, just before our Christmas vacation, I recovered. I asked the Cramers if they could find another home for me, a warm home with a spare bedroom at or above ground level. That was my only request. I prayed that when I returned after the new year, I would have another place to stay— one with a warm, well lighted room.

For the next twelve days, however, I didn't have to worry about that or any thing else except studying for my exams scheduled to begin on January 3, immediately after I returned from Sheho. Now I was going home for the Christmas holidays. What a relief. At the railway station, I couldn't wait for the train from Edmonton to arrive. When it did, I was the first one in line to get on the train. And when I got on, I couldn't wait for it to start moving. The truth is, I was homesick. I hadn't seen my family in over three months, and I had them missed them all—Mom and

Dad and Etta and even Sylvia. But especially Mom. I couldn't wait to get back.

The next twelve days were the happiest of my entire life. Although it was so cold outside that the storm windows were perpetually covered with frost, I didn't care. All I did was stay in the house with Mom, near the potbelly stove in the dining room, or near the kitchen stove, and talk to her about everything or nothing at all. It's easy to talk about nothing when you love that person more than anyone else in the world. I also spent much of the day studying for my exams.

In the afternoon, I went to the store for a couple of hours to be with Dad and Etta, both of whom had managed the store quite well in my absence. Etta told me that the village had sponsored a home-coming party and dance in the town hall for our returning veterans. I was sorry that I had not been home to join the celebration. A day or two later, Eddie Grumetza, who had recently received his discharge from the Army, came in to see me. He knew I had been away to university and greeted me as though I were a hero. How ironic, I thought. He needed an over-coat and some fleece lined underwear, which was still in short supply. I sold him the overcoat and, to his surprise, as much underwear as he wanted. I thought that was the least I could do.

I also waited on the odd customer who wanted to buy little toiletry gifts for the upcoming Ukrainian Christmas, two weeks later than December 25. And I also helped customers who needed wool socks and wool mitts and ear muffs. Otherwise, there weren't too many customers who braved the frigid weather to come into the store if they didn't have to.

I got to visit Mr. Leckie, and I even spent some time with Sylvia without quarreling.

But most of the time, I just stayed in the house with Mom. She seemed especially happy to see me. Dad felt the same. He bought some beer from the hotel and gave me a bottle. He had hardly ever drunk beer before, but I suppose this was his way of celebrating. It's impossible to describe how happy I was during this time. I hoped I could stay home, so the feeling would last forever. But of course that was impossible. In the meantime, I would enjoy the happiness for as long as I could because I had a fleeting premonition that this might be the last time we would all be together.

We all celebrated New Year—1946—quietly. And then it was over. I took the train back to Saskatoon.

At Wynyard, Lyonel Fishman a second year predental student joined me. He was wearing a handsome gray donegal tweed suit. I had only one suit which I reserved for special occasions. But since his father owned a clothing store, Lyonel had quite a wardrobe. He joked continually and was not worried about money or about his upcoming exams or about anything. He seemed as if he didn't have a care in the world. I asked him if he had spent much time studying during the holidays. "No, I'll study tomorrow." I asked him if he was worried. "No. I've applied to Dental School in Portland, Oregon. Eppy (Epstein) and I both applied. We should be hearing from them this month. Maybe we'll get in this year. If not, maybe next." Two weeks later, both were in dental school. In the words of Maurice Faigen, "They were brains."

The Cramers, in my absence, had found another home for me. My prayers had been answered. Just as the Almighty in His infinite mercy delivered the Children of Israel out of bondage from the wicked Pharaoh and led them under the command of Moses out of Egypt, so, too, did He deliver me out of the damp, dingy, darkness of the cave in which I, too, had suffered unbearable misery for three months. True, maybe my plight wasn't quite as long and quite the same as that of my forebears. No army pursued me as I walked, suitcase in hand, all of two blocks from Avenue E to Avenue G; therefore, God did not have to part the waters. Also, I did not have to eat matzos all my life and get lost in the desert for forty years. But that's a different story. I was delivered out of the darkness and misery of my cave. Thank God! He looked after me. He got me a room in the home of Mr. Spector, the kosher butcher.

My upstairs room had a large bed and a dresser. No desk. Who needed a desk? I hadn't asked God for a desk. I could study for my exams and later—when they were over—write my assignments in a notebook balanced on my knee when I sat in the large, soft, velvet armchair that matched the chesterfield in the sitting room. Next to the armchair was a slim, tall standing lamp whose large lampshade focused the brilliant light from the 150 watt bulb onto my notebook, as I calculated what percentage of potassium permanganate was required before the solution first turned purple. Or I could dream of Tennyson's "Locksley Hall," or get lost in the world of Egdon Heath and sympathize with Eustacia Vye in Thomas Hardy's *The Return of the Native*, as she cried out to heaven: "How I have tried and tried. . . and how Destiny has been against me."

The house was warm. The bedroom was warm. The sitting room was warm and cozy. And it was quiet all afternoon when I came home except when Mrs. Spector, in the hallway, was on the phone for half-an-hour. But since whatever she had to say was so boring, it wasn't worth my time trying to figure out what the other person was saying in return. So I learned to ignore her monologue and pretended that her words sounded like a boiling tea kettle letting off steam. Eventually, she took the kettle off the stove. Otherwise, it was quiet. The entire family, including their teen-age daughter, didn't talk much, even at the supper table, when Mr. Spector was home. He was a big burly man with a loud, gruff, commanding voice, which at first intimidated me. But that was just his voice. He didn't know how to talk softly. Fortunately, he didn't say much, even after supper, or even after he came back from a hockey game, except when the Saskatoon Quakers won. Then he would say, "It was a good game. We won, 5-4."

Every night he brought home the choicest cuts of meats—kosher of course—more than enough for the entire family, of which I was now a member. On Friday night and Saturday we had chicken. Otherwise beef. It never went to waste.

My social life increased from the odd Hillel brunch to attending a University of Saskatchewan Huskies hockey game. I was surprised to see two of my friends on the team, Jack S. Katz and Milt Spector. I hadn't seen Milt in ten years, ever since he had moved from Springside to Watrous. I didn't know a great deal about hockey at the time, but I thought our Sheho senior hockey team—even without George Homeniuk—could have beaten the Huskies easily.

I also attended my first operetta, the university's production of Sigmund Romberg's *The Student Prince*. Except for the professional tenor in the leading role, all other singers were university students. I found the production absolutely delightful. I thought back to that day in early October, when I had been walking on campus after classes with a pretty girl from Wilkie. She was also a freshman, quite friendly, and I was just tagging along. "Where are you going?" I asked her.

"I'm going to try out for *The Student Prince*. Want to come along?"

The only prince I had ever heard of was the Prince of Wales. "What's *The Student Prince*?"

"It's an operetta. They're auditioning for singers and the chorus. It might be fun."

Inside the building we joined about a hundred other students milling around until an older man, the conductor I assumed, said, "All right now, I'm going to separate you into groups. Ladies on my left and men on my right. Tenors on the left and baritones on the right."

I didn't know if I was a tenor or baritone because I never sang. Although my sister Sylvia had a beautiful soprano voice, whenever I tried to sing at home, imitating Bing Crosby, 'When the blue of the night meets the gold of the day,' Dad would shout, "The bull *burchit*." [is bellowing] Since I thought my voice resembled Bing Crosby's more than Richard Tucker's, I joined the baritones.

"Come boys, let's all be gay boys." Then later, "To the inn we're marching, cause our throats are parching." Then much later I left.

I never went back, not because I didn't enjoy the singing, but because I thought it took up too much time. Besides, I thought I wasn't good enough. Months later, when I saw the thrilling performance, I knew I had been right. There was no way I could have made the chorus. Although I have since seen top notch professional productions of that operetta, with obviously better singing and more elaborate sets, they don't hold the same thrill for me. For one thing, that pretty girl from Wilkie is missing, but more important, the lyrics have been changed to appease politically correct fanatics. The word *gay*, as in "Come boys, let's all be *gay* boys," means happy. That's what the author intended it to mean, and that's what it meant when I saw the operetta. As a writer and an author, I am extremely offended when somebody has the audacity—the gall—to change or prostitute the original words of the author. If one is offended by certain words, don't read them or don't listen to them. Or write a different operetta or book. But don't tamper with somebody else's work.

The days passed quickly, and so did the weeks, and soon it was spring. But it was still cold. Gradually, reluctantly it seemed, the snow melted and the ice in the shaded yards behind the two-story homes, protected from the sun all these months, began to soften and melt around the edges, leaving tiny streams and small puddles, sure signs of the death of winter. Now it was April. Our final examinations were only two weeks away.

Like a bucket of ice cold water abruptly splashed into my face, the news hit me. Etta was on the telephone. "Mom just had a stroke."

That's all I remember. Apparently I have blocked out the details. I don't remember if I took the train back immediately or if it was the bus. I don't remember if I first went to see her in the Foam Lake Hospital or if I went on to Sheho and saw her later that night or the next morning. I don't even remember what she looked like when I saw her. But I did see her. I do remember that she was conscious but unable to speak, and she appeared happy to see me. She was paralyzed on her arm and leg. But she was still alive. That's all I remember about my visit.

I also remember thinking about Dr. Miller's prediction the year before. "If she has another stroke, she'll die." I had assumed that her second stroke would kill her "immediately." I guess that's why I was surprised that she was still alive. I also remembered my prayer to God the particular morning I learned of her first stroke. I had asked Him to spare her life this time. If He did, He could take her any time afterward. I had made Him a solemn oath. He had answered my first prayer. Now, I could not go back on my word. God could take her any time He wanted to, and I would not be mad at Him. I had made my peace with God.

I hoped Mom would recover. I hoped for the best. She was still alive when I returned to Saskatoon a few days later. She was still alive, but I was not optimistic. And I did not pray. I had accepted the inevitable.

Now, on April 17, it was time for our three-hour final examinations. Final as in "finale"—the end. The university operated on a full year's term, from September 28 to April 24. Part of the final mark (grade) for each subject was based on the January exam, but the greatest weight was usually given to the final three-hour examination. One exception was botany, which counted for half of the final biology mark; zoology counted for the other half. In most of my other classes, the results of our entire year's work hinged on the outcome of these finals.

A week before the exam, Jack S. Katz began growing a beard for good luck and vowed not to shave until after the exams. Other students let their hair grow or wore the same clothes every day. All kinds of superstitions were visible during those final days. And then it was over.

I knew I had done well in English and probably in zoology. But I would not have spent my entire savings account betting on the other subjects. I would know the results within a month.

I sold my books to the bookstore, then said good-bye to the Spectors and to the family of friends I had met during the year. I had grown to feel that we were all part of a special family—a family of students privileged to be able to attend the University of Saskatchewan. I felt a tinge of sadness. I knew I would not be seeing most of them again because I would not be returning to this university. When I did resume my studies, hopefully within a couple of years, it would be in Winnipeg, where my family would eventually move. In the meantime, any plans for my future education were put on hold for at least a year.

Now, as I was about to leave Saskatoon, I felt that despite the unpleasant living conditions I had experienced for the first three months and my constant worries about my family back home—and my future— I had for the most part enjoyed my first year away from home. Attending the University of Saskatchewan was an experience I knew I would never forget.

Toward the end of May, I received a letter from the University. I knew it contained my marks. I hastily tore open the envelope. I could not believe the results. Transposed from percentage marks, these were my letter grades: English, B; Biology, C; Chemistry, D; French, D; Political Economy, F.

I was stunned. My mouth suddenly went dry. I felt as if the floor had suddenly collapsed. All my countless hours of hard work and study had been in vain. For a long time I wandered around in a daze. Then I made up my mind that the next time I would work harder. I had lost the battle. But I would not lose the war.

CHAPTER TWENTY-SEVEN
Life Goes On

In March, about a month before Mom's stroke, my sister Sylvia entered an amateur talent contest sponsored by the Tuberculosis Association of Saskatchewan. Held in the Sheho town hall on a Saturday night and broadcast live over radio station CJGX, Yorkton, its purpose was to raise money to fight tuberculosis, commonly known as TB. Local contestants proud of their achievements in music and undaunted by stage fright and standing in front of a real microphone, officially lettered CJGX, did their best to impress the audience by performing musical selections on their favorite instruments. These included the accordion, banjo, guitar, mandolin, mouth organ (harmonica), piano, and violin. In addition to these virtuosos, a few of whom could even read music, many of the contestants strummed their guitars and sang cowboy songs at the same time, followed by yodeling. There were also a few high school girls who would sang their version of the latest song to reach number one on the "Lucky Strike Hit Parade." And then there was Sylvia.

After each performance, everyone in the audience would clap, some louder than others, depending on how much they liked the performance and the contestant. But it was not the loud clapping or whistling that determined the winner. Otherwise, the yodeling cowboy singers with their guitars, or the mandolin or accordion players would have won hands down. Those performances might bring down the house, but they didn't count because they hardly ever raised any money. What counted was the amount of money raised by each individual contestant.

As each performance ended, members in the audience who liked that performance had an opportunity to immediately pledge money for their favorite contestant. In addition, listeners in radio-land also had an opportunity to do likewise by telephoning their pledges to our local telephone operator, or if they were closer to Yorkton, to CJGX, which had an open telephone line to the operator in Sheho, and hence to the announcer in Sheho's town hall. Thus, within about fifteen minutes following each performance, both the local audience and listeners throughout much of Saskatchewan and Manitoba would know how much money they, themselves, had raised in the name of their favorite performer, and more important, the total amount raised by that contestant. The contestant would then be called back for an encore. Those were the rules. Whoever raised the most money was the final winner.

Although Sylvia had never taken singing lessons, she often sang at school and at home, in a promising lyric soprano voice. This time she was accompanied on the piano by her classmate Mickey Haluke, who had taken lessons from Etta , and who was now an excellent pianist. Sylvia's first song was a "teaser." She flirted with the audience as she sang:

"I'm in love with you, Honey. Say you love me too, Honey."

She brought down the house and raised as much money from the audience as did anyone else. But that was only the beginning.

From near and far, radio pledges began to roll in. In Foam Lake, Dr. Rubin was playing bridge. Someone told him about the radio program. He caught the tail end of it, and both he and his bridge partners immediately phoned in a substantial pledge in her name. Then they phoned their friends. By now, she had raised more money than anyone else.

She sang an encore. This time it was a lilting aria, "The Laughing Song," from Strauss' operetta *Der Fledermaus*. (The Bat.) She sang it in English. Once more she brought down the house. The pledges mounted. In Inglis, Manitoba, a neighbor rushed into Uncle Abe's store and shouted, "Hurry, tune to CJGX. Your niece from Sheho is singing on the radio."

The telephone lines to Yorkton were suddenly overloaded. By the time the pledges were added up, it was clear that Sylvia had won. She would represent Sheho in the final talent contest to be held in Yorkton on Sunday, July 8th, 1946.

When I returned home from Saskatoon, toward the end of April, Mom was still in the Foam Lake Hospital, under the care of Dr. Rubin. He had received his discharge from the Army and had resumed his practice in Foam Lake following Dr. Miller's departure. The stroke had left her paralyzed, but she could talk. That's all I remember. My mind has blocked out not only the details of her condition but even my visits with her. To be perfectly honest, all I remember is that while I was home, she was in Foam Lake about a month before Dr. Rubin decided he could do nothing more for her. He recommended that she be sent to the Winnipeg General Hospital, the most prestigious teaching hospital in Western Canada, whose specialists were among the best in the country.

During those weeks in May, while she was still in the Foam Lake Hospital, I wondered what would happen to her. I suppose I already knew there was no hope for her recovery because Dr. Rubin had already warned us that we would probably have to take her to Winnipeg. Would the specialists there be able to do something miraculous, or at least something that might help her? Would she ever be well enough to come home? That seemed most unlikely. Or would she merely exist as an invalid for months or possibly years and suffer a slow, lingering death? Or was it only a matter of time—perhaps a couple of months —before her misery would be ended? I wondered about many things. I needed to be alone with the Creator's handiwork so I could think.

I remember going down to the creek that flowed beneath the bridge where years before I had spent some of the happiest days of my life with Walter Lys, roasting potatoes along the banks of "our" creek. Now I had come back again to be alone and to think. As I sat on a log near the bank and watched the minnows and tadpoles swimming back and forth, and swirling around in the cold, clear, shallow water, with the warm sun overhead, I thought about many things, not necessarily one at a time and certainly not in order of importance. For who was I to say what was *most* important? Important to whom? To me? What about Mom? What about Dad? What about my sisters? In the end, however, even though my thoughts were so mixed up that I had a hard time concentrating, I did think about all of them. But I spent most of my time thinking about my future. Would I be able to continue my studies in premed? And if so, when?

Since my future depended upon what our entire family would do after Mom was transferred to the hospital in Winnipeg, where she might survive for a couple of months or linger on as an invalid even longer, my main question was, how long would it be before Dad would sell the store and move to Winnipeg? It was not a question of *if* but *when*. Then, what would happen after that? What could he do in Winnipeg to make a living? Or would he have to live on his reserves, the ten or fifteen thousand dollars he might have after he sold the store and the house? And as Mr. Leckie pointed out, if Mom continued to linger in the hospital for even a year, the medical costs would eventually bankrupt us. Was there a solution? It all seemed overwhelming. I wondered what life had in store for us.

I reached into the shallow water, hoping to catch a tiny minnow circling about the tadpoles; but just as it was almost within my grasp, it squiggled out and swam away.

I couldn't think any more. As I walked home along the gravel highway, the sounds of the croaking bullfrogs in the water-filled ditches brought back memories of the year before, when Mom and I used to take walks along this same gravel road, listening to the same bass baritone tune: Croak -croak. Croak croak. Croak-croak. I now realized that I would never be able to take a walk with her again. Never.

Toward the end of May, Dr. Rubin finally decided that Mom should be sent to Winnipeg. According to my sister Sylvia, she was transported by ambulance to the railway station and then to a lower sleeping birth on the overnight train to Winnipeg. When it stopped in Sheho, again according to Sylvia, all four of us in our family (Dad, Etta, Sylvia, and I) boarded the train to visit her for about fifteen minutes before the train departed. Mr. Leckie also joined us. He had come to say good-bye to my mother, who had treated him as one of the family ever since she had come to Sheho. Dad and Etta stayed aboard with her. When the train arrived in Winnipeg next morning, Mom was once more transported by ambulance to the hospital. That evening, or the following one, Dad boarded the train back for Sheho, but Etta remained in Winnipeg. Those are Sylvia's recollections.

Mine differ entirely because I have almost none. All I remember is being notified that Mom would be on the train one particular evening on the way to Winnipeg since there was nothing more that could be done for her in Foam Lake. I also have a very vague recollection of being aware of that evening—the particular evening when the train carrying Mom would be stopping in Sheho. She was on her way to Winnipeg for the last time. And she would never return. She was going there to die. I guess I was so traumatized that my mind has taken the easy way out by blocking the details from my memory.

About a week or two earlier, Dad received a letter from Bill Laskin. He had recently sold his store in Rose Valley and had moved to Edmonton, along with his wife and Shimon, to be near his only daughter, Merle. The second oldest in the family, she had graduated as a pharmacist from the University of Saskatchewan some years before and had been working in the Misercordia Hospital in Edmonton. Mr. Laskin's letter, in Jewish, was written to share his blessed news with his dear old friend. As Dad read the letter to me, he was as happy as any close friend could be. Merle had met a wonderful Jewish doctor where she worked and had just become engaged. DR. Maurice Weinlos and Merle Laskin would be married in two months, on July 14th.

On May 24, Victoria Day, also known as Empire Day, Dad received even more wonderful news. His own daughter Merle, my oldest sister, had just become engaged. Dad was absolutely delighted. He sat down immediately and as Mr. Laskin had done, wrote his own letter in Jewish, which he gleefully read to me. Although my translation is not even remotely accurate, the main idea was something like this: "I want to wish you *Mazltov* [congratulations] on the engagement of your daughter. Now I have some wonderful news to share with you, so you can wish me *Mazltov*, too. My own Merle has just become engaged to a wonderful Jewish boy. His name is Arwin Goldstein. He just got out of the Army. His father has a factory making brushes from horsehair. She met him last December and they are planning to get married July 1."

Although my sister Merle and her fiancee had not yet announced their engagement when Mom arrived at the Winnipeg General Hospital, two or three days before Victoria Day, and although they originally had planned to be married in the fall, they immediately decided to move ahead with their plans as soon as they saw how frail and helpless the stroke had left Mom. They realized she had not long to live. They told her they would announce their engagement on Victoria Day, and they would be married on Dominion Day, Sunday, July 1st. They felt that now Mom had something to look forward to and to live for—the knowledge that her oldest daughter would be married within five weeks. They hoped Mom could hold on until then. They wanted her to know that they had gotten married while she was still alive.

A few days before the wedding, I went to Winnipeg to visit her. She spoke softly, and her mind was clear; but she seemed to be getting weaker every day. Larry Lackman accompanied me. He had been discharged from the United States Navy some time after the Japanese had officially surrendered to General Douglas MacArthur, and he was now in Winnipeg, along with his mother, Bessie, whom we called "Bee." They accompanied me every day, and every day Mom seemed to be getting weaker. On one particular morning, I thought the end was near. But the following day, after she had been given oxygen, she looked completely different, perky and full of life, as though she were on her way to recovery. I was astounded. "It looks like a miracle," I said to Larry. He agreed. But by the time Dad arrived, just before the wedding, the miracle had vanished. She was now weaker than ever.

"Is Merle married yet?" she whispered.

"*Morgen. Zee gate hasene hooben morgen, ziben a zeyger.*" he said. ["Tomorrow. She will be getting married tomorrow, at seven o'clock."]

"She will be getting married tomorrow," I repeated. The wedding is at seven o'clock."

A faint smile crept over her mouth. "Good. Tell her good. I wish I could be there. Let me know when she's married."

Dad told her he would definitely let her know when Merle had been married. She nodded. Then, with a faint smile once more on her lips, she fell asleep. She knew that her daughter would be married tomorrow. And she must live to see that day.

Merle and Arwin had decided to follow an old custom practiced by Orthodox Jewry in Eastern Europe that required the groom to "bedeck the bride," that is, lift her veil to make sure that she, not somebody else, was the one he wanted to marry. This custom originated because of the trick played upon the Biblical Jacob by his father-in-law, who had tricked Jacob by covering the face of the homely daughter Leah with a veil and pawning her off to the unsuspecting young groom. From that time, the custom of unveiling the bride had been part of the pre-marriage ceremony, to insure that the groom got the right bride.

At the big Goldstein house on Ethelbert Street, in the West end, I joined a number of Arwin's close single friends and relatives, as well as a few young men on Merle's side of the family, including Larry and my cousin Maurice Shnider.

The last time I had seen Maurice was when he had visited us on embarkation leave, just before being sent to England. After flying convoy escort and anti-submarine patrols over the Atlantic, Flying Officer Shnider had been transferred to India and Ceylon, where he participated in air-sea rescue of American crews whose B-29s had been shot down by the Japanese. On one of these missions, he had navigated his Catalina low over the waves of the enemy infested Andaman Sea, for one thousand miles without any points of reference whatsoever, landing at the exact spot for a perfect rescue; then flying back safely and returning after twenty-four hours, with only one hundred gallons of fuel left. He had set a record. It was the longest air-sea rescue of the war. For this remarkable feat and others, now Flight Lieutenant Shnider was awarded the Distinguished Flying Cross by the Royal Air Force.[15] But although The United States Army Air Corps made a general reference to such rescues, it did not even mention this one, let alone his name. After returning to England, before being discharged, he married the sweetheart whom he had met two years before. Now they were both in Winnipeg. Maurice was completing a special premed class for returning veterans, and had taken the day off from his studies to attend the wedding. Since he had already been married for almost a year, he was giving Arwin some friendly advice.

"You've still got two hours to wait before you pick her up," he said. "I know how nervous you must be. I remember the day I got married. I was so nervous I took a bath right before the ceremony to calm me down. That always works."

"I don't need a bath," said Arwin. "I took a shower this morning. I'm not nervous. Another hour or two won't kill me."

I thought that Maurice should have given his advice to me. I was the one who was becoming nervous. It was my sister who was getting married, and I would be participating in the ceremony, and everything about it was strange. In fact, I had never been to a Jewish wedding ceremony that I could recall. This was a first and it made me nervous.

The Goldstein house had just been painted but, unfortunately, nobody told Maurice, or else he forgot. Suddenly it was too late. In a relaxed mood, since he wasn't the one getting married, he leaned against the screen door. When he straightened up, we all saw his mistake. Both his suit coat and pants had a broad green stripe running down the entire length of each, from the shoulders to the cuffs on the pants. He hurried home to change.

Our cavalcade drove across town to the home of Bill and Mabel Cutler, my (second) cousins, on Pritchard Avenue, where Merle was awaiting her bridegroom; then we continued a few miles farther to the Peretz Hall on Main Street, in the heart of the Jewish district.

In compliance with Jewish Law, a canopy had been set up, under which the rabbi would soon perform the marriage ceremony of Arwin Goldstein and Merle Katz. As soon as I saw that canopy, I began to perspire. I knew it was only a matter of time, perhaps half an hour or less, before my sister Sylvia would sit down at the piano to play the Wedding March. Then, in a matter of minutes, with Etta and I waiting in the wings, Merle and Dad would begin walking down the aisle toward that canopy. Then, only seconds later, with Etta—the bridesmaid—on my arm, I would follow. Yes, for a few minutes I would not only be part of that ceremony, but I would be the very center, and the entire audience would have their eyes focused on me. I began to sweat. What if I made a mistake? What kind of a mistake? Maybe I would be out of step with Etta. I might even trip and fall. It's not easy to be the only brother of your big sister who is about to get married and you're in a big city and you have to walk down the aisle, while a hall full of strangers are staring at you, their eyes focused on every step you take.

Arwin saw how nervous I was. "Don't worry," he said, "You'll be all right." It's reassuring to have a bridegroom about to get married tell his future brother-in-law there's nothing to worry about.

Etta saw how nervous I was. "Why are you nervous," she said. "You're not getting married."

"You'd better believe it. And it's going to be long time before I do. Are you nervous?"

"Sort of. I only hope Sylvia plays the Wedding March straight. Maurice has been showing her how to jazz it up. He thinks that's funny. I told her, 'Don't you dare jazz it up! Don't even try.' That's the only thing I'm worried about."

Fortunately, her fears were unfounded. Mendelssohn would have been proud of Sylvia. She played it straight, and neither Etta nor I fainted.

The tone of the wedding was dignified and subdued. Everyone knew why. It was not a formal affair, with the groom and his party dressed in tuxedos and the bride in a long white flowing gown attended by numerous bridesmaids, all in fancy gowns. Not this wedding. Arwin had ordered a made-to-measure English wool worsted suit, but since it didn't arrive on time, he bought a light weight tan one off the rack. Merle's cousin Bee Lackman helped her select a beautiful light blue suit and a white frilly blouse and white gloves.

As Merle walked down the aisle with Dad by her side, she carried a Bible on top of which were three white gardenias.

Etta and I followed them, both keeping in step to Sylvia's "straight" rendition of "The Wedding March" from Mendelssohn's Incidental Music to *A Midsummer Night's Dream.*

Except for the names *Goldstein* and *Katz*, the entire ceremony was performed by the rabbi in Hebrew. Finally, the penultimate moment was at hand.

To mark the conclusion of the ceremony, a small, thin drinking glass had been heavily wrapped in a towel, then placed on the floor. To symbolize the destruction of King David's temple in Jerusalem, and the survival and continuation of the Jewish people and their religion, the groom must stomp on the towel hard enough to break the glass. It must be broken with a single stomp of the foot. Just in the event that the glass was thick, Arwin took no chances. He brought down his foot with a hard bang that left no doubt in anyone's mind about the outcome. The glass had been utterly shattered. Then he lifted the veil and kissed his bride.

Although the original plans were for a very small wedding because of Mom's critical condition, the final count for invited guests turned out to be approximately one hundred. Arwin's relatives on both sides of his family filled the hall.

His mother, along with Merle, had made the arrangements for the wedding. Because of the Dominion Day long weekend, all the kosher caterers were out of town at Winnipeg Beach. And since Merle wouldn't even dream of serving any food that was not kosher, they contracted with Peggy's Pantry to serve vegetarian sandwiches, soda pop, coffee, and of course a big wedding cake. Finally, for anyone who might want a drink of hard liquor, there was a bottle of Scotch whisky available. This was not exactly a drinking crowd. We lingered for a while after the bride and groom left, and then the crowd gradually thinned and it was over. It was a lovely evening, but very subdued.

Around ten o'clock, a few of us decided to go to a night spot on Pembina Highway. One of Arwin's cousins and I joined Larry and Etta and Maurice and Renee Shnider. We drank soft drinks and danced and listened to Larry telling us what mischievous tricks he would have played on the married couple if he had known where they were staying. "I would have slipped into their bedroom ahead of time and put pebbles and crackers underneath the mattress." We all knew he was serious. Fortunately, he didn't find out where they were staying until the next day. By then, they had taken the bus to Clear Lake, Manitoba, to spend a week on their honeymoon.

But it was not to be.

The next morning our entire family except for Merle went back to the hospital. There was little change in Mom's condition except that she was a little more tired and a little weaker than before and also quite drowsy. She barely spoke, even after Dad, speaking into her ear, told her that the wedding had indeed taken place. She looked at him for confirmation. "Are they married?" she whispered.

"Yes. They're married," he repeated, both in English and Jewish, nodding his head to make sure she understood.

"You were at the wedding?" she whispered to me.

"Yes," I said. "We were all at the wedding."

"Then they're really married?"

"Yes. They're really married," I repeated. "They're went to Clear Lake on their honeymoon."

"I'm sorry I wasn't there," she said. "Was it a nice wedding?"

"It was a nice wedding," Sylvia said.

"It was a lovely wedding," I said. "Everyone said it was a lovely wedding."

One by one, we all described the wedding to her. She listened for a while, then with a smile on her lips, fell asleep.

On Tuesday, she seemed only slightly weaker; but towards evening, she took a turn for the worse. The doctors warned us that the end might be near and it would be advisable to notify Merle.

Realizing that Arwin and she had not spent even an entire day together in Clear Lake, we nonetheless followed the doctors' advice. Mabel Cutler made a telephone call to the lodge where they were staying. When she learned they had gone to a movie, she phoned the movie theater and explained the emergency. The movie was interrupted so that Merle and Arwin could be paged. When they learned about the sudden turn of events, they decided to return immediately. However, since they had just missed the bus connections back to Winnipeg, they did not get back until the following day, Wednesday.

Bleary eyed, they joined us in Mom's room. There was not much change in her condition. At least she seemed to be holding her own. The end now did not necessarily appear to be imminent. Bee Lackman, decided to return to California.

On both Thursday and Friday, her condition seemed to be about the same. We thought she might linger on for several days or perhaps weeks. There was no way of knowing. We did know, however, that we simply could not afford to leave the store closed much longer. It was now over a week since Dad had closed the store to come here. He had expected to return shortly after the wedding. But now, on Friday, realizing that although Mom might pass away any day, yet might linger for days or possibly a week or two, he decided that Sylvia and I should return to open the store. He would stay here with her until the end.

On Friday afternoon, realizing that this was the last time I would ever see Mom, I told her that I had to go back to Sheho to open the store. I fought to hold back my tears because men don't cry. I leaned over and kissed her, then held her hand and told her how much I loved her.

She nodded, gripped my hand and said, " You will become a doctor." She paused, then whispered, "Don't marry a *shiksa*."

"I won't," I said. Then I hugged her and kissed her again. Finally, without looking back, I turned around and left my beloved mother behind.

A few hours later, Sylvia and I took the overnight train back to Sheho and arrived there after ten. As soon as we got home we opened the store and waited on customers. They were all anxious to hear about Mom and expressed hope that she might still recover. I thanked them. But I did not share their optimism. I knew it was only a matter of time—perhaps a few more days. Perhaps a week at the most.

That night I slept in the bedroom facing the kitchen. I was still asleep early Sunday morning when I heard a knock on the kitchen window. "Jack, wake up." It was Mr. Leckie. He looked sad. I knew immediately why he had come. I went outside. "I'm sorry," he said. Then he paused before continuing. "Your mother passed away last night."

I nodded. "Sylvia and I will take the one o'clock bus to Winnipeg."

It was Sunday, July 8th, the day Sylvia had been scheduled to appear at the amateur talent contest finals in Yorkton. With tears in her eyes, she went to see her classmate and accompanist, Mickey Haluke. She told her what had happened. Her eyes were still red when she returned. Mom was only forty-four. Sylvia was only fourteen, barely a teenager. Now her mother was gone.

We arrived in Winnipeg late that night and went to the home of our cousins Mabel and Bill Cutler, where Dad was also staying. They told me Mom had passed away early Sunday morning, shortly after midnight. The funeral would be held the next day. I still had not cried. For the past week, I had been expecting Mom to die any day and was therefore prepared for the inevitable. Besides, I told myself, I was now a grown man and men don't cry.

Early the next afternoon, as we prepared to go to the Jewish Funeral Home, Dad and I were given black neckties to wear. According to the Jewish funeral custom, these would be cut off to symbolize the shredding of one's garments over grief shown by the bereaved. I still had not cried.

I remember being with Merle and Arwin in particular when we arrived at the funeral home. A couple of ladies dressed in black, with black shawls, were sitting in the front row, wailing long, loud, terribly mournful cries, as though someone were torturing them to death. I had never heard anything like it. "Isn't that awful?" said Arwin. "They've got professional wailers." I recognized the one who was wailing the loudest. She was Mom's Auntie Leachman. I had never even seen the other one. Dad, my sisters, and I were the ones who had suffered the greatest loss, yet we weren't even crying. Not at the moment. But here was Auntie Leachman wailing as if she had lost her entire family. As for the other one, I wondered if she had ever known my mother. Although I realized they weren't professionals, I thought it was disgusting to put on such a spectacle, pretending to be so grief-stricken.

I looked around and quickly recognized several Jewish travelers who had always eaten at Mom's table whenever they were in Sheho. I also noticed other representatives of the wholesale houses and garment factories we dealt with, as well as their owners. I assumed it was they who had ordered the wreaths now covering Mom's casket. I felt gratified to see that so many of Mom's business associates were paying their last respects. She would have been deeply honored by their presence and overwhelmed by the flowers. I thought of the flowers I had bought her on Mother's Day, just over a year ago. Flowers were a symbol of my love, but only a symbol. However, when I treated her with loving kindness, that was the *real* thing—something that money could not buy. That's why I always say, "Be kind and show your affection and your love. Give flowers to the living."

A rabbi whom I had never seen gave the eulogy. He spoke in Jewish from notes he had apparently had taken a few hours before, summarizing her life in about ten minutes. He complimented her on being a devoted, dutiful, loving wife and mother and even mentioned the name of her husband and children. Then he said some prayers in Hebrew, after which we all stood up as Dad hurriedly recited the Mourner's *Kaddish*, the Mourner's Prayer for the Dead. I accompanied him, slowly, mumbling along as best I could, since I had almost forgotten how to read Hebrew. "*Yis-gad-dal v'yis-kad-dash sh'mey rab-mo, b'ol-mo di'v-ro chir'oo-sey ...*" ["Magnified and sanctified be the name of God throughout the world which He created according to His Will. May He establish His kingdom during the days of your life and during the life of all the house of Israel, speedily, yea, soon; and say ye, Amen."]

[The *Kaddish* does not mention the deceased.]

We all filed past the closed coffin. Dad and my sisters were sobbing. I swallowed hard. Men aren't supposed to cry. Then we went outside, got into several cars and drove to the outskirts of the city, to the Hebrew Sick Benefit Cemetery.

We gathered at the edge of the freshly dug large hole, the graveside, where the rabbi conducted a brief burial ceremony. Dad and I once more recited the *Kaddish*. Then the rabbi approached us with a scissors and cut Dad's black necktie in half, and then mine. The rabbi uttered a short prayer. And then the pine box coffin was slowly lowered into the grave. Finally, some men began to quickly shovel the mound of earth over the coffin, higher and higher, until the hole was filled. That's where Mom would lie, in that hole, forever and ever, through eternity. She would lie there, buried in the cold, wet earth, without blankets to keep her warm when the snows fell and everything froze. Even when it got to be fifty below. She would spend eternity in that hole, covered only by the yellowish-brown thick clay at the bottom, with the moist black earth at the top. A year later, at the unveiling, a gravestone would mark the place where my mother was buried, six feet beneath the earth.

We returned to Bill and Mabel's home. All the mirrors had been completely covered in accordance with Jewish law, to observe the period of bereavement, normally lasting seven days, during which time we would sit *shivah*. [in mourning] A tray of delicatessen foods and pastries had been prepared to offer the many visitors who also brought sweets. They had come to offer their condolences, and to cheer the bereaved. I wanted none of this. I was repulsed at the thought of anyone trying to cheer me up. I was tired and I was *really* in mourning for my beloved mother. All I wanted now was to be alone. I retreated to my bedroom, undressed, and went to bed, trying not to listen to the buzz of voices and sounds of occasional laughter. I had not cried at all, because men aren't supposed to cry. That's what I had thought up until this very moment. Suddenly I lost control, and I burst out crying.

I could not help myself. I cried and cried aloud, unable to stop. I did not want anyone to hear my cries, so I stuffed a pillow over my mouth to absorb the sound. And I just kept on crying and crying, and sobbing in bursts, uncontrollably, with tears streaming down my cheeks and down the pillow case until it was soaked. I was only eighteen and I had lost my beloved mother. She was too young to die, but she had died and I would never see her again. My pain was unbearable. I would have gladly given anything in the world to have her back, to tell her once more how much I loved her, and how sorry I was for the many times I had misbehaved and upset her. But it was too late now. She was gone. So I just kept on crying until at last there were no more tears to shed and my sobbing stopped. Then I went to sleep and did not wake up until the next morning.

And that was the last time I ever cried over the loss of my mother—the last time—until these last few days, fifty-three years later, as I write these very words. Even now, at this very moment, while I try to record my final memories of her, I must stop with every few words I write in order to wipe my glasses and wash my reddened cheeks. The bitter tears continue to fall. And since I no longer believe that men aren't supposed to cry, I no longer swallow hard and try to hold back my tears. I simply let them fall. And they just keep on falling. They have had a long time to accumulate. But at last I can express my grief, not only on these pages, but more important, through these bitter tears.

We sat in mourning for three days, then returned to Sheho. The rabbi, realizing that we had already lost a great deal of business while the store had been closed for over a week and could not afford to keep it closed much longer, gave Dad a dispensation. Instead of sitting in mourning for the full seven days, the rabbi decided that three days would be enough. Life must go on.

CHAPTER TWENTY-EIGHT
Exodus

On Friday, three days after Mom had been laid to rest, Dad, Sylvia, Etta, and I boarded the train for Sheho, accompanied by Larry Lackman. It was now obvious that Etta and Larry were very serious about each other.

With Larry around, the house did not seem so empty. It was like having a real cousin as part of the family, even though he would eventually become my brother-in-law. He showed me some judo tricks which I assumed he had learned in the Navy. I was startled to learn that with practice, I would be able to smash an opponent's head, gouge out his eyes, or even kill him, in a matter of seconds. He also showed me the proper way to handle Dad's .32 caliber revolver, which he referred to as a lady's toy because of its small handle. I decided that since I had never held a revolver in my hand before and had no intention of ever using one, I would let him handle that toy. And I decided that I would never get into a street fight or any fight, just in case my opponent also knew a little judo. It was not something to play around with. He stayed with us for a week before returning to Winnipeg, and then taking the bus back to his home in Long Beach. Etta would stay home and help in the store until Christmas. Then she would leave us to join him in Long Beach, where she would stay at his parents' home until they got married.

Sylvia, too, would move away after Christmas. She would go to Winnipeg and complete high school, while living with Merle and Arwin. That would leave Dad and me alone in Sheho. And since neither of us had any intention of remaining in Sheho, we decided to promote a "Selling-Out Sale" in the fall, after which we would sell the store and the house. Then, hopefully in six months or less, we, also, would move to Winnipeg.

Every time our customers, as well as others who shopped elsewhere, came into the store to tell us how sorry they were about our loss, Dad would momentarily break into tears and sob, "She was too young to die. Too young."

I was gradually coming to grips with our loss and had decided to get on with my life. But in the evening, after the store closed, the house seemed empty. It no longer felt like a home even though Dad, Etta, and Sylvia were still living with me. Someone was missing. It was not the same as when Mom was alive. It was like walking into an empty house. That's the only way I can describe it. Empty. I felt alone. Terribly alone.

Slowly, that aching feeling of emptiness began to ease, and I adjusted to our new circumstances. Life must go on. I had important things to do. I went to Winnipeg on a buying trip for the store. This would be the last fall we would spend in Sheho, and I needed to prepare for the biggest fall-and-winter business we would ever do. Now, at eighteen, I was completely in charge of all the buying for the store except for groceries and hardware, which I never liked anyway. In fact, I hardly ever worked behind the grocery counter. Dad bought the groceries and hardware. I bought everything else. Our suppliers—wholesalers and manufacturers—treated me with kindness and respect, and all expressed their condolences. Many of them had known Mom for over fifteen years. It was their loss also. I spent only a few days in Winnipeg, just long enough to stock up on everything we needed for our forthcoming "Selling-Out Sale," including many items still in short supply.

I had thought about the death-bed promise I had made to Mom. I had every intention of keeping it, but I was curious about what Dad would do if I ever intermarried. So one morning when there was nobody in the store and he and I were sitting on the cement step outside, I asked him what he would do if I ever married a shiksa.

Without reflecting for even a second, he said, "I would take out mine 'revoiylver' and shoot you. Then I would shoot myself." That ended any discussion about the subject, and I never brought it up again. But I continued to think about my promise. I had no intention of ever intermarrying. Nevertheless, I was troubled. I already knew that life does not always go according to one's plan. And one never knows what the future has in store. If two people love each other, the accident of birth should not prevent them from getting married. It certainly should not be a taboo. But I kept my thoughts to myself.

One evening in August after the store closed, I went to the fairgrounds across the railway tracks to watch a baseball practice and decided to try out as a catcher. I put on the huge catcher's mitt, stood behind the plate, and for a while caught every pitch that George Homeniuk threw. My coordination was perfect. But George was barely warming up. And he was not yet throwing curves. So I just stood there, catching everything he threw at me. Finally, he threw a fast ball. It was the fastest ball I had ever seen. But I wasn't afraid, not with that huge padded mitt on my left hand. Besides, I had perfect coordination. Until now. Suddenly that ball began spinning. It was hurtling toward me out of control. I turned my mitt slightly downward, just a tiny bit, instead of upward. Instantly, I realized my mistake. But before I could correct it, that bullet-like curve ball hit my mitt dead on before glancing off. I threw off the mitt and howled in pain. One of my fingers was blue. Mr. Leckie's oldest daughter, who was a nurse and was visiting him, said it was only a sprain. But after the pain persisted for days, I went to Yorkton to see Dr. Portnuff. He had it X-rayed. It was broken, so he set it in a cast. When I asked him how much I owed him, he replied, "How's business?"

"It's O.K. I just got back from Winnipeg on a buying trip."

"How was it?"

"Good."

"Was it *very* good? "

I knew what he meant. Was I able to buy a lot of goods that were still in short supply? "Yes. It was a very good buying trip. How much do I owe you?"

"Twelve dollars."

I was astounded. I had expected a five dollar charge maximum. I was glad I hadn't needed an appendectomy. We would have had to sell the store. Perhaps I should have told him it was a terrible trip and I had come home empty handed. I was getting an education in some economic aspects of medicine. Those who can afford to pay, pay more. Those who can't afford to pay, give promises. When I told Dad about the incident, all he said was, "He's a good doctor. But he shouldn't have charged you that much."

The weather was good that fall. As soon as the crops had been harvested, I sent out our flyers to every village and town within a twenty-four mile radius. Large bold-face, all-capital letters headlined the flyer:

KATZ' STORE, SHEHO

SELLING OUT SALE.

The promotion worked. That fall as I had predicted, we did more business than ever before. Since Mr. Orloff was no longer in business, we were now getting some Foam Lake customers. They were buying parkas, ladies' dresses, coats and other big ticket items. Three and four hundred dollar days were common, and on some Saturdays we rang up over $600. Compared to the grim days of the Depression, when we were lucky to take in a hundred dollars on a Saturday with total sales of only $12,000 for the entire year, on a razor- thin profit margin, and then most of it on credit, our annual business now had doubled, with almost all of it in cash. Dad was amazed. For a time he had some misgivings about moving away. What would he do in Winnipeg? But he realized that before the year was up, both Etta and Sylvia would be gone, and the two of us would be left alone.

With Mom gone and with all of my close friends having left Sheho, I really felt lonely. Fortunately, I was busy. During the day, I spent almost all of my time in the store. Even after supper I would usually return to prepare for the next day's business. If I did remain in the house, I would occasionally try to read a book or magazine. But I couldn't concentrate, not even on a magazine. So I usually went back to the store, or I would visit Mr. Leckie. But it just wasn't the same.

The only social event I attended that fall was the wedding of Olga Kereliuk. Her father owned a small grocery store on the main floor of the two-story red brick building that had once been a bank and later the provincial liquor store. The family lived upstairs. She had transferred to our school from the farm eleven years earlier, when her father had gone into business, and she had graduated from high school the year before I did. After that, I simply lost contact with her, as I had with many of my classmates. Both Dad and I were therefore delighted when Bill Kereliuk, Dad's minor competitor, threw a wedding party for her in the Ukrainian hall and invited the entire village to the celebration. It was the first time either of us had shared in any joyous occasion since Mom's passing. Everyone in the village attended, as well as Mr. Kereliuk's friends from the outlying areas. It was the biggest wedding celebration I had ever attended, and both Dad and I felt honored to be part of it. Although some of the food was not kosher, there were enough cheese sandwiches, as well as cake, to satisfy Dad's appetite.

The celebration reminded me of the many times I had accompanied Dad to the weddings of his Ukrainian customers on their farms. Whatever furniture there had been in the small dining and living room of the house had been removed to make way for tightly packed rows of benches on which the numerous guests sat and dined. At the head table, below a picture of a blonde, long-haired, blue-eyed, bearded Jesus, sat the groom or bride, along with the parents, the priest, and other honored guests. Large platters of meat and vegetables and a cake lay on top of the table. Dad was always seated at the head table of the groom or bride, since there were two celebrations, one at the home of the bride and the other at the home of the groom. After he had toasted the groom or the bride and the parents with one shot of homemade vodka, he filled up on bread and cake. That was all he ate. Then he left. But he always put in an appearance at the wedding celebration of the sons or daughters of his customers, and it was always the same. One shot of vodka and all the bread and cake he could eat. Besides giving a generous wedding present, he would also present the couple with their first pair of baby shoes free, as soon as their infant began to walk.

But here at Olga Kereliuk's wedding celebration, there was more than just bread and cake to eat. There were also sandwiches, including some that Dad could eat because they were made without meat. Neither Dad nor I went away hungry. Now, for the first time in my life, I felt that both Dad and I were accepted by the Sheho community. Jewish or gentile, it didn't matter to Bill Kereliuk or to anyone else. I felt that we were a "part" of the community. But more than that, for the first time I also had a sense of my father's standing in the community. In a word, it was "respect." It made me feel proud.

The months passed. We had hoped that somebody in our area who had enough money would buy our business. George Lys had sold his store quietly, without even advertising. But we had sent out hundreds of flyers, so everyone in the entire area knew we were going out of business. Yet nobody had even approached us. I suggested placing an ad in the *Jewish Post* and *Western Jewish News*, widely circulated English language weekly newspapers about Jewish life that were published in Winnipeg. We got one bite. Two brothers from Winnipeg arrived by train, looked at the store and at our books, then took the train back that night. It appeared that we would eventually have to sell everything to the bare walls unless we could get a buyer.

Christmas was approaching. Etta had fulfilled her promise. She had done more than merely fulfilling her obligation. She had stayed home for the entire time I had been away to Saskatoon, and even longer. She had come home after the funeral to help us in the store. Soon it would be time for her to leave. As planned, regardless of whether we sold the store, she would be leaving us on December 26, the day after Christmas. Then there would be only three of us left.

About two weeks before Christmas, Fred Klewchuk came into the store. He had recently become the new section foreman, replacing Mr. Wolkowski, who had moved away. He spoke to Dad in Ukrainian, but the conversation went something like this: "Louis, I'd like to buy your house. How much do you want?"

"Two thousand dollars."

"Is that the best you can do?"

"It's worth more than that. Two thousand is a bargain."

"Okay. I'll buy it. I'll be in with the money in two days. Will you hold it for me until then?

"Sure."

"Do you need a deposit?"

"No. Your word is good enough. "

They shook hands. There was no written contract, nothing. It was a gentleman's agreement, the only contract my father ever required. His word was his bond. He would hold the house for Mr. Klewchuk.

The very next day somebody else came into the store and wanted to buy the house. "It's too late," said Dad. I promised Fred Klewchuk that I'd sell it to him for two thousand dollars."

"I'll give you an extra hundred."

That was five percent of the total value of the house, a lot of money. But without even considering it, my father replied, "No, I've given him my word."

"Did he give you a deposit?"

"No, just his word. That's good enough. That's the way I always do business."

A day later, Mr. Klewchuk came into the store as he had promised and thanked Dad for keeping his word. "I always keep my word," said Dad.

"That's what I've heard. Thank you." He gave Dad a check and requested that his family be allowed to move in immediately after the new year.

The next week was hectic. While Etta packed her belongings for her trip to California, and Sylvia packed for Winnipeg, Merle came home to help us prepare for the auction sale of all our household effects—dishes, furniture, the piano—everything in the house. We would have to vacate it on the first Saturday after Christmas. That was the date scheduled for the "Auction Sale."

On December 26, Etta boarded the train in the morning bound for the West Coast, on her way to California. A few days later Frank Wunder conducted the auction sale. Our front yard was packed with farmers from the entire area who had come to buy our furniture and household items for a small fraction of what they had originally cost. One by one, every item in every room in the house was hauled out on the snow- packed front garden for Frank to auction off. He began with every item in the summer kitchen, then the kitchen, the dining room, the bed rooms, and finally the living room.

First to go was the ice box, which originally had cost about sixteen dollars. Frank was not nearly as fast as the Lucky Strike tobacco auctioneers, but he was fast. "How much am I bid. Two dollars, Who'll make it three? Do I hear three, three-fifty, four, who'll make it four, four dollars, do I hear four- fifty? Four, four dollar bid. Going for four dollars. Going once. Going twice. Going three times. Gone. The ice box gone for four dollars."

After everything in the (outer) summer kitchen had been auctioned off, the indoor kitchen items were next. First came the big kitchen clock, the one I had set after guessing the time by estimating how many horse droppings we had used in a hockey game. My kitchen clock. It went fast. I was sorry to see it go. Then came the kitchen stove, the kitchen table and chairs, the kitchen cabinets, the dishes, pots, pans, and so on, until every item in every room in the house, from the clock to the beds and dressers and chesterfield set and piano had been sold.

The house was finally empty. If I shouted, my echo bounced off the walls. It's the weirdest thing to stay in your empty house. That's the only word I can think of. Weird. That evening we left the doors unlocked. There was nothing inside to steal.

That very night Merle and Sylvia boarded the train for Winnipeg. Now only Dad and I were left in Sheho. We moved into the hotel. I ate all my meals in the big dining room, but Dad ate only breakfast there, toast and tea. For dinner he opened a can of salmon or sardines and added lemon juice. Bread and cheese from Mr. Leckie's store completed his meal. For supper, he cooked corn meal on top of the big potbelly stove in the store. After supper he would visit Mr. Leckie and then go to our room upstairs in the hotel. We were both very lonely.

As if sent by Providence, Bill Kereliuk's brother Fred, who owned a farm not far from town, came into the store a week or two later and bought it. Just like that. Dad did not charge him "goodwill," as some other merchants did. Dad, Mr. Kereliuk and I "took stock" of all our merchandise, recording the wholesale cost of each item in a book, then totaling the cost of our entire inventory. It amounted to approximately $15,000. We sold him the entire inventory at our cost, and threw in the huge safe and fixtures for a token price, and also the building for a fraction of its value.

Dad had never had a bank account, only a small savings account in the Post Office. Whatever money was left over after paying our bills to the wholesalers and manufacturers was put into this postal account. As a result, almost all our money had been tied up in inventory. Until now. So when Fred Kereliuk paid cash for our inventory, it was high time for Dad to make use of a strange institution—the Royal Bank of Canada in Foam Lake.

Although I could hardly wait to leave Sheho, both Dad and I remained and worked in the store for a few weeks to show the new owner how to run it. The days crawled. Seven days more. An eternity. Six days more. Every so slowly each day went by. Five. Four. Three. Only two days left. It reminded me of when I had waited for my bike to arrive.

And then came the final day. I ate breakfast slowly. I didn't have to be in the store. Mr. Kereliuk could now manage on his own. But I still felt a sense of obligation. So both Dad and I went back to keep him company. But I was too impatient, too nervous to stay. I went back to the hotel and made sure our trunk and both suit cases were properly packed. I lingered. Then I ate dinner. Slowly. Afterwards I went back to Mr. Fred Kereliuk's store. I stayed for a couple of hours. Finally, enough was enough, and I said good-bye to his wife and to him. I then went across the road to the elevator, shook hands with Bill Finley, and thanked him for all his help; then across the road to the Red and White Store, where I said good-bye to Mr. Tansley and Frank Wunder. It was still only five o'clock. I went to the post office and thanked Mr. and Mrs. Merritt for their help. They wished me good luck. Everyone was wishing me good luck. It made me feel good.

As soon I entered Mr. Leckie's store, he smiled at first; then his expression changed. He seemed sad. "I'll be joining you soon," he said. "It won't be long. I'm going to sell out, too, as soon as I can."

"There won't be any Jewish storekeepers left here," I said.

"No. Nobody's left in Foam Lake, either. Eventually, there will be very few of us left in the country."

I shook hands with him, as I had done with everyone. "Good luck," he said. I'll be joining you soon." I was glad that I would be seeing him again.

Back at the hotel I had an early supper. Finally, it was time to go. I walked up the road to Mr. Grumetza's store, said good-bye, then back to the hotel to get my suitcase, and on toward the station. My final stop was at Bill Kereluik's store, where we shook hands and said good-bye. Then I walked across the road and down to the station.

I was glad the train was on time. Dad and I put our suit cases on the overhead rack, then sat down on the green plush, felt-covered seats facing the railway station sign reading "Sheho." As the train began to move, first with a jerk, then more smoothly, gradually picking up speed, I saw the sign, the railway station, the school, and finally the skating rink disappear behind me. I wondered about the village I had just left. Although I was too young at the time to realize it, everything changes. Everything. I had absolutely no idea that half a century later, I would write a book about the world I had known for eighteen years on the Great Canadian Prairies. Only by then, that world had vanished forever.

IN FOND REMEMBRANCE

I thought I had seen the last of Sheho when I moved away, but something kept drawing me back—several times. In 1955, just before moving from Edmonton to California, I again visited Sheho for what I thought would be the last time. But I could not forget about my home town. In 1971, on our tour from Vancouver to Winnipeg, my wife and I stopped in Sheho for an all-too-brief visit. Then twenty-one years later, when I began writing this book, we again toured Western Canada, this time looking up everyone I had known. Once more we stopped in Sheho, this time on our way west; and while in Calgary, I met a number of old friends living there and initiated the idea of having a Sheho mini-reunion. Two years later, a group of us gathered during the Calgary Stampede for a wonderful get-together, after which word spread about the possibility of having a large reunion of everyone originally from Sheho in our home town itself.

Finally, in July of 1998, the tiny village of Sheho, now less than two hundred population, hosted a three-day reunion of anyone who had ever attended Sheho Public School since its founding in 1904. Almost nine hundred people came from all over Canada, as well as from the United States, and even from as far away as Australia and Pakistan. It is impossible to describe how elated I was to see so many acquaintances and friends, many of whom I had not seen in almost six decades. It was certainly one of the happiest get-togethers of my life, made especially so by having perhaps fifty or more people come up to me and tell me how fondly they remembered my parents, and how kind and generous they were during those long ago "hard times." I could not have been prouder had I been the son of the most well-known man or woman on the planet.

For the words that best described how these Shehoites felt about my parents were "respect" and "esteem." What better way to be remembered!

Because he was a Jewish immigrant in a British dominated country known for its anti-Semitism, my father had always considered himself an outsider in the community. The irony, however, was that like thousands of other Jewish general storekeepers throughout the Great Canadian Prairies, he was actually an insider—the center of the farming community he so generously served. Neither his foreign accent nor his different religion mattered to the farmers who often needed his help to survive. He was a kind and generous man. And that is how he is fondly remembered.

He died in Winnipeg on November 11, 1954—on Remembrance Day.

ADDENDUM

Introduction

1. Jane McCracken, "Homesteading," *The Canadian Encyclopedia*, 2nd ed.,Vol. II, (Edmonton: Hurtig Publishers), p.1002.

CHAPTER TWO

2. At the very bottom of the acceptable immigration list in Canada were Blacks and Asians, whom the British considered alien, inferior and unassimilable. "Chinese Immigration was curbed by a 'head tax' and was stopped altogether by the Chinese Immigration Act of 1923." Howard Palmer, "Prejudice and Discrimination," *The Canadian Encyclopedia*, 2nd ed., Vol III, p. 1741.

CHAPTER EIGHT.

3. The plural of *Kohayn* is actually *Kohanym*.

CHAPTER TEN.

4. Two of the four Saskatchewan stations were still fairly weak: CJGX Yorkton, with only 250 watts; and 1000 watt CFQC Saskatoon, which was beamed toward the north and west. But 1000 watt CKCK Regina was beamed toward the east, toward us, and its programs were loud and clear.

5. This program featured the Burns Chorus, consisting of four young ladies—the Nabobettes—and three young men, with Juliette, Susan's sister, as soloist. The group also went on the road and even

performed at the world famous Calgary Stampede.

6. His mother was supposed to be a fountain of wisdom who always gave everyone excellent advice whether it was asked for or not. But her voice and manner were so soft and syrupy that she sounded like an overbearing mother whom I would have loved to drown. The story took place in Elmwood. I could just imagine their home on a lovely tree-shaded street in the summer. What I remember most about that program is Pepper Young's voice; it was so distinctive, it was unique. It had an odd nasal quality that sounded as though he were speaking through his nose after gargling with lukewarm water containing a mixture of half a spoonful of fine sand and half a spoonful of loose gravel. In fact, long after that program ended, the owner of that voice continued to broadcast voice-over commercials on television. But despite his hundreds of commercials, I never saw him. And whenever I heard his commercial, I would say, "That's Pepper Young." So in my mind, I imagined him to be in his late teens or early twenties. Then one day, a few years ago, I saw him on T. V. Was I disappointed! He looked older than I. Then I realized that even for Pepper Young, time had not stood still.

7. Still another announcer would introduce his program with the sound of someone whistling, followed by these words: "I am The WHISTLER. I know many things, for I walk by night. " Yet another thriller, but much less frightening, was *The Green Hornet*. First came the sound of a hornet's buzz, followed by a violin and piano rendition of "Flight of the Bumble Bee." Then came the announcement: "He hunts the biggest game of all— public enemies that even G-men can't reach. Red Reed, daring young publisher with his faithful servant Kato." But the second most frightening program, second only to *Lights Out* was *The Shadow*. Like most mysteries, it began with several resonating chords on the organ, more than enough to set the mood. Then in a demon-like voice came this challenge: "Who knows what evil lurks in the hearts of men? The shadow knows. Ha Ha Ha." And as his sardonic laughter trailed off, my imagination painted a vivid picture of "the shadow" lurking in the darkness to uncover some evil deed that would otherwise go unpunished.

8.   We heard all kinds of wonderful music. *Texaco's Radio Broadcast of the Metropolitan Opera Company, The N.B.C. Symphony Orchestra*, conducted by Arturio Tosconni, The Robert Simpson Company's *Singing Stars of Tomorrow* (over the C.B. C. network), *The Kraft Music Hall*, starring Bing Crosby, *Your Hit Parade* starring Frank Sinatra, *Kay Kaiser and his College of Musical Knowledge, Major Bowes Original Amateur Hour*, "Round and round she goes, and where she stops nobody knows," and even cowboy music—the grand parents of today's Country and Western.

We listened to variety shows, which almost always included comedians: *It Pays to be Ignorant, Fibber McGee and Molly, The Great Gildersleeve, Amos'n'Andy, The Aldrich Family, George Burns and Gracie Allen, Duffy's Tavern, Bob Hope*, and many, many others.

We listened to dramas and mysteries: *Lux Radio Theater* ("Lux Presents Hollywood"), *Mr. District Attorney* ("Champion of the people, defender of truth and guardian of our fundamental right to live, liberty, and the pursuit of happiness"), *Grand Cenral Station* ("Crossroads of a million private lives"), *Philip Morris Playhouse* ("Johnny presents Call for Philip Mor-rees"), *The Campbell Playhouse* ("starring Orsen Wells"), and *Chando the Magician*.

CHAPTER TWELVE.

9.   Following is the translation of *Kol Nidre*, Rabbi Morris Silverman, editor, The Joint Payer Book Commission, *SABBATH AND FESTIVAL PRAYER BOOK*, The Rabbinical Assembly of American and United Synagogues of America. "All vows, oaths, and promises which we made to God from last Yom Kippur to this Yom Kippur and were not able to fulfill—may all such vows between ourselves and God be annulled. May they be void and of no effect. May we be absolved of them and released from them. May these vows not be considered vows, these oaths not be considered oaths, and these promises not be considered promises." p. 399. Note: TO SEEK ATONEMENT: "For transgressions between a human being and God, repentance on Yom Kippur brings atonement. For transgressions between one human being and another, Yom Kippur brings no atonement until the injured part is reconciled." p. 399.

10. In Biblical times the *shofar*—a ram's horn—was blown as a wind instrument for battle signals and for religious events.

CHAPTER NINETEEN.

11. Along the second and third shelves were one-pound packages of Salada, Red Rose, or Nabob orange pekoe tea and one-pound packages of Nabob Coffee for customers who insisted on a famous brandname instead of our own ground-to-order coffee. Next came one-pound packages of Burns and Swifts lard, packages of Nabob or Red Rose jelly powder, boxes of Royal yeast cakes, small bottles of vanilla extract and lemon extract, small cans of black pepper and other spices, and cans of ready to eat fish. These included large fishy-tasting cheap sardines from New Brunswick, tiny delicious tasting King Oscar sardines from Norway, awful tasting Monterey pilchards from California, and delicious tasting British Columbia red salmon. Finally, came Libby's canned vegetables: peas, creamed corn, and tomatoes.

Stacked upright, on top of the highest shelf, were boxes of Quaker puffed wheat, puffed rice, and—the biggest seller—the yellow and black boxes of corn flakes at three for a quarter. Alongside was the more expensive Kellogg's corn flakes at ten cents a box. Occasionally, the prohibitively expensive Nabisco shredded wheat at fifteen cents a box was also stacked atop this shelf. Since my father had no intention of climbing up on the counter to reach the boxes of cereal, he became very adept at using a broom to knock them down.

12. Running along half the length of the store from the shoe department (at the back) to the front was a long counter behind which was the dry goods section—its shelves filled with dozens and dozens of bolts of cotton, rayon, and satin fabrics in all kinds of colors and weaves. In the fall and winter the top of these shelves was stacked high with white packages of Penman's fleece lined cotton underwear for the whole family. At the beginning of this counter—from left to right—lay boxes of caps for boys and men, as well as fur lined leather helmets during winter. Behind this counter the pullout drawers were filled with sewing needles and

spools of cotton thread and balls of woolen yarn and everything one needed to sew or mend clothes. Also, inside this counter were men's and ladies' combs, small mirrors, wicks for coal oil lamps and lanterns, and mica mantles for Coleman gasoline lanterns. At one time there were even some gold band wedding rings inside one of these drawers. Continuing (left to right) from the caps and helmets on this drygoods counter to the front of the store was a high-top glass showcase filled with boxes of ladies' silk stockings, panties and brassieres, slips, corsets, and brightly colored *babushkas* (ladies' shawls), bed sheets and bed spreads, towels, as well as men's dress shirts, ties, belts, and socks, and almost anything else that was either too small or too expensive to risk losing through stealing.

The shelves on the right-hand side of the yard goods were filled with men's cotton doeskin jackets, men's black denim and blue drill pants, blue denim overalls, and work shirts—cotton chambray during spring and summer and solid colored cotton doeskin and brightly checked flannel during fall and winter. High above this counter, also running almost the entire length of the ` store, was a narrow metal rod suspended only inches from the metal ceiling. Attached to this rod hung parachute-like bundles of men's cotton gloves, cotton work socks, men's handkerchiefs (both white and brightly colored red or blue), and ladies' cotton hose and bloomers. In the fall and winter, bundles of lumbermen's heavy woolen stockings and woolen gloves and mittens were added. From these bundles the customer could see and feel the merchandise and help himself by pulling down, one-at-a-time, any item he wanted. These bundles of low-and-moderately priced merchandise were the only self-serve items available. Since the bundles were somewhat higher than even the tallest customer, it was usually easy to see who was handling this merchandise. However, when the store was full of customers and nobody was around to watch, some of them helped themselves without paying. But my parents, like many storekeepers at that time, were philosophical. This was the price for progress.

13. Robert Knuckle, *IN THE LINE OF DUTY: The Honour Roll of the RCMP since 1873* (Bumstown, Ontario: General Store Publishing House, 1995), pp. 155-158.

CHAPTER TWENTY-SIX.

14. The Hayes Censoring Office during this time imposed its own ab surdly strict rules of sexual morality upon movie makers, going so f a r as to mandate that bedroom scenes require married couples to sleep in separate beds. Sexually suggestive and offensive language were taboo.

CHAPTER TWENTY-SEVEN.

15. Excellent stories about Manitoba World War II RCAF aircrew can be found in *Memoirs on Parade: Aircrew Recollections of World War II* (Wartime Pilots' and Observers' Association, P.O. Box 1702, Winnipeg, Manitoba, R3C 2Z6).

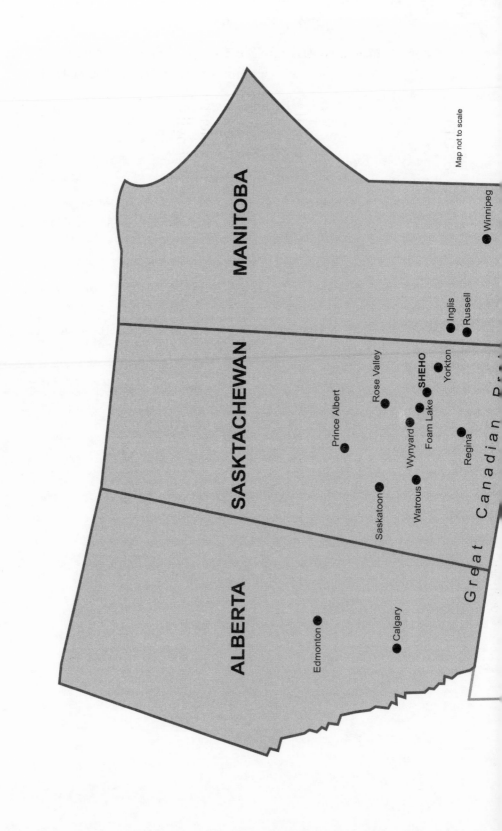

ALBERTA

SASKTACHEWAN

MANITOBA

Edmonton

Calgary

Saskatoon

Prince Albert

Rose Valley

Watrous

Wynyard

Foam Lake

SHEHO

Yorkton

Regina

Inglis

Russell

Winnipeg

Great Canadian Pra

Map not to scale

UNITED STATES

MONTANA   NORTH DAKOTA   MINNESOTA

Great Falls

Bismarck

"I knew all about the United States. On our map in Miss Griffiths's room, it was green. It was not nearly as big as Canada, which was a huge red country, part of the mighty British Empire on which the sun never set. I was proud to belong to the British Empire because we had a king and queen... Not like that little green country—the United States— which didn't even have a king or queen. Only a president whose name was Roosevelt. ...Even though it was much smaller than Canada, it had a lot more people. They were called Americans. And they all spoke English—without accents."